Praise for *Victory at*

"The novel colorfully and accurately portrays Washington and other figures as they struggle with tactics, logistics, intelligence, meddling politicians, and petty rivalries . . . Exciting historical fiction, offering insight into just how close George Washington and the Americans came to losing the war." —*Publishers Weekly*

"Augmented with character sketches of lesser-known patriots, the book brings Washington to life as a resolute and bold general. The authors shine brightly in describing the depth of his emotion flowing from the victory at Yorktown." —*Kirkus Reviews*

Praise for *Valley Forge*

"This second title in the George Washington series (after *To Try Men's Souls*) offers an energetic dramatization of the Continental Army's grim winter bivouac at Valley Forge, Pennsylvania, in 1777. . . . Gingrich and Forstchen re-create the sights and smells of the Continental Army's hand-to-mouth camp life and the battlefield action around Valley Forge with a brisk panache that should bode well for future entries." —*Publishers Weekly*

Praise for *To Try Men's Souls*

"Grim, gritty, realistic, accurate, and splendid, this is a soaring epic of triumph over almost unimaginable odds." —*Library Journal*

"A new novel is taking us back in time to examine some of the pivotal events in our nation's history and it gives readers an up close and personal look at American heroes like George Washington and Thomas Paine. . . . The book is fascinating." —Sean Hannity

Praise for *Pearl Harbor*

"Masterful storytelling that not only captures the heroic highs and hellish lows of that horrific day that lives on in infamy—it resonates with today's conflicts and challenges."

—William E. Butterworth IV, *New York Times* bestselling author of *The Saboteurs*

"A thrilling tale of America's darkest day."

—W. E. B. Griffin, *New York Times* bestselling author of *The Shooters*

"A politician and a novelist, each an accomplished historian in his own right, are emerging as master authors of alternative history. In this 'what if' treatment of the attack on Pearl Harbor, Newt Gingrich and William Forstchen combine their talents to make the diplomacy as suspenseful as the combat, even for readers who know what happens next—or think they know. The authors' mastery of both the broad sweep of events and the details of naval war and military technology give their counterfactual scenarios an unusual degree of plausibility, concluding with a version of the Japanese attack that guarantees a fictional Pacific war even more terrible than the one that began on December 7, 1941."

—Dennis Showalter, former president of the Society of Military Historians

Victory at Yorktown

NEWT GINGRICH,
WILLIAM R. FORSTCHEN,
and ALBERT S. HANSER,

CONTRIBUTING EDITOR

THOMAS DUNNE BOOKS

ST. MARTIN'S GRIFFIN ⚌ NEW YORK

THOMAS DUNNE BOOKS.
An imprint of St. Martin's Press.

VICTORY AT YORKTOWN. Copyright © 2012 by Newt Gingrich and William R. Forstchen. All rights reserved. Printed in the United States of America. For information, address St. Martin's Press, 175 Fifth Avenue, New York, N.Y. 10010.

www.thomasdunne books.com
www.stmartins.com

The Library of Congress has cataloged the hardcover edition as follows:

Gingrich, Newt.
    Victory at Yorktown / Newt Gingrich, William R. Forstchen, and Albert S. Hanser, contributing editor.—1st ed.
        p. cm.
    ISBN 978-0-312-60707-4 (hardcover)
    ISBN 978-1-4668-0250-6 (e-book)
    1. Yorktown (Va.)—History—Siege, 1781—Fiction.   2. United States—History—Revolution, 1775–1783—Fiction.   1. Forstchen, William R.
II. Hanser, Albert S.   III. Title.
    PS3557.I4945V53 2012
    813'.54—dc23

                                                        2012028307

ISBN 978-0-312-60708-1 (trade paperback)

St. Martin's Griffin books may be purchased for educational, business, or promotional use. For information on bulk purchases, please contact Macmillan Corporate and Premium Sales Department at 1-800-221-7945, extension 5442, or write specialmarkets@macmillan.com.

First St. Martin's Griffin Edition: September 2013

10   9   8   7   6   5   4   3   2   1

There is only one dedication that is truly fitting for the conclusion of this trilogy. To the memory of those who fought by Washington's side, from Boston to Yorktown, and our all but forgotten allies, the French troops and sailors who insured our victory at Yorktown. In a world where, at times, friendships of old can be forgotten, we should always honor the memory of the aid France gave us in our struggle for liberty, and in turn, the sacrifice we offered back in the great struggles for freedom of the twentieth century.

Acknowledgments

GEORGE WASHINGTON CAN BE A HARD PERSONA TO TOUCH emotionally. It is easy to picture an evening with Abraham Lincoln, him leaning back in his chair, long legs stretched out and resting atop his desk, spinning out stories, some funny, some profound, some deeply emotional. He is easy to picture as "one of us." This was due, in large part, to the advent of the new technology of photography that left us with hundreds of images of him, which captured, as Carl Sandburg wrote, this "Hoosier Michelangelo." Consider the world before photography, how anonymous the lives of even the famous could be. It explains in part why kings once wore crowns so that all recognized the king, and there were strict laws restricting you to wearing clothing only of your social caste so we could sort out "who was who." It can rightly be said that Abe was our first modern-media president, and thus seems far more "reachable" and familiar to us.

Forty years later it was even more so with Teddy Roosevelt, of whom we have motion pictures and sound recordings. All toothy grin, more than a touch of bombast, but a man you could easily tag along with as he hiked with John Muir through what would become our glorious National Parks that are his legacy, or yes, even charge with him up "San Juan" Hill. With FDR we know we could be charmed and maneuvered as he mixed a martini, his warm patrician voice so familiar from his fireside chats. Then there is Ronald Reagan, a film star before he became president, his motion picture images already casting for so many of us, his admirers, as the embodiment of the quintessential goodness, strength, and wisdom from the Old West and apply it so correctly and forcefully in the confrontation with an evil empire. Here, as well, was a man we feel we could sit back and chat with. With all these great leaders we can build an image, real or not, based upon photographs, printed newspapers, and as early as T.R., recordings of their voice and moving images.

But George Washington?

Our only image of him comes from the posed and formal paintings of the era. There is no recording of his voice. His features are even hard to define, except as marble busts like those of the ancient Romans. Even much of his personal side is lost to history. While there survives the lively, warm, at times, even passionate correspondence between John Adams and his "dearest friend" Abigail Adams, which spanned decades, upon the death of Washington, Martha burned over thirty years of personal correspondence. What a rich treasure, like a burnt offering on a pyre, went up in smoke that day! It could have reshaped the marble bust into a man just like us, and just as accessible to historians and writers as melancholic Lincoln or a grinning Teddy Roosevelt.

When my coauthor Bill Forstchen and I decided to write a trilogy about George Washington and the Revolution the task seemed daunting. We are historians, but we also love a good story and believe that neglect of good stories has always been the failure of most traditional histories, which turn such exciting adventures and personas into dull and lifeless facts. The challenge? How do we bring Washington alive?

The glimpses of him as a man, just like us, are indeed rare. As a general in command of an army desperately hanging on against near-impossible odds, he had to remain aloof, calm, and ever-confident. For any show of weakness or doubt could have, most definitely would have, caused a collapse of that heroic, starving, and ragged "band of brothers." As president he was aware that he was being watched by the entire world. He was the central actor on the stage of an entirely new form of government. The slightest comment or gesture carried grave significance. He knew he was establishing precedents and he played his role to perfection.

But what of the man within? As trained historians we of course had to adhere to facts, but as historians who believe that novels can enrich and broaden our knowledge of the past, our quest became one of trying to delve within, and at the same time, reveal the nature of the men who fought by his side, and as well, those who fought against him.

Consider that wonderful movie, *The Last of the Mohicans*. Beyond its grim story of the brutality of the French and Indian War, we had personalities that engaged us. The brave and appealing "Hawkeye," the pompous British major who in the end comes through with a noble sacrifice, and even the villain Magua, who carries the realization of the tragedy that made him thus. Few realize this was, as well, the world and the war in which George Washington matured to manhood. Few can picture him, as he was in his early twenties, out on the frontier of the 1750s as a scout, a leader of a tough band of borderland "rangers." We tend to picture Washington toward the end of his life, living in the stately mansion of Mount Vernon, rather than as a young man as much a frontiersman as Hawkeye, Daniel Boone, or his friend and comrade in arms Dan Morgan. Few can picture him as a powerfully built man, considered nearly a giant for his time at 6'2". He was known as the finest horseman in northern Virginia. First in any race at breakneck speed, admired even by his Native American foes, who believed that the hand of God protected him, for how else to explain his reckless courage in battles from which he always emerged unscathed. He was even a man, like "Old Abe," capable of outwrestling any of the local frontier toughs. Long before our Revolution, he was admired and respected. When the great crisis finally came, there was near-unanimous assent that he should be our military leader. Such trust does not coalesce around marble statues, pompous fools, or wax images. In the Americas of the eighteenth century such trust was earned by a man's reputation, his gravitas, as the Romans would have defined it, and by his moral strength. Only such a man could have pulled together such a divergent group of true revolutionaries, from Georgia to New Hampshire, and ultimately welded them into an army that against all odds humbled the greatest empire in the world.

This is the Washington we sought to capture in our trilogy that concludes with the story of Yorktown. This is the man who startled the world, when not once, but twice, he renounced the prospect of absolute power, as an army commander and later as a president, to return back to private life, saying he had merely performed the service that any citizen of a free republic should embrace. Little wonder that his greatest foe, King George III, would finally proclaim that Washington would be remembered as the greatest man of his century.

Prior to our trilogy about Washington, Bill Forstchen and I enjoyed writing what we call "active history" and most call "alternative history." But for Washington? His story is so astonishing and inspiring that we knew we had to write it "as it was." Our goal was to delve into the heart and soul of this enigmatic figure and try to bring him to life. Most certainly he was one of the greatest leaders in history, but what of the man within?

On the night before his crossing of the Delaware, during the freezing nights of Valley Forge as he watched his army all but collapsing from starvation, disease, and cold, on the boiling hot plains of Monmouth, New Jersey, in what we believe was the turning point battle of the war, and on the long desperate march, a near-forlorn hope, to Yorktown, were there not moments of fear, of hesitation, of near-crushing fear that all would be for naught? What inner struggles were there with the Titan-like weight placed upon his shoulders, when a single mistake could have doomed our efforts, and with every decision, the lives of thousands of men who followed him were put in the balance?

This is the Washington we wished to reach for and we hope that you, the readers, believe we have reached that mark.

To have achieved this required five years for three books, in which other efforts at times held our attention as well, such as a bid for the presidency, along with our roles as parents and citizens. Thanks are owed to many. Of course there is Steve Hanser, our technical editor, who resolved many a difficult question. For Bill Forstchen there was his ever-patient daughter, Meghan, who, while this series was being written, went through her teenage years and knew so often that when her father said "just let me finish this chapter," a day might pass before he emerged from his office. As always for Bill there are thanks to his school, Montreat College, with an ever-understanding staff and president when he was wrapped up in research or writing, and, on occasion, wandered in late for a class, or needed several days off for research travel. As he worked on the series he shared parts of it with his history classes and drew inspiration from their responses. Thanks, as well, to his close aviation friends Don Barber and Danny McMullen, who kept him safe when he sought a few hours of relaxation, flying his World War II–era plane in order to "clear his head." Thanks, as well, to friends such as Maury Hurt, John Mina, Frank Smith, and fellow author Bill Butterworth, who were always there with encouragement.

I'm grateful to our agent, Kathy Lubbers, and to our advisers, Randy Evans and Stefan Passantino; the talented staff of Gingrich Productions and other members of the Gingrich team, including Alicia Melvin, Joe DeSantis, Anna Haberlein, Vince Haley, Jorge Hurtado, Bess Kelly, Christina Maruna, Kate Pietkiewicz, Michelle Selesky, Liz Wood, and Ross Worthington.

We extend our deepest thanks to Pete Wolverton and Tom Dunne for their partnership and support of this book. Anne Bensson is tremendous asset, as are the copyeditor, Bob Berkel, the proofreader, Ted O'Keefe, and the production editor, David Stanford Burr.

We hope that you find this third work of our trilogy about Washington and the Revolution to be as engaging as so many have said the first two were. We part from this series with one final thought. All along, from the first day we started, and in fact, far back to earliest childhood, we both knew how the story ends. We win at Trenton, we endure Valley Forge, and we achieve triumph at Yorktown. General

George Washington will become President George Washington, indeed, "first in the hearts of his countrymen." In a sense, it was therefore easy to tell his story.

Consider it from his perspective. Like all of us, we know not what tomorrow will bring, be it fulfillment of hopes and dreams, or a darkness filled with tragedy and loss. Consider the moral, the spiritual strength of George Washington the man. On the freezing stormy night before Trenton, or the long grueling march to Yorktown, not sure if it was a final futile gesture. Consider the strength within his soul. Regardless of inner turmoil and potential doubt, he knew that as a leader who all turned to for hope and inspiration, he must indeed lead and offer inspiration. He did his duty admirably well and thus created the nation we have today. We owe him all, as a general, as a leader, and as a man. Let us work together to insure the legacy he gave us is passed, unsullied unto generations of Americans yet to be born. That is our duty to them; it is our duty as well to that most remarkable of men, George Washington.

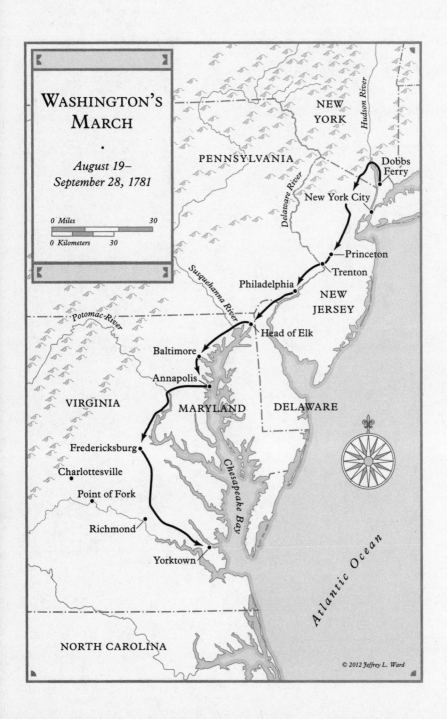

WASHINGTON'S
MARCH

•

*August 19–
September 28, 1781*

0 Miles   30

0 Kilometers   30

NEW
YORK

Hudson River

PENNSYLVANIA

Dobbs
Ferry

Delaware River

New York City

Princeton

Trenton

Philadelphia

Susquehanna River

NEW
JERSEY

Potomac River

Head of Elk

Baltimore

Annapolis

VIRGINIA

MARYLAND

DELAWARE

Fredericksburg

Chesapeake Bay

Charlottesville

Point of Fork

Richmond

Yorktown

Atlantic Ocean

NORTH CAROLINA

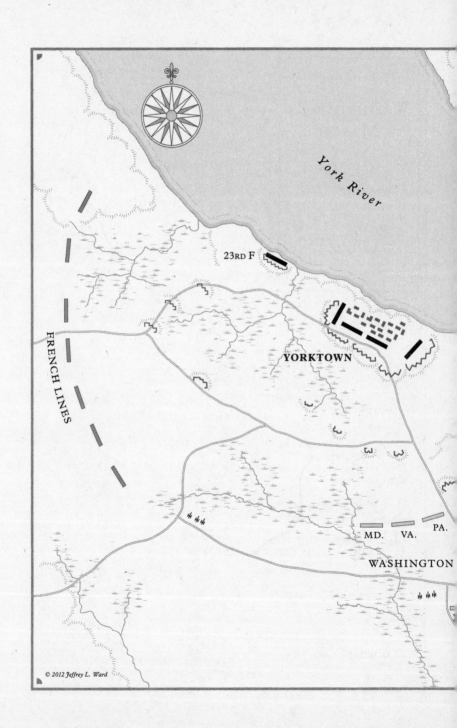

York River

23RD F

YORKTOWN

FRENCH LINES

MD. VA. PA.

WASHINGTON

© 2012 Jeffrey L. Ward

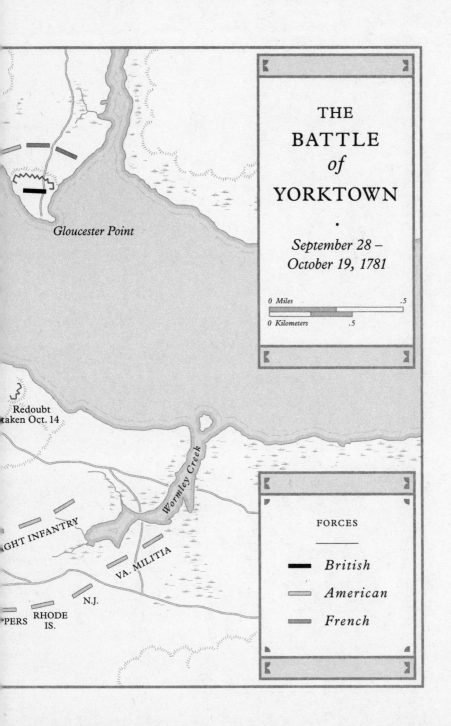

Gloucester Point

THE
BATTLE
of
YORKTOWN
·
September 28 –
October 19, 1781

0 Miles   .5
0 Kilometers   .5

Redoubt
taken Oct. 14

Wormley Creek

GHT INFANTRY

VA. MILITIA

N.J.

PERS RHODE
IS.

FORCES
───────

━━━ *British*
━━━ *American*
━━━ *French*

Part One

MAJOR ANDRE,
UPSTATE NEW YORK,
SEPTEMBER 30–OCTOBER 1, 1780

Prologue

DARKNESS BLANKETED THE HUDSON RIVER VALLEY, THE glow of hundreds of campfires reflecting off the low scudding clouds, passing in the wake of this afternoon's rain. He left the window open to admit the fresh evening breeze even though if Martha were here, she would slam it shut, cautioning him about the danger of chills and fever borne on such a breeze.

It was a strange silly notion. As a young man he had spent years out on the edge of the frontier, either campaigning in the last war or surveying after the conflict had ended. He would go for months at time with only a bit of canvas over his head, but once back in the house where Martha held sway and even on the most sweltering of nights, she held religiously to the belief that night air coming in through an open window was dangerous. Of course he indulged her, there were some things, even though he was commander in chief of all

American forces in the field, he nevertheless deferred to his wife and usually did so gladly.

He wished for her presence this evening with a deep longing. Whenever presented with what he felt was not a military question but instead a moral decision, it was her advice he always turned to. The decision he had just made, the paper he was about to sign was, indeed, a military decision, that was and would always be how he defined it, and yet it was, as well, a moral question forced upon him by this never-ending war.

General George Washington stood up, stretching, his towering six foot two height nearly brushing the low beams overhead. Opening the door to his office he stepped out, the guards flanking it snapping to attention. Alexander Hamilton, busy at work in his office across the hallway with the door open, looked up, ready to be summoned. Washington shook his head and gestured for him to remain at ease, then headed for the front door, opened it, and stepped out into the night, the guards posted outside coming to attention as well.

Hands characteristically clasped behind his back he started into the night. He had barely taken a dozen paces and then heard footsteps trailing behind him. A bit annoyed, Washington turned to see Hamilton racing to catch up, half a dozen guards following.

"Alexander," he sighed, "I'm just going for a walk."

"Sir, after the events of the last week, I must insist that a guard accompany you at all times. One cannot be too cautious."

It was obvious Hamilton was filled with concern for his well-being, at times too much so, but he knew the young man to be right. After the events of the last week . . .

"All right then, Colonel Hamilton," he sighed and looked at his guard detail, "but no need to hem me in, young sir. Indulge me by just following along at a decent interval."

The men encamped near his headquarters, having finished their evening meal of salt pork and whatever they could forage on the sly or barter for from nearby farms, were settling down for the night. He did not enter the encampment area, that would simply trigger all the usual calls to attention, rousting men out, with nervous young officers trying to put on a show of having their men properly attired and lined up to present arms. When serving with the British during Braddock's disastrous campaign back at the start of the French and Indian War, he had endured such foolery often enough. British main line infantry were used to such, as part of the ordinary annoyances of life, but volunteers, especially militia, detested it all after the first few times, and saw it as yet another bloody officer lording it over them and disturbing the one time of day they could call their own and relax.

He took a wooded path instead, his usual evening stroll, down to a knoll that looked out over the magnificent Hudson. He knew that following this routine had set off Hamilton, who softly ordered a couple of the guards to angle off into the woods to either side, run ahead, and act as flankers, in case someone, be it assassin, ambusher, or even British agents intent upon snatching him as a prisoner, might lay in wait.

Two weeks ago he viewed such as bordering on insanity, but no longer.

A man he had trusted as a brother, a man of whom he had more than once said should replace him in command if he fell in battle, had, indeed, betrayed him.

Benedict Arnold.

He had been unable to dwell on little else these last two weeks, it was almost obsessive, but such a base betrayal could not help but wound him to the core, with thoughts of it filling nearly every waking moment.

"Benedict Arnold," he whispered under his breath, paused and then added "damn your soul, damn your soul."

These were was words he so rarely used. He rarely felt such even toward those whom he saw as his mortal foes, men such as the British Howe, who did attempt to fight an honorable war. Even the now pathetic Hessians, who when they first arrived here had shown such haughty arrogance and brutal treatment to his captured wounded, but now were terrified of their own shadows for fear of falling into the hands of a Rebel, who might remember the slaughter on battlefields past and slowly take revenge.

But Benedict Arnold? Here was a man he had clasped to his heart like few others. This was the man he had met back in those first heady days of 1775, detailing him off to try to capture Quebec and bring a fourteenth colony into their cause. Arnold had set off, leading six hundred gallant men, through the autumn storms of Maine and the freezing cold of a Canadian winter, nearly dying in the assault on Quebec with a bullet in his leg. He was captured and finally exchanged, but eager for more action.

Arnold had fought the British in their campaign of 1776 down Lake Champlain to a standstill. Fought them throughout 1777, while saddled, thanks to the politics of Congress, with the self-serving Gates as his superior. At the climactic moment of the struggle around Saratoga, Arnold, who technically was under arrest for having dared to argue with Gates, and stricken with illness, had risen from his bed when word came that the battle, typical of Gate's actions, was turning in the wrong direction. He mounted his horse and dashed to the front. Then in a mad display of bravado, he had charged straight at the British lines, screaming for any and all with courage to follow him in. He had rallied the men, led them to a smashing victory, only to be wounded at the supreme moment in the leg, the ball striking nearly at the same spot as his wound at Quebec.

He had saved the battle and created victory. That victory had swayed France into the fight. It had saved the Revolution, for at nearly that exact same moment Washington's own army was being hammered to pieces by Howe and forced to abandon the national capital of Philadelphia. The news of Saratoga arrived in France before word of his own defeats, and had given Benjamin Franklin the argument to bring France into the war. Arnold, in that one gallant moment, had saved the Revolution.

Tragically, it was Gates who had galloped south from Saratoga to parade before Congress, aggrandizing unto himself the glory of Saratoga while Arnold languished for weeks, arguing with his doctors, refusing to let them hack his leg off. He had survived, kept the leg, but needed months, more like a year or more, to slowly recover. He was no longer fit for command in the field when Philadelphia was taken back from the British. As Washington looked out across the Hudson he remembered that moment all so well, the joy of recalling Arnold to some form of duty and without hesitation slotting his friend into that strife-torn capital as its military commander. Given the politics of Congress, he knew he could trust Arnold in all things, unlike Gates, and made it clear that if a bullet or disease should end his own command, his nomination for commander in chief would either be Greene or Arnold. He firmly believed, that given another six months to a year for Arnold to recover fully, he would be ready to again take the field and create yet more victories.

With the British all but driven from New Jersey in 1778, and the theater of war shifting to the Hudson Valley, leaving Arnold in the rear, it most likely had begun. He had heard rumors about the young woman Margaret "Peggy" Shippen. One of his more effective and gallant spies in that captured city, a brave lass believed by most to have Tory leanings, had been able to use her friendship with Peggy to smuggle out information regarding British plans. Especially the crucial news that they were preparing to abandon Philadelphia, thus giving him the lead for the long anticipated confrontation that climaxed at Monmouth Court House.

While the British occupied Philadelphia during the winter of 1777, this "Miss" Shippen, at seventeen, had an affair with a well-placed Major Andre, but after the British abandoned the capital in 1778, her attention, if not her loyalties, suddenly shifted to the new military governor, Benedict Arnold. As a gentleman he never communicated to Arnold his concerns about who he had chosen to fall in love with and had even sent along a silver tea set as a present from Martha and himself when they were wed in 1779. To his growing concern, the spy had passed along warnings that she believed that "Miss Peggy" was still in touch with her alleged lover, Andre.

Arnold, a brilliant battlefield commander, was no political general. He was besotted with a girl less than half his age, and soon ran afoul of the politics of Congress in the city he was meant to govern in time of war. Repeated charges of financial chicanery were brought against Arnold, but never proven. He languished in frustration, like a fighting bear locked in a gilded cage, openly took to drink, and finally begged for a transfer that Washington had readily granted his old friend as commander of the garrison and fortifications at West Point.

Then, at last, it unraveled. At some point Arnold, after losing the laurels of his victory at Saratoga, the rumors that the pain in his crippled leg were so severe he had taken to laudanum, his marriage to Peggy, and his growing rage and frustration with Congress, had turned coat.

Only by the slenderest of margins had the plot been discovered at the very last minute. Arnold had opened communications, via Peggy, with Andre. He had been promised a generalship, the command of his own forces, and after the Revolution was suppressed, title, rank, and high position in the postwar government of the Americas. He had succumbed, offering back secret maps for the approaches to West Point, the stripping out of troops from the position on the day the British would launch the surprise assault, and to Washington's disbelief at first, Arnold had even offered him as a prize, promising to lure him into the trap just before it was sprung.

An untrusting sentinel had caught Major Andre, in civilian garb, carrying the final details of this elaborate plot and trying to slip through the lines as a courier from Arnold. It would have been sprung before the end of the month. As for his own fate, Washington cared little. He had assumed more than once that he was fated to die in this war, but if by so doing, he could inspire the cause to continue, he would gladly lay such a sacrifice upon the altar of his country. The fall of West Point, the guardian and barrier of all of upstate New York, while at the same time, the commander in chief was killed resisting capture? The war most likely would have ended here, especially after the unrelenting series of debacles Gates had suffered in the Carolinas.

Arnold had not only betrayed him, he had betrayed his country, and that action Washington could never forgive.

Now the orders that he hesitated to sign were lying upon his desk. By all accounts, Major Andre, the contact for Arnold, was a man of honor, though caught out of uniform while behind enemy lines. By two thousand years of military tradition the doomed man could face but only one fate. Yet all of those who sat at his court-martial, even General Greene, had made appeals for some form of clemency rather than death by hanging, so impressed were they by Andre's soldierly bearing, his personal sense of honor, and display of gentlemanly behavior. They saw him almost as a victim of Arnold as well, caught up in a web not of his own making, and on the night of his capture simply doing what any officer would do to further the cause they fought for, even at the risk of being caught out of uniform. As he looked out across the river Washington mused that he, too, had knowingly sent more than one of his own to such a potential death. When in desperate need of intelligence, he sent agents under his direct order straight into the heart of Manhattan to ascertain what the enemy might be planning. If Andre had been on his staff, he might have ordered him to do such a risky deed and from all that was said of the man, he would have followed orders without hesitation.

Washington stood atop the knoll looking out over the Hudson, the surface of the river dark as the night sky above. It looked as if not a ship was upon it, a river that had swarmed with traffic night and day, before the war, but they were out there. His own picket boats and a light schooner armed with four pounders, and at times British boats would slip up on the tide to try to take one of his pickets by surprise, raise havoc with an alarm, or as happened but a few days ago, slip an agent ashore. He could barely see Hamilton standing off to one side, pistol out, looking down toward the river, most likely filled with anxiety that Arnold's plot had not yet been fully laid to rest and an attempt would still be made upon "the general."

He disdained the concern, but then again, if he was to sink so low as to attempt to assassinate his opponent General Clinton in New

York, what better time to attempt such than after a plot had been unmasked, followed by a week or so of alarms, followed by a gradual lowering of guard.

But he felt no fear. If fated to die, he had trained himself long ago to believe that such things were ordained by God and to leave fear behind. He had gone into every battle of his life, now nearly countless, with that fatalistic assumption, which he found calmed his soul while other men, brave men, inwardly fretted and thus could not concentrate upon the life and death decisions to be made, in an instant and without hesitation. To die here though, by an assassin's bullet while standing silhouetted upon the knoll, would be a useless, ridiculous fate.

Nevertheless, he stood silent for about five minutes, just gazing off, pondering the order that rested on his desk.

"Damn war," he finally muttered, and turning, headed back to his headquarters, a much relieved Hamilton trailing just behind him. Returning to his office he saw that someone had started a fire, set a light snack of bread and two eggs on a plate and, of course, closed the window. It was a standing order that his servant, Billy Lee, had received from Martha years ago, and that it was senseless to argue against.

He picked up the document, written out in Hamilton's neat hand. It concurred with the findings of the court-martial and ordered that Major Andre, found guilty of espionage and behind the lines of a belligerent while out of proper uniform, was therefore condemned to death by hanging. Earlier in the day he had received a missive from General Clinton appealing for leniency in the case of Major Andre with an offer of exchange of several score prisoners of rank held by the British in New York. To which he had replied that the only exchange he would consider was that of the traitor Benedict Arnold for Andre.

He looked down at the appeals sent privately by every member of the court-martial, asking for him to find some way to at least spare Andre's life temporarily. Though not driven by vengeance now, he thought of the foolish young Nathan Hale, and how he was hung without delay or ceremony, and left to dangle at the end of the rope for an entire day.

He tried to tell himself his decision had nothing to do with the shock and rage that still burned over Arnold's betrayal, made even more base by the manner in which he fled, leaving his young strumpet of a wife behind at West Point, and Andre to face his fate alone. Regarding "Miss" Shippen, who had wailed with terror that she knew nothing about the plot, he of course let her go to rejoin her husband, though before leaving, her luggage was taken apart piece by piece, and several reputable ladies of the camp had searched her carefully for any hidden documents. She shouted indignations that such effrontery and treatment of a proper lady would soon be the talk of all of America and the courts of Europe. He was told that when she was asked if she had any feelings for the fate of Andre, she reportedly gave a shrug of dismissal and announced it was none of her concern. He prayed word of that did not fall on Andre's ears before his ending. At least let the man die with some illusions intact.

For it certainly must be an ending he now realized. There was no room for hesitation. Though privately he wished different, he was as bound by military law as any other general; though he took no pleasure in this act, it had to be done. Placing the document on his desk, he drew the pen out of its inkwell and signed the order with a firm hand. He let it dry, then crossing the hall back to Hamilton's office he handed it to the Colonel.

"An extra day should give him time to set his heart and spiritual concerns in order, any longer would simply be an act of torture," Washington said.

Hamilton nodded in agreement.

"Sir, a courier just came in. There was a communication at the picket line," and he handed a folded note to Washington who opened it.

He scanned it quickly and put it down on Hamilton's desk.

"No need for a reply. I approve."

"Sir, that is letting a British officer into our lines?"

"According to this note he's actually a Loyalist. I'm familiar with his name. He is reported to be an honorable man and will not violate the rules of war by reporting anything he sees while within our lines other than to witness the formalities of Major Andre's . . ." and he paused.

"His fate. Besides it would be unchristian to deny Andre the comfort of a man this note states is one of his closest friends."

"Sir, there could be some secret communication between them," Hamilton replied forcefully. The fact that part of Arnold's plot had been either the capture or death of Washington by a ruse rather than on the field of combat had filled him with a rage. It was evident that Hamilton, unlike most of his other officers, held little pity for any involved in it.

"I have come to believe everything said about Andre. Besides, I want you to assign one of our staff to be with this visitor the entire time he is within our lines. It should prove to be an interesting matchup and might even bear fruit for us."

"Who is that, sir?"

"Our visitor's friend from before the war. Find Major Wellsley, brief him that he is assigned as an escort for this visitor, that if possible to pick up what information he can and to insure none is transferred from Major Andre."

Washington returned to his office, looked at the tray Bill Lee had set out. He had no appetite tonight. Unbuckling his belt, he doused out the candles and stretched out on his cot, but sleep would not come. Too many thoughts raced about. Arnold, his decision regarding Andre, a wish that Martha was here, even if just to talk about the entire affair, and then with it, all the other issues that had bedeviled and haunted him across five years of war, the ever-constant worry about supplies, food, shoes, pay, and the near-daily humiliation of begging officers and men to stand firm in spite of all privations with not even a real shilling of payment in way of thanks from their nation. Now all this was compounded by the debacle Gates had created in the Carolinas and his decision to remove him from command, regardless of the repercussions from his friends in Congress.

To think, *I volunteered for this task*, he thought with a wry smile, but then again, that was precisely why he would see it through to the end. It was not just that he had volunteered, it was, as well, his duty to see it through, regardless of outcome, and to face it honorably. Such thoughts did not still the racing of his mind, and he would lie awake most of the night.

One

NEAR TAPPAN, NEW YORK
OCTOBER 1, 1780

DESPITE THE SUN SHINING BRIGHTLY THROUGH THE autumn leaves on the Hudson Valley, he felt cold, cold and weary. They had given him a mission, and it was almost a curse that it should have fallen on him. Since this damn war had started for him, nearly four years ago, he had never felt as alone and depressed as he did now.

Major Allen van Dorn was posted to the staff of General Sir Henry Clinton, commander in chief of all of His Majesty's forces in North America. He looked over at his sole escort, the rather nervous sergeant riding beside him.

"Sergeant O'Toole, keep that white flag up high, and be waving it, not hanging limp," he sighed. "We're most likely inside their lines now. You want one of their militia to blow us out of the saddles and only then figure they made a mistake?"

"No, sir, sorry, sir." The sergeant took to waving the white banner with exaggerated vigor as they continued along the road to Tappan on the Hudson.

It was a path well known to Allen, a scene of near-daily skirmishing since the two armies had settled into what appeared to be positions of permanent standoff and waiting. The British army in New
York City faced off against the Continental army, which was under
direct command of George Washington and garrisoned near West
Point. The land in between was often fought over, but never with any
serious intent. Both sides were waiting on events transpiring seven
hundred miles away in the South. The emphasis of the war had shifted
to the South after the reversal at Monmouth Court House over two
years ago, after the splitting off of a significant number of Clinton's
best troops, who were placed under General Cornwallis to try an alternative plan to break the deadlock. They had realized that New
England, the birthing place and hotbed of this rebellion, could never
be taken by the British with the forces at hand. The campaign to take
back upstate New York in '77 had turned into a debacle under Bur-
goyne. Clinton realized that pressing a campaign into Pennsylvania,
as tried three years ago, would degenerate into a wild-goose chase
with Washington forever drawing back deeper into the hinterland
and the wilderness beyond.

The British leaders had concluded that the South was now their
best chance. Reports indicated that a high percentage of the resi-
dents were, at heart, if not outright Tories, at least wishing to be
loyal to the Crown and see this bloody stalemate come to an end.
Split the Southern states off and bring them back to the Crown, offer freedom to slaves if they would fight, close the war off there, with
Loyalists in control in the field, they reasoned. As they restored colonial governments, they thought, the Middle States would crack
wide open and collapse as well. That would leave just upstate New
York and New England. With their allies to the South gone, the
northern states would finally seek agreement. Unfortunately, the
French were now in this as well, expanding it to a global conflict. It
was all madness.

It felt on this day like it would just go on forever. He was tired. He
was cold, though the sun shone warmly, and he dreaded what the day

ahead might bring, though Clinton had dispatched him with some little hope that all might yet be well.

He heard the deadly sound of a musket being cocked.

"Don't you lobsterbacks move another damn inch!"

Sergeant O'Toole, by his side, seemed close to panic.

"Don't move," Allen hissed.

He looked over his left shoulder to where the sound had come from. A soldier wearing the uniform of the Connecticut militia stepped out from behind a tree. He was thin and lanky, in a dirty and thread-bare uniform. Three more came out behind him, led by a sergeant, all of them with muskets leveled.

They had ridden straight into the Rebels' picket line and had not even realized it.

Allen slowly raised his hands, and nodded to the white flag O'Toole was holding.

"We are under a flag of truce, sergeant. You could see our approach was in the open."

The sergeant just gazed at him. Why was it that all these Rebels chewed tobacco, a disgusting habit? The sergeant looked straight at him as he expelled a stream of dark spittle, striking the hoof of his mount.

"A courier came to this place yesterday under a truce flag, to inform your General Washington that I would come today bearing a note from my commander, General Clinton."

"I ain't heard nothin' of it," the sergeant drawled. "Now get down slow and easy. A lot of strange things been going on around here the last two weeks. So slow and easy. Make a wrong move and, by God, you are both dead men."

"I do like them horses," declared the first soldier with a grin, musket still aimed directly at Allen. "Bet they'd fetch a half dozen pounds sterling each, no questions asked."

Allen carefully dismounted, the sergeant drawing closer.

"Now let's see this letter you're talking about."

"Sergeant, I am under orders to deliver it personally to General Washington and to no other."

"Look, you bastard, I'm the one with the gun aimed at you, and not the other way around. I suggest you do as I'm telling you."

"My orders from my general were clear," Allen said, trying not to let fear take hold, using his best clipped officer-in-command tone.

"You ain't one of 'em," the sergeant said. "You sound like Jersey or Pennsylvania."

Allen nodded.

"I'm a Loyalist. I was born in Trenton, New Jersey."

"We got ourselves a damn Tory no less," the first soldier announced. "I say, shoot them and take their horses. We can be drunk for a week on what we'd get."

"I am carrying a dispatch, under flag of truce from General Clinton to General Washington. You do that and all four of you will be dancing at the end of a rope."

"Just like that bastard Andre does tomorrow."

With that Allen stiffened, anger showing.

"Major Andre is an honorable soldier," he replied sharply.

"Oh really? That ain't the way we see it, and we're gonna snap his neck like a twig for being a spy." The sergeant cradled his musket and made the gesture of breaking something with both hands, while behind him the private who had first stepped out held one hand up over his head as if clutching a rope, then cocked his head to one side, rolled his eyes, and stuck his tongue out. "Just wish we had that son of a bitch Benedict Arnold doing the rope dance next to him."

"You bloody bastards."

"What did you just call us?" the sergeant snapped again, training his musket on Allen. At that instant he knew they were, indeed, going to kill him and O'Toole. Easy enough to hide their bodies, take the horses, and sell them later. When inquiries were finally made, most likely days from now, all would shrug their shoulders and say nothing.

"All of you, stand at ease!"

The sergeant looked past Allen, stiffened slightly, and sighed. "Damn officer," he muttered under his breath.

"You men, uncock your pieces carefully, then shoulder your weapons, now! These two are under a flag of truce."

The four reluctantly did as ordered.

"What command are you?" the officer behind Allen snapped.

"Second Connecticut militia, Captain Randell's company."

"Clear out of here before I put all of you up on report and have you flogged. I'll take over for these two. Now clear out!"

There was a moment of hesitation, the sergeant looking past Allen. He let a squirt of tobacco juice loose, striking Allen's boots, then turned.

"Come on," was all he said to the other three, and they drifted back into the woods.

Allen could hear the man behind him sigh, then the click of a pistol being uncocked. He turned to face the man who had just saved them and felt as if stricken a visceral blow.

It was his childhood friend, Peter Wellsley, wearing the uniform of the headquarters company of Washington, the braid of a major on his shoulder. With him were two troopers, mounted, but with pistols still raised and casually pointing in the direction of where the militiamen had retreated. They were taking no chances.

"My God, Peter," Allen whispered.

He could see Peter's eyes widen in recognition, but there was no exchange, no acknowledgment.

"I've been sent down to meet you," Peter finally said coolly.

There was an icy chill to his voice, a distant look to his eyes.

"Get mounted and let's get the hell out of here. Men like that can be dangerous when hungry and smelling booty."

Allen did as suggested without hesitation. Hell, two minutes ago he had figured himself a dead man.

Peter and the two troopers set the pace at a sharp canter for a quarter of a mile or so until they passed through another picket line of Continentals. This position was obviously the "official" forward outpost for the Americans, thus the road was barricaded, a company of men guarded the approach, actually well-uniformed for Continentals. Peter slowed long enough to show a slip of paper, a few words with the commander there, a nod to the white flag held by a trembling O'Toole, and a quick exchange of words. Several of the men then moved the barricade so they could pass through.

Once past, Peter slowed the pace to a walk, said something to his two escorts, who dropped back half a dozen paces, looked over his shoulder, and motioned to Allen to come up by his side.

The two rode in silence for several minutes. Allen still felt chilled, inwardly a bit shaken by the experience with the first troops he had met. There had, indeed, been murder in their eyes, and if not for Peter's timely arrival, he knew with utmost certainty he would have been dead by now, stripped, buttons and braid clipped from his uniform along with any identification, the dispatch he carried read, if those men could, indeed, read, then shredded.

To his right the broad Hudson reflected the afternoon sun. The rising hills on the far shore were a riot of autumn color that should have brightened any man's day, but he looked at them vacantly, his soul torn and empty.

His closest friend on the British side, Major John Andre, was scheduled to be hanged tomorrow morning, and his closest friend from before this damn war, now a major like himself, but wearing the uniform of his sworn enemies, was riding by his side.

It was Peter who broke the silence at last.

"Your mission is futile, Major van Dorn. General Washington refuses to accept your letter from your general."

Startled, Allen looked over at him. His old friend's features were taut, thin, so unlike the round-faced boy, the "youngster" who would tag along with Allen and his brothers as they went afield. Was it really all that long ago, when they'd venture out to play, to hunt, to snitch apples in the fall, or darn near drown themselves in an old punt boat, fishing on the Delaware when the shad were running in the spring? He wondered if he had aged as much through these last five years.

"Peter?"

His friend finally shifted and turned to look straight at him.

"It is good to see you again."

Peter nodded, but did not reply.

"You saved my life back at Monmouth Court House. I will never forget that kindness and the debt of life I will always owe you," Allen said.

"You would have done the same for me, but things change."

"Not all things."

Peter could not respond for a moment.

"Allen, if not for Loyalists like you, your side would have given it up years ago and gone home."

"I could say the same about your side. The king has offered you fair terms repeatedly."

"Fair terms for slavery."

"For reunion, for peace."

"So the response is to continue to ravage the land in revenge? A wonderful way to convince us to fight on, knowing the treatment we would receive if ever we were to lay down our arms, were defenseless, and threw ourselves on his mercy and that of his hirelings."

"Both sides are ravaging the land," Allen said. "You get the same reports we do out of the South. How the war is being fought there. Farms burned, men hanged in their own front yards, women and children driven out as refugees."

"If you were not there it would not be happening," Peter retorted sharply. "Allen, there's no sense in arguing that. We're seven hundred miles away. Neither you nor I have or would take part in such things.

"Up here, instead, one of our generals is suborned, turns traitor, and tries to sell out our entire army. What your army could not win through honorable warfare, your side now tries to win through bribery and backstabbing."

There was no denying the truth of that and Allen fell silent.

"Were you part of it? Did you know about it?" Peter asked sharply.

"I am under a flag of truce," Allen replied a bit defensively. "You know I cannot answer that. Nor would I."

Yes, he did know. It was his job to know as the Loyalist officer responsible for intelligence gathering in the region. He had been one of the last to see Andre before he had departed on his fatal mission. He had begged him to show caution, warning that it could be a trap, and to stay in uniform concealed under a cloak in case he was captured. At least then he would have some grounds to argue that he should be treated as a prisoner of war rather than a spy. Andre had smiled, even laughed, patted him on the shoulder and said he would be back in little more than a day, and within the week the war along the Hudson would be all but over.

There were several minutes of tense silence until Allen finally broke it.

"My family. They are behind your lines. Have you heard anything about them?"

Peter seemed to relent slightly.

"I was home in Trenton early this spring, carrying a dispatch from the general to Congress and stopped over. Your brother is prospering." He paused. "Of course."

"And my parents?"

"They're alive, though I doubt they will ever recover from the death of your brother, James."

Allen stiffened with that. James had gone with the Continentals at the start of the war, and had died of exposure after the battle for Trenton back in '76. Allen had been captured in that fight, helped carry his dying brother back when Washington and his men withdrew across the Delaware after their stunning victory, and then helped them to bury James the following day.

He knew it was Peter's and James's comrades who had personally appealed to Washington and convinced the general to have him paroled and exchanged through the lines because of his young brother's sacrifice.

"They can't find the grave. They want to return him to the family plot," Peter sighed.

"After this is over, I know where to find him," Allen whispered. "I marked the spot well, remember I helped to dig his grave alongside you."

"It's all washed away now. Looks like a potter's field, with several hundred sunken-in holes now. You can't tell one from the other. Perhaps it's best he stays with his comrades anyhow. I think he'd prefer that."

Allen lowered his head.

"I still can't believe you went Tory," Peter finally sighed, a sharp edge to his voice. Your brother died on our side. We were once friends. You love this land as much as I do. I still cannot believe seeing you in that damn uniform."

Allen looked over at him sharply.

"Yes, I do love this land as much as you do, and I ask you this: If you win, then what? You know history as well as I. Nearly all revolutions end in just replacing one ruler with another, often far worse. The king made mistakes, but was it really all that bad as compared to how you might fare and suffer under another ruler afterward?"

Peter looked at him sharply.

"We have General Washington to guide us."

Allen shook his head. "Washington may turn into another Cromwell, another Caesar."

"Damn, how dare you," Peter said. "Remember, he gave you your freedom to go back and wear that damn uniform, otherwise you'd be sitting this one out in some prison camp out on the frontier with your Hessian friends."

Peter paused for a moment.

"Remember Garth Williamson, Vincent van Hoek?"

"Yes. Hell, they used to go exploring with us as kids," said Allen.

"They're dead."

"What?"

"Oh, I thought you might have heard since they died within sight of you. They were taken prisoner at Brandywine then locked up in your damn prison ships in New York. We've all heard about those ships. How the bodies are just dumped out a gun port when the tide is going out. Tell me, when the wind is blowing from the east, can you smell the death at your headquarters?"

Allen bristled at that, but knew there was no defense. More than a few had made appeals to Clinton to abandon the charnel houses of the prison ships, to establish a proper camp on dry land, but he refused, saying it was all that bloody Rebels against the Crown deserved. Word was that nearly four out of five men confined there died within a matter of months, and yes, their bodies were unceremoniously dumped into the river when the tide was running out.

"It's this war, this damn war that is doing this to us," Allen finally offered, "but you and I, Peter. I thought there was no hatred between us."

"Live what I've lived through for four years while you and your comrades sit fat and happy in the city and maybe you'd understand better. At Morristown last winter, I watched comrades who had served from the beginning, dying by the hundreds from starvation and the cold. Hard to believe, but most of us say it was worse than Valley Forge. Meanwhile you and your Clinton were most likely sitting rosy faced by warm fireplaces, stuffed to bursting, and but a few hundred yards away your prisoners were huddled together without even a blanket and dying in their own filth."

"I did not do this," Allen replied.

"But the side you fight for did," Peter snapped.

"There have been atrocities on both sides. We could argue this all day. That is what war does to all of us. There've been reports of our men nailed to trees and scalped."

Peter, whose eyes had formed cool narrow slits, widened them slightly and he turned away.

"Not with my command."

"Those four back there were only seconds away from performing the ritual on my sergeant and me. You can't deny it."

Peter sighed and nodded.

Again, long moments of silence. The road ahead curved up and to the left, following the bank of the Hudson, its surface shimmering with the red and gold reflection of autumn trees lining its banks. A company of troops was marching toward them and they edged to the side of the road. The passing infantry wore relatively new uniforms, hats adorned with sprigs of pine or hemlock, muskets polished to a sheen. No rabble, this. They were regulars, lean and hawk faced, even if some had seen only seventeen summers. Though they maintained marching discipline, nearly everyone looked up at him with a cold eye, muttering comments about "damn lobsterbacks." These were not the type of men he recalled facing when this war had started. These men looked as tough and seasoned as any British or Hessian regular, even tougher now, in fact, because Peter was right: For two years his army had languished in near luxury in New York City, compared to this army encamped in the rain, mud, heat, and freezing cold of Morristown and now on the banks of the Hudson.

The company marched on and they resumed their ride, Peter urging his mount up to a gentle canter, Allen following suit.

"Peter?"

"Yes."

"Do you remember Miss Elizabeth Risher?"

Just saying her name caused Peter's throat to tighten.

Peter was silent for a moment remembering her only too well. Then he just nodded, stifling his emotion, not wishing to reveal what he had in fact carried in his heart for years, ever since meeting her long before the war.

"Her father was a merchant in Philadelphia," Peter said, trying to act calm. "We're distant cousins. You must remember when she used to visit us in Trenton before the war. Pretty lass. Why?"

Allen hesitated, Peter looking over at him.

"It's just that while we occupied Philadelphia, I met her . . ." and his voice trailed away.

He could sense the sudden tension in Peter.

"And?" Peter finally whispered, voice tight, even trembling.

"It's just that, well at that time . . ." and again he fell silent.

"Something happened?"

"No, not really," Allen replied, though that was something of a lie. A lot had happened, and she had never left his heart after two and a half years.

Any attempt at friendliness of but a moment before seemed to have evaporated as Peter gazed at him.

Allen tried to smile.

"Peter, don't tell me that you . . ." and his voice trailed off.

Peter just looked at him coldly.

"Don't tell me," Allen said softly. "My God, she's nearly two years older than you and I just assumed . . ."

"Two years might be a big difference when I was fifteen," Peter snapped, "but not now at twenty."

"You do have feelings for her then?" Allen asked. He was trying to sound like an old friend, kidding a comrade about a girl both were interested in, but it came out awkwardly.

Peter, still stiff as if struggling for control, looked back at his escort, two old troopers nearly twice his age, both of them grinning over this conversation that they were obviously "eavesdropping" on.

"I don't want to speak of it with you," Peter finally said.

"I've tried to send at least a dozen letters through the lines, Peter," Allen replied, "but never a word of reply. I worry for her. After our army evacuated Philadelphia I feared she might face reprisals as a Loyalist, especially because her father fled to New York, claiming he was going there to oversee the family business interests and leaving his daughter to oversee their home, legally signing it over to her name. Their friend Doctor Rush was supposed to keep an eye on her and vouch for her if need be.

"Peter, regardless of your personal feelings, as a gentleman may I ask a favor?"

Peter nodded, not replying, making no offer.

He took a deep breath.

"She was close friends with Peggy Shippen. I fear that association compounded by the fact that her father has fled to New York, now puts her in harm's way."

"That traitorous bitch Shippen!" Peter snapped. "My God, if Elizabeth is friends with her, she better lay low until Judgment Day. If Shippen wasn't a woman, she'd be dancing at the end of a rope tomorrow morning as well."

Allen instantly regretted telling Peter that bit of news. At this moment Peggy was the most infamous woman in North America—the wife of the arch traitor Benedict Arnold, and beyond that rumored to have been the mistress of his friend Major John Andre when they had occupied Philadelphia back in '77. Some even saw her as the link of communication between the two.

"Could you at least make sure for me that Elizabeth is all right and inform her that I still think of her daily and," he hesitated, "that I still love her?"

"I'm making no promises on that score," Peter replied sharply. "As to your personal concerns, Miss Elizabeth is perfectly safe. Neither of us makes war on women and children."

"Not what I've heard from along the frontier and down South," Allen retorted.

The tension triggered by mention of Elizabeth stilled their conversation and the attempts by both, at some level, to try to show some level of friendship for a childhood friend evaporated. It was, of course, compounded by the fact that both faced each other, not just at this moment, but across the years in the game of point and counterpoint of spying in New Jersey and New York.

The road ahead dipped down into a broad open expanse, a field of several dozen acres, covered with tents, and a two-story stone farmhouse was set back a hundred yards from the road.

Alongside of it, carpenters were busy erecting a simple gallows— not the trapdoor kind, recently developed and claimed to be more humane since the victim's neck was usually snapped, bringing instant death, but the old-fashioned kind of just vertical uprights, a crosstree, the rope already dangling from it. Next to it, shovels rose and fell rhythmically from out of the ground, the grave digging detail at work.

Allen all but came to a stop, staring at it.

"Andre is in there," Peter said, nodding to the farmhouse. "It takes place the hour after dawn tomorrow."

Allen, throat again tightening, could not speak for a moment.

"My orders are to proceed to General Washington's headquarters and present a missive from General Clinton."

"And I have told you, his Excellency the general will not receive you."

"Major Wellsley, we are both bound by our orders, please escort me to General Washington's headquarters. If rejected, I can at least tell my general I had made the personal appeal and that your general acted directly toward me as you claim he now will."

Peter sighed, finally nodded, and without comment spurred his mount, Allen taking a moment to catch up. For an instant there was a childhood memory of having "borrowed" two horses from the barn of the Snyders, who lived beyond the edge of their village, and racing them bareback across the pasture. He recalled Peter falling off and cracking a rib, and how the Snyders, good people that they were, had actually rigged up their carriage to take Peter home.

They rode for a couple of miles, passing more and more troops camped in fields or out drilling, and woodcutting parties working on the stockpiles for approaching winter. It always amazed him how an army of just several thousand could devour acres of woods in but a few days. Allen took note of their appearance, and sensed their morale was high. Most were somewhat raggedy, but they were not the ill-uniformed scarecrows he had faced at Germantown and Monmouth.

The French supply ships, able to run the blockade, had brought in uniforms, new muskets, tentage, artillery, and ammunition for thousands. It showed. There was even a company of French troops, in their distinctive and somewhat absurd white uniforms, impossible to keep clean in the field, out drilling with absolute precision. He could not help but see all this, but of course, by the rules of war, while under a flag of truce he was forever forbidden on his word of honor to report on anything observed. Peter could have required him to wear a blindfold, but had not done so, at least a small concession to a memory of honorable behavior dating back to childhood.

At last, General Washington's headquarters loomed into view, made obvious by the commander-in-chief flag flying in front and by the guard details, which had, without doubt, been doubled and doubled again since the Arnold incident started, and with it the revelation that part of the plan was to have Washington himself captured or killed.

Peter reined in, and an orderly briskly stepped forward to take his mount's bridle, then offered the same service to Allen. It had been a long day of riding up from Manhattan, and he wished he could just walk around and stretch for a few minutes, but knew that all eyes, most of them hostile, were upon him. Peter's two escorts and Sergeant O'Toole, still carrying the flag of truce and looking about, obviously still frightened, came up and dismounted as well.

Peter approached the door to Washington's residence, a strongly built home, typical of this region of the Hudson Valley, influenced by Dutch designs, constructed of sturdy fieldstone with a high sloping roof. The two guards directly at the door came to attention. The door was opened and a young officer stood there, barring the way. Allen had some recollection of him. It was the Frenchman, Lafayette. Peter spoke to him for a moment. Lafayette looked past Peter to Allen and to his surprise actually bowed slightly and offered a salute; Allen instantly stiffened and returned the gesture. The door closed behind them, and Allen suddenly felt awkward, indeed. Still at attention from returning Lafayette's salute, he just stood there for a moment, knowing nearly all eyes were upon him. O'Toole came up to his side and that at least gave him a diversion to turn and speak to him.

"Are you all right, sergeant?"

"Well, sir, we are now in the belly of the beast, are we not?" O'Toole whispered, and he could not help but smile at this comment.

"They'll honor the flag," Allen said.

"Those first ones weren't about to."

"This is General Washington's headquarters, these are men of honor," he said, deliberately loud enough so that those nearby could hear, "not those militia scum who nearly murdered us back on the road."

He said it loud enough so that Lafayette and others would hear of the incident.

"If I'm granted an audience, you just remain here, go over to those trees over there so you are in the shade, and stand at ease. Don't talk unless spoken to. Remember we are under a flag of truce so be careful of what you say. They might try and get information from you."

"Soul of caution it is, sir," O'Toole replied.

"Good man," Allen replied, patting him on the shoulder to reassure him, even though the sergeant was an enlisted man nearly twice his age.

"Major van Dorn?"

He turned. It was Lafayette. Allen stiffened again to attention and saluted, the two following proper European custom.

"I hope your journey here was without incident?"

"No problem at all once I finally met Major Wellsley. Major Wellsley is a childhood friend."

"So I have heard. It was your brother who helped to successfully guide the attack at Trenton."

Allen could only nod.

"On that indulgence of memory, his Excellency the general has agreed to meet with you, and to receive your letter. Your friend pleaded your case most persuasively."

"I thank you, sir."

Given Peter's cool reception, this information surprised him. He followed Lafayette into the house, the main corridor filled with half a dozen officers who turned and looked at him. Lafayette went through the ritual of formal presentations, nods exchanged to each—Generals Greene, Stirling, the now legendary von Steuben, and the rotund artillery commander Knox. Except for the polite words of introduction, no comments were exchanged. He scanned each of them quickly, trying to imprint the memory of them into his mind if ever a day should come when they met on the field of battle.

Lafayette tapped politely on a dark green door facing the main corridor, then slowly opened it. Within, General George Washington was looking up from behind a desk, and Peter Wellsley was standing stiffly at attention by his side.

Lafayette led the way in, then closed the door behind Allen.

"Your Excellency, I have the honor of presenting to you Major Allen van Dorn, of the staff of General Clinton. Major van Dorn, may I present to you General George Washington."

Allen stiffened to rigid attention, doffing his hat and bowing low. Washington rose from his chair, hatless and offering a salute.

Washington then sat down, but no chair was offered to Allen.

Allen studied the man closely. They had met once before, the day after Trenton when the general had offered him parole and exchange because of his brother's service. The impression on him then was memorable, a towering man of muscular build, still young-looking in his early forties. The only imperfection in his features was the deep scarring of smallpox, but then again, that was true of a fair percentage of people in this world.

General Washington had aged greatly since then. With wig off, his hair had gone nearly entirely to gray, his eyes were deep sunk, features slightly gaunt, a sense of weariness about him as if he had endured a sleepless night, yet nevertheless gaze fixed unflinchingly.

"Young Major Wellsley tells me that we have met before," the general finally said, breaking the silence.

"Yes, sir. The day after the first battle at Trenton. You offered me parole and exchange because of . . ."

His voice trailed off for a moment and the general finished the sentence ". . . because your brother died a noble Patriot in service to his country."

Allen wondered if there was the slightest hint of rebuke in Washington's tone, questioning how he could still serve the Crown after the sacrifice of his own brother to the Rebel cause.

"I had already informed your courier yesterday that I would refuse any appeal from your General Clinton to spare the life of Major Andre unless it was to exchange him for," he hesitated as if there was a bad taste in just saying the name, "Benedict Arnold."

Allen watched his features closely. Yes, the general loathed Arnold now, but only weeks before, Arnold was rumored to be among this man's closest friends and confidantes, and that if Washington should ever fall in battle it was his wish that either General Greene or Arnold assume full command of the forces in the field.

"As the party making the request, sir, may I have your permission to give to you a letter from my commanding officer?"

Washington nodded, saying nothing.

Still rigid at attention, Allen took the final three steps to Washington's desk, reached into his uniform breast pocket, and drew out the heavy envelope, sealed with wax and bound with waxed cord. Washington, using what looked like a paring knife, cut the cords, broke the seal, and opened the letter.

His eyes darted down the page, taking not more than half a minute. With a sigh he put the letter down, leaning back in his chair, rubbing his eyes.

"As I already had sent to your general, the only consideration I will offer will be the exchange of Arnold for your Major Andre. That was refused, which was why I initially declined to even meet with you, Major van Dorn. If anything, this meeting now is a courtesy more to you than to your commander who . . ."

He hesitated but then continued.

". . . refuses to hand over an outright traitor, for a man, who by all accounts, even from those who sat at his trial, is an honorable officer, a gallant man of noble spirit."

"Sir, he is," Allen blurted out. "He has been my closest friend in the army for three years, and it gladdens me to hear that even those who sit in judgment of him see that nobility of character."

He regretted this breech of protocol even as he spoke, but his emotions had taken hold.

He caught a glimpse of his old friend Peter looking at him, stand-ing slightly behind Washington, and subtly shaking his head.

"Yet, nevertheless, no matter how honorable his character, he was caught behind our lines, in civilian garb, and attempted to bribe his way past our pickets when stopped."

Allen knew it was not his place to present the argument that An-dre had, indeed, gone to meet Arnold, right in the middle of his own encampment, by necessity forced to disguise himself in civilian cloth-ing. It was an action at which he had expressed doubt, but was or-dered to do so by Clinton in order to consummate Arnold's betrayal. He had, indeed, tried to bluff his way past the pickets manned by troops most likely similar to the ones who had surprised Allen on the ride in. Andre had at first mistaken them for a Loyalist unit, then, realizing his mistake, had fallen back on the subterfuge that he was just a civilian visiting a friend behind the lines, and offered a bribe to be allowed to pass. One of the guards, searching him, had found the secret plans to coordinate the betrayal and offensive strike by Clin-ton to take West Point and to capture General Washington as well.

Now his noble friend stood condemned.

"There is no offer here in this letter for a fair and proper ex-change, as I knew there would not be," Washington finally said, voice weary.

Allen wanted to express his contempt for Arnold, a man who had left Andre to his fate, who had even left his wife behind when he re-alized the plot had been unmasked. Now residing in New York, even though he had come over to the Loyalist side, his manner of betrayal made him a social pariah. He was useful to their cause, but never to be accepted into polite society—if a man would betray once, he would, without doubt, betray again. At least those Loyalists who had stayed with the Crown, such as himself, had done so openly, at the start of the conflict rather than switch horses in midstream.

Allen was, as an officer bearing a message, not graced with the latitude of discussion, debate, or appeal that would perhaps have occurred if Washington had been at a meeting of equal rank with Clinton.

"I have received the letter you bear, Major van Dorn. You have fulfilled your mission. There is no need to send a reply to your general, since there has not been an indication on his behalf of the slightest change other than an appeal to my sense of humanity."

He sighed, looking up at the ceiling and then back to Allen.

"Do you think I relish this task?" Washington asked coldly. "I want you to know that every officer you saw out in the corridor, even General Lafayette here, was impressed by Major Andre's nobility and seeing he was simply caught in the machinations of another, have appealed for some form of leniency."

Allen knew better than to offer a reply.

"Regardless of my personal feelings in this case, I am in command of all armies in the field fighting for our independence from your Crown. Personal feelings must not hold sway, must never hold sway. Such personal sentiments must never overrule what must, however regretfully, be my duty.

"By the rules of war, a spy may be exchanged for an enemy of equal value, and that equal value is Arnold. If not, then he is to be hanged."

Allen could sense Lafayette stiffening slightly, drawing in his breath. Washington shot the young French general an angry glance, and Lafayette went rigid.

"I will say this, and you may convey it to your General Clinton: Every member of the trial board spoke to me of some form of leniency, or if execution was, indeed, necessary as required by the rules of war, and that same board voted for unanimously, urged that your Major Andre face execution by firing squad rather than hanging."

Washington fell silent for a moment, shook his head, and then lowered it.

"This is not revenge, Major van Dorn, but no such choice was offered to Nathan Hale, or many another man captured behind your lines in this conflict. In some cases our people have been strung up within minutes of being captured."

He sighed.

"This is not revenge. These are the rules of war. I am honor bound to uphold them and it must be so."

Allen stood silent, and General Washington finally looked up at him and nodded.

"Go and tell General Clinton my reply."

Allen swallowed hard, and was about to remove his hat again, bow, and withdraw, but then nerve took hold.

"Then a personal request, sir, an indulgence I beg of you."

Washington looked at him with flash of annoyance.

"Go on then, Major."

"Sir. Major Andre was my closest friend in this conflict. It was he who taught me so much about the code of honor of a soldier. May I remain with him in his last hours as a comfort."

Washington said nothing.

"Sir. It would enable me to report back to my general, as well, that though he was hanged, all proper military honors were observed by you and your men, which I am certain will transpire, and perhaps in some way might make this easier for both sides."

Washington's gaze drifted from Allen to Lafayette, and Allen, not daring to look, sensed that Lafayette was nodding an assent. Washington's gaze fixed on him, and again there was that look of infinite weariness. Allen sensed that the betrayal of Arnold was an emotional shock from which he had yet to recover. He knew this man was educated in the classics and wondered if in his heart he was saying over and over, "et tu, Brute?"

There was finally the slightest of nods.

"You may spend the night with your friend. I regret to go through this formality, but do I have your word of honor that if there are any secrets Major Andre has kept concealed, that you will not allow him to speak of them?"

"Yes, sir," Allen replied.

Washington looked over his shoulder at Peter.

"I am not questioning your adherence to honor, Major van Dorn, but you will be accompanied by Major Wellsley here throughout. You may remain with your friend until," he paused, "until it is finished."

Allen fought to hold back his emotions. This man was his enemy. On a field of battle if ever given the chance to bring him down, he would do so without hesitation. He was the heart and soul of their Revolution. Yet he could sense as well the inner conflict that Washington must be suffering at this moment, on the one hand compassion, wishing that these decisions did not confront him, and on the other, his sense of gravitas, of duty that demanded the response, ameliorated by this small act of compassion.

Again removing his hat, he bowed low. Washington, half standing, returned the salute.

Two

NEAR TAPPAN, NEW YORK
OCTOBER 1, 1780

AS THE DOOR OPENED, ANDRE, WHO WAS SITTING IN A COR-
ner of what was actually a rather comfortable room, staring into a
crackling fire, turned, looked back, and for once the formalities of a
military life fell away entirely.

"Allen!"

The chair fell backward as he leaped up, came up to his old friend,
and eagerly embraced him, patting him on the back.

There was wetness in the eyes of both men as they hugged—a
most unusual act for the normally reserved Andre—until he, as if
remembering himself, broke the embrace, stepped back, nervously
clearing his throat, wiping his eyes, and then mumbling that he must
have gotten a cinder in his eye.

He looked past Allen and saw Peter standing tensely in the doorway.

"John," Allen announced formally, "this is a friend of mine from
before the war. Major Peter Wellsley, may I introduce Major John
Andre."

The two exchanged polite bows.

"A friend of Allen is, of course, a friend of mine," John offered, and pointed to a couple of straight-back chairs positioned by the fire-place, which was the only illumination in the room, as he lifted his own chair from the floor, motioning for them to sit.

"General Stirling was so kind as to send over a delightful bottle of claret. May I offer you some?"

"Of course, John," Allen replied, again struggling to control his emotion, recalling so many evenings of John, ever the gracious host, offering to share whatever he had, even if huddled in a miserable tent while icy rain fell outside. Peter nodded in assent, but said nothing.

"Delightful, then. Wish I had some remnants of dinner, some roasted goose. I was told General Washington personally sent it down from his table, but alas, gentlemen, I did not expect guests and hunger dominated my thoughts."

He poured some wine into two crystal goblets, handing them to his guests, and poured a third for himself. Allen noted the bottle was now little more than half consumed. If Stirling's kindness was with the hope that John would consume the bottle in order to calm his nerves, John was maintaining his inner discipline even though at many a party at headquarters he had consumed bottle after bottle, and rarely shown an effect.

John turned his chair to face his friend, smiled, saying nothing, looking expectantly. Allen realized that some sort of hope had sprung in John's heart at the sight of him.

He drew a deep breath, struggled to control his voice, trying to offer a comforting smile.

"Nothing has changed, John. You will face your fate in the morning."

There was barely a flicker of emotion, a slight widening of the eyes, a drawing in of breath, nothing more. He looked down at his glass of claret, took a sip, and just stared at the fire with a strange distant smile.

"General Clinton made every effort for your release, but would not agree to the exchange of Arnold as demanded by Washington."

"Well," John sighed and actually chuckled, "exchanging a mere major for a general is rarely the form, you know."

"Gentlemen, may I interject?"

Both turned to look at Peter.

"I have served directly under General Washington ever since Trenton. First as a private in his guard, promoted along the way, and now . . ." he fell silent.

Allen did not fill in the rest. He knew exactly what Peter's position was. He served as an intelligence officer for Washington, the same way Allen served Clinton. During the campaigns in Jersey both knew details far beyond anything traditionally serving officers had from overseas or from other states. They shared a grasp of local personages, their loyalty to one side or the other, and thus both had risen quickly. The ever-backward and -forward movement of spies, be they professionals or amateurs, had revealed Peter's position to him a year ago, and he assumed Peter knew the same about him.

It was, without doubt, why Washington had sent him down to meet him as an escort, why Washington had acquiesced to his appeal for an audience, and, of course, why Peter was sitting here now as their companion for the night. If John should in any way be indiscreet, Peter would pick up on it.

"What I am saying, gentlemen," Peter continued, "is that General Washington is not a bloodthirsty man nor a vengeful man. Major Andre, in this tragic case of yours, he is constrained by the traditions and rules of war. There is no personal anger in him toward you. In fact, it is quite the opposite. All know that you have borne yourself as a gentleman of honor throughout this ordeal."

Andre smiled and pointed back to the remains of the roast goose, well plucked over.

"Be certain to thank him for me for this excellent repast, and yes, I do know the positive qualities of his character, and what constrains him now."

There was another moment of nervous silence.

"Another round, my friends?" he asked, standing and picking up the bottle to refill their glasses, though he poured only a small amount for himself.

He sat back down, picking up a couple of split logs of hickory, and set them into the fire. Within seconds they were crackling and sparking.

"Tending a fire is a most relaxing pastime," he said, smile never vanishing. "I detest boors who just throw the logs in, sparks and ash flying. It shows no respect for the fire itself. Each log should be carefully set to complement the others already aflame, to catch their heat, ignite properly, and add to the symmetry. A good fire is a work of art in and of itself, and I consider myself something of a Rembrandt with such things."

"I remember the night after Brandywine," Allen chuckled. "Pouring rain, and yet you got one going to heat our cold hash."

Andre nodded, gazing at the flickering flames, holding his glass of claret up to the flame as if to examine the color of the wine before taking another sip.

"'Tis a comfort at least we do not live in medieval times. I will confess there would be a bit of a dread if fire was to be my fate."

Both looked over at him, shaking their heads, and Allen knew what the hint was.

"John?"

Andre looked sidelong at him.

"It will be by hanging, but you already know that."

"As a soldier you know what I would have preferred. I had hoped our good Clinton could have influenced that."

"Sir, I can attest that every officer of your court-martial appealed for it . . ." Peter hesitated, "the other way, but rules of war, as you know."

"Of course, of course," Andre said and for the first time Allen could sense a bit of a falling away of the facade.

Then, strangely, Andre chuckled.

"Perhaps a last-minute reprieve as in the dramas. Courier gallops up crying, stop the hanging, shoot him instead! That would be rather droll don't you think?"

"One can hope," Allen whispered looking over at Peter who remained silent, just staring at the fire.

"Could stand for a bit of music right now," Andre quickly said, changing the subject as if he had allowed his wish to venture too far outside his outwardly calm demeanor.

"Wish we had Franklin's glass harmonica right now," Allen replied. "Such a fascinating instrument. What fun we had while living in his house."

"Glass harmonica?" Peter asked, obviously trying to make conversation to help shift the topic to other things.

John went into a lengthy description of the instrument, the other two laughing as he tried to imitate the strange ethereal sound. Allen and he together hummed the Mozart piece written for the instrument.

They were interrupted by Jenkins, Major Andre's manservant, who had been allowed to come through the lines to attend to him, bearing another bottle of wine, this one a port with the compliments of General Greene. Uncorking the bottle Jenkins refilled their glasses, even though John's was only half empty, stood there woodenly for a moment, and then actually broke down into a sob.

John stood, went over to Jenkins, and put his hands on the man's shoulders.

"Now none of that, Jenkins."

"But, sir, you all seem so jovial. Sir, 'tis a great wrong, this, what they are doing, I can hardly bear it."

John patted him on the shoulder.

"A gentleman does not lament his fate in public, Jenkins, he faces it as a gentleman. For after all, all our candles are but brief flickers of light in eternity. Especially for a soldier. Remember our old barracks toast?"

He held up his glass.

"Gentlemen, to a long war, or a bloody plague and rapid promotion."

This time he at least drained half the glass. Allen, slightly bleary-eyed, but fearful of his own emotions, drained his entire glass, and motioned to Jenkins for another, while Peter just took a polite sip, obviously aware of his duty tonight to stay sober and attentive.

Jenkins did as requested, and then just stood there, tears coursing down his cheeks.

"Now Jenkins, cast not a dim pall over this night. It is my last upon this earth, and I want to fill it with life, the companionship of comrades, and not with tears. You are excused, Jenkins, and please compose yourself before you leave this room."

His servant left, wiping the tears from his eyes with a damp sleeve.

So the long hours of night, the last night Major John Andre would know on this earth, passed in song, the telling of soldiers' tales, sips of wine, and a midnight repast of cheese and bread sent from an anonymous benefactor. Several times Allen or John had to nudge Peter awake in his chair, joking that he was duty bound to stay awake so that no secrets might pass.

Peter just sat quietly as if lost in thought, letting the two friends talk through the night, until finally a couple of hours before dawn, John stood up, went to the window to look out at the early autumn morning sky.

"Orion is up high," he whispered. "Strange to think, tomorrow night it will rise, and I will not be here to see it."

"At least from here," Peter replied.

John said nothing, just gazing out the window, morning mists beginning to rise off the Hudson.

"All of this, the river flowing by with all its majesty, Orion rising, the first birdsongs of dawn, and I will not be here. I've had just over thirty years and how swiftly it flowed, just like that river, but now I am at an end."

Hands behind his back, Allen could see they were clasped, clenching and unclenching, as if he could only let the inner tension and fear show when not directly facing others. Andre lowered his head for a moment, as if in prayer, then turned, features fixed in a smile.

"I pray you do not think me rude, but think I should sleep for a while. I do want to look fresh and proper for my stroll through the valley of death."

Neither Allen nor Peter spoke as John stretched out on a narrow cot tucked up in the far corner of the room. As he settled down he looked over at Peter.

"I am certain our friends out in the corridor can guide you to a place to rest."

"Not at all," Peter replied. "I am not sleepy."

He looked over at Allen who simply shook his head, and then stood up to place an extra log on the fire, as Andre would have preferred it.

To Allen's amazement, John actually fell asleep, and within minutes was snoring lightly. He stood up to fetch the bottle of wine, offering to fill Peter's glass, and this time Peter accepted and drained half of it. Allen topped off his glass.

"My God, that man has nerve," Peter whispered.

"He is my friend, and yes, he does have nerve. To fall asleep like that with only a few hours left."

"This is worse than waiting for a battle to start," Peter sighed, sitting back down to stare at the fire.

"Suppose he was your comrade or friend, what would you think then?"

Peter, leaning forward, drained the rest of his wine.

"As we carried your brother—my friend—back from Trenton, I knew he was dying."

"What's that supposed to mean?" Allen replied sharply. "Remember, I was there and he was my brother."

Peter held up his hand, as if to ask for silence and to forestall an argument.

"Sorry, just remembering."

"Death watch for a friend, who deserves a better fate," Allen whispered. "Damn it, in your heart, is this fair?"

"You know I can't answer that," Peter replied. "If all was reversed and your Clinton was going to hang one of my comrades, do you think any appeals by Washington or me would change it?"

"Andre is different."

"Andre was caught as a spy."

"Andre is different," Allen retorted, voice choked with emotion.

"Gentlemen, please." It was John, half rolled over, looking toward them. "If you wish to argue my fate please go elsewhere and let me rest in peace."

The two friends from long ago, now divided, looked at each other.

"Rest in peace," John whispered, as if dwelling on the irony of the request. He rolled back over to face the wall.

Peter lowered his head. Allen, silent, just stared at the fire, occasionally putting in another log, while outside the first birds of dawn were chirping, the eastern sky shifting from darkness to indigo, then to golden red, and finally the light of approaching dawn.

A knock on the door caused the two to stand up, startled.

"Surely, not already?" Allen gasped, as he went to the door and opened it. It had aroused John as well, who sat up on the cot, looking about a bit hazily, like any man roused from deep and peaceful slumber. Allen wondered if the full reality of what he was awaking to this morning had dawned on him, or if John was still half lost in some final pleasant dream.

He opened the door and to his surprise and relief it was not the guard detail, but Jenkins, bearing a silver tray, covered with a dish.

"Excuse me gentlemen," Jenkins whispered. "It's breakfast for the major, sent with the compliments of General Washington himself."

"And nothing else?" Allen whispered hopefully.

Jenkins could only shake his head as Peter opened the door wide, the corridor outside empty except for two sentries who were leaning against the far wall, barely awake.

John was already standing up, rubbing the sleep from his eyes, yawning, running his hands through his hair. Jenkins set the tray down and uncovered it. It was a meal of fried ham, potatoes, scrambled eggs, and of all things, a steaming pot of coffee.

John smiled as he went over to the table and sat down.

"Would you gentlemen care to join me? The general in his largesse has sent more than I can possibly consume."

The two shook their heads. Though hungry, how any man could eat at a time like this was beyond Allen. He feared if he took a single bite he'd vomit it back up. It was just the same as he always felt in the final moments before battle was joined.

Jenkins stood silent, drawing a napkin around John's neck.

"Not too tight, now," John said, trying to joke, and again Jenkins begin to fill up with tears.

"Jenkins, none of that. I know your tears come straight from the heart, but do not unman me with them."

Jenkins nodded, unable to speak.

"Would you be so good as to fetch some hot water? I wish to be freshly shaved for the occasion, brush down my uniform, and I'm not sure of the protocol here: Should I wear my wig or not?"

He actually looked over at Peter as he spoke.

Peter, remembering previous hangings, swallowed hard.

"May I suggest, sir, no wig."

He did not add that often the wig came flying off, or shifted to an unsightly angle, especially if the victim's neck was not broken and he began to instinctively kick and struggle in his death agonies, as he slowly strangled at the end of the rope.

"Fine then, forget powdering the wig, Jenkins. Now please be quick with the hot water and razor."

He actually ate a fair part of the meal, then asked for a moment of privacy to relieve himself. John and Peter stepped outside to do the same. A long column of troops was coming in from the encampment behind the residence, and started to deploy around the gallows on three sides. A group of officers came down the road from the direction of Washington's headquarters, the judges of the court-martial, required by tradition to witness the carrying out of the sentence imposed. Allen looked toward General Greene hoping that somehow there would be a last moment reprieve. He caught the man's gaze. Greene looked straight at him and gave a subtle shake of his head.

The two went back into the room. The breakfast tray was set aside, Jenkins already shaving John, his face red from the effect of the razor. How tempting, Allen thought, more than one man had escaped the terror of the hangman's noose by, at such a moment, just seizing the razor and cutting his own throat. But that would be so out of place for John that there was not even a guard posted directly alongside Jenkins. The two sentries were just standing by the door, curiously looking in, one whispering to the other a comment about Andre's nerve.

A drumroll could be heard, growing louder, approaching from the encampment.

"I think it is about time, now," John said, standing up after Jenkins wiped the last of the lather from his face, letting Jenkins help him into his scarlet coat, his uniform jacket, Jenkins brushing it off with a whisk broom, the man obviously having polished the gold buttons to a mirrorlike sheen. He lifted the neck cloth and cravat from the chair where he had placed the uniform. Peter coughed politely, caught Jenkins's eye, and shook his head. Jenkins stood as if stricken and then folded them up, looked around desperately, and then just tucked them into his pocket.

The drumroll was now just outside their window, and shifted from a march beat to the slow steady beat of a funeral march. A moment later there was a knock at the door.

John, already facing the door, took a deep breath.

"You may enter."

Four guards were standing in the corridor, led by a young captain who saluted.

"Sir, it is time."

Just behind them was a minister, who stepped forward, looked at Peter, Allen, and Jenkins without comment, and the three left the room to wait out in the corridor.

Several minutes later the door opened and John stepped out, still forcing a smile.

"Gentlemen, I am at your disposal," he said, voice cool, even, and not breaking.

Flanked by the four guards, the captain in front, the minister behind, they started for the door, and John held up his hand.

"A momentary indulgence, gentlemen," he said, coming to a stop and looking back at Allen, beckoning him to his side.

He reached into his breast pocket and drew out several sheets of folded paper.

"My friend, would you be so kind as to see that these are delivered. One to my parents, the other to a young lady," he paused, and smiled. "Well, her name is atop the note."

He looked back at Peter.

"If your duty requires you to examine them you have my permission."

Peter shook his head.

"You are a man of honor, sir. I know the correspondence is private. I will not examine them."

"Thank you, Major. They are just simple sentiments of farewell."

Allen took them with shaking hand.

"Good-bye, my friend," John said, and grasping Allen's hand he leaned over to embrace him.

For Allen, it was the hardest moment of his life, struggling not to lose control. When he had laid his beloved young brother into the ground on that cold freezing day along the Delaware, that had been different, but at this moment, he did not want to let John see him weep, and perhaps unnerve him, nor would he let any of these Rebels see him lose control. They were about to see how two British officers would face what was to come.

The captain opened the door. The guards stepped out, with John and the minister following, then followed in turn by Allen, Peter, and Jenkins. All awaiting him stood silent, a thousand or more men forming three sides of a square around the gallows, the officers of the court-martial the fourth side. John did slow at the sight of the gallows, as if even at this final moment hoping against hope that he would be granted the honor of a firing squad rather than a too often squalid death at the end of a rope.

Two young officers now stepped to either side of him, each putting a supporting arm around his elbows, ready if need be to help brace him up if he faltered or, as had happened in more than one case Allen had witnessed, the victim began to struggle or try to turn away.

"Why this emotion, sir?" one of the two asked, as John, having slowed, gazed at the gallows.

Peter wondered if there was mockery or insult in the young officer's voice, and he wanted to step forward and strike the man down.

John simply smiled and looked straight into his eyes.

"I am reconciled to my death, sir, but I detest the mode," and he stepped boldly forward almost as if dragging along his two escorts. None could fail to notice, and as he passed his judges nearly all saluted him. It was obvious several had tears in their eyes.

A high two-wheel cart had been backed up under the gallows, and Peter thanked God for that. Rather than be hoisted up to die by strangulation, chances were the fall would break his neck and end it quickly.

Reaching the back of the cart, John broke free of the embrace of his two escorts and deftly mounted the back of the wagon unassisted and stood rigid. The executioner, an elderly sergeant, drew out a handkerchief, and, with trembling hands, wrapped it around Andre's eyes.

He then took the rope but fumbled, leaving the opening of it too small to get it over John's head.

Allen watched, wanting to scream out to just get it done right.

John apparently whispered something to the sergeant, and then actually took the rope himself and drew it over his own head and slipped it down around his neck, reaching up to tighten it.

This gesture sent a gasp through the assembled ranks.

"Merciful God," someone cried from the ranks. There was the clatter of a musket falling, a young soldier having collapsed in a faint.

The officer directly in charge now stepped up to the base of the cart, drew out a sheet of paper, and read the findings of the court-martial with its sentence, ending with "May God have mercy on your soul, sir. Do you have any final words."

John, still with that enigmatic smile, actually reached up and raised a corner of his blindfold, looking out at those assembled, and Allen knew with aching heart that there was a momentary glance to him as his gaze swept across the gathering.

"This shall be but a momentary pang. Just tell all that I died bravely, as befitting one of His Majesty's officers."

With his own hand he drew the handkerchief back down. He put his hands behind his back and the executioner bound them tight. John nodded to the executioner and whispered something to him.

The sergeant, shaking with emotion, stepped off the back of the wagon, walked around to the side of it, picking up a heavy strap of leather, and looked to the officer in command of the execution, who stood with arm raised.

"Major Andre, today you shall sup in paradise," someone from the ranks cried as the officer let his arm drop.

The sergeant raised the leather strap and slashed it across the back of the horse hitched to the cart. The beast whined with pain and fear and leaped forward.

Major John Andre tumbled from the back of the wagon and Allen was torn to the soul, but also relieved when there was an audible crack, the sound of John's neck breaking.

He swung slowly back and forth, legs twitching spasmodically for a moment, and then was still.

Several more in the ranks collapsed, others turning their heads away. There was a bit of ragged cheer from others, met by officers shouting for silence in the ranks.

Allen turned and looked back at General Greene, who, still mounted, was only a few feet away.

"And was this justice, sir?" Allen snapped bitterly.

Greene looked down at him sad eyed.

"This, young major, is war."

THE LAST SHOVELFULS OF EARTH WERE HEAPED ATOP John's grave, which had been dug and waiting within feet of the gallows. They had afforded him a simple coffin. Jenkins, again sobbing, had affixed John's cravat and neck cloth around the bruised and torn neck and carefully set his wig and hat on him along with his decorations before the lid was hammered shut.

The assembly had long since marched away, this final detail attended to by the sergeant who had been the executioner. The last shovelful was smoothed out over the grave, and the six enlisted men working on the task stepped back, not sure what to do next. The sergeant ordered them to return to camp.

The sergeant looked at Allen, who had stood at the foot of the grave, flanked by Jenkins and Sergeant O'Toole, who apparently during the night had found some Rebels willing to share a bottle of what smelled like whiskey.

The sergeant in charge of the detail looked at Allen, came to attention, and saluted. "Sir, I've never seen a man go as bravely to his death as he did."

Allen could not reply, just merely nodding his thanks, and the sergeant turned and walked away. The day had a definite chill to the air, the early morning sun now obscured by clouds rolling in from the east, a certain sign of a cold rain to come. Allen looked over to where Peter waited, again flanked by his cavalry escorts, each of them leading a horse. Allen came to attention, saluting the grave.

"Farewell my friend, I pray I shall meet my death with but a fraction of the bravery you have shown. If there is a heaven, I shall look for you there."

He mounted and the small cavalcade rode south, finally reaching the barricaded road where Peter reined in. Allen looked over at him. "Would you mind riding with us to within my own picket lines. Your militia most likely is just waiting for my return, and I'd prefer a better death than to be murdered for a horse and the buttons on my uniform."

Peter nodded in agreement, ordered one of his escorts to take the flag of truce from O'Toole, and they rode on, passing the place where Allen had, indeed, nearly been killed less than eighteen hours before. There was a faint rustling in the woods, a muffled curse echoing, but no one was visible. They rode on for another mile and, coming about a bend in the road, Allen could see an advanced picket guard of half a dozen mounted dragoons of his army, the army of the king. He reined in, and Peter did the same.

"Fine then, they will see us through, you can go back now." The first light drops of rain were beginning to fall, chilled, the cold seeping into him.

"Allen?" Peter looked at the man who had been his childhood friend. "Allen, I am, indeed, sorry. He was an honorable man."

"Yet your bastards hung him anyhow," he snarled, his anger surfacing at last. "For God's sake could you not have shown him the dignity of a firing squad? He was an honorable soldier."

"I will not argue that with you now," Peter replied.

"But I will not forget."

Allen hesitated, as if struggling with a comment, and then it spilled out.

"At least keep your promise to look-in on Miss Elizabeth if you can. Tell her I love her and always will."

At this moment, Peter's own feelings regarding that were buried. Peter nodded an assertion and extended his hand. Allen glared at Major Peter Wellsley of the Continental army.

"Thank you Peter for doing that. But as for us, for you and me? War changes all things," he snapped, turning away, and spurring his mount back to the safety of his own lines.

It was a contemplative ride back for Peter, barely noticing the salutes as he passed through the picket lines, then whispering a dismissal to the escorts who had kept watch over him and Allen. Their lieutenant saluted and drew closer.

"Tragedy, nothing but damn tragedy, all of it. I wish I could have voiced condolences to your friend."

"My friend?" Peter asked.

"Yes, that British officer. It was obvious to all of us. Heard you and he knew each other before the war."

Peter looked at him blankly. Then just rode on. He passed where the gallows had already been knocked down, the grave freshly piled and even smoothed over, a guard placed on it so it would not in any way be defiled. He rode on, at last turning the bend in the road that led to Washington's headquarters, where he felt he should make a brief personal report on his conversations with Allen over the last day.

"Major Wellsley?"

He was startled out of his thoughts by the sight of Nathanial Greene riding toward him, a cold mist swirling about them. Peter reined in. Nathanial Greene brought his mount around and motioned that the two of them turn aside from the headquarters road and continue to ride up to the heights of West Point. They rode on in silence for several minutes until finally it was Greene who spoke.

"Hard day for you, young man," he said softly.

Peter simply looked over at Greene. Here was the man who had emerged as Washington's most trusted officer and comrade in the wake of these last few tumultuous weeks. It was a rank and honor well deserved. A Quaker by birth and upbringing, he had nevertheless picked up the sword even before the Revolution, enlisting as a private in a Rhode Island militia company; within months he was a general.

Gallant, audacious, he had led one of the assault columns at Trenton and had even urged a midday pressing on to Princeton after their triumph, which Washington had to rein in. He had stood by his general's side at Brandywine, was credited by Washington with saving the army from starvation when he took over as quartermaster general at Valley Forge, but had repeatedly begged to be return to field command. He managed to slip another battle in at Springfield, New Jersey, in which he handily turned back a British and Hessian raiding column while still serving as quartermaster general, supposedly foraging for supplies in that much contested state when the British attacked. Peter had been at that battle, taken impromptu command of a militia unit on the flank along what the locals called the "Mill Burn," and Greene had personally cited him in dispatches for his rallying of the troops and coolness under fire.

"I want you to know, Major, I would have preferred a different outcome to this morning."

"Sir?"

"It is obvious to me and others that there is some sort of personal connection between you, and the British representative and friend of Major Andre. If only Andre had been wearing some semblance of uniform, we could have found reason to hold him prisoner and then when all this madness is over exchange him. It grieved the entire court to condemn a man obviously of such courage. The fact that you were friends with someone close to Andre speaks of your character as well."

"Sir?" and he wondered if there was a note of reproach in what Greene had just said.

Greene extended a hand in a gesture of reconciliation.

"No insult," and he hesitated, "may I call you Peter?"

Peter, a bit surprised, nodded.

"I recalled you well from the Battle of Springfield and your rallying of our flank. I spoke of you this morning with General Washington after reporting back to him after the execution."

They rode on together to the crest of a rise that overlooked the plains of West Point, far below them the serpentine turning of the Hudson River, the hills and mountaintops ablaze with autumn's glory, and the mist like rain enhancing the glow of the autumn leaves.

"Lord this is a beautiful country. I wonder what it must of looked like before we came here, what it might look like a hundred years hence. So peaceful now, hard to believe there is a war going on."

Greene took off his hat and wiped his brow even though a cool breeze greeted them atop the heights.

"I've been given my own command again," Greene said, not looking at Peter, gaze fixed on the valley.

"Congratulations, sir," Peter replied, not sure if Greene was musing to himself or actually speaking to him.

"With all that has transpired these last few weeks this has neither been the time nor place to make it public, but it will be announced shortly."

Greene dismounted, letting his horse's bridle fall so that it could crop on the high autumn grass, Peter doing the same, feeling that Greene wanted him to follow.

"Gates has made a botched affair of things yet again," he announced coldly, still gazing at the river. "Even as we hold and block up here, that old man has allowed Georgia and the Carolinas to fall under British control. Good God in heaven, at Saratoga if it had not been for . . ."

His voice trailed off. Peter did not need to fill in the rest of that sentence. The name that could no longer be mentioned in any way and given credit for that incredible victory. It was Benedict Arnold who had saved the day at Saratoga, it was Gates who aggrandized unto himself the glory, galloping south to parade before Congress, while Arnold, immobilized by the wound to his leg suffered in his gallant charge, was pushed aside. Though no one would say it now, this was the start of his slide into the madness of what he had just done.

"Then Congress gives him the Southern command and in short order we lose Charleston, Savannah, the fight at Camden, Georgia all but subdued, the Carolinas torn apart by bitter civil war as Loyalists and Patriots fight with utter savagery against each other, while Cornwallis runs riot over our few remaining forces. That is my new command, Peter. I leave for the Carolinas within the week to take command of the wreckage that is left and try to forge a new army."

His words were now the one faint bright moment of this otherwise heartbreaking day.

He whispered congratulations but could say no more, and then wondered why Greene had sought him out to share this news. There was a long pause and then Greene looked back at him.

"I had a long talk with General Washington this morning, laying out plans and as mentioned, your name came up."

"Why so, sir?"

"I want you to come with me."

"Sir?"

Now he was, indeed, confused. His focus of effort and dedication these last several years had been the ever-constant war in New Jersey, of raid and counter-raid, planting of information and misinformation, the ferreting out of spies in a dark and ugly manner at times, and placing spies in turn into the British lines.

He wanted to raise this point but Greene interrupted him.

"Since our victory at Springfield, the enemy has pretty well conceded Jersey as their ground to raid upon, holing up in Elizabethtown with a quick line of retreat to Staten Island if we should push them hard enough. Winter is setting in, Jersey is secure. Clinton is too timid to try yet another winter overland campaign against Philadelphia. Jersey is secure, your work for the moment nothing more than that of a watchman."

He wanted to reply that after all that had transpired, perhaps a winter of relative peace would be a blessing. On the journey South there would even be time to see Elizabeth. "The general and I have decided that we would like a personal liaison we both can count on, especially with such a distance between us. It might entail but one journey, perhaps several, but we want someone savvy enough to know the grounds of New Jersey to pass safely, who both of us trust to personally carry dispatches to be handled by no other. Old Gates will try to derail my efforts and might even stoop to intercepting sensitive communications and twisting it to his own use. He will not give up easy. Cornwallis as we both know from the campaigns of 1776–77 is a wily foe, but by God I think I have his number and know how to beat him. When that time comes, I want you with me, to observe and be able to report back accurately, without distortion, to General Washington back here in New York.

"Will you take the job, sir? By the way, a promotion to colonel comes with it," he offered, smiling.

After such a tragic day, filled with dark foreboding, this man had just offered him an escape, a hope, a belief, and an honor of trust as well.

He nodded and gladly clasped hands with the Quaker turned general.

Part Two

THE BATTLE OF GUILFORD COURT HOUSE

NORTH CAROLINA

MARCH 15, 1781

Three

**IN FRONT OF GUILFORD COURT HOUSE,
NORTH CAROLINA
MARCH 15, 1781
AN HOUR BEFORE DAWN**

"GENTLEMEN, ARE YOU CERTAIN YOU ALL KNOW YOUR POSITIONS?"

Nathanial Greene looked about those gathered before him. Peter stood silently to one side, saying nothing.

When he had ridden South with Greene last fall, there had been days of simply cantering alongside this imposing man, often just engaged in casual conversation. His own years on Washington's staff, essentially in command of part of Washington's spy network, had taught him a certain degree of reticence. Answer a question when put directly to him by his general, otherwise just sit back, listen, gauge, and remember.

Greene talked of his strategy, glad that Peter had some knowledge of classical history when he referred to "Fabian Tactics." He was drawing his inspiration from a Roman general, who, facing Hannibal, knew that Hannibal had the better trained troops, and he could not beat him in a stand-up, knock-down fight, but he could wear him down to exhaustion.

Cornwallis was deep inside the Carolinas, unable any longer to hold a supply line hundreds of miles back to Charleston thanks to the efforts of irregular fighters like Francis Marion, the "Swamp Fox," who regularly pillaged the British line of supply. It was forcing the British to live off the land, which meant they had to keep moving, because five thousand hungry mouths and several thousand horses and mules could strip a county clean within a few days.

So like Fabius, his plan was to avoid a full pitched battle, unlike Gates, and instead, when Cornwallis advanced, he'd retreat farther back into the hinterlands, but as he did so, he would strip the countryside clean, leaving empty barns and fields in his wake. It was a strategy that would win few allies for the Revolution after his army had passed, stripping out the countryside and handing back "vouchers" for payment after the war, but that could not be his concern of the moment, even for one such as he, raised as a Quaker. It was about driving Cornwallis's army to desperation.

In the months after Greene took command, he had been rigid and unyielding with his plan. Now before this village of Guilford in central North Carolina the test was at hand. Cornwallis, driven near to distraction with rage and frustration that he could not corner and finish off his foe in open battle, had taken the desperate measure of ordering his army to throw aside all baggage, tentage, and nearly all supply wagons. The army was to strip down and then lunge forward with the hope of catching up to Greene and his ever-maneuvering army, and bring it to a final annihilating battle of decision.

No sooner had Cornwallis set forth on this desperate march and even those in the ranks who professed no belief in God started to wonder if Divinity itself had decided to show His hand. The weather had turned absolutely wretched. Any army that tried to campaign in the winter was taking a risk; to strip down, without adequate winter clothing, tents, and bases of supply to fall back on, was, indeed, tempting "Fate," and that fate had shown its cards.

Torrential rains, freezing ice storms, even snow—rivers swollen over their banks, and every which way Cornwallis turned, empty barns and fields stripped of crops and forage, those still loyal to the Revolution fleeing ahead of him as well.

Then far to Cornwallis's rear, twin victories. A thousand, very angry "Over the Mountain Men" as they called themselves, had swarmed out of the high peaks of western North Carolina and Tennessee and directly offered a challenge to battle to one of Cornwallis's reserve columns and thrashed it to pieces at Kings Mountain. A few weeks later, the ruthless commander of Cornwallis's cavalry, Tarleton, was soundly thrashed by Dan Morgan and his riflemen down on the border with South Carolina at Cowpens. That fight had lasted less than fifteen minutes. Tarleton was lured into a charge and was suddenly confronted by several hundred well-trained marksmen, who stood up out of the tall grass and fired a volley at less than ten paces.

Tarleton unfortunately had survived, and fled with his remaining few stragglers to rejoin Cornwallis. Many was the man around Peter this morning who prayed for the chance to have him in their sights within the hour.

"Remember," Greene said, pacing back and forth now on the steps of the small county courthouse, "this is not a stand and die battle, though if we see the chance to finish that bastard we will. Keep in mind this is big open country here. We're going to meet and fight this morning, but for all of us to die to hold this one little place?" He shook his head violently.

"He is the one who is desperate now. Not us. Let him come on. He is desperate and keep that word in your mind, he is the one who needs this fight more than we do. Let him come on. He will be driving his regimental commanders relentlessly to close in, regardless of loss, thinking he has us.

"Gentlemen, by day's end, if all goes perfectly, Cornwallis's army will be smashed and he our prisoner. But in war, we should all know after six years against this foe, nothing ever goes perfectly. This is not about holding the field against what are, indeed, his elite troops. It is about making them pay for the field, to maul him, and even if he holds the field, at sunset he will look at the wreckage, his blood now chilled, and wonder why he charged without regard of loss. That is the battle I want."

Peter looked around at those gathered about Greene. He could see that Greene's strict orders connected with some, but others grumbled under their breath that they wanted it finished today.

"Gentlemen!" Greene snapped, and all fell silent.

"Trust me on this. Now follow my orders and all shall be well."

His features eased and he smiled.

"Trust me the way I have so happily come to trust you, my hearty comrades."

He had that touch about him, Peter thought concealing any hint of a smile. In a way a touch Washington did not have. Washington ruled by the magnitude of the man, that sense of a Roman-like gravitas that could only but elicit admiration, even at times in the hearts of his foes. Greene, a man raised in the most gentle of religious traditions, was known to be a hard warrior, but he had as well that "common touch" that could reassure a frightened private with a fatherly word of encouragement. He was also a regimental commander who was a man of his word and knew what the hell he was doing, very unlike the last man who commanded this army.

"Now, to your posts and God be with you all this day."

The group broke up, Peter remaining still, looking to Greene and waiting. His blood was up, the same as it was last summer at Springfield in New Jersey when he had taken it upon himself to rally a wavering line of militia. He had hoped Greene might have a field assignment for him.

Greene caught his wistful glance, smiled, and shook his head.

"Young sir, you stay by my side this day. Last thing I need to do after this fight is to send a letter to Washington saying I allowed you to get yourself killed. Your duty, Peter, is to observe and then report what happens here today."

Peter could only nod, then salute.

Greene patted him warmly on the shoulder.

"Stay close and remember what you see here today."

THE BATTLE OF GUILFORD COURT HOUSE
MARCH 15, 1781

"My God, here they come!"

The long battle line of Cornwallis's elite infantry regiments had at last crested the rise of a low ridge a quarter mile away. At the double time while holding perfect formation, flags fluttering in the morning breeze, the sound of fifes, drums, and bugles echoing, they pushed straight into the forward line of General Greene's battle formation, made up entirely of Carolina militia.

General Greene seemed unperturbed as his forward line fired off but a single volley, then broke and ran under the frightful, unrelenting pressure of Cornwallis's men. As the militia ran, the heavy infantry and grenadier guards that made up the elite cadre of Cornwallis's Southern army moved forward in serried ranks. Many of the militia were in such a mad a panic that they were throwing aside weapons and backpacks.

"Should I try and rally them?" Peter asked hastily, coming up to Greene's side. The general made a dismissive gesture.

"I told you, young sir, stand by my side. It is what I expected and will only embolden Cornwallis to press in."

Peter could not help but admire the discipline of the advancing British line of grenadiers and heavy infantry, but gone were their once terrifying light infantry, Loyalist riflemen, and most of Tarleton's light dragoons, lost at Cowpens two months ago. They had no ability for rapid pursuit and thus no way to ride down and slaughter those trying to escape.

With every battle fought, Cornwallis had fewer and fewer men in his command, spreading out yet farther to try to control the vast region. Greene, unlike Gates, knew the real weakness here, to bait and withdraw, bait and withdraw, cut up smaller detachments such as at Cowpens, and now, deep into North Carolina, turn to offer battle.

Peter, though dismayed at the sight of the thousand or more militia turning about and fleeing, knew that they still outnumbered Cornwallis nearly one and a half to one.

After the way he had personally led militia at Monmouth Court House and again at Springfield, it was hard upon his soul to see militia flee thus, but he knew that was all part of Greene's plan at this moment. The sight of their enemy fleeing, but nevertheless in that one volley dropping several dozen of Cornwallis's precious elite troops, now propelled the British charge forward, a few buglers, filled with bravado, urging the men on with derisive foxhunting calls, as if the battle were already won, and now it was simply a game of chasing down and killing. A few British deserters, lads press-ganged out of Ireland and fed up with it all, had come through the lines over the last few days with warnings that Cornwallis's men, pressed to the limits of endurance by this endless winter campaign, were now swearing vengeance. Any who begged for surrender on the battlefield would be greeted with a bayonet in the stomach. This would be a death match, according to them.

Greene posted Morgan's skilled riflemen to the flanks, not to hold, but simply to kill and wound as many as possible with oblique fire into any attack on the center. Thus as the militia ran from the field, the riflemen began to pop up, ghostlike out of the tall grass, pouring a killing fire into the enemy flanks at a range of 150 yards, twice that of the muskets carried by the heavy infantry and grenadiers. They could not turn the battle, but they sure as hell would make Cornwallis pay. That was his intent now: to make him pay far more than he ever expected while routing the militia out of the Carolinas yet again.

The deadly fire caused the regiments to either flank to begin to waver, and Peter wondered if that part of the trap had been sprung too soon. That the enemy might turn, shake out into skirmish lines, and try to rush forward and overrun Morgan's hearty men. To his amazement they did not. They continued to press straight for the center of the American line, feeling that once that was shattered, they could deal with the damn riflemen harassing their flanks, but with each shot taking yet another deadly toll.

Peter remained silent as he watched the disintegration of the Rebels' first line of defense. Within minutes, more than a third of Greene's army was running for the rear, more than a few tossing weapons aside and surely never again to show for muster after this fight.

Greene seemed unperturbed.

The charge of Cornwallis grenadiers and elite infantry, driven forward with the obvious desire to at last close with their elusive foe after so many months of rainy marching in the fields, within minutes had reorganized their front. Though dozens were dropped by long-range rifle fire as they did so, they drove forward and smashed into Greene's second line. This line had been braced with some regulars and Greene appeared to be dispassionate, almost detached as they delivered several volleys at close range, dropping scores of the enemy before breaking as the first line had.

The advancing foes were now less than two hundred yards distant, disorganized but their momentum carrying them irresistibly forward. He could see that Greene's staff was looking about nervously. It seemed as if the battle was devolving into yet another utter rout and defeat, as the grenadiers, their ranks thinned but still game, reformed and now advanced at the quick step with bayonets leveled. He caught a glimpse of Cornwallis himself, riding along their line, urging them forward.

To their flank, along the Saulsbury road that led to the hinterlands and the rear, there was a flurry of gunfire, and Peter turned to see that an advanced guard of British infantry had actually pushed up the road and was threatening to envelop their flank.

The Maryland line of Continentals held directly in front of where Greene stood. This Peter knew from the prebattle briefing was to be

Greene's "stonewall," to hold and trade it out at close range for at least half a dozen volleys, inflicting maximum damage on the elite that England had shipped four thousand miles and kept in the field for five years in their vain attempt to suppress the Revolution. With the loss of even one of these men, another weakening blow would be struck, and Greene's plan was now dropping them by the scores and soon by the hundreds, as an intense firefight now exploded, volley traded with volley at a range of fifty yards, dozens dropping on both sides. Smoke roiled about Peter and General Greene, all but blinding them as to the effect of the blows traded back and forth at deadly range. Men were cheering, screaming, cursing, as they fired, tore open cartridges, reloaded, shouldered weapons, and fired again into the blinding smoke until the flanking British force began to swing about to either side of the Maryland line. It was a masterful move by Cornwallis, who even in the heat of such a bloody battle still had some of his old skills of tactical sense that had seen him through many a fight, his men reforming ranks around their shot-torn flags and now beginning to close in.

Greene seemed unperturbed as ever, calmly surveying the stricken field where in little more than an hour the British had gained six hundred yards of ground, smashed two of his lines, and were poised to envelop the third.

"Gentlemen, it is time to concede the field," he said calmly.

Peter looked at him in surprise. This was no defiant stand as he had witnessed at Monmouth. Did Greene really mean to withdraw?

"Colonel Wellsley, look about you. Tell me later what you think General Cornwallis has paid for this piece of useless ground."

Stunned, Peter was not sure how to reply. The heat of battle was upon him and for the first time since joining Greene's side on the day Major Andre was hung, he found himself doubting the moral strength of this man. All of his fighting instinct was telling him that they still outnumbered the British. Surely a single solid line could have held and dealt a sharp, even destructive blow. Yet, now orders were being passed for the men of Maryland to pull back in good order.

For a moment, Peter found himself alone on the low crest look-ing across the stricken field at the now advancing grenadiers, faces contoured with rage, but their advancing line disorganized, ragged, the men obviously exhausted. Then it struck Colonel Wellsley what Greene was about. The British ranks, good Lord, how thin their ranks truly were, the field behind them carpeted with hundreds of dead and wounded.

Greene was still by his side though the advancing British were now within musketry range; a number of them, sensing that the two mounted men before them were of high rank, levelled their muskets to fire.

"Come on, Wellsley," Greene cried, leaning over to grab Peter's reins and turn him about, urging their horse to a near gallop, "It's one thing to die for your country; it's another thing to die uselessly for your country."

EVENING OF MARCH 15, 1781

"Peter, do you drink?" Greene asked, holding up an earthen jug of the ubiquitous "corn liquor" of this region.

"At times, sir."

"Sit down and join me."

It did surprise him that a Quaker, whose sect did not hold with hard drink, now took a long sip on the jug before offering it over to Peter, who gladly took a warming gulp. In the last few hours a cold tor-rential deluge had been unleashed from the heavens and all were half frozen and soaked to the bone.

"God pity the wounded lying out on that field tonight," Greene whispered. "I've sent a flag of truce over to Cornwallis, suggesting we mutually offer aid to the wounded of both sides and they be ex-changed without regard to numbers."

He could not help but smile.

"I rubbed a bit of salt into his hide by saying that in the name of

Christian humanity I had a surplus of medical supplies and would gladly offer what he might need to succor his numerous casualties."

He chuckled softly, took the jug back, and indulged in a long drink.

"Most unchristian of me, my real intent, but what the hell. It made its point and actually I'd have done so if not for that damn stiff English pride that haughtily refused the offer."

Peter said nothing, looking at the ground, not sure how to react as the thin canvas of the tent leaked steady dribbles of cold rain on both him and Greene.

"Burdens them," Greene said, and his voice was cold now. "We can scatter our wounded back as far as Saulsbury if need be, but he has hundreds this night, so I am more than glad to see him gather them in and offer to help. Each one that lives rather than dies of exposure is one more man for him to tend to—without wagons, ambulances, and supplies."

Peter looked up at Greene and said nothing, motioning that he would like another drink that Greene readily offered to him.

"You think we lost today, don't you, Peter?"

"It sure looked that way," Peter replied honestly. "Our lines, sir, if I may be so bold, were not in mutual support range. As they bowled over the first one it encouraged them to take out our second and then our third, at each point of impact the numbers even or on their side."

"Let me ask you something," Greene retorted, fetching the jug back and taking another deep swallow.

"A battle is an agreement by both sides to face off and have it out, young sir. Neither side will ever seek battle unless he thinks he can gain something, or on those rare occasions when one side is backed into a corner from which he cannot escape. I was certainly not backed into a corner. We could have continued to fall back. But Cornwallis? He wanted this battle, he needed it after months of ballyhooing and chasing us back and forth across hundreds of miles. He wanted to finish it today."

Greene smiled.

"If I had presented an impregnable front, outnumbering him two to one, and dug in on the heights as I recall you and some others of my staff urging the night before, do you think he would have attacked us? I wanted my opponent to think I had misdeployed, that I had made a fatal mistake, and thus lure him in. But as to our holding the ground and my risking a close-in brawl with the few solid Continental regiments under my command against half a dozen of the most elite regiments in their entire empire?"

He chuckled sadly and took another sip.

"There's a hundred thousand square miles of land out here. Let him have it. I wanted him to attack, and attack he did. But what was my purpose today? I asked you earlier to try to count their losses— and your report?"

"Hard to say, sir, but maybe four hundred, five hundred or more on that field before you pulled me back."

"If I hadn't you'd of stood there, gap mouthed, or worse yet, with your blood up and tried to lead a countercharge and gotten your fool head blown off. Dulce et decorum est pro patria mori," Greene whispered looking over at Peter.

"But better still, Colonel Wellsley, to live for your country and help build an even stronger one after this damn war is over."

Peter nodded, knowing he was right.

"Victory is not always about holding a field and being the last man standing!"

He stood up, his head brushing against the canvas ceiling, triggering a cold drenching downpour of rain into their leaky tent.

"They have no tents, no wagons, no supplies, no medicines. God pity them. Yet now he has four or five hundred wounded—a quarter of his army to take a useless piece of ground. Good heavens, give him one more victory like that and he will lose everything, and he knows it now this night."

It was as if a door was beginning to open, and Peter finally did see what this man was driving at.

"War is about winning a war, not a battle. If he wants to attack me like that again tomorrow, in this driving storm, let him. I will apparently misdeploy and again retreat. Then lure him twenty miles farther from the coast, their navy, resupply, reinforcements, and help. I am willing to bet in that miserable camp of his this evening he realizes just what he won today . . . nothing."

He chuckled softly.

"Oh, he will write his dispatches claiming a great victory, but some wiser heads, either back in New York or London, will look at the butcher bill, if he reports it honestly, and realize that one or two more alleged victories such as today will mean ultimate defeat."

Greene sat back down and patted Peter on the knee.

"We will sit back and wait for a day or two to see if he wishes to come farther into our wilderness in pursuit, but already I am sending militia round his flank to the south while trying to lure him deeper in here."

He smiled after taking another long sip from the jug.

"Three hundred miles or more of back country, flooded roads, perhaps even ice- or snow-covered at this time of year, separate him from his base of supply at Charleston. If he now tries to turn in that direction, I will dog him every inch of the way. He can turn toward Wilmington, but what is there? No supplies or reinforcements to speak of.

"Cornwallis will eventually turn north toward the Chesapeake Bay, which is what I want."

"Sir?"

"I think I have a grasp of his thinking. If he tries to pull back through the Carolinas it will be a concession of defeat, surrendering ground every step of the way, and doubtful if he can even gain Charleston now, after this battle today.

"There is a combined Loyalist and regular force of several thousand harrying Virginia, some of them led by that damn Benedict Arnold. Cornwallis will be drawn to them like a lodestone. They are the only viable force he can link up with, while at the same time not conceding all that he thinks he has won here in the Carolinas these

last two years. He will be filled with the belief that if he can drag the
war into Virginia, leaving the Carolinas while claiming to have con-
quered, he can retrieve what happened here. Yet realize that he is
not supreme commander here in the Americas, his reports must go
back to Clinton in New York and all the way back to London, a month
or more away, where armchair generals and politicians will simply
push pins into maps without any grasp of the true reality out here tonight in this freezing rain.

"That is why I will send you off at first light tomorrow, after you
have had some rest," he smiled, "and sobered up, to report back to
General Washington, and to him alone, what you witnessed here and
what my thinking is regarding future plans to finish off Cornwallis.
Not just to defeat him on a battlefield, but to truly bag him, lock, stock,
and barrel, and every damn lobsterback and Hessian with him."

"I am not sure I follow you, sir," Peter replied, now thoroughly
confused.

"I will not write out a dispatch to General Washington as to the
events here. There will be plenty of dispatches flying about, of course,
one of them being my own official report to Congress. I want you,
though, to carry back to him your personal observations of what we
did here this day and my thoughts as to how I think Cornwallis will
next jump. I am entrusting it to you personally, no one else to hear it,
not even members of Congress. If they should somehow waylay you
and demand an accounting of this battle, that I shall send to them by
separate post. Oh, I am sure Granny Gates, if he finds out about your
mission, will try to waylay you. So you are to change out of uniform,
I'll have someone find the uniform of a rifleman or something. I'll dig
up several pounds of hard money to see you on your way, the only
note you'll carry is an order for the military postal relay authorizing
you to exchange mounts, and I expect you then to ride hard, damn
hard. Get to Washington in a week at the most."

Peter took that in. Close to five hundred miles. This was going to
be one hell of a ride.

"I want your word of what happened here to Washington before all the usual rumors flood out. Convey to him it is important as well that he immediately tell our French allies what happened here, because in the future, their actions must play into this as well if we are to win a final victory as a result of today.

"Gates, his cronies, and those in Congress ready to get out of this war because it is now truly hurting their pocketbooks will call this a defeat, but I want Washington to know my thinking and my intent here. We spoke of this very concept of battle before I left West Point.

"God blessed our arms at King's Mountain with a damn good victory before we even arrived here. Our victory at Cowpens all but destroyed Cornwallis's ability to move rapidly and fight an irregular war. So now he is stuck with having to resort to the kind of bloody head-on confrontation that we gave him today, a damn good bloody fight. His only recourse now is either to fall back to Wilmington, and wait for a fleet to pull him out, which he will never do, for it would be a full concession of defeat, or to turn north to link up with that renegade Arnold, and somehow make all this look like a victory in his reports."

"Will you follow him north?" Peter asked.

Greene smiled and shook his head.

"I will demonstrate south as I have already said, making it clear to Cornwallis that if he should try to regain Charleston he will have to fight every inch of the way, burdened with hundreds of wounded and no supplies. I want him to go north, to reinforce Arnold, perhaps even think he is winning there, while I retake the Carolinas and Georgia that he perforce must abandon."

Greene smiled.

"Convey to General Washington what I have told you and to him only. Cornwallis moves into Virginia thinking to secure that state now, but with God's good grace, come summer or fall, General Washington, perhaps even with the support of our supposed French allies, can move into Virginia, join forces with Lafayette who is opposing Arnold, pin Cornwallis against the Chesapeake, and finish him.

"Achieve that," Greene said excitedly, "and the entire British designs for the South collapse. Collapse those designs that they can at least win back some of their former colonies, then broker a temporary peace, and they will be forced to concede the whole thing. They know they can never conquer New England without garrisoning every city and village with an additional fifty thousand men. With New England holding and New York, too, once outside the city, then Jersey and Pennsylvania will hold out. Their last remaining hope was to split us off and I think, young sir, that we just might have dashed those hopes today. I hope you do not think me full of hubris, but do report clearly to General Washington my thoughts, that we could be on the verge of winning this war if he can take the gamble I am suggesting."

Greene looked at Peter, eyes filled with fire and belief.

"Get a good night's rest, Peter. I want you off before dawn. I'll roust out a good mount for you and an escort of several of Dan's men to ride with you, at least as far as Wilmington, Delaware."

Peter left Greene in a state of confusion. He was calling what looked to be a defeat a victory. He had laid out a plan that would cover hundreds of miles of marching even if Washington should see a hope in this. Either they were all mad, or maybe, just maybe, there was a real hope of ending this war, after so many bloody years of stalemate that would lead to inevitable victory.

Four

ON THE POSTAL ROAD, TEN MILES
SOUTH OF PHILADELPHIA
MARCH 20, 1781

PETER WELLSLEY, DRESSED NOT IN FORMAL UNIFORM BUT instead in the brown hunting frock and leather breeches of a Virginia rifleman, had been in the saddle nonstop for over four days, from the battlefield of Guilford to here. As ordered by Greene he traveled in secret, to report only to General Washington; other couriers riding at a somewhat slower pace would carry official word to Congress of events in North Carolina.

Exhausted, begrimed with mud because of the cold spring rain that had soaked and turned the post road into a quagmire, he was now amazed to learn that somehow word had raced ahead of him of the battle.

Stopping in a tavern to given his exhausted mount an hour's rest and himself a quick predawn breakfast, a real meal of roasted mutton and boiled corn, all the tavern was already swarming with those seeking news, all abuzz about the "defeat at Guilford."

He wanted to scream with outrage, to announce he had been on that stricken field, and though retreating, Greene had dealt Cornwallis a crippling blow that forever ended him as an offensive force. Cornwallis would have to either fall back on to Wilmington or turn north to try to link up with Benedict Arnold in Virginia if he was to remain an effective fighting force.

To the tavern generals, whoever held the field at the end of the fight, no matter how much blood was spilled, was the only criterion to judge victory or defeat. He ate his meal in silence, feeling a bit awkward that the importance of his duty had entitled him to actual real shillings and a couple of Dutch thalers as hard currency money to wing him on his way to Washington. He paid for his meal, more than a few turning to gaze at him when the tavern echoed with the sound of real coins clinking. He went out to the stable behind the tavern after silently eating his meal, the stable boy having rubbed down his mount and fed him.

"Poor horse," the boy said, "mister you be riding him like you fleeing the devil himself. Perhaps give him a rest."

He patted the exhausted animal's neck affectionately, having traded his previous mount with the hefty price of an additional two pounds for this animal yesterday evening in Baltimore. The trade had been almost honest, though the gait of the animal was discomforting and for the first few miles it had tried to throw him several times so it could flee back to its stable, but then, resigned to its fate, had given good service. It was just a few more miles into Philadelphia where he would quietly trade him at the military postal headquarters and then quickly get out of town for the ride across Jersey before being waylaid by some overbearing officer who would try and force news from him.

He gave the stable hand a few coppers as thanks for his care and mounted; the animal actually seemed to sigh with disbelief that he would be forced to push on. It was ten miles to Philadelphia and exhaustion for both horse and rider was transcended by duty.

. . .

IT WAS WELL PAST DAWN WHEN HE FINALLY REACHED THE outskirts of Philadelphia. A middle-aged man, dressed in a raggedy uniform, one legged and leaning on a crutch, was holding up a bundle of newspapers.

"News of the defeat at Guilford Court House in Carolina," he shouted over and over, citizens out early gathering around to buy the paper. Peter reined in, drew out a penny, and handed it over.

"When did this come in?" Peter asked.

"Last night, some special courier for Congress and word sent down to the papers to print it up," the one-legged man replied.

He wanted to curse. There was no possible way the official dispatches could have arrived ahead of him. It must have been someone else, perhaps even Gates with his own people in the field to undermine Greene and thus win back his position. There was no sense in arguing the point with a half-crippled veteran, and he just shook his head as he scanned the supposed dispatch, saying that Greene had fled the field of battle, leaving the victory to Cornwallis.

"Who you with?" the veteran asked.

"First Continental," Peter lied.

"My old unit," the veteran said, "don't remember seeing you in the ranks."

"Must of joined after you. Where'd you lose the leg?"

"Valley Forge," and there was bitterness in his voice. "Foot froze, rotted, fell off, and then had to take the leg with it."

"Sorry for that."

"So now I sell papers and get a quarter of a penny profit for each. Take a good look at me laddie. You'll be like this in another year or so."

Peter hesitated, reached into his haversack, fished out one of the last two thalers and tossed it to the man, who holding the silver coin looked up at him stunned, unable to reply as Peter rode off. It would mean an empty stomach for the last part of his ride, but how could he eat and leave a man like that hungry. At least at Valley Forge, as part of Washington's personal guard and then von Steuben's first training company, he had a barn to sleep in and rations better than most.

His mount was all but stumbling with exhaustion, and frankly he needed at least a few hours out of the saddle before pressing on. Therefore he did not feel any sense of guilt or dereliction of duty as he turned off of Market Street and rather than immediately barter an exchange with the military postal remount officer, who typical of their kind eyed the mount they were expected to replace sharply, and usually traded in kind, he rode on a few blocks up toward what some now called the Independence Hall, then turned onto a side street.

The last half block he suddenly felt a tightening in his gut. There was part of him that chuckled inwardly with his reaction, going into battle seemed to hold less fear but he pressed on, dismounted, took a deep breath, went up to the door, and knocked. There was no immediate answer. He knocked again and saw a closed curtain in the parlor flutter, the sound of footsteps, and the door opened a crack.

"Merciful God, Peter Wellsley?"

He forced a nervous smile.

"Good morning, Miss Elizabeth."

She opened the door wide but stood blocking the way.

"Peter, pardon my rudeness for being so direct, but after two years, what in hell are you doing here?"

Elizabeth, so typical of her, and he actually chuckled.

"Well, for a weary soldier, perhaps beg for a cup of tea and toast?"

She smiled, gestured him in, closed the door and then to his amazed delight actually threw her arms around his shoulders and hugged him tight.

"By God, it is good to see an old friend," she sighed.

He nervously returned the hug, not wishing to soil her white linen morning dress with a muddy embrace, and then she slipped back from his arms.

"My Lord, you stink like a dead goat, Peter Wellsley. Not to be too personal but when was the last time you bathed or had a change of clothes?"

The question shocked him, but after five years of war, so many of the old and proper customs of conversation between the sexes had, indeed, slipped by the wayside. Change of clothes? The hunting frock and breeches had been issued to him before he set out. His now tattered ragged uniform from Washington's headquarters would only draw unwarranted notice. But he had no idea when the previous owner, a man who died in the hospital after Guilford, had cleaned them. As to bathed? When? Fording that river in January might count.

"Never mind, Peter, and yes, I think I can find some toast and tea for you," and she gestured for him to follow her out into the kitchen. As he passed the parlor, once all so ornate, he was shocked. The rich carpet, imported all the way from the land of the Ottomans, was gone, while in the dining room to the other side, the heavy mahogany table, always properly set for the next lavish entertainment, was missing as well. As a boy he had remembered visiting here, the country bumpkin from Trenton visiting with his parents the home of a wealthy distant cousin who had made good in trade, even though some of that trade was in slaves.

She looked back over her shoulder, her green eyes and blonde hair, the way she looked back at him, striking a near-visceral blow. She said nothing, gesturing for him to take a seat in a high-backed chair near the kitchen fire.

Its warmth was luxurious after the cold rain of the day before and a sigh escaped him as he settled down. He could not help but lean forward, extending his chilled hands to the fire and rubbing them.

She stood on the far side of the fireplace, now suddenly a bit distant it seemed, hands on hips, gazing at him.

"All right, Peter. The truth. Why are you here?"

"Carrying dispatches."

"From?"

He hesitated. Regardless of his adoration at such a distance she had, indeed, been friends with the damned Peggy Shippen and was the center of Allen's attention now as well.

"Might I ask first what happened here?" and he nodded back toward the empty dining room.

She did not reply for a moment. First going through the formality of pouring some tea, no fancy china, instead an earthenware mug filled nearly to the brim, but taking a china cup for herself and sitting down in a chair she pulled up by the opposite side of the wide fireplace.

"The war of course."

"I don't understand," Peter replied, trying to be polite but unable to hold back as he drained a quarter of the scalding mug, the warmth flooding through him.

"Well, if you haven't heard, I am now branded a Tory. If not for our friend Doctor Rush, who vouched for me, the house would most likely have been confiscated and though they don't ride women out of town on rails, or tar and feather them, I would have been driven out and sent to join my father in New York, abandoning our property."

"But why?"

"Remember. I was once friends with," she hesitated but then spat the words out, "that bitch Peggy Shippen. I was bridesmaid at her wedding to you know who."

She sighed bitterly and leaned back in her chair, and said, "Oh, well Arnold was still the hero, any rumors about my behavior during the British occupation forgotten it seemed. Once the table was turned yet again, those damn two-faced types, who have both American and British flags in their attics and hang them out accordingly, like the Havershams and van Dykes, were screaming I should be driven out and the house auctioned off, of course to them, at one tenth its value before the war.

"So it is live as best one can. The mahogany table fetched two pounds sterling, the Ottoman rug, which father brought back before the war and paid fifty pounds for, did fetch five and thus I get by."

He looked down at his half empty cup of tea, feeling a twinge of guilt as she took it from his hand and refilled it, wondering if she was offering the last of her larder to him.

"You look like a drowned kitten who has been tossed in the gutter, Peter. Can I make you breakfast?"

"No thank you, Miss Elizabeth, I ate on the road; I'm fine for the day."

"It's Elizabeth, dear Peter," she said with a smile, "and don't be going telling no tales if your stomach is empty."

"Truly. I did eat a couple of hours ago."

"All right then, but I did offer."

"I remember a house full of servants, Elizabeth, where are they?"

She laughed and shook her head.

"For a while there, it was being said that a real Patriot sent their manservants off to help the war. When father fled to New York, I could not abide any slave in this house and gave them their papers. Old Ben stayed on, God bless him."

She lowered her head and, try as she might, a shudder ran through her.

"He died last month of a winter fever."

She looked back up and there were tears in her eyes, the sight of them all but breaking his heart. Stink as she said or not, he was out of his chair, came to her side, knelt down, and put a reassuring hand on her shoulder.

"Ben filled some of my first memories," she sighed, fighting to hold back her tears, "I was his 'Little Missus,' and he would carve me little playthings and take me for long walks, always protectively by my side. Now, even he is gone."

She brushed away her tears, and then she looked straight at him.

"I'm no damn Tory," she said. "Ben helped to prove that to Doctor Rush, who tended to him as he lay dying. Yes, I stayed around that traitorous bitch Peggy, but whatever I could find out as she flittered about with Major Andre and would blather to me, I would pass on to Ben, who risked his life again and again to slip through the lines and carry that information to General Morgan, who hovered outside the city during the Valley Forge winter."

This was something he never knew about, or heard a word of from anyone, though without doubt General Washington knew.

"And now even he is gone."

"I'm so sorry, Elizabeth."

"So your treading into the house of a damn Tory, who when the British were here was all so accepting of their presence, it might taint your reputation, Peter Wellsley."

"I don't give a damn what others say, Elizabeth. You always knew I cared."

Her features were suddenly fixed as she gazed into his eyes.

"So why are you here? To spy on me. I heard rumors to that effect that you work in Jersey as a spy."

He could not lie to her as he could to near anyone else. Besides, the truth now was harmless and might actually help in some way.

"I was assigned to General Greene's command for the winter, to be a liaison to General Washington. I am carrying a report of what happened at Guilford Court House and General Greene's thoughts."

"Good God, not in writing I hope."

He smiled and just tapped his forehead.

"Up here."

"I heard the news crier just after dawn saying we had been defeated again."

"Damn liar," and he hesitated, blushed slightly for using a profanity in her presence.

"Oh stop it, Peter, I know soldier talk."

Now it was his turn to hesitate.

"What is it?" she whispered.

"I was asked by a mutual friend, perhaps a former mutual friend to inquire after your health and safety."

She blushed.

"You mean Allen. You actually saw him?" and there was a touch of eagerness in her voice that left him crestfallen.

"Yes."

"Is he safe?"

"Last time I saw him, yes."

"Thank God. When did you see him?"

He told her all, and she sadly shook her head when he asked if she had received any of his letters.

"Only one came through, right after the battle at Monmouth."

"And?"

Even as he asked he wished he had not pressed so hard.

She lowered her head.

"He wrote that he loved me, and begged me to wait for him, and we would wed after this horrible war was over."

"And will you?"

She looked back up, her gaze holding him.

"Oh, Peter, I suspect why you ask. You know I love you as well . . ." her voice trailed off.

"But not in that way," he sighed.

She tried to smile, and leaning over she kissed him lightly on the forehead, not saying a word.

"Now tell me what really happened at Guilford," she said, and there were tears in her eyes again.

He returned to his seat on the other side of the fireplace, heart filled with sad longing as he gazed at her, telling her all of being with Greene, the winter campaign, the lies of the report that had raced ahead of him, her interjecting that it obviously had to be part of the old Gates's "cabal" but the truth would come out.

He suddenly felt very weary. Was it the long days of riding, or the sad shock of looking at Elizabeth, realizing more than ever how much he loved and idealized her, but that her heart had been captured by Allen.

He at last fell silent and then was startled by a light touch on his shoulder, a kiss to the top of his head, the scent of her body and perfume.

She laughed softly.

"You dozed off in midsentence there my young hero, come with me."

Yawning he stood up and followed her into the living room where she motioned to the sofa.

"You have a long day ahead. Sleep for an hour or two. Don't worry, I'll wake you up in plenty of time. I already took that poor exhausted mount of yours out to the barn and got the saddle off him."

"Elizabeth, I should have seen to that."

"Can't a lady know something about horses? When Ben used to tend to father's mount I would help him. Now get some rest."

He did not resist, even accepting her loving gesture of helping him take his boots off, though embarrassed that his socks were little better than rags. When he awoke two hours later, she was sitting on a chair by his side, a simple repast of yet more tea, toast, and several thin slices of bacon waiting for his attention. She had also laid out fresh socks, riding breeches, and a freshly boiled shirt.

"The pants belonged to my father. They are a bit portly but seriously, Peter, you can't appear before your general in those stinking leathers. Now eat and change and I'll leave you to your privacy."

He did as ordered as she retreated to the kitchen. He was embarrassed to take off his shirt, for it was full of lice and fleas, the same as the breeches. After changing he picked up the filthy gray shirt, pants, and tattered socks and nervously walked into the kitchen where Elizabeth appeared to be busying herself with tending the fire.

He did not even have time to ask before, with a wrinkling of her nose that he found all so loveable, she gestured straight to the fire.

"Not even worth handing over to the rag man," she announced as he tossed them into the fire, and she even managed to laugh as she shifted them deeper into the flames with an iron poker.

"Just that one hug, I most likely caught a few of your traveling companions."

"I am so sorry," he stuttered.

"I'm not, even though Doctor Rush is convinced they carry disease."

"Elizabeth, I am so . . ."

"Stop apologizing to me, Peter Wellsley," she snapped. "That one time we danced together, every time you trod on my toes you kept muttering apologies."

Then she stepped forward and kissed him yet again on the forehead.

"You know something, Elizabeth," he began, unable not to stammer.

"Don't say it," she whispered, even as she gave him a gentle hug then stepped back.

"Now get you on your way, I dare say our general needs to hear the truth as to events."

He smiled at the way she said "our general," a touch of reverence in her voice.

She followed him to the back door, opening it, but before doing so, she again embraced him.

"You will always hold a special place in my heart forever, Peter."

He could not contain himself any longer.

"Elizabeth, I do love you and always will."

"Peter, don't."

"I know about Allen. Even though now he is my enemy, out of love for you I pray that all shall be well for him and for you."

His voice began to choke.

"If need be, I will help him on his path to you, once all of this madness has ended."

Her eyes filled with tears, and she was unable to reply as he left her side. He looked back as she slowly closed the door, knowing he would be forever haunted by her gaze. Saddling his poor weary mount he trotted back out on to Market Street. All was abuzz with rumors about Guilford Court House, people gathered around the office of the *Gazette*, snatching up copies as quickly as they came off the press.

He felt all so weary at the sight of it all, and heartsick now that he had left Elizabeth's side, his longing, he believed, forever to be unanswered. He felt shaken to the core, the thought of dickering with the remount officer and then the long ride across Jersey filling his soul with exhaustion. He still had a couple of shillings and a thaler in his haversack and in spite of his sense of duty and urgency, there was no harm in taking a few minutes for a cool mug of German beer to fill his stomach after the thin repast with Elizabeth. Spotting a tavern, one of many lining the waterfront, he dismounted and walked in.

Of course all were talking loudly about the supposed news from North Carolina. Taking a frothing tankard, which would have cost him five dollars Continental but only a few pennies of hard coin, he looked about for a place to sit for a few minutes to gather his strength before moving on. A table near a fly-splattered window had but one occupant and approaching he motioned to the empty seat on the other side, the thin, somewhat bedraggled man sitting there offering a smile and a welcoming gesture for him to sit down.

The man looked at him appraisingly.

"Pennsylvania Rifles? First Continental?" he asked.

"Yes, sir," Peter offering the usual lie.

"Hmmm," was the only response as his host drained the rest of his glass of dark rum, and slamming it down, slapped the table, calling for the barman to bring him another.

The service was surprisingly prompt Peter thought, the barman taking the genuine shilling gladly and nodding his head.

"Thank ya, Mr. Paine."

"Mr. Paine?"

The hawk-faced man, features flushed obviously from too much drink, simply nodded then in the gesture that had become common and showed the egalitarian nature of a revolutionary by extending his hand.

"Thomas Paine at your service, my young rifleman."

Peter could not help but contain his shocked surprise. Before him sat "the" Thomas Paine. The author of the immortal words that he had listened to, while shivering on the banks of the Delaware, waiting to cross. "These are the times that try men's souls . . ."

Yet the man who sat before him now? He would have expected

Thomas Paine to have the look of a scholar, an intellectual, a young Benjamin Franklin or Thomas Jefferson. Instead his coat was seedy looking, stained, his face covered in stubble, the classic look of a man lost in drink, clouding his eyes, pinching in his cheeks.

"Don't look at me with such surprise, young Patriot," Paine said with a chuckle before downing half the glass of rum. "I am mere mortal as any other."

"I remember your words, sir," Peter replied, unable to hide his awe, "I crossed the Delaware with Washington, your words filled our souls with fire."

"That was, let's see, that was over four years ago and still it goes on," Paine sighed now looking into his glass. "So you were one of the gallant few, the winter soldier and not just the sunshine Patriot."

He laughed softly.

"If there is a God, may He not hold against me all who died with my words in their souls."

Peter could not reply.

"Now news of yet another defeat," Paine sighed, taking another sip of his rum.

"It was not a defeat, damn it," Peter snapped.

Paine looked straight at him.

"Well pray, sir, do you carry some winged message from heaven to the contrary of what all are crying in the streets."

Peter hesitated.

"I've become a good judge of truth versus falsehood if I dare to praise myself," Paine said, "and you, sir, do not look like a rifleman. You don't have that hardened steely eye and sinewy, at times, murderous look about you, and good God, sir, those breeches you wear are the pants of rich man and not a rifleman who has been the army for four years."

Peter looked down at the pants Elizabeth gave him and inwardly sighed. Sure enough, to a practiced eye it was a dead giveaway. They were not velvet, thank God, he would have rejected that, but they were, nevertheless, good riding breeches of rich material.

And this was Thomas Paine.

"I know it is the oldest question in the world, sir, but can you keep a secret, at least till I am clear of this town."

Paine smiled.

"I'm a stranger, why would you trust me thus?"

Peter looked down into his own mug. Thomas started to call to the barkeep to bring a fresh one, but he held out his hand in refusal. The last thing he needed at this moment was to fall drunk, shoot his mouth off, and fail in his mission.

He hesitated, and Paine smiled.

"I am who that barkeep said I am, and, good sir, one of the reasons I am good and properly half-drunk this hour of the day is that I am to take ship with the tide for France. I am to accompany the young son of the president of our confederation, Colonel Laurens, bearing dispatches to Mr. Franklin, God bless him, and John Adams to beg the French yet again for more help. So if you have some secret intelligence, let it sail with me on the tide rather than news of yet more disaster."

Peter nodded and could not help but draw a bit closer, having made his decision. Besides, in another hour he would be out of this town and on the postal road to West Point.

"I'm bearing a dispatch from General Greene to General Washington."

Paine sat back and laughed out loud.

"Go on and tell another."

"If you don't believe me, sir," Peter sighed, and he motioned as if to finish his drink and then depart.

Paine laughed and gestured for him to stay.

"Let us share conspiracy, and if I think you tell the truth, I will tell you truth as well."

For the next half hour Peter told him all of what he had witnessed in what was called the "Southern Campaign," and his own firm belief that Greene, having lured Cornwallis to the edge of disaster while keeping the bulk of his army intact, would now swing south, abandoning Cornwallis to whatever fate he might decide upon, with the goal of winning back Charleston, Savannah, and forcefully pulling back the Southern states, which had been wavering, to the revolutionary cause.

"You place great trust in this Greene," Paine finally said, and though he had drained the rest of his glass and called for another, he now seemed cold sober.

"Only one man I trust more and that is General Washington himself."

Paine nodded thoughtfully.

"Young sir, Peter, isn't it? I believe your words and they are heartening after listening to the ballyhoo of that confused crowd, egged on even by some members of Congress this morning."

"I tell you, sir, Greene believes victory could be in sight if Cornwallis either is bottled up in Wilmington or turns north into Virginia and is trapped there with his back to the sea. Such will be impossible as long as the British control access to those ports and can either resupply him, or simply pull him out, and transport him back to New York, or reaffirm his hold on Charleston before Greene can march his army there."

Paine nodded after Peter fell silent, and then smiling, wearily shook his head.

"They actually think I can somehow hold some sway with the French court. Silly creatures many of them, for even as they support us, the very system they live on I would see brought down as well, but there are some there I hope are of good heart."

He shook his head, a bit bleary eyed and looked at Peter.

"I'll believe your story, young sir. Perhaps because it is so fantastic. I've learned in this war to believe the near unbelievable. So if, indeed, you will be in the presence of General Washington by tomorrow, carry this to him from Thomas Paine."

Paine ordered another glass of rum and then looked about the room as if fearful of being overheard, then leaned forward, his voice barely a whisper.

"Congress totters on the edge of giving up this fight. Except for the elder Laurens, the president of this so-called confederation, many of the delegates of the deep South are ready to break away and seek some sort of accommodation with the British with the vain hope it will end the slaughter and destruction. Nevertheless, the wounds there run too deep now, it must be total victory for one side or the other, otherwise it will be a perpetual running sore of civil war. If they do break away while the rest of our states hold true, there will be another war in short order, a belligerent border we would have to guard from the Atlantic to the Mississippi. Even some of the northern delegates mutter that a treaty now with England, with some concessions by both sides, will open the ports back up to trade and to hell with the Southern states. Others, as always, mutter against Washington."

"Who?" Peter asked angrily.

Paine smiled.

"I dare say he knows and to recite the names? It would just be the usual list and he most assuredly knows them after five years, otherwise he would not have kept his saddle. Now there are rumors floating in from Europe that the Czarina of Russia, Catherine, has offered to broker a peace and even some in the French court are turning to listen to her."

"Catherine of Russia?" Peter asked, and there was confusion in his voice.

"The old game of European politics, my young friend. A war involving the powers of western Europe does not fit her own game. While England, France, Holland, and now even Spain struggle because of a shot fired, most likely by accident at Lexington Green, she would rather see one or more of them grateful to her and to lend support for her own designs. To throw the Turks out of the Balkans in some sort of holy crusade to free Constantinople from the Turks, which of course gives her far better access to trade. Or to turn against Sweden or whatever she is scheming. So, she is sending her agents to Paris, London, and here, with honeyed words that she will bring about peace between all, acting as if she is giving a holy offering to help negotiation. Just tell your general that some in Congress are turning their heads and seeing it as a way out. That unless there is a firm conclusion in the field by the end of this year, they will broker a compromise peace before next spring."

Paine stared straight at Peter.

"There is fear in Congress as well that Washington barely has control over his army, that it is on the verge of mutiny yet again, as it did at Morristown a year ago. That," and now he hesitated, "some whisper that Washington is another Caesar or Cromwell, biding his time and waiting for the right moment to sweep down on this city and seize the government for himself, and then it will be 'all hail Caesar Washington.'"

Peter sat back in his chair now absolutely confused. He had come into this tavern an hour ago to have a single mug of beer to fill his stomach and settle his nerves regarding Elizabeth before riding on. Now this additional burden?

"That fear, sir," Peter snapped, "is obscene. I have been part of his headquarters guard and staff since Trenton. That man would die rather than do such an ignoble thing. He would die first."

Peter had raised his voice in anger so that several turned to stare at him.

Paine extended his hand in calming gesture.

"But the state of the armies?"

"It is true some mutinied and many deserted, your sunshine Patriots, sir," Peter replied sharply, "but there is still a hard core of us winter soldiers left who would stand by our general's side if such a crisis ever came. Which it will not if only Congress would pay men who give all at least a few shillings to send home to their families rather than more paper that is fit for only one use."

Paine laughed softly at that, reached into his pocket, and pulled out a wad of such money.

"A couple of thousand last time I counted, and like you, I see it fit for but one use. If you care for some to ease your comfort while you ride, do take it," and laughing Paine tossed more than five hundred dollars of currency on the table.

Peter angrily brushed them off, sending them scattering, hardly anyone stirred except for an old drunk with rheumy eyes who cackled his thanks and taking the supposed money tried to negotiate with the barkeep for a drink.

"As to real money. All plead that the government is broke," Paine sighed, "and frankly, after living in this city all these years, I half believe them, though I know of more than a few who have slipped out to country estates to bury what coin they have and then sit things out."

The two fell silent for a moment.

"What would you have me tell my general?" Peter finally asked.

"Tell him this is the year he must end it. If he does not, Congress will end it for him, that or the coalition of confederation will fall apart into separate peaces for the South, Middle States, and North. If this scheme of Greene's has even a remote chance, grab for it with the audacity he showed on the Delaware. This nation of basically good people has fought itself to exhaustion against the greatest power on earth, but no struggling republic can endure a war that appears to drag on forever. I leave for France today, I'll carry over the truth about Guilford Court House, and maybe even prod along the idea that if the French want out of this, which I know they surely do after three years of little return and tens of millions of livre spent by them, that now is the year for them to coalesce around a unified plan and act with audacity."

Paine smiled.

"Audacity. Yes that is the word. Audacity, to risk all in '81 on a single throw of the dice might be the only chance we have, otherwise we shall lose this war."

The door to the tavern opened, a brawny sailor half stepping in.

"Tide turns in the hour, those shipping out, get aboard."

Paine sighed.

"Damn how I hate sea travel, damn near killed me last time."

He pulled a shilling out of his pocket and tossed it to the barkeep as he headed to the door, pointing to the old drunk, and motioned for him to give the old man a drink. Peter followed by his side.

"Audacity," Paine muttered, and stuffing his hands into his coat pockets he staggered off.

An hour later Peter was mounted on a halfway decent mount and thankful to be out of the city, though as conflicted now about Elizabeth as he was about everything else he had heard this day.

WASHINGTON WATCHED AS THE DOOR CLOSED, THANKING the young colonel yet again for his diligence and speed in bearing his reports. To ride the distance from North Carolina to here in just five days was a remarkable act of endurance, and of youth, one he might have attempted twenty years ago, but not now. It was still two hours before dawn, Hamilton having awakened him feeling that Wellsley's news was worth interrupting the general's sleep.

He had ordered that Hamilton draw up a quick announcement, to be immediately circulated to all the troops, along with the firing of a salute in honor of General Greene and his gallant men, and a dispatch to be drawn up and sent over to the commander of French forces in North America, Rochambeau, who was based near Newport, Rhode Island. It was essential to get his own version out first before the false rumors that Peter claimed were racing about reached this camp.

He laid back down on his cot and stared at the dark ceiling. Wellsley was to write up a full report and return with it tomorrow after taking a bed upstairs and rest the entire day. He had, though, shown a sharp sense for detail and memory under rapid-fire questioning as to the state of Greene's men, their morale, and why he had decided to abandon the field rather fight it out to a bloody finish. Then the additional disturbing news about the conversation with Thomas Paine.

Of course some in Congress, still part of Gate's supporters, would denigrate Greene and call it a defeat. Combine that with word that some in Congress were, indeed, now sniffing the air for a negotiated peace was what struck the hardest.

Peter had even quoted Paine directly, saying he urged "audacity." But audacity where? Any attempt to take Manhattan while a British fleet lay at anchor in the harbor was utter folly. He had learned that in the near-fatal mistake of trying to hold the city back in '76, forced to try to defend everywhere, and thus holding nowhere as the British so easily moved men and artillery back and forth, nearly cutting him to pieces. Yet if he moved from here to try to force the issue in the South, then Clinton, backed by the fleet along the tidal waters of the Hudson, could launch a summer campaign to take the fortress at West Point, sail clear to Albany, cut off New England, and take New York out of the war.

He had hoped Clinton would try another campaign against Philadelphia for on the open fields of New Jersey he would come storming down on their lines of supply and seek then a battle of decision.

Audacity? But audacity where? Greene offered a scheme but it was based on so many ifs. If Cornwallis marches north rather than east or back south, if he can at least be contained, if the French fleets stir and come north as he has begged for two years for them to do.

Audacity. He sighed. The hardest thing in war, and his personal nature was to wait. He would have to wait. But for how long? While waiting, would Congress fold first?

Five

PHILLIPSBURG, NEW YORK
AUGUST 14, 1781
6:00 A.M.

"IF WE DO NOT WIN THIS WAR BEFORE THE YEAR IS OUT, WE
will most certainly lose it."

That thought, which he never dared to voice to those around him,
had come to haunt nearly every waking moment.

As was his custom, General George Washington, before taking
breakfast at headquarters, would walk alone through the encampment area of his army, the Continental army of the United States. It
was a way for him to collect his thoughts before the start of another
laborious eighteen-hour day, to observe his troops and in that inde-
finable way, "sense" their mood, their morale, their willingness to
keep on fighting. It was, as well, a time to try to purge away the nightmare thoughts of impending defeat. He had to keep his outward appearance calm, in control, for a commanding general was, indeed, an
actor upon the stage. One misspoken word, one display of depression

and fear of defeat could shatter an entire army within hours as surely as any battle.

This morning, however, it felt impossible to shake the terrible realization of the reality confronting him. After six years of bitter struggle, the will of the army of the nation was at low ebb, perhaps worse even than in the weeks before the victory at Trenton. Then, it had been the result of the shocking blows endured by the loss of New York City to the British and their Hessian hirelings, but it was a morale Washington had been able to rebuild with one risky shake of the dice that resulted in victory. What he faced now was more lethal, like a slow-growing cancer. It was pure exhaustion and war weariness. After six years, the end was nowhere in sight. The will of his army and of Congress to continue the fight was collapsing.

The report carried to him by Colonel Wellsley of his conversation with Thomas Paine, that peace feelers were out, via Catherine of Russia, was, indeed, true, and more than a few in Congress were openly sniffing at the bait.

A negotiated peace in which there would finally be a craven collapsing, a return to the empire in exchange for an offer of pardon for the temerity to seek independence. All the years of sacrifice of life and treasure for a quick selling out.

While after that selling out, a gradual tightening of the screws of repression. Leaders would flee in spite of the offer of pardons, generations might pass before the same war would have to be fought again by our grandchildren at a far more bloody cost.

Washington had received General Greene's private thoughts via Peter Wellsley, who he had reassigned back to his role of keeping watch on New Jersey. It had all sounded so clear and optimistic at that moment, but in that same report of Greene's victory were his words, according to Paine, and then reinforced across this summer by other still trusted advisers in Congress that there was, indeed, a leaning toward a negotiated peace.

Many in that body, encouraged by Gates, were denouncing

Greene for what they called a lost opportunity at Guilford Court House. It had devolved into a massive defeat, a rout, allowing Cornwallis to now venture freely into southern Virginia while Greene just marched off in the opposite direction back into the Carolinas.

Greene's dreamlike plan had captivated his imagination, but faced with the current reality, it seemed to be nothing more than a dream. Cornwallis, as Greene had predicted, did, indeed, finally move into Virginia to establish a base on the Chesapeake, and with the claim that having all but subdued the Carolinas, his intent, by linking up with the forces led by Benedict Arnold, was to take Virginia out of the war. By last reports Cornwallis had soundly checked Lafayette, who he had dispatched with some of his own best troops to counter this new force led by the traitor Arnold,

The thought of what was now transpiring was sickening, intolerable, reminiscent of the interminable struggles that wracked both Greece and Rome throughout their long-storied histories. If he could not bring this war to a close, or at least a clear decision this year, Congress would seek peace. One war would but settle the issue for the moment, and then within a few years, a generation at most, yet another war would erupt to consume another generation, until finally Greece had collapsed from the global stage and Rome had devolved into an empire. This war seemed destined not to end as a clear definitive win that settled it once and for all, but at best, a half victory. Now he felt that hope of victory slipping further and further away with this damnable stalemate of the last two years.

Clinton was ensconced in comfort and heavily fortified in New York City, as dug into that as deep as a tick on a dog. Supplies flowed in from England to them on a daily basis. A reconnaissance force he had sent out just a few days before was easily repulsed. The report was that even if he had three times the number now directly under his command it would be a doomed bloodbath to try to take the city by storm.

The English controlled the seas, and with Cornwallis united with Arnold on the Chesapeake, with a deepwater port at his back at Yorktown he could hold out there forever, if need be, reinforced with supplies and whatever additional troops England might finally send.

Clinton in New York City and Cornwallis on the Chesapeake were their two main forces and strongholds. Though Greene soldiered on gallantly in the Carolinas, the enemy still held Charleston and Savannah, with Loyalists throughout the South and as far north as New Jersey engaged in brutal murder and countermurder by avenging Patriots, both sides tearing each other apart. Washington wondered, even if they won, could the wounds ever be healed now? It had all plunged a nation, filled with such high and glorious hope but six years ago, into sullen depression, like a patient fighting a long illness who could not muster the strength to recover, but who after such a long painful struggle, just simply wished to let life slip away.

He walked through the encampments of the New York and New Jersey "lines." The troops were respectful enough. Men hunched around campfires cooking their morning ration of salt pork and hardtack, coming to attention, saluting, but saying little. Few smiles, just the formality of salutes returned, but after he passed more than one voice whispered, just loud enough to be heard, "When in hell are we gonna get paid?"

Pay, shoes, and uniforms: His bane ever since the start of this war. The winter before, encamped in Morristown, New Jersey, three brigades had mutinied at one point. A regiment still somewhat loyal had deployed to face them with loaded muskets, bayonets fixed, and for a terrifying moment he had feared the entire army would disintegrate into a full pitched battle against one another. The rebellion had been suppressed and its two ring leaders hanged, but in the days afterward men by the hundreds had simply deserted and gone home. When pay was offered with the usual Continental scrip, the paymaster was met with derisive howls and most of the alleged "money" burned or used for more practical purposes. After years of his appeals, and endless wrangling through various committees, the creation of an office of a single treasurer and paymaster for what was now called "the Confederation" had actually passed. Robert Morris, a man who was rumored to have been made rich through war profiteering, now held that coveted post. Whether it was for his own personal gain or for the good of this army had yet to be seen.

As he continued his walk, his furtive glances at his troops were not heartwarming in the slightest. Uniforms were dirty and threadbare, barefoot was the order of the day, though in camp and with this hot weather, many of the men went barefoot to spare their shoes for hard marching, if, indeed, that would even come again before winter set in. They were lean, pinch faced from poor rations, and a general feeling of malaise could be sensed easily. The army had sat here, month after endless month, keeping at watch on New York City and guarding the approaches up the Hudson, but doing nothing else. For the more aggressive, such as himself, it was maddening. For the timid, boredom, interlaced with drilling and yet more drilling, sapped morale. The number of men on report for insubordination, petty theft, drunkenness, brawling, and attempted desertion was soaring ever higher, a clear indicator that the army, if he still had an army, might not make it through another winter. Clinton, by his mere inaction in New York, could very well win this war.

The only bright spot in this sea of misery was the presence of their French ally, Rochambeau, with nearly five thousand men. Their old position in Newport, Rhode Island, was finally conceded to be useless thanks to the blockading Royal navy, and the French troops had moved to an encampment nearby—but not too close, out of fear that his own "Continentals" might not take kindly to the "Frenchies," especially since some of the older men had fought them twenty-five years before, out on the frontier. He had one additional worry: They could be recalled to France or the Caribbean at any time. France had, indeed, entered the war but it was now a global war, and for both sides, possession of but a couple of the sugar islands of the Carib were deemed far more important than the entire North American continent, and both sides had concentrated their fleets and some of their elite troops there. He sensed that unless there was some dramatic turn, once the hurricane season in the Caribbean had passed,

Rochambeau and his five thousand would be ordered out of this theater entirely, and then surely his miniscule army of less than seven thousand would collapse.

Reaching the edge of the encampment, he turned sharply and started to walk back. It was only now, at this time that he allowed himself to dwell on these things. By the time he reached headquarters again he would have to affix the look of outward calm and confidence, offer praise where it would help, and pretend an optimism that soon all would change for the better, even if in his heart, exhausted from six years of this, he himself had all but given up hope.

"General, sir!"

He looked up to see young Alexander Hamilton, running toward him in a most uncharacteristic manner. His years as staff officer and even a field command had matured him quickly, but this morning? Had he been drinking?

He slowed as Hamilton, breathless, dashed up, came to attention and saluted, the eyes of hundreds of men around the camp turned his way. He was grinning like a delighted child.

"A dispatch has just come in, sir."

Washington extended a calming hand; too many of the men were standing close by, straining to hear every word. Already rumors would fly through the camp, and perhaps, before the day was even out, have crossed into British lines.

"No more of it until we are inside," he said softly, as if any dispatch that could excite Hamilton was of no real concern. Dispatches arrived by the score every day, most of them mundane, some depressing, some enraging—especially those from Congress that offered the usual excuses about pay, rations, supplies, and demands that he recall Greene or better yet dismiss him and return Gates to command.

He braced his shoulders, measured his pace, commented that it was going to be another scorching day, and to pass the order that the men were to drill in the morning but then have midafternoon off for their leisure, making sure that was overheard, and continued on.

Headquarters guard, turned out smartly in their buff and blue, sweat already trickling down from beneath their powdered wigs, snapped to attention and presented arms at his approach. Tied to a post beside the house he saw a lathered horse, an excellent mount with fine lines, which obviously had been ridden hard. A half mile back, on the road that led to the French encampments, he saw a small cavalcade approaching, the flag of their commanding general held aloft.

Something surely was up, and he actually swallowed nervously as he stepped into the cool exterior of the heavy fieldstone home that was his headquarters. Had Rochambeau received orders to prepare to be pulled out? The French general had, ever since his arrival, shown the utmost decorum and sense of protocol, deferring to the American as "mon Général," insisting before all that the French presence was under Washington's direct command, only to be superseded by direct orders from France.

The courier, without doubt, had first ridden to him, and he, without opening the dispatch, had ordered him to go to the commander. Yet curiosity could not contain the French general who was now riding in to hear the news.

The courier, a French officer, his white uniform dust covered, hatless, most likely lost in the hard riding, wig slightly askew, snapped to rigid attention as Washington stepped into the corridor. The courier held forth the envelope, wrapped in wax-impregnated string in case of threat of capture, so that it could be burned quickly. It bore a red seal, which Washington could not identify. He motioned for the courier and Hamilton to enter his office, picked up a paring knife, cut the cord, the seal, and opened it up. It was in French, and without his spectacles hard to decipher, he handed it to Hamilton.

"Just tell me what it says, Colonel."

"To His Excellency, General George Washington,"

"My general, it brings me the greatest joy and pleasure to send this missive to you. I cannot begin to express the honor . . ."

There would be the usual flourishes for another paragraph or two before the meat of the issue was laid out.

"Just tell me what it says," Washington interrupted.

Hamilton nodded, fell silent, lips moving as he read, and then his eyes widened.

He looked up at Washington for an instant, then back down at the sheet of ornate paper but now his hands were trembling, and then looked back up again.

"It is from Admiral de Grasse! Commanding a fleet of ships of the line in the Caribbean and dated nearly two weeks ago. He is abandoning his station in the Caribbean and at this moment is sailing north," Hamilton was nearly sputtering with excitement, "it states here, 'with twenty-eight ships of the line, aboard as well, three thousand troops of three of France's finest regiments, supplies, siege equipment for land operations, and currency of silver and gold.'"

"To where?"

Hamilton looked back down at the letter, tracing out the sentences with one finger. "To the mouth of the Chesapeake, there to blockade the British army of Cornwallis and he prays that sufficient troops shall meet him by land to effect a siege and the defeat of said army!"

Hands shaking, Hamilton handed the letter back to Washington, who stood silent, shocked beyond the ability to speak.

Ever since the victory of Saratoga and the French entrance into the war their help had been more than could be expected—for after all, regardless of their more liberal philosophers' platitudes about the glories of liberty and self-rule, France was a monarchy that just might not wish to see the seeds of liberty planted too deeply in another nation, lest it just might pollinate in their own land. England, a sworn enemy for centuries, was now too good a target, tied as it was to a bloody land campaign on the far side of the Atlantic, to let off scot free. Help had, indeed, come. Rochambeau, at this very moment dismounting outside his doorstep, was proof enough of that, but far more effort had been expended by the French in trying to snatch up some of the precious spice islands of the Caribbean, to join the Spanish in an attempt on Gibraltar, and with skirmishing and battles ranging far out to the other side of the world in India, prize taking in the Indies. France had weighed in, but did so with a global war in mind, and perhaps even, when the dust had settled, hoped to regain her lost possessions of Quebec, control of the lucrative trade along the Mississippi from New Orleans to Saint Louis, and the junction of that river and the Missouri. Distant fabled lands of riches from the shores of those rivers to the Pacific.

As he contemplated these thoughts, trying to gather his self-control after receiving such astounding news, he heard footsteps behind him. He struggled for control, realizing he was actually trembling with excitement, Hamilton standing before him grinning like a child.

He forced himself to regain a look of calm composure and turned about.

Rochambeau, with his typical touch of ceremony, entered the house but then stopped at the doorway into Washington's office, removing his hat with a flourish and bowing low, to which Washington responded in kind, but as he rose, Washington could see that this man did not need be told. Without doubt, the courier was a loyal Frenchman even while serving as an allied courier.

Rochambeau presented nearly as imposing a figure as Washington, standing over six feet tall, still young-looking though he was several years older than the American general, and disdaining the courtly look of some. He wore no rouge and skin lightener and the "birth," or "beauty mark" on the cheek or jaw, which was all the rage in the courts of Europe. His features were ruddy from long years under the sun, shoulders straight and still strong. The deep tan, a "look" that none of the usual aristocrats would have accepted, but in this war was the mark of a man either in the field or on the quarter deck of a man-o'-war.

He did not say a word as he came in, though his grin revealed all, as Washington handed him the dispatch. The French general feigned surprise, then open delight, and with a most un-Gallic-like gesture reached out and warmly clasped the American general's hands.

"I knew he would do it," Rochambeau cried excitedly, "I knew he would see where the real victory was waiting to be snatched."

Washington, knees actually feeling a bit weak, sat down, motioning for the French general to sit by his side. He looked up at Hamilton.

"Would you please be so kind as to summon a pot of coffee, maps of the Chesapeake region, Colonel Smith to take notes, Colonel Laurens to translate as needed, and Colonel Wellsley.

"Yes, him. He was there last winter and I want him to sit in as well."

Hamilton rushed from the room. Within minutes, as if reading his general's mind, the ever-faithful Billy Lee came into the room bearing a tray laden with coffee pot, china cups, and even some fresh baked biscuits smothered in butter. General Washington had been tempted increasingly of late to send Billy back home to Mount Vernon—the rheumatism from long years of campaigning in the field was taking its toll. Yet even the hint of it would send Billy into a defiant silence, with dark mutterings later, just barely within hearing distance, about "All these years of service," "Who in hell will see he eats right," and "The Missus herself told me to keep watch." Washington always relented.

Billy poured the coffee, stood expectant for a moment as if hoping to hear the gossip, for it was obvious by the behavior of Rochambeau's staff outside and the way young Alexander was running about that something was afoot. Washington just smiled at him and nodded a dismissal, suggesting he sit by the fire in the kitchen to ward off the morning chill in his bones.

Hamilton was back minutes later with the large portfolio, containing scores of maps of every theater of operation in this war, and shuffling through them started to lay out the pertinent ones on the dining table by the large south-facing window. Standing, he could see that a bit of a crowd was gathering outside. Word did, indeed, travel fast that something was afoot and he looked to Rochambeau.

"I regret having to ask this, sir," he said slowly, knowing that the French general understood English when spoken clearly and carefully enunciated. "Do any of your staff know of this development?"

"I assure you, sir, I am, as you Americans say, as mum as a cat. The courier first reported to me, and me alone, and gave me verbal news of what the courier ship had brought in to Newport and I ordered him to hurry on to you."

"Newport?"

Rochambeau grinned with delight.

"The English have abandoned the blockade of that harbor. For some reason the ships based there have apparently sailed for New York harbor. That is, according to two deserters, pressed men, who went over the side just before they sailed."

"Reliable men?"

"The Americans on my staff said they were Yankee men, born and bred, taken a year ago and pressed off a merchant ship captured trying to run the blockade. The Newport fleet is concentrating with the New York fleet in anticipation that our fleet will strike there."

"Apparently so."

"But not to intercept at Newport."

Rochambeau shook his head emphatically.

"Your reports and mine from yesterday clearly indicate that the British ships protecting New York harbor are still anchored off Staten Island. If they were to effect a rendezvous for a sortie to the south, they would already be maneuvering to clear the channel of Sandy Hook. Foretop masts and yards on many of the ships are struck down; crews freely wander the city on liberty. The hundreds of tons of supplies to feed such a fleet have not been ordered or loaded on board. It would take a week or more for them to prepare for a sea venture. Years of service there with no action other than the boredom of blockade and the occasional chase of one of our ships trying to slip by them has weakened their readiness for swift preparation and action. They must have received news by now that our good admiral has left the Caribbean, but as to where he is heading, it is apparent they do not yet know and are waiting for more information before acting."

Washington smiled with open approval, even as he motioned for

Hamilton to close the shutters to the window, and then close the window itself as well, so no curious eyes or eavesdroppers could see or hear what they were about.

Hamilton laid out maps, based on the latest information from Lafayette, Cornwallis was in Yorktown. It was easily defendable, readily open to supply from the sea via the Chesapeake Bay, always a British lifeline, and from there could raise havoc all across the fertile lands of eastern Virginia, while at the same time blockading any support coming up from North and South Carolina.

The prophetic report that Colonel Wellsley had carried to him back in early spring had, indeed, come to pass. Cornwallis's campaign to subdue the huge landmass of Georgia and the Carolinas was an exercise in folly that Greene had immediately learned to exploit, all but begging Cornwallis to venture into Virginia.

Why he had not made such an obvious move earlier, Washington wondered? The fertile belt of Virginia, Pennsylvania, and New Jersey was the breadbasket of the Revolution. Some of the strongest contingents of troops had come from these states as well. Ravage their homelands, and the Virginia line would have collapsed. Why had he not done so earlier and with the forces he had at his command prior to Kings Mountain, Cowpens, and the bruising confrontation Greene had offered him at Guilford Court House?

Again, was it because of a war office trying to run a continent-sized conflict from nearly four thousand miles away that they were so hampered?

All the British really had to do was simply to dig in at New York and some place in the mid-South, raid out when possible, wear us down as they had been doing. Then a meddlesome Empress Catherine or some other monarch would announce a grand peace conference and many in Congress would fall all over themselves to rush to it. As for himself, if such was the case, he would resign, take those men who would never surrender, head out to the Ohio lands, and perhaps in a generation, try again.

But now, this? This undreamed of turn of events? It seemed that finally a French admiral had pierced the veil of the true grand strategy of this war? He sat back in his chair, in front of Rochambeau, Alexander, and even the courier, who still stood rigid as if expecting to immediately receive a return dispatch. He put his spectacles on, something that only a trusted few ever witnessed him doing, and slowly read through the letter, stumbling here and there, a bit embarrassed asking Alexander to provide translation.

There was one line that Alexander, in his enthusiasm, had not announced. Admiral le Grasse said that upon arrival off the "Cape of the Bay of the Chesapeake" he would hold station for six weeks, but then orders from his own admiralty office and the king would compel him to return to the Caribbean once the hurricane season had passed. He looked at the dating of the letter, dispatched by fast courier frigate at the start of August. It was now August 14, so it was fair to wonder if some unforeseen disaster in his passage—a hurricane or violent storm or misnavigation that could put half a fleet aground on a dark night, or an encounter with an unsuspected British fleet—might have prevented him from being there at all. At this moment the twenty-eight ships of the line, the three thousand troops, the chests filled with freshly minted livres to pay his troops, and twenty thousand sailors, might be lost in a storm off Cape Hatteras, or have turned back or fled to safety in France.

There was no clue to their whereabouts, other than this one note.

He hesitated, then handed it to Rochambeau.

"I regret to question the veracity of this letter," he said, "but can you verify it?"

Rochambeau nodded, carefully taking the letter, holding it up to the shaded light from the window to examine the watermark and the secret coding within the water mark personally assigned to each admiral of the French fleet and no other, holding it close to examine the script, looked at the courier and asked if he had personally received it from the captain of the French ship. The courier said he had, and Rochambeau, smiling, handed it back.

"It is the truth."

He had never been demonstrative, but this time Washington let out a sigh of relief. His hopes had soared in the last few minutes, but then long years of war, of spy and counterspy, ruse and counter-ruse of which he himself was a master had come rushing in. This could be an elaborate British forgery to try to stir him into an action, and into a trap that could be disastrous. One defeat of his army in the field would be a disaster that would, without doubt, end their cause.

If de Grasse's promise was true, contrary to all the nightmares he had harbored but a scant hour ago, there was just a chance—a vague, one-in-a-hundred chance. Throughout history all military men knew that the coordination of land to sea forces, especially across vast distances, challenged even the best of generals and admirals. The vagaries of wind, tide, storms, faulty charts, miscommunications, the often tragic inability of one service to understand the needs and timing of the other, had seen to it that few such plans come to fruition. What about this one?

When the dispatch had been sent forward, de Grasse was nearly three thousand miles away. Who knew what he might have encountered since then to thwart his promise?

To make a decision based on this one letter? He stood up and stared out the upper panes of the window not concealed by the shutters. Could he ask this army to endure one more winter without any hope of an end in sight? Then another Valley Forge, another Morristown, when nearly half the army had mutinied because of no pay and lack of food, or even shoes, and had afterward deserted by the hundreds, declaring the cause was lost? What Lafayette and Greene had positioned against Cornwallis in Virginia could in no way stop him if he decided to launch an early fall spoiling campaign to ravage the harvests from Fredericksburg to Petersburg and perhaps, as well, lure Lafayette into a defeat against superior odds.

It all came down to this letter.

There was a polite tap on the door. Colonel Laurens, whose father was president of Congress and who had just returned, himself, from service as ambassador to France, entered, followed by his secretary William Smith and Peter Wellsley, who again handled spying and intelligence in his native state of New Jersey.

Hamilton, invoking the strictest confidentiality, read de Grasse's dispatch to them and all stood silent, awed.

He could see Colonel Wellsley barely able to contain his excitement, like a child gazing at a long anticipated missive that promised some great reward.

"Your thoughts, Colonel?" Washington asked.

"It is exactly as General Greene had hoped for after the battle at Guilford. To drive Cornwallis north and now into this trap," he quickly looked over at Rochambeau, "that our gallant French allies now give unto us the opportunity to complete."

He did not add in front of Rochambeau that it was what he hoped Thomas Paine and Laurens would urge the French king to do as well. Perhaps they had played a hand in this as well.

Washington nodded deferentially to Rochambeau, then turned to those gathered and uncharacteristically, he smiled.

"Gentlemen, in light of this startling news, I propose the following plan."

Six

NEW YORK
AUGUST 16, 1781

THE DAY WAS ALREADY TURNING SCORCHING HOT AS LT. Colonel Allen van Dorn, of the staff of General Clinton, slowly rode up the "Broad Way" of New York City. It was a typical marketing day. During the night, drovers from New Jersey and Long Island had ferried across pigs, goats, sheep, and a score of cattle, and were driving them to the holding pens where they would be slaughtered. This evening, they would be on the plates of the seven thousand men of His Majesty's army who occupied this city and the ten thousand sailors idling at anchor aboard the score of ships of the line and dozens of lesser craft, from light sloops to frigates, lying in the lower harbor off Staten Island.

Carts, loaded with the early harvest of late summer and drawn by slow oxen, made their way up the road, piled with Indian corn, cabbages, and other fresh vegetables. Also sacks of wheat for the bakeries of the army and the nearly thirty thousand civilians who lived under military occupation and military law.

It was nearly five years ago that His Majesty's army had occupied this city after the pathetic resistance of Washington's rabble. A fair part of the city had burned only days after Washington's retreat. Both sides blamed the other for the conflagration, but after five years, with the king's money pouring in, the trade created by an occupying army, and the need to support and supply the armada of war and supply ships, the city had actually prospered under military rule. The hundreds of burned houses, mansions, taverns, dives, brothels, and warehouses had long since been rebuilt, and with each passing year the city spread another block or two northward up from lower Manhattan.

The only signs of war here were the fortifications and batteries in what even before the war was called "Battery Park," the ever-present ships of war at anchor, the hundreds of red British uniforms and blue Hessian garb of soldiers granted leave for a day to quench their thirst for rum, beer, schnapps, or women. Officers, far more refined, had taken to early morning or evening carriage rides with their mistresses, and even, in some cases, their new American wives. They rode up from their quarters to the lush countryside around the Harlem Heights for a dignified picnic and to watch the sunset beyond the Palisades of New Jersey.

Before the horrific affair with his friend Andre, Allen's missions often carried him across the river to those heights and beyond, venturing at times as far as the Watchung Hills and the Short Hills a dozen miles west of Elizabethtown, especially when Washington's army was encamped but twenty miles farther on at Morristown.

He had been present at the disastrous Battle of Springfield in June of last year, the last foray with significant troops into New Jersey. It was a bungled affair—humiliating, actually—as Continentals led by Mad Anthony Wayne, still thirsting for revenge for what they called the "massacre" at Paoli, along with a swarm of Jersey militia had driven them back. He had barely escaped with his own life when Light Horse Harry Lee had led the Rebel cavalry in a charge around the flank. That, and the base capture of his friend John Andre, had

led General Clinton to order him to remain in Manhattan for fear of
his own capture or death. Among the New Jersey militia in particular
he was recognized as "that damn Loyalist from Trenton," and contrary to the profile he needed, all knew that he was now responsible
for coordinating efforts of British spying and the blocking of Rebel
spies in what had once been his home colony.

Before dawn, he had met with his "usual agents" in an upper story
room of a slop house just off of Battery Park, typically frequented by
drunken sailors and those who preyed upon them. The crowd included the drover known to him only as "Crazed George," a slatternly
woman, "Fat Dianne," from Elizabethtown, an honest preacher from
Chatham disgusted with the God-cursed depredations of the Rebels
upon honest men and women still loyal, and a shrewd lad simply
known as Edward, who did odd chores around the militia camps
occupying Elizabethtown and Newark, and would then slip across the
river at night for his half crown pay in exchange for the latest gossip.

Allen had labored over his daily reports, now neatly tucked into
his breast pocket. He trotted past a couple of carriages at the edge of
the city, filled with officers and their "ladies," more than a few already
in their cups though it was not even midmorning but observant to salute a superior when necessary. After all, even after five years of service, and his known friendship with Andre, all knew he was "merely"
a Loyalist—a colonial—and the slightest breech of etiquette would
surely be spoken of loudly within earshot of Clinton.

Sprawled under an apple tree just outside the limits of the city
he saw two soldiers passed out cold. He edged off the road and approached them, wondering for a moment if they were dead. It was a
common enough occurrence, usually blamed on Rebel scum and spies,
but more often than not it had been a "soldier's fight" to settle a score
over a hand of cards or some woman. Other times, the notorious cut-
purses and thieving gangs, who did not give a damn which army was
in this city, would fall upon a couple of drunks to rob.

These two were simply drunk and sleeping it off.

"You two, wake up!" he snapped.

One half-opened his eyes, shading them against the early morning sun, and groaned.

The man sat up, kicking his companion in the side as he came to his feet, looked at Allen, and realized he was an officer.

"Beggin' your pardon, sir," he said as he offered a wobbly salute.

"Get back to your regiment."

"And the time, if I may ask, your honor?"

"Long past morning roll."

"Christ in heaven," the second soldier sighed, barely able to stand. "'Tis a flogging for sure."

"Worse, if you don't get back now," Allen replied without rancor. If they were lucky, maybe a sergeant had covered for them at morning roll and the usual bribe paid afterward. If not, it was twelve lashes for being drunk and absent without leave.

He rode on, looking back over his shoulder at the two pathetic men, one of them stopping to lean over and vomit, the other then pulling him along. From the sound of them, they were Irish, had taken the king's shilling to escape the poverty of that isle, with little heart in this war other than the fact it was what they were paid to do.

As he rode on and crested a low rise, morning mist was rising off the Hudson to his left, and the East River to his right. The view to his right was not a pleasant one. There were the prison ships, in which thousands of men had died of starvation, disease, and neglect. His old friend Peter had legitimately spoken of them with heartfelt bitterness when last they met, on the day John Andre died.

Allen, as a Loyalist now trusted by Clinton himself, had appealed several times, trying to persuade the commanding general that removing the surviving men to dry land, to offer good rations, clothing, and medical care, to parole home those men who were obviously too infirm or injured to ever fight again, and to symbolically burn those damn ships to the waterline would be a message of reconciliation that would echo far and wide. It would even serve as an indicator that their side wished for this war to end with a fair peace.

His last appeal had been met with incredulous disbelief, mockery, and even reproach. General Grey, under whom he had served at Paoli, had snapped, "I thought you were Andre's friend? After what they did to him, I thought you'd want to see every damn Rebel hanged, or are you growing soft, van Dorn?"

From an officer of equal rank, not just the remark but also the taunting voice would have required a challenge of honor. Received from a superior, he had just fallen silent.

He turned away from that place of agony and let his gaze linger on the Palisade Heights. Thin coils of smoke rose every mile or so, marking the forward picket lines of the Rebels. He paused for a moment, dismounted, took out his telescope, and focused on one after another. Several had observation towers of rough hewn timbers, rising twenty to thirty feet to offer a better view of the city. Every few months a raiding force of light infantry and grenadiers would be sent across during the night, to scale the heights and scatter them, and try to bring back a few prisoners. It served little purpose other than to add a few more names to the casualty lists of this war.

As he let his gaze linger on one of the towers, he saw a man leaning over a tripod-mounted telescope that appeared to be aimed straight at him. On impulse he raised a hand to wave, and the gesture was repeated back by the Rebel a few seconds later.

He sighed, closing his telescope. Who was the man? Jersey militia, from the look of him. On random chance, one in a thousand he thought, they might even know each other from before the war. Now they waved back and forth in a friendly manner, but up close, neither would hesitate to kill the other.

Strange, how war is. Before this started or afterward, if he had met this man, perhaps down on his luck, he would have offered him a pint and even a shilling out of a sense of charity, yet now he would kill him if need be.

That, at least, was one thing he was somewhat sure he had never done. Though in action in the major battles of Brandywine, Germantown, and Monmouth, and a score of smaller skirmishes, the last being Springfield, he was never really sure if he had actually killed a man.

In all the smoke and confusion he had fired many a shot, but kill a man? Some of his comrades boasted of the dozens of Rebels they had put in the grave, but any real veteran looked at them with disdain. Unless you actually drove a blade into a man, which was actually rather rare except for the cavalry—that when unleashed in pursuit could be heartlessly vicious—few knew for sure what they had done in all the smoke and confusion of a major action.

He thought of Peter Wellsley. At Monmouth, he was part of a unit overrun as it retreated in the suffocating 105 degree heat. Peter had captured him, stood with musket leveled, then turned it aside and told him to run.

Peter. . . . Could he kill him?

After what they did to John, he knew he could, if need be.

He mounted back up, pulling out the silver pocket watch, imported from London, which had cost him two months' pay. In a few minutes he would be late for the morning briefing and he urged his mount to a loping gallop, glad for the cooling air, the pleasure of riding, of letting go of the war for a few minutes as he rode past the rich farmlands of Manhattan Island. At last the headquarters of General Clinton was in sight, down near the banks of the East River.

It was, indeed, a strange location the commanding general of all His Majesty's troops in the Americas occupied this day, a mansion a good four miles north of the city. Clinton had five such homes at his beck and call, a couple within the city, the others out here in the countryside. Some said it was in a vain attempt to conceal his liaisons with one of several mistresses, the deference of a gentleman since his favorite was married to a wealthy merchant in the city. A few said it was actually a wise move, for with every summer the city became a breeding house of contagion. For every man killed on the battlefield in the last five years, half a dozen had died here of disease, especially in mid to late summer. Others whispered, though never in the general's presence, that he actually harbored a morbid fear of Rebel plots to assassinate him, and thus moved his headquarters, suddenly and without notice, to throw off such plots. None would ever dare to say that out loud. Allen was one who tended toward this belief.

Nearby, the headquarters of a battalion of troops, Clinton's personal guards, were enduring their morning inspection. Sergeants barking out orders, dressing down a man if there was the slightest smudge to the lily white strap of his cartridge box, or the slightest speck of rust on sparkling gun barrel or bayonet. He thanked God fate had not cast him as a soldier of "the line." Discipline and humiliation were constant, relentless, and he wondered if the two soldiers he had roused from under the apple tree, at this moment were enduring similar treatment, or perhaps were already stripped to the waist and being caned or flogged for their drunken offense.

He circled along the now graveled lane that led to the mansion. The guards, familiar with who he was, came to attention at his approach. A black orderly ran up to take the bridle of his horse as he dismounted. He took his watch out, realizing he was barely in time, and as he mounted the front steps, from the distant city he could hear church bells ringing out the hour.

Clinton was holding court in his usual location in this house, the dining hall of which had a massive mahogany dining table, imported, most likely at great expense, all the way from the East Indies before the war. A servant who was leaving the room as he entered slowed, and whispered "tea, sir?" Allen nodded his thanks. The ever-present William Smith, Clinton's secretary, sat to one side, gazing out the window while absently munching on a slice of toast. Clinton looked up from his own repast of coffee and fresh baked ham, his morning glass of sherry half drained. Peter snapped to attention and with absent wave of his free hand, the general motioned for him to be seated by his side, the servant returning only seconds later with a steaming cup of tea—no toast, ham, or breakfast. He was here to report, not to join in the social circle of a general and his staff and friends.

On the table there was a scattering of maps. After years of the type of work Allen did, he could not help but scan them with a quick glance. It was, after all, his job to gather intelligence. Only one map was of their tactical situation here in New York, and there were no changes or notes upon it, indicating shifting positions. The others, though, were of the Atlantic coast clear down to the Sugar Islands of the Caribbean.

Clinton caught his glances and cleared his throat.

"Your morning report, sir," the general said.

He was, as always, a polite man. Rare was the dressing-down of a fellow officer, a display of the kind of rage or tantrum for which General Grey was somewhat infamous. He was always calm, almost too calm, even deferential for a general in command. Whenever a question of the moment arose, he tended to counsels of war, with his various brigade commanders and the admiral of the fleet anchored in the harbor. That was hard to keep track of at times. There were Hood, Rodney, and others, who had kept the sea lines open, moving back and forth between Halifax, this harbor at New York, and clear down to Jamaica.

Of the ships in the harbor there had been some movement back and forth in the last few weeks, and he had picked up rumors in the taverns from drunken young midshipmen and lieutenants that something was afoot at sea. Reports of a battle lost in the Caribbean and that the main French fleet could not now be found. One was so open with his blathering that a major fight was in the offering, right here outside of New York harbor, that he had learned the young man's name and sent over a report to his captain the following morning. If a Rebel agent had been in the tavern and if the boasting was true, busting his rank to common sailor and time "before the mast" would be light discipline, indeed, for such open and foolish talk that the Rebels could expect their French allies to appear off the coast any day now.

He doubted if his advice was taken. The ever-existing tension between the navy and army was as old as history, both looking down on the other, both claiming always that if there was victory they were responsible for it and if there was defeat it was the fault of the other. He had learned after five years that, hidebound though this army was with its tradition and rituals, the navy was far worse. Every captain was terrified of offending his admiral, and the admirals, often frozen like a rabbit, would be pointing to the printed manuals of instructions from the admiralty office in London, which tied their hands no matter where they were at sea. All were ever-mindful of the fate of Admiral Byng, a generation before, who had actually been executed because he had won a battle but failed to prosecute the victory effectively. There had been little daring in this navy ever since. All strictly followed rules and procedures, from common seaman to admirals, never with a creative thought or taking chances. It was the safe bet to be sure, but it was not the kind of thinking that won wars.

"Your report, sir," Clinton asked with that ever-so-correct tone of a gentleman addressing an officer, but also the implication of boredom with this daily ritual.

Allen opened his uniform, reaching into his breast pocket and drew out the several pages of notes, carefully sealed. After writing them, he was always extremely cautious with these reports. If he were ever waylaid, or—far worse—accidentally dropped them, it would put at risk the lives of four agents. Young Edward was readily identifiable and if "smoked out" would without doubt be dancing at rope's end in spite of his tender age of sixteen.

They had shown no pity for John Andre; they would show no pity to a youth who was actually a rather skillful spy.

He drew the notes out, placed them on the table, and Clinton broke the seal while sipping his tea, Allen letting his go tepid. He began to read, and chuckled slightly.

"Why do you put trust in that woman?" Clinton asked after scanning the first page.

"Sir, it is amazing at times what a man will boast of in bed, even with a woman of such low virtue."

He damn near bit his own tongue as Clinton shot him a sidelong glance. He did not make eye contact, realizing that the general might take personal insult. It did set him at the same instant to wondering. Was one of the mistresses of this man a spy? He had not dared to consider the question before, but it was in front of him now by that glance, for perhaps the general had spoken when he should have been silent and the look was one of defensive guilt.

He dared the thought of perhaps putting a watch on the general's mistresses but instantly ruled it out. If found out, either rightly or wrongly in his inquiry, it was a definite sentence to some fever-ridden island thousands of miles away. No one ever dared to inquire too closely into the affairs of generals in command. Even if a dangerous truth was discovered, how to approach and explain it? The end result would be the same, a fever-ridden island on the other side of the world.

He looked away from the man, picking up his cup of tea and sipping it, putting on his best display of innocence, and after a few seconds Clinton went back to reading the reports.

"Interesting, so they are building a bakery in Chatham for making hard bread. Oh, that is, indeed, interesting." There was a touch of sarcasm in his voice.

"It comes from a minister, a reliable source."

"And it means what? How do you see its importance?"

"Perhaps an army preparing in advance for a march, laying out supplies and rations ahead of the route they take."

Clinton said nothing.

"This young Edward, in whom I do put trust, overheard two militia officers discussing an order from Washington's headquarters to find as many boats capable of carrying heavy loads such as horses or artillery, and to prepare to maneuver them down to the channel that divides New Jersey from Staten Island. If need be, to go as far south as the Sandy Hook in search of them, then ferry the boats along the coastal shallows at night to avoid detection, and hide them by day."

"So?" asked Clinton.

"It could mean planning for a maneuver for Washington to bring his army down from their current position. To then seize Staten Island that, sir, we both know is held only by a light garrison. If done swiftly enough, they could take the battery positions from the landward side at the Narrows, and close off the harbor."

Clinton sighed and shook his head.

"Colonel van Dorn, you do have an active imagination but then again that is your job."

"Sir?"

"Surely we would detect their march, and, if they did take Staten Island back, the ships in our harbor mount more than five hundred guns. Even if they did set up a battery on land, it would be flattened within the hour and the navy's vaunted marines would storm it and bag the lot of them."

He could sense the disdain as Clinton spoke of the navy's marines. If there was little love lost between the navy and army there was even less between the navy's marine infantry and the army. So many brawls had broken out between the two that certain taverns and houses of "amusement" had been set aside for marine use only down by the Battery at the tip of Manhattan to avoid fights, some of which had proven fatal to one side or the other.

Allen did not respond.

Clinton read the rest of the report, and with a languid gesture handed the papers over to his secretary, with a comment about properly filing them. The secretary, equal in rank to Allen, took a moment to read the report, shot a quick glance as if this report, like nearly all the others, was not worth notice, and pushed the sheets of paper over to a pile of other paperwork, the daily returns of regiments, requisitions for supplies, reports to and from England, the myriad of paperwork that haunted any general in command.

"And your analysis today, Colonel?" Clinton asked almost as if just being polite but having already reached his conclusions as to the worth of Allen's nightlong efforts and interviews in smoky dives and taverns.

"I think, sir, something is afoot at last."

"Pray tell why?"

"That report from Chatham, New Jersey, caught my attention. I've known the minister for years, a good man with keen insight. He said a courier came riding in with great haste, handed the orders off

to the local militia commander, demanded a fresh horse, then said
he was pressing on to Princeton and that 'things were afoot,' as the
minister said, having overhead the conversation."

"Well?"

"Sir, if it was simply to build ovens to keep the army supplied if
they should decide to winter again nearby in Morristown, why the
haste? It would have come as a standard order, a month or two from
now, not with such haste within the last day. To me, that indicates a
preparation for a march by a large force, perhaps the bulk of Washington's army."

"What, pray tell, does that have to do with your equal concern
about this Edward lad and his story of gathering boats with the intent
of attacking Staten Island?"

"I agree, sir, that building ovens in Chatham, twenty miles from
the coast, bears no relationship, but we both know that General Washington is a master of subterfuge, to have one plan but to lay out several
false trails to confuse us."

"You confuse me, good sir," Clinton said and now there was an
indulgent smile. "First you speak of Staten Island and their seizing the
Narrows, an absurd move, and now you speak of this godforsaken
village named Chatham and their army building a bakery of all things
to support them as they march. March to where, sir? To where?"

Smith, who had been all but ignoring the conversation, turned and
now looked at Allen with what appeared to be interest.

Allen hesitated; he had been grilled often enough before like this.
He was simply doing his job, providing daily intelligence reports
about what was transpiring in New Jersey, much of it trivial, he knew
as well as Clinton, but beneath those trivial facts, there might be concealed a nugget of truth.

This war had dragged on far too long. There were rumors of peace
feelers, that some in their Congress were even greeting such talk
after so many years of exhaustion and destruction. Would Washington
accept such an outcome? He had stood before that man twice, and
both times had left on him a marked impression. He kept his compo-

sure but as he looked at Clinton the contrast between the two was all too evident. Clinton, though a good general, a man who even showed a higher degree of consideration and concern for his infantry, the common soldier, than most of the officers of this army, was a man of languid airs. He lacked a certain boldness, a "joie de vivre," a zest for command, a challenge, and the willingness that Washington had shown for action and risk-taking if he detected an opportunity. Allen had witnessed that personally at Trenton and again at Monmouth.

From his daily intelligence, Allen knew that Washington's army was spiraling downward, with no pay for months, no action, nothing that could even remotely be called a battle in this theater for more than a year. That had been at Springfield; in which only a fraction of the Continentals were involved. His army was increasingly disgruntled, and had damn near mutinied into full rebellion the winter before last. The only thing still propping them up here in the North was the support of the French. Washington's army, in its current condition, most likely could not stand another winter like Valley Forge. Washington was a man of action. Between now and the advent of winter he would have to seek action, as he did on Christmas night of 1776. Most men feared battle to one degree or another, but Washington did not. Washington was a bold leader ready to stake all on a single roll of the dice, "the random chance of battle," as one put it, the way Caesar, Alexander, and William of Normandy had.

He would seek some bold move before winter and all instinct told Allen it was about to begin. Yet this general, his commander, sitting across from him, sipping his tea, was content to let another year of boredom, of no action in the North, play itself out. It was the safe bet, a slow winding down of the war, and finally he would return to England honored with titles, an estate, and ten thousand pounds a year. He was not willing to risk that. Washington, with nothing more to lose, was willing to risk everything.

He cast a glance back at the charts on the table.

"Perhaps not here," he finally said, breaking the long moment of silence.

"What do you mean, Colonel?"

"Sir, we both know, and Washington does, too, that the defenses you have designed for this city are perfect."

It was a deliberate compliment and Clinton swallowed it whole and smiled.

"That, sir, is the problem here, now."

"I do not understand your meaning."

"Sir, with my compliments you have laid out fortifications ringing this city that even if outnumbered four to one, we would hold and repulse the attack with ease."

He did not add that, of course, the major card in that equation as well was the presence of ships of the line of the Royal navy that from here, clear up to the barrier at West Point on the Hudson, gave their side complete mastery of any approach to the city. It would be sheer insanity or the final lunge of a madman to venture an attack on Manhattan.

But somewhere else?

"Thank you for your report, Colonel, but I have others that now await me. I will expect you again same time tomorrow."

He stood, saluted, and started for the door, again glancing at the charts. Opening the door he was surprised to find himself confronting an admiral. It was Rodney himself, and he stiffened, offering a salute. Rodney, followed by a long trail of staff, walked past him as if he were a servant, holding the door open for him. Clinton actually came to his feet, offering a warm greeting.

Rodney had not even noticed him, and a few captains shot him sidelong glances as they followed their commander in.

There was a call for tea with something to "stiffen" it. Allen stepped outside looking for his mount, and walked around the ornate carriage that had most likely borne up Rodney from a dock down by the Battery. His duty done for the day, he looked forward to a good breakfast, a good stiff drink or two, and a few blessed hours of sleep before repeating the same damn ritual yet again, from nightfall until dawn.

"Colonel?"

He looked back to the entryway into the mansion. It was Colonel Smith.

The man came bounding down the steps and approached. It caught Allen slightly off guard. This man had always been diffident, apparently bored whenever present as Allen reported.

"A moment of your time, sir, before you depart," Smith said and motioned for Allen to join him on a walk down across the open lawn that led down to the East River.

"I have but a few minutes before the meeting with the Admiral begins, may I beg your indulgence as to a few thoughts."

This did, indeed, catch Allen off guard. Smith had dropped the outward display of effete superiority nearly every officer on Clinton's staff showed toward a "mere Continental, even if on our side," especially one who dealt in the distasteful world of spying and counter-spying, with the exception of course of his old friend, John Andre.

"I am at your disposal, sir," Allen replied cautiously.

Smith actually took him by the arm, guiding him away from a knot of officers, the hanger-ons, who always lingered about army headquarters, hoping to pick up tidbits of news, or to be noticed.

"I am curious, sir."

"However I may be of help," Allen replied, still cautious.

"You implied more than my general was willing to discuss with you."

"I am not sure I follow you, sir," Allen said, voice even, showing no emotion, something he'd had to learn in order to survive, whether in this world of headquarters or back during the time when his life was on the line if he misspoke one word while behind enemy lines.

"I think, Colonel van Dorn, you were trying to warn my general that General Washington is planning some bold stroke. You are not yet sure what it is, but your sense of things, your knowledge of our opponents has led you to that conclusion."

"I did not say that, sir."

Smith laughed softly.

"Let us exchange confidences, sir. Say it is for the good of our king whom we both serve. I shall keep your words, as coming from you, in strictest confidence and upon that, sir, you have my pledge of honor as a gentlemen. So I do pray, just be frank with me."

He looked into Smith's eyes and at that moment did feel somewhat disarmed. The gaze was the same as his old friend Andre. Open, frank, noble to be certain, but one of honesty and integrity, even if he, Allen, was merely a "Continental" who had thrown his lot in with the Crown.

He forced a smile in reply, his smile greeted in turn by Smith, who, still holding him by the arm, squeezed him tightly as a sign of confidence, and then released his grasp.

"Washington knows his army will not hold together for another winter," Allen said. "Six years since 1775 have exhausted the will of nearly everyone to continue the fight. They believed at the start of this war that it would be over in six months; it has now been six years. Washington knows he must risk all, in one bold stroke, to revive the will of Congress, his army, the people, and their allies the French to continue the fight. I think it shall happen here, or pass before our doorstep within the next few weeks."

"What then?" Smith asked.

"As I said to our general, and he did not catch my full meaning . . ." Allen hesitated.

"Go ahead, sir, I have pledged on my honor that this is in confidence."

He hesitated, then nodded, thinking of the old saying "in for a penny, in for a pound."

"The defenses here are too perfect. I did mean that in one way as a compliment, but combine that with the support of the Royal navy, and Washington knows he cannot attack with even the remote hope of a victory as he achieved at Trenton."

Smith nodded in agreement.

"Dare I say he should have left some point weakly held. At least to outward appearances. A point to lure Washington into one of his bold ventures. We have seen before there is no weak point. That leaves

Washington with only one alternative. To seek a bold stroke in another location, another theater of operation entirely, to win a battle
he must win, no matter what the risk, before the onset of winter. If he
hesitates in this, he knows he will lose this war by spring."

Smith stood silent, not replying.

"The charts on the table. May I ask why they were there. Charts
more for the navy, extending clear to the Caribbean and our coast
clean up to here. That indicated something to me."

Smith still was silent but he could see by the narrowing of the
man's eyes that he had hit on something.

"You know that the campaign in the Carolinas has all but failed.
Cornwallis has pulled back to Virginia, under the guise of taking the
war there, but essentially he is in a defensive position at this moment."

"But still supplied by sea?" and Allen said it more as a question
than a statement of fact.

Smith hesitated, then nodded.

"As long as His Majesty's navy controls the approaches to the
Chesapeake, yes."

Allen took that in and finally nodded.

"In order for Washington's and Rochambeau's armies to link up
with that of Greene and Lafayette, to then have a superior force to
challenge Cornwallis, they first must pass through New Jersey."

He let the words slip out in one quick rush, a thought that had
been forming ever since he walked into Clinton's office and saw the
maps on the table. Was that what Rodney and Clinton were talking of
even now? Was something in doubt? He had heard, of course, as all
had, that the French admiral, de Grasse, was in the Caribbean raising
havoc. But . . . but perhaps, with the advent of the hurricane season,
when most fleets wisely withdrew from that region, his destination
was this campaign in North America. Where would be the logical
place to strike?

Smith looked at him and seemed to draw in, as if he dare not say
more of what he felt.

"I really must get back in, the meeting with Rodney has started by now and I am needed there," he finally said.

Allen nodded with understanding.

"Of course, sir."

There was a moment of hesitation.

"Perhaps, if you permit, I may call on you later in the week. Ever since the murder of our friend Andre, the general has hesitated to send officers behind enemy lines, but I would like to discuss some thoughts with you."

"But of course, sir," Allen said, and he offered his address, a rather lowly place down near the wharves off of the Wall Street, but a convenient location for the work he was engaged in.

Rather than salute, Smith actually shook his hand, so uncharacteristic of the British, then turned and ran back to the mansion. An orderly led up Allen's mount, freshly groomed while he attended to the general, and held the lead as he mounted and started back to the city.

As he rode along the Broad Way, passing several parties of officers accompanied by their ladies of the day, out for picnics in the countryside, his gaze lingered on the Palisades.

What exactly was going on behind that ridge?

He had a feeling that in a few days, he would be seeing for himself what was afoot, and the thought filled him with anticipation, and as he remembered the fate of his friend John, it filled him with fear as well.

Seven

TAPPAN FERRY ON THE HUDSON
AUGUST 19, 1781

THE FIRST BOAT CAST OFF AS NIGHTFALL BLANKETED THE river.

For Washington this was not like the nightmare of evacuating after the horrific defeat at Long Island, or the lunge of desperation that Christmas night on the Delaware. After receiving word from Admiral de Grasse to expect him by month's end at the mouth of Chesapeake, Washington had made his decision in less than an hour and the die was cast. He would take more than half his ragged army on a five hundred mile march, to be covered in less than a month, down into Virginia to link up with his old comrades and friends, Lafayette and Dan Morgan, whom Greene had detached to reinforce the young French general, while he took the rest of his intact army south to retake the Carolinas and Georgia. Rochambeau had agreed without hesitation to Washington's plan, eager for action at last, to place four thousand of his elite troops at "mon Général's" disposal.

The gamble would settle things one way or the other, once and for all, before winter. Though the odds were long, nevertheless it was a far better chance than a slow flickering out and dying of the cause for which he had given the last six years of his life.

To coordinate land and sea forces separated by thousands of miles? Yet the thought lingered in his nightmares that in spite of Rochambeau's reassurances, the letter from the French admiral could be an elaborate forgery, a ruse of war. Then there was the vast array of other unknowns upon which he was now gambling all. Hurricanes were known to strike the tropical isles as early as May. At this very moment de Grasse, along with his twenty-eight ships of the line and twenty thousand sailors, might be cast up onto the shores of a tropical atoll or the barrier islands of Florida, nothing but splinters and marooned men surrounded by floating, decaying corpses. The history of over two hundred and fifty years of fleets sailing the Caribbean was replete with stories of elaborate plans, smashed by the whimsy of fate and an ill wind.

Beyond the random acts of fate and wind, to underestimate the power of the Royal navy was madness as well, even though in this war, admirals of the king were almost pathetically timid, influenced still by Admiral Byng's execution in 1757. Surely they had kept tabs on the French movements, from the time de Grasse slipped out of the harbor of Brest in March. Surely Hood, Rodney, and others, with an estimated forty or more ships of the line, at this very moment would be on a course of interception, though his intelligence reports of this morning indicated that the force covering New York City was still at anchor on the leeward side of Staten Island, or docked in Manhattan for maintenance and resupply. No emergency orders had been issued to purchase and load necessary supplies aboard, to round up drunk and missing sailors, and immediately make for sea.

Though that appearance itself could be a plan within a plan. Clinton, after years of inaction, might be just as frustrated as he was by inaction, thus a ruse of war to let him believe that de Grasse was on his way to the Virginia coast and commit his army to meet him, leaving the defense of the Hudson and West Point all but naked. Then he would sally forth, and while Washington was campaigning in Virginia, Clinton would smash the gateway into upstate New York, or swing about to the south of New Jersey and take Philadelphia once again. If Philadelphia fell yet again into British hands, he knew with almost utter certainty that Congress would remove him from command, Gates would be placed in charge, and the government would then seek a negotiated peace under English terms. The cause of freedom would be lost in dishonorable disintegration.

There were too many "ifs" to even begin to contemplate. He had struggled with that ever since the initial enthusiasm after the arrival of the courier. As usual, he decided that to ponder the "what ifs" would cause him to freeze into inaction. He and his army had faced worse odds at Trenton and seen it through to victory. Make the decision, then stick with it, and the hell with wasting time on listening to some nagging voice of an inner fear. He had made his decision and as surely as Caesar had crossed his Rubicon, and Alexander the Hellespont, he was now preparing to cross the Hudson.

Before dawn of this day, he had sent the best of his light infantry and dragoons southward, as if an advance guard, pushing toward the outskirts of New York in preparation for an assault from the north. Skirmishing had been light throughout the day. The British were ready to pull back those few crucial miles, not willing to sacrifice lives in a game that across the last year had been back and forth a dozen times in the fought-over zone between his own encampments and Yonkers, just north of Manhattan Island.

A cordon had been established: Anyone known to be of Loyalist leanings and still residing behind the lines had been politely but most firmly ordered to pack and head for the city with the promise their property would not be looted.

"The first boat—it is going," Rochambeau announced in the falling darkness.

Washington focused his attention back to the broad expanse of the Hudson, here nearly five miles across. The Tappan Ferry was the first significant crossing point north of the city that was out of sight of the British forward lines, chosen because with its broad expanse, the current was placid, and usually a breeze could easily be caught for the wide-beamed ferryboats carrying a single large lateen-rigged sail. A single boat could carry a hundred or more men, or half a dozen horses, or a fully loaded artillery piece with crew and draft animals. Amazingly, they had been hired with real money and not useless scrip. In spite of his doubts about the honesty of Robert Morris, the new treasurer and paymaster had, indeed, come through. A wagon, burdened down with three heavy barrels, and guarded by half a hundred picked dragoons, had arrived in camp the day before. To his stunned disbelief, when the barrels were cracked open, concealed under a load of fresh hay, they contained over forty thousand dollars of money—real hard money.

Morris had pledged his own credit and his entire fortune on those three barrels, and suddenly, miraculously, money lenders and banks in Philadelphia "discovered" that there was money, in real silver, to be found somewhere in that city. The hard task was to figure it all out. It was an insane mix of English pennies, shillings, half crowns, silver guineas, and even some ten guinea gold pieces, French "louis," Spanish dubloons, and a fair mix of pieces of eight, even some German and Dutch thalers, and Russian rubles. Blacksmiths with cold chisels finally had to be rounded up, to carefully split more than a few of the coins, as his entire army was lined up, with each man receiving a month's pay of real money in hard currency, the first they had seen in years. Morale had soared, though more than a few, with typical American defiance, pointed out that several years of back pay were still waiting. Yet for the moment it had served its purpose, with enough set aside to purchase supplies for the march, stockpile more foodstuffs along the line of march, hire the ferrymen, and leave sufficient funds to be doled out for bribes, payment of spies, and spreading misinformation.

Another boat cast off, and then another. The first three were carry-ing the advance guard of light infantry and a company of heavy infantry, to deploy down the river road toward the Palisades, by dawn to be clearly visible near what had once been Fort Lee. They were to be the diversionary force and draw the attention of the British in New York, while the main bulk of his army steathily moved farther inland. Behind them were half a dozen more boats, loading up infantry, the first of the artillery pieces, a dozen dragoons, then more infantry.

The interweaving of infantry, artillery, and cavalry had been carefully calculated. If, indeed, a trap was waiting on the far side of the river, he wanted a fighting force in place as quickly as possible to secure the position, and then to make the decision whether to press ahead with the landings or retire. It was always a risky operation, to retreat back across a river under fire, especially this one, deep drafted enough that even a ship of the line could venture this far north, and with one broadside devastate the entire operation. Still, he had planned this for when the tidal currents were running down to the sea, and his luck was holding. There was a gentle breeze from out of the northwest, which favored his crossings, both coming and going. It made it all but impossible for an enemy ship to tack up the river and try to stay in the middle of the stream without being detected from either shore.

French army engineers, ever-efficient, had constructed an observation platform for himself, General Rochambeau, and other observers who were to keep a careful watch southward, downriver, in case the British did attempt to strike during the night. Yet no signal fires were lit along the river banks to either side by the British. From his own troops on the far shore there were occasional flashes from hooded lanterns, which indicated all was going according to plan. A secured perimeter was established around the ferry landing, the advance decoy column already on the march toward Fort Lee.

Shortly after midnight a pale waning moon rose in the east. The timing of even that had been taken into consideration. If discovered now in the moonlight, sufficient forces were across to hold their position, with artillery already dug in to lay down fire across the river, the moonlight silhouetting their targets out in the river.

It was almost too perfect.

He looked over at his comrade, General Rochambeau, and in an uncharacteristic gesture, extended his hand, which the French general clasped.

"I think it is time I cross," Washington announced.

"God's blessing go with you, my General," Rochambeau replied in his heavily accented English. "As planned, I will cross within three days, and follow you on the march. I pray all shall go well."

He felt he did not need to add that Rochambeau should continue to pressure the reluctant Admiral Barre, anchored in Newport Harbor, Rhode Island. The British had, indeed, abandoned their blockade of Newport, Rhode Island, the week before and there was sharp speculation that they were gathering their own fleet together, perhaps having word as well that de Grasse was heading north. With the path to the sea wide open now for Barre, he seemed to be afraid of his own shadow, and had not yet committed to taking aboard his army's heavy siege train and food supplies, both crucial if anything was to be accomplished at Yorktown. He was leaving it to Rochambeau to dislodge the reluctant admiral and get him moving. Rather than haul a heavy siege train of the larger eighteen- and twenty-four pound guns, and the precious sixteen-inch mortars provided by the French, along with all the entrenching equipment needed for a siege, plus additional rations, Barre had so far indicated a refusal, saying his posting and orders were to "keep watch" on the Royal navy guarding New York.

If he did so, he served no purpose. It was, perhaps, the only failing in de Grasse's letter explaining his intentions. Unfortunately, by a technicality of precedent de Grasse was in one sense of lower rank than Barre, even though charged to coordinate naval operations along the North American coast. He therefore could not order him to move, but could only "suggest" it, as proper etiquette the French navy required.

Barre's capital ships would surely give de Grasse the upper hand if the two fleets could unite, but it would be a risk for him to venture forth with only half a dozen ships of the line, carrying such essential supplies only to fall afoul of a superior British force possibly holding the weather gauge if they should sally forth from New York harbor.

Then again, Washington reasoned, as he had ever since the note from the Caribbean had arrived, this entire venture was one mad, insane risk.

Removing his hat in formal acknowledgment to Rochambeau, who returned the gesture, Washington climbed down from the observation platform. The grounds were visible in the moonlight but no torches were lit. He sensed more than saw his personal guard falling in around him. Ever since the Arnold affair there had been rumors of plots either to assassinate him, or to snatch him in a raid and take him back to England for trial and a good public hanging. Though he kept no pistol at his side, as a show of bravado, Billy Lee knew what the final order was if surrounded, his guard down, and about to be taken. Billy Lee carried two pistols for that grim task.

He sensed Billy by his side, limping slowly, the night air afflicting his rheumatism. There was no sense in asking. Of course the man would deny any discomfort.

The only light visible was a single lantern down by the ferry wharf. In peacetime or war, that light would be there as a marker for a nighttime crossing, by someone willing to pay the extra shilling in hard silver for a midnight crossing rather than wait till dawn. Tonight thousands would make that crossing.

All was going in orderly fashion, so different than that nightmare of Trenton. Companies of infantry, troops of dragoons, artillery pieces, their draft horses and crews, and the first of the supply wagons carrying extra ammunition were stretched out in a leisurely manner from the wharf clear back to the main encampment. The weather was mild after a hot day. Fires were forbidden, men had cooked their ration of fresh beef or pork during the afternoon and had placed the meat back in their haversacks. Of course, having seen their first real pay in six months, thanks to Robert Morris, gambling now consumed many of them, though in the darkness a game of whist or dice was difficult, so it tended to just be whoever threw down the high card that won the pot. As any wise general knew, there were times to break up such vices, and times to turn a blind eye, and tonight was a time to turn a blind eye. A strict cordon had been placed around the camp ever since this campaign had started to form in his mind, and one of the strictest orders was to block all liquor from coming in, along with women of dubious virtue who might actually be spies.

As to the legitimate women of the camp, some who had been with the army since before Valley Forge, his orders had been strict as well. They were to be left behind with the small garrison he was leaving in place to bluff the British into thinking his entire army was still north of New York. There had been howls of protest over that, with more than one of the women directly confronting him, even the famed Molly Pitcher of Monmouth Court House, but they had at last seen some reason. The march—and he did not reveal to a soul where they were marching—would be swift and hard. The fact that they, the women and children of the camp, remained here would help delude the enemy into thinking all of this was a bluff if detected, for surely the army would not leave their wives and children behind.

Some recognized him as he approached the road down to the wharf, coming to their feet, saluting, a few wags asking questions from out of the darkness. "Where we headin' to, General?" "Gonna kick 'em out of Staten Island!" One, his Virginia accent clear, did chill him with the question, "I bet we'uns are going after Cornwallis, ain't we, General?"

If he had reacted to that one, it surely would have been a giveaway. He ignored them, moving along the side of the road. At last they reached the wharf, one of the broad-beamed Dutch-designed ferry-boats, shallow of draft, with a removable keel, and a single large sail drifted up out of the darkness, sail luffing in the light breeze. One of his staff announced for the next group waiting to stand aside, that the general was about to cross.

The men were silent as he passed, but he could hear their whispers after he passed, that if he—the general himself—was crossing the river this night, then something was, indeed, up.

He smiled at that. It meant that so far the truth of what he intended had not leaked out and all was speculation.

It only took a few moments for his guards and staff to board. As was typical of him, he was the last to board, spotting an officer of the next company waiting to go over, accepting the man's salute, offering a few words of encouragement, and telling him, loud enough so that others would hear, that when the time came, all would be made clear, and he had full trust in the men of this army to end this war soon.

The two crewmen of the ferry poled off from the wharf, the pilot putting the helm over as they hoisted up the lateen sail, the boat heeling slightly as it caught the gentle night breeze, the cheery sound of splashing water echoing from the bow, a faint shimmer of a white wake spreading out to either side. The sail above fluttered for a moment until sheeted home.

"A few of you men to windward," one of the crew announced, and some moved up to sit along the railing. In the presence of the general, there was no foolery of splashing up water, or playful threats of pushing a man overboard.

The river was wide here, nearly five miles, and this ferry spot chosen long ago because in the broad shallow they would not have to run tight against a swift-moving tide. Rare was the day when the low hills on the distant shores blocked out all wind. It took somewhat longer to cross, but for the boat crews it was far easier work.

A pale glow ahead from a hooded lantern revealed one of the ferries, eastbound on return passing, a low murmur of greeting from the pilots, a comment from the eastbound man that the wind was coming about more northerly for an easier run.

Halfway across, out in the middle of the river, his prediction proved true, with a slight increase in speed, and a few more men were asked to sit on the windward side railing.

Bracing against the mast, Washington stood up. There was a glare on the distant horizon. Were those the lights of the city? Picket boats had deployed a couple of miles downstream, to intercept and pass any warning of a foray by the British to ghost up the river, even though it was against the tide, in any attempt to attack the ferry crossing. There had been no warning, but still he felt uneasy.

A third of the forty-five hundred men marching with him had crossed by now. If there were a moment for a surprise attack it was now, catching his men divided, with four defenseless boats crisscrossing at midriver. Even a light sloop—let alone a brig, or far worse, a frigate of forty guns—could raise havoc and shatter this entire plan before it had even started.

All was silent, except for a whispered order from the pilot to his crew to ease out the sheet a bit, and a whispered hail from another boat on its return voyage.

The shadows ahead darkened. It was land, and he saw the single lantern light the pilot was making for.

He heard more whispered commands to ease sheet, a suggestion for the "gentleman to please sit down," rudder over to run before the wind for a moment, then a luffing of sails as they turned straight into the eye of the wind. The center keel was winched up, and a line cast to the wharf and the boat hauled up snug against the wharf.

They made it all look so simple. Of course, his Massachusetts fishermen would have found some fault or other, that these were not real sailors, plying a river crossing while they had known hurricane gales and forty-foot seas—the usual bravado of any professional men observing the work of another in their craft—but he was impressed with how effortless it all seemed in contrast to the nightmare of the icy crossing at Trenton.

Though he was not prone to such thoughts, was this not a good portent, he wondered? Or because it all seemed to be going so effortlessly, would he soon be in for a rude shock?

He ignored the offer of a hand of assistance as he leaped to the dock, even before the boat was snugged in tight for offloading. His guards, staff, and Billy Lee followed. In less than a minute the boatmen had cast off for the return journey to the far shore.

"General Washington, sir?"

He looked about in the semidarkness illuminated by the single lantern and the waning moon.

The man inquiring as to his presence approached and saluted.

"Colonel Wellesley, sir," he announced as Washington returned the salute.

"All goes well?" Washington asked.

"Yes, sir."

Washington motioned for him to follow as he stepped off the wharf. The men on this side had done their work well, throwing up a final defensive position fifty yards out from the wharf, and a forward position a hundred yards beyond the inner line and thus out of effective musket-fire range.

Once past the outer line, walking along the road that led southward, Washington stopped, looked around, motioned for his guards and staff to remain in place, and walked up a narrow country lane for several dozen paces until he was sure the two of them were truly alone.

"Your report?"

"Sir, all is going according to your orders. The decoy companies are marching along the river road. I already have my people out ahead of our dragoons. We have fairly reliable lists of any Loyalists along our line of march, and they will either be placed under guard by local militia, or, if thought to be of significant risk, they will be detained until three days after our passing."

Washington nodded with approval. The hidden game of war, of subterfuge, of spy and counterspy, of gathering of intelligence and of spreading false rumors was one he would not admit to in public. Yet it was this part of it all that fascinated him. A well-placed rumor that diverted a brigade of British troops, that sent a ship bearing a false dispatch clear back to England, or that spread any kind of confusion was an effort well made. Even when the army was literally bankrupt, he had somehow managed to keep a small amount of hard cash always on hand to pay or bribe those who were motivated by less than patriotic motives.

"And your spreading of 'tall tales'?" Washington asked, and he smiled, a rare luxury these last few days, in which, like an actor on the stage, he had plotted out the most complex maneuver of this war, based upon but one letter from thousands of miles away. Throughout he had to act calm, confident, but not too eager and excited. It was actually a pleasure for him, this moment to be alone with a soldier he trusted, and talk of the ancient game of spying and not have anything to conceal.

Wellsley's smile was visible in the moonlight.

"There is, how can I say this delicately, sir? A woman of, shall I say, dubious virtue who the British think works for them."

"And she is in your pay for information."

"Even now, someone, a militia officer, is boasting about getting ready to lead an attack across to Staten Island. The boats, as you suggested as well, sir, are being moved into the bay on the Jersey side and will be visible from time to time. I have some other things afoot as well."

"Sir?"

Washington looked back down the lane. It was Alexander Hamilton. The young officer, all so eager for battle, approached with a jaunty step, stopped, and saluted.

"I have the honor to report that the first entire brigade is now across, sir, and moving out. Can we request the honor of your company for a while?"

He considered the proposal and then agreed. He would not actually leave this area for another day, until the last of his men and supplies were across, and fully assured that Rochambeau was moving and had convinced Barre to do so as well. "I'll ride along to start your men off," Washington announced. It was obvious Hamilton was delighted with the response.

He turned back to Wellesley.

"I trust you, Colonel, with much, but I also caution you to take no extreme risks with yourself. One can only tempt fate or the devil so far."

If Billy Lee had heard that comment there would have been a barely suppressed cough and clearing of a throat. His servant had said the same to Washington a hundred times or more during the heat of battle when his general would go literally into the volley line to encourage the men.

Washington turned and disappeared into the shadows, Wellsley coming to attention and saluting his receding form.

Perhaps it was best not to discuss too much what some of his plans were, Wellsley thought to himself. The general had enough worries to deal with this night.

NEAR YONKERS, NEW YORK
AUGUST 19–20, 1781
3:00 A.M.

Allen carefully braced the telescope on its mount, barely touching the focus. It was a "night scope" versus the standard field telescope, with a wider front lens to gather in more light. Frankly, he didn't see much difference using it, but then again . . .

Yes, a sail, a momentary glimpse, as a boat five miles away up the Hudson appeared to come about, the sail broadside against the moonlight. Only a moment, but it was enough. What appeared to be horses on board the boat as it slipped up against the wharf, on the west bank of the river, illuminated by its single lantern.

"Note, boat carrying an estimated half dozen horses."

After the obvious terror that Sergeant O'Toole had shown the previous year when they had ventured through the lines in the vain attempt to try and intervene for Major Andre, he had the man reassigned to his regiment, even sent him back with a warm letter of recommendation to keep him in good graces. His assistant now was a street urchin, picked up off the wharves of the city, a native of the city since the start of the war, who knew its alleyways and darker secrets. Jamie O'Neal, at sixteen, actually had some education behind him until both his parents died in the smallpox epidemic, which had left him badly scarred as well. Of course, his kindly schoolmaster, without tuition payment in hand, had cast him out onto the street before his parents were cold in the ground. The lad had damn near starved to death until he learned more of the school of harder knocks and had fallen in with Allen when he had tried to rob him last year after a night in the "stews" picking up gossip. Allen had wandered out acting as if he were drunk, and then had thrashed Jamie half to death, when the lad fumbled a bludgeoning attack from behind. He took pity when a guard detail, hearing the commotion, rushed to the rescue of an officer and was ready to haul the boy off to prison. Assaulting an officer, in an occupied city during wartime, would be construed as a Rebel plot of assassination and the boy would be doing the "midair jig" from a gallows within a day. For his skin and bones and ragged appearance, Allen felt pity. Twice before there had been attempts to kill him in alleyways at night, by hardened men, either real Rebels or those hired by someone to eliminate a man suspected of running spies. He had seen Jamie was only a pathetic lad trying to survive.

He had dragged the boy into a nearby tavern, ordered a meal for him, kept a wary eye, and as he ate his fill the youth collapsed into tears. As the boy stuffed himself like a voracious wolf, Allen learned his family had come over from the north of Ireland ten years before, purchased a farm and orchard just north of Springfield, across the river in Jersey where the battle had been fought the year before, and prospered there until the war. Some ill-advised public statements by his father—"to hell with all Rebels, God save the king"—and in short order they were refugees in New York. With their deaths in the great smallpox epidemic, and no other kin, and no home to go back to since it had been sold in auction at a fraction of the fair price, the boy had barely stayed alive, Too scraggly and weak-looking, even for a recruiting sergeant, and obviously not skilled in his latest craft of strike from behind and rob, he was near death.

He had an instinct about the lad. As they talked, he learned the boy knew the declensions of Latin, even read a little Greek. He had a sharp eye for details and a keen mind, once fed to near bursting, and spoke of his parents' desire that he become educated. The story resonated with Allen since it was so much like his own.

The only reason his own father's business survived in Trenton was that all knew that Allen's younger brother was considered a hero from the battle there five years ago. Otherwise he most likely would have been driven out because of Allen's decision to serve the king; but for a slight twist of fate, this boy's story could have been his own.

He tossed a shilling on the table, gave his address, told the boy if he wanted work to come to his place at dusk tomorrow. If not, then take up some profession other than trying to rob officers in alleyways, for it was a certain quick trip to the gallows.

Allen sat back from the telescope to rub his eyes. A slight mist was beginning to rise off the river, making observation difficult. In the silence of night by the river, sound carried, and he could hear the muffled stroke of oars, hoarse whispers, one of the Rebel picket boats pushing a lot farther down river than they usually did, keeping watch against any foray by the Royal navy.

The mere thought of that filled him with frustration. It would have been easy enough to run a couple of light brigs up with the tide, perhaps even a frigate before nightfall. With rumors of something afoot, he had even suggested it in his report the previous morning. Of course, that would now be lost in the piles of paper on Clinton's desk, and the army would never ask the navy for such a thing, anyway. They had to stand ready to sally if de Grasse did show up off the passage out to Sandy Hook, which was now the latest concern. The Royal navy feared that the French might appear here and join with Barre. They would then far outnumber the ships of the line keeping the sea lanes open back to Halifax and England from here. Chasing after a few Rebels on boats on the Hudson was beneath their dignity and not their task.

He sometimes wondered just exactly who was on whose's side when it came to the rivalry between the army and navy, as to which branch was to perform what task and the hell with bloody pride.

Without bothering to ask, Jamie relieved Allen at the telescope, adjusting it slightly, carefully, slowly sweeping it along the river, then paused.

"Another one, sir," he whispered.

Allen resumed his position, looked but couldn't see anything.

"You sure?"

"Certain, just a glimpse, heading to the west shore."

The mist continued to rise, turning all northward into an opaque haze.

He set back down, opened his haversack, pulled out a thick slice of ham, cut it in half and tossed one half to Jamie, who grunted a thanks. Even after all these months the boy devoured food like a wolf believing he was having his last meal.

"So what do you think?" Allen asked.

"Oh they're moving, sir. How many boats have we counted crossing?" he held up his sketch pad of notes to the moonlight. "We observed sixteen, chances are we missed twice as many until the moon came up."

Allen nodded in agreement.

"Pack up the telescope and let's head back."

The boy silently set to work, after finishing the ham and licking the grease off his fingers. Minutes later they were walking the half mile back to the village where they had left their horses. Yonkers was the outer line dividing Rebel territory from that held by the army in the city. A forward skirmish line had been pushed up after dark in order to give him a vantage point for a look up toward Dobbs Ferry, with orders to pull back before dawn. First light would begin to rise in another hour or so.

Gaining the village, and making sure the telescope case was concealed under a heavy horse blanket so as not to arouse notice, the two mounted, thanked the innkeeper for tending to them with a silver shilling, and headed down to the bridge across the Harlem river and back to Manhattan Island.

To the east the first indigo glow of dawn was showing, the morning star of Venus shimmering bright above the horizon.

"Ever look at Venus through a telescope, sir?" Jamie asked.

"Can't say that I have."

"We had one out on the farm. My father helped me to make it, ground the mirror for weeks on end. 'Tis a beautiful sight," the boy sighed wistfully.

"Your farm, you still miss it?"

"Aye. We called where we lived the 'Mill Burn.'"

"For a burning mill?"

The boy laughed.

"Lot of Scots were in the region. A burn is another name for a creek and there were several mills near our farm, just to the east along the headwaters of the Raritan. Yes, I miss it."

"Care to see it again?"

There was hesitation for a moment, the implication clear. The boy finally just nodded.

Allen smiled. It would be good to get out of this damn city, and be off on an adventure again.

Eight

THE BANKS OF THE HUDSON NEAR DOBBS FERRY
AUGUST 23, 1781

IT HAD BEEN A VERY DIFFICULT, EXHAUSTING FOUR DAYS but the last of Rochambeau's men were finally across the river. For General Washington it had been, perhaps, the most intense, tension-laden four days of his life. Though Rochambeau was all but explosive with enthusiasm over this audacious plan, they were all still tied hostage to whether the French fleet at Newport would, indeed, sally forth, skirt around the British in New York, slip away into the vastness of the Atlantic, and then rendezvous with de Grasse. Barre remained sitting on the middle of the fence and not committing. Feeling he could wait no longer, Rochambeau had agreed with Washington that their armies would march regardless, praying their departure would ultimately shame Barre into getting off the damn fence and doing his job, which was to sail and seek action.

Then finally, only an hour ago, thank God, word had come. Barre had agreed to take aboard his fleet the heavy siege train of French supplied eighteen- and twenty-four-pounder guns and the score of heavy mortars absolutely essential for a proper siege operation against a heavily fortified position, which Cornwallis would surely have built by now, each of which weighed several tons and would have taken months to haul overland to Virginia. He was also taking along fifteen hundred barrels of salted beef, enough to feed the entire army for several weeks, an additional regiment of French infantry, siege engineers, and artillerymen to handle the heavy weapons that could be as dangerous to the user as the target if not handled correctly. In short, he had signed on to the plan, and Washington felt at last that he could gallop forward to the head of his army, already halfway across New Jersey.

The campaign had now truly begun.

"I will see you in Philadelphia in six days, sir!" Washington announced, leaning forward to grasp Rochambeau's hand, the French general grinning.

"Do promise that my men may enter the city marching with yours, mon Général. It is good for morale, yes, and the ladies will certainly cheer and offer their personal thanks to their noble allies from France."

Despite the ribald intent of the general's comment, Washington, with his usual taciturn sense, decided to let it pass without comment. As he looked at the famed French regiments, arrayed in marching order, and contrasted them with his own ragged lot, there was nothing that could be said. There was many a "lady" of Philadelphia whose gaze would rest upon the neatly attired soldiers of France and head straight to them, and even the heads of the more virtuous would most certainly be turned.

Some of the most famed and ancient regiments of the French army, with proud lineages dating back over a century to the Thirty Years War, had crossed the river during the previous night, along with their mountains of baggage, what the Romans called "impedimenta" with just reason, for it would surely slow their march. Nevertheless, these regiments were, indeed, fighters—many of the men in the ranks were veterans of the brutal Seven Years War, either against his own side, or against the British and Prussians on the continent—but they also expected a proper repast at dinner, tents for all, even soap and whitening to cover over the stains of their lily white uniforms for morning inspection or for a formal parade in front of the ladies of Philadelphia.

Compared to his "scarecrow" army, the contrast would be startling and most noticeable.

Returning Rochambeau's melodramatic salute and bow, while mounted, Washington turned his horse and set off at a canter that was soon up to a gallop. The head of his army, weaving along back roads on the far side of the Watchung Hills, thus blocking any observation from New York City, was approaching the passes out of those hills and would be in Princeton by day's end. It was a ride of nearly sixty miles, and he took delight at the prospect. It had been a long time, indeed, since his army had been on the march. As he headed out to a gamble and an uncertain fate, inwardly he rejoiced in the long day's ride ahead, the type of ride he so often indulged in when young.

He spared a quick glance over his shoulder and, of course, Billy Lee was behind him, well mounted, with the ever-hovering guard detail trailing close behind. A wave of exuberance swept through him for a moment after these long years of stalemate. Now in this heady moment they were again on the march, a march of nearly five hundred miles on a mad insane gamble with all the odds against them.

Angling off the side of the road, he urged his mount to vault over a five-rail fence into an apple orchard.

Though technically it was against his own orders, he slowed, came to a stop, reached up, and plucked an apple—green, but near ripe—and bit into it. It was tart, yet so refreshing. He relished the moment, giving his guard time to catch up, and then turned about, vaulted back over the fence, and set off at a swift trot southwestward for the Jersey hills.

They were on the road to Virginia, to a final victory or death, at last.

ALONG THE KILL VAN KULL NEAR STATEN ISLAND
AUGUST 23, 1781, DAWN

Colonel Peter Wellsley was making a great show of it and having a delightful time after so many months of boring inactivity since his return from North Carolina. The decoy troops he had planned out with General Washington had marched down from Tappan over the last four days, making the most of their diversionary efforts, finding great fun in disappearing from view, marching out into open view on the east shore of the Hudson River so observers on the other side could see them, and once out of view, taking off uniform jackets, backtracking along a hidden path, then marching by again, looking like militia, following a quickly fashioned banner made out of a bedsheet "borrowed" from a nearby farmstead.

Peter had been directing the effort, while at the same time, taking in reports from his agents, spread out along the line of march. He knew, of course, that his cordon could never be airtight, but at least he could try. Hundreds of Loyalist families had either been placed under guard in their homes, or the more rabid of them, rounded up and detained.

Peter had passed the strictest of orders that no family was to be abused and no property destroyed. If supplies were taken they were to receive proper vouchers, payable upon acknowledgment of independence and the ending of hostilities for any cattle, pigs, chickens, or stock of grain confiscated for the army along its line of march. Someday, when this was over, if it was ever over, he did not want it to be said in his home state that he had been party to looting and pillaging, as was the habit of their enemies.

With telescope raised, he scanned the far shore of Staten Island, at this point less than three hundred yards across the swampy tidal river from the Jersey shore. A cordon of Hessian Jaegers followed his movements, pointing and gesturing, and several dozen shots had been fired by their riflemen, one of them nicking his horse's ear, nearly dismounting him and causing gales of laughter from the other side. He had responded with a cheery and obscene salute, which had elicited even more laughter and several more shots.

He had just made a show of a group pushing along a heavy boat, mounted on wheels and pulled by half a dozen oxen to become visible to the far shore, and then mimicked wild rage, had ridden over to them, shouting that they were damn idiots and to push the boat back into hiding.

A random long range shot by the riflemen on both sides might hit someone now and again, but a major battle was not in the offing, so it was all something of a lark with only a hint of danger.

Damn them, some rascals had, indeed, managed to find a forty-gallon barrel of good rum, and were selling five seconds on the spigot for fifty dollars Continental or one shilling silver, and a fair number were now drunk. Even though he knew his business well, trying to spy out where the barrel was hidden was beyond even his skills.

If the men were too merry and carefree, rather than acting as men bent on a mission they knew would be deadly. If they tried to seize Staten Island, and then blockaded the British fleet with its hundreds of guns, then the subterfuge was falling apart.

Another puff of smoke from the far shore. A couple of seconds later he actually heard the flutter of the bullet zip past his head.

Whoever the Hessian was, he was damn good. Perhaps too good.

He raised his hat in salute, turned his horse about, and rode back from the marshy shore, insults, clear in intent, carrying from the far shore.

"I'm looking for Colonel Peter Wellsley?"

He could barely see the rider approaching through the tall swamp grass of the Jersey marshlands, but the man was riding hard. Peter stood in his stirrups and shouted for him to come over.

The courier, a militia man, reined in, and saluted.

"Sergeant Robert Arnett, 4th New Jersey out of Springfield, sir," he said as they exchanged salutes.

"What's your report?"

Arnett, however was looking past Peter to the Hessians on the far shore. They had brought up a light fieldpiece, unlimbered it, and now the first shot was being fired, the four-pound ball singing past them so that Arnett ducked down against the neck of his horse.

There were distant shouts and laughter.

"Sergeant Arnett, never let them see that you are unnerved," Peter announced, loud enough so that others would hear, but nevertheless he motioned for Arnett to follow him down toward a fold in the land that concealed them from the opposite shore, waving a farewell to the Hessians. Since he did know Dutch and a good sprinkling of Rhineland German, he clearly understood what they were shouting back about his courage and his legitimacy.

Arnett, a bit crestfallen, recovered as Peter leaned over and patted him on the shoulder.

"First time under fire?"

"Once before, sir, last year at Springfield," he replied, and fell silent. Peter could sense the young man was not of the stoutest stuff, but then again, if that gunner on the far shore had shifted the muzzle of his fieldpiece but a fraction of an inch, both of them would now be dead or writhing in agony.

"Your report."

"Sir, I was told to look for you specifically. You are, sir, Colonel Peter Wellsley?"

"That I am."

There was hesitation, as if Arnett was about to ask for proof, but he noticed more than a few looking on with bemused glances and relented. He leaned forward.

"Sir," he spoke with a stage whisper. "Do you know of a British officer by the name of Allen van Dorn?"

Peter felt his heart go cold. He fixed his features, struggling not to show reaction, but wondering with a fearful heart what would be said next.

"Yes, I do. Go on."

"Sir, he was recognized this morning on the road from Springfield to Chatham, heading toward the Watchung pass. Before he could be intercepted, he disappeared but is believed to be in the area. Sir, my colonel requests your presence since it is said that you know this man personally, and if captured, can confirm who he is before we hang him."

Arnett hesitated but then smiled, "Sir, my colonel said we'd hate like hell to hang the wrong man and rumor is that you'd want to see the show if we catch him."

Peter could only nod, saying nothing.

"Will you come with me, sir? With luck we might have already captured the bastard, but we want to make sure before we hang him."

He was silent, time seeming to stretch out, memories of the year before, watching Andre, hearing his neck snap. Would he now be forced to condemn Allen to the same fate and then witness it?

He realized in this same instant, as well, that if Allen was poking around behind their lines, it meant he was on to something, perhaps the entire secret of the plan, and had to be stopped.

"Lead the way, Sergeant," was all he could say, working to control his voice and seem unemotional.

NEAR CHATHAM, NEW JERSEY

They had concealed their horses in the woodlot of a Loyalist who Allen trusted, as far as he could trust anyone in this region given the way the fortunes of war shifted back and forth. To go boldly riding into the village after a near run-in and pursuit with some militia guarding the pass through the Watchung Hills would be suicide. Word would be out now to keep a close watch for two men, most likely Tories, both of them well mounted.

The day was hot, and swarms of mosquitoes were tormenting them as they had skirted along the banks of the Passaic River, at last finding a muddy ford. He and Jamie had stripped down to cross, and wandering about in soaking wet breeches would certainly draw notice. The crossing had been unpleasant, the Passaic was here a muddy creek and stunk of tanning bark from an upstream mill. The banks were muddy and there had been a startled moment when they kicked up a copperhead that had nearly bitten Jamie. The lad was still a bit shaken.

The village was just a few hundred yards ahead, and all seemed quiet, though several militiamen were lounging in front of a tavern.

"Stay here, boy," he said softly. "If anything happens to me, just get the hell out. Get back. Your best bet would be wait until dark and set out on foot. You know which ferryman to trust once back to the Hudson. Report to General Clinton."

He paused.

"No, find his secretary, Colonel Smith, and report to him. He'll believe you."

As he spoke he handed over a purse filled with a couple of pounds of silver Spanish coins to buy his way across.

Jamie grinned at him.

"You know, if I lit out with this much money now, you'd be in a fix, wouldn't you?"

Though the boy had been working for him for more than half a year, he did feel a slight hesitation, but then Jamie laughed softly.

"I'll wait for you here, sir."

With his breeches back on and nearly dry, he took a bottle of rum from his haversack and doused himself liberally with it, and for good measure took a strong tug on the bottle as well. Coming out of the woods and brush bordering the creek he struck out on to the main road, carefully checking first to make sure no one saw him emerging and then fell into one of his old routines of weaving a bit drunkenly, bottle in hand, and, nerving himself, headed straight into the village.

Chatham was not all that much—several mills along this, the upper reaches of the Passaic, and the farmland not as good as on the far side of the Watchungs down into Springfield—but it was on the main road from the coastal plain to Morristown, where the Rebel army had twice gone into winter camp. It was a main thoroughfare back and forth between Rebel territory and Loyalist-held Elizabethtown and thus patrolled by both sides.

As he weaved his way into the center of the village, the militia "guarding" the tavern barely stirred, several chuckling as he made a bit of a show of staggering about and then with a friendly gesture holding up the bottle of rum. One of them motioned him over.

"Started early today, didn't you?" one of them said as he took the bottle without comment, took a long swig, grunted with approval, and then passed it to his friends.

He sat down on the edge of the porch in a shaded corner, took off his broad brimmed hat, and fanned himself.

"Got more of that," he said with a slur, and patted his haversack so that the half dozen bottles inside clinked significantly, conveying the message that was his standard cover, a petty rum runner moving between the lines, smuggling bottles of blockaded rum, which flowed freely from the Carib to New York harbor.

He reached into his haversack and held a full bottle up for them to see.

"Jamaican, the best," he announced proudly.

The four didn't speak, just looking at the bottle and then glancing down significantly into their mugs, filled with local whiskey and most likely distilled only the week before.

"How much?" one of them asked, coming straight to the point.

"Fifty dollars Continental or a silver shilling."

"For all of them. You got more in there—I can hear it," announced the man who had taken the half-empty bottle from him.

He shook his head with an exaggerated gesture.

"Per bottle, friend."

"You son of a bitch, that's more than four months' pay."

"In paper, which we know ain't worth a damn."

"Suppose we just take what you got and the hell with you."

Allen held up a finger and wagged it with an exaggerated manner.

"Then I won't be back in a few days with more. Long walk it is from where I get this."

"We most likely won't be here in a few days anyhow, you thieving son of a bitch," one of the others announced and there were grunts of agreement. One of them stood up threateningly.

Allen stood up, swaying.

"I'll break 'em all before I'll let you steal 'em." As he spoke he fumbled in his haversack, pulling a bottle out and holding it up threateningly.

"If you do, damn it, we'll break your skull."

"Gentlemen, gentlemen, we can settle this and everyone will be happy," he replied. "I spoke rashly. How about twenty-five a bottle?"

The four looked at each other.

"Ten," their leader replied, but not coming any closer to Allen, obviously fearful of his threat.

He acted as if debating.

"Fifteen, that is ninety for the six I still have."

The four huddled together, looking back at him as he held the bottle up over his head. Even as he did so, he took in the details around him. These were the only four militia about and, thank God, no officer who might be sober and question him more carefully.

The deal was struck at twelve and a half a bottle, the scrip handed over, coming out to eighty dollars for the six bottles since no one had any notes for less than ten dollars, and within minutes the four, joined by their new friend, were happily drinking and blathering away.

In another fifteen minutes he had all the information he needed, though he was feeling more than a bit lightheaded. The belligerent soldier of but minutes before, pouring a quarter of a bottle into a mug and insisting he join them in a toast to General Washington and the damn Congress and was not satisfied until Allen had drained the mug. Though, he tried to spill as much of it as possible as he downed it.

There was, indeed, a new bakery for hardtack built down by the river, with a call out for farmers to bring in their grain for a fair price, which was actually being paid. The miller and several bakers were now hard at work. As fast as the unleavened bread was coming out of the ovens, it was not going into storage but being shipped west.

Then one of them spilled it.

"Poor bastards, marching in this heat, gotta pity them, you do."

"How's that?" Allen asked, feigning disinterest as if more intent on getting another drink out of the bottles he had just sold.

"They're pushing fifteen, twenty miles a day, just ten miles up that road," one of them announced pointing to the west and shook his head. "I said to myself, Vincent lad, they only march like that when there's a fight coming on. I had my fill of it, did my part years ago at Monmouth where I took a bullet," he said, making a dramatic show of pulling his shirt up to show the scar, where a ball had, indeed, hit him in the lower chest.

"Still in there, it is," and the others nodded sagely as he showed off his wound.

"So I convinced Captain Butler that the old wound had me down again." As he spoke he hunched over and put on a good imitation of wheezing, which set the others to laughing, even though Allen could tell it was not entirely an act. "So he ordered me to fall out and guard this place."

Allen looked off to the road that led toward Morristown. He was half tempted to push his luck, get back with Jamie, fetch some more bottles from their saddlebags, and perhaps try to ride farther up after dark by keeping to the fields and back lanes, though it would be very be risky.

"Anyhow, I'll be damned if I'm going to march all the way to Virginia, like some are saying," and he was silent now, just looking into his mug, not urging the loquacious veteran to say anything more that might arouse suspicion.

The others muttered approval.

"Joined to fight here in my home state, not go wandering off. There's nothing but ague, snakes, and swamps down where they're heading, and besides, I don't like them damn Virginians. All haughty, just 'cause the general is one of them. Still, we heard the Continentals got their pay in good silver last week to bribe them to march, while all we got was some damn paper scrip, as usual."

"Folks in Elizabethtown are all astir," Allen finally ventured. "Word down there is the army is gonna swing around, cross over to Staten Island, and trap the damn navy in the harbor."

"Oh yeah, with what? The pop guns we're dragging along? Besides, the damn Frenchies got all the heavy guns and they took them off to Newport to put on their ships is what I heard. Bet they're skipping out on us anyhow, even though word is they got thousands of them coming up behind our men on the road toward Princeton."

"I'll place a bet on Yorktown," one of the group muttered. "Join up with Lafayette and ole Dan Morgan down there to take care of that bastard Cornwallis good and proper. I say let them; those that want to go. We've done enough fighting up here. Don't see why we have to go all the way down there anyhow."

"So that's where all that hardtack is going," Allen ventured, motioning to where he could catch a glimpse of wood smoke down toward the river.

No one spoke for a moment and the soldier who was so open-mouthed looked over at him.

"Why do you want to know?"

He could see that though rather drunk, the man was now giving him appraisingly glance.

He stood up, putting on his own drunk act.

"Gotta figure out how far I gotta hike with my next load of rum. Will you be guarding the bakery and this flea-bitten town or be ordered to join the march to Yorktown like you say, or is it Staten Island? I gotta know where my market is going."

"How the hell did you get your hands on good rum like this anyhow?"

"I stole it, a whole case, being off-loaded."

"Where?"

Now the other man was standing up, drunk but fixing him with a steady gaze.

"Down by the wharf in New York, got it yesterday."

"That's a long walk in a day, and why only six bottles with you? You could of sold it for damn near the same, at half the walking you did to get here."

The somewhat drunk soldier was now turning interrogator as he looked down at Allen's feet.

"Nice riding boots for a man who claims he walked all the way."

The boots, damn it! He should have put on some old walking clogs or even gone barefoot. His boots were of the finest leather and craftsmanship, Andre insisting that a friend of his should always be turned out proper. It was a stupid mistake.

As his interrogator spoke Allen looked back to the road heading east and as he did so, his heart froze. Two riders were coming across the bridge, coming on fast, and instinct told him in that instant that the game was up. He had ridden too many races against Peter not to recognize the way he could barely keep a saddle, even now.

"I feel the flux coming on," he muttered and without further comment he started up the alleyway alongside the inn, asking where the privy was.

"Hey you, hold on a minute!"

Fortunately they were far more drunk than he was. As he reached the end of the alleyway along the side of the tavern, he turned off into the back garden, out of sight to the road, and then took off at a run. It was long seconds before he heard the hue and cry go up behind him and he was already a good hundred yards out of the village before he looked back. None had shouldered their muskets. He was already out of range and thanked God they didn't have a sober rifleman in their group. Besides, they were just staggering drunk, but pointing in his direction as the two horsemen came riding into the village.

The riders slowed to get information, giving him valuable seconds of lead time as he tried to keep low, running behind a split rail fence piled high with summer honeysuckle that acted as a shield. Reaching the end of the fencerow, he saw it was going to have to be a dash across an open field to the woods. Now he set off at a full-out run. He turned to look back, and it was, indeed, Peter in pursuit, drawing a short barrel musketoon out of a saddle holster. He dodged into a couple acres of corn, nearly head high in the August heat, crouching low, weaving back and forth, but realizing that as a horseman mounted up high, Peter should be able to see the wavering corn as he stumbled and shoved it aside. He came out the far end of the cornfield and saw Peter was galloping along the edge of the corn, his other mounted companion riding along the opposite flank to try to cut him off. He vaulted a low split-rail fence, gasping for air as he reached the edge of the woods where Jamie, still loyal to him was still waiting, pistol out, leveling it toward Peter, who was still a hundred yards off. The range was too far. Better to run for it, and besides . . .

He knocked the weapon up.

"Run, you damn fool!"

Together they sprinted for the narrow river, downstream from the bridge. If Peter had posted men on the other side he feared it was about to go bad, but only his old friend and whoever was with him were in pursuit, their mounts lathered and blown. Jumping into the river they half swam, half waded across, gaining the far bank, scrambling up it. Jamie looking around nervously, obviously more afraid that the snake might be lying in wait rather than Jersey militia.

"Allen!" he heard.

It was more a question, as if Peter was not sure who he was pursuing. Allen did not look back, running hard, weaving through the brush and bramble into the next woodlot where they had left their horses tethered, fortunately still saddled. He could hear Peter cursing as he splashed across the muddy river, stinking of refuse from the tannery, his exhausted mount struggling to get up the muddy bank even as Allen swung into the saddle of his mount, leaning over to grab Jamie by the shoulder and helping him to mount as well.

There was a crack of gunfire and he heard a ball clip through the branches overhead. That startled him and he looked back to see Peter, half concealed in dirty, yellow gray smoke, short-barreled musket recoiling.

Was he shooting to kill?

He was not about to hang around to discuss the issue, as he kicked his mount to a gallop, taking a farm lane that would swing wide of the Rebels guarding Springfield. It was obvious they were onto him and he'd have to head north, up through the Short Hills and the crossroads of the Mill Burn on the forward slope of the Watchung range. He could lose Peter, who obviously could not keep up, then wait until dark, leave the horses behind and hike it back to the Hudson.

He had some of what he wanted, but not having actually seen the troops on the march, he knew Clinton would dismiss as unreliable a report based on conversation with four drunken Jersey militia. He'd have to come back for more, and he actually felt a thrill of excitement when it became evident that Peter had given up the chase.

PETER WELLSLEY, CURSING SOUNDLY, GAVE UP AFTER SEVeral miles. It was, indeed, Allen and he was far better mounted. Peter was furious with himself for having come in as impetuously as he did to Chatham. He should have rounded up some militia and put out a cordon on the far side of the river before rushing in. He had only half believed the report, increasingly annoyed that he was riding all this distance on what was most likely a fool's errand. Also, he could not fully believe that Allen would be so reckless as to try to penetrate the American lines on his own when without doubt he had more than one informant. Or had his own efforts been so effective as to dry up the British sources while the army traversed New Jersey and so Allen had been forced to look for himself?

He had spared his friend's life at Monmouth Court House, but now? It was a bit of a shock to realize that when he had fired at his old friend, he had shot to kill and regretted that he had missed. He would have to report to the general that the cordon had been penetrated and chances were that unless Allen was stopped from getting across the river, that by tomorrow, Clinton and the Royal navy would know that Washington was on the march and heading south.

Nine

OUTSKIRTS OF PHILADELPHIA
AUGUST 29, 1781

WASHINGTON HAD RIDDEN HARD FOR THREE DAYS IN ORDER
to move up to the front of his column. In one day he had made nearly
fifty miles over the farm lanes and back roads beyond the Watchung
Hills, of course, completely avoiding the open pike that swung south of
those hills from Newark, down the Raritan, and along flat open ground
clear to Princeton. It was the road he had retreated along when falling
back from New York after the disasters of 1776, and that his army had
surged along in the boiling heat of a summer day in 1778, looking for a
fight that would lead them to Monmouth Court House.

Three more years of war had passed since then. He had thought
about that more than once as he rode into Princeton, and then the following morning when he had passed through Trenton. The two
battles that had been fought there were still clearly evident from the
bullet-scarred buildings. Across the ferry at Trenton he had ridden
along the west bank of the Delaware, passing the supply train bring-

ing up the rear. North of the city he had ordered his army into camp for a day to rest, in order for stragglers to catch up, form ranks, and wait for their French allies to join them before marching into the capital city. Knowing they were about to parade through the capital city of their allies, the entire French column was busy preparing for the event. After hard days of marching on the dusty back roads of New Jersey, their white uniforms were a mess. Under the baleful watch of corporals and sergeants they had obviously devoted hours to cleaning up, scrubbing out stains, using white pipe clay to polish gaiters and leather straps, neatly combing out and reweaving the pigtails of the enlisted men, while servants were dusting the wigs of officers with flour, and trimming moustaches. Musket barrels were polished to a high sheen, horses curried, the tails and manes of some braided with ribbons.

Long years ago he had fought against some of these same regiments on the frontier and had viewed such fussing with disdain—and besides, a white uniform in a dark forest did make such an ideal target. But now? These were his allies. Without their fleet, if it was moving as promised, this campaign would end in disaster. He had come to learn the mettle of these men, first with his friendship with young Lafayette, whom he viewed now as a substitute for the son he would never have. Then working with them for years around New York City. They were every inch as tough as any Hessian or British grenadier.

As he trotted past the columns of French troops, all proper respect was paid to him and it was, indeed, pleasing as these tough professionals snapped to attention and saluted. There were even shouts and cheers of "Vive Washington!" that he would studiously and austerely ignore if offered by his own Continental line, but courtesy of alliance demanded he acknowledge with grateful bows from the saddle and lifting of hat to the flags of the various regiments that he passed.

At last he found his friend Rochambeau awaiting him at the front of his column, word having been sent ahead requesting the "indulgence" that they enter Philadelphia together.

It was, of course, a show that they both knew they had to put on. The commanding American general riding into the capital, side by side with the commanding general of their allies.

Rochambeau and his staff were absolutely glittering in fresh uniforms and immaculate. As he approached he was aware of his own rather travel-worn look. Dusty, face sweat-streaked after the hours of riding in the heat from Princeton, and Billy Lee muttered more than once that they should at least stop so he could curry the general's horse and dust him off as well.

He had refused. Though he admired the look of the French troops, somehow he sensed that his own entry into Philadelphia, at the head of the column should demonstrate that this was an army moving swiftly and hard, an army looking for, and eager for, a fight. He felt his own "look" was appropriate to convey that sense. Now safely across New Jersey without an attack or even a feint by Clinton on their flank, the time for subterfuge was past. He had received young Colonel Wellsley's report that their secret had been penetrated with some trepidation. If, the following day, Clinton had actually shifted his army to Staten Island under the cover of the navy still in New York harbor, and moved across to intercept him somewhere near Princeton, he would have been forced to turn and fight. It would have shattered any hope of bringing his strength to bear within the six-week window that de Grasse had offered him in his message.

There had been a tense two days after that report, but amazingly, Clinton had not stirred, and now it was too late to stop Washington. After this march through the center of Philadelphia, there would be spies aplenty to report it back. Unless Clinton had pulled some remarkable sleight of hand, and was even now embarked to come to the relief of Cornwallis, it did not matter what was reported back in New York after this day.

Rochambeau and his staff offered a formal Gallic salute that Washington returned with style, and staff officers on both sides saluted each other as well, with more than one American offering their new tradi-

tion of a handshake, and accepting with some embarrassment at times
the kiss on both cheeks offered in reply.

"Shall we proceed, gentlemen?" Washington offered, and there
were smiles of agreement. The French had obviously been awaiting
this parade with eager anticipation.

The two generals set off down the road, side by side, flag bearers
before them holding aloft the banners of France and of this new republic, followed behind by more flag bearers carrying the individual
colors of their headquarters and various regimental standards.

It was all a showy parade, the type of thing he normally disdained,
but knew it was essential for his army, their army, and for the citizens
of Philadelphia, all of whom were so weary of war after six bitter
years. This show was especially for the Congress, which had better be
ready with the pay and supplies for his men that Robert Morris had
promised to him.

The spires of the churches of Philadelphia stood out clear in the
dusty heat as they rode at a swift canter down the main thoroughfare. His own regiments of his Continental line were now in view.
These were "his men," and he felt a swelling of pride at the sight of
them, the men of the Pennsylvania, New Jersey, Virginia, and Maryland line. They were hard-bitten veterans of so many years of war.

They, too, had been spending the morning preparing for this
moment, but with far less elegant results—as Washington felt was
befitting this new kind of army for a new world and hopefully a new
republic.

In the three years since Valley Forge, French largesse had included
shipments of new uniforms, turned out by hundreds of French tailors,
seamstresses, and weavers, but the long years had worn them thread-
bare as well. The buff, blue, and tan of Virginia; the brown and red
of Maryland; while some of the men of Pennsylvania shunned such
finery and still insisted upon brown or green hunting frocks and tan or
deer skin leggings. On many, knee and elbow patchings of various
hues had just been sewed on this morning, and they were patches over

patches for many of them. Deep stains from marching and camping in rain, mud, and snow were evident, and for the old veterans, some just barely out of their teens, these were worn as marks of pride in their service. Many, long ago, had come to disdain the traditional tricorner hats, having broken them down into broad brims to ward off summer sun and icy rain. Barely a man of the line sported a wig as he now did, most had hair tied back in short ponytails, and more than a few of late had just simply taken to shaving their heads to ward off the lice and fleas with which nearly all were afflicted.

Some shouldered battered backpacks of leather. Many had come to adopt "horse-collar" blanket rolls slung over their left shoulder—one or two threadbare blankets, wrapped within an extra shirt if they had the luxury of one, and a treasured change of socks or knee-high stockings. On the left hip most wore a canvas haversack for rations, although those haversacks were now thin and depleted after days of marching, but all knew that tonight they would be feted by the citizens of Philadelphia. Come morning, before setting off toward Maryland, fresh supplies of five days marching rations would be issued on the far side of the city. Wooden canteens rested atop the haversacks, and as he rode past the men, he could only surmise that more than a few had been greeted by grateful citizens with a fresh supply of rum or corn liquor (or perhaps "foraged" from reluctant nearby farmers). Those men were grinning, and a couple of them collapsed and stretched out behind the columns lining either side of the road. On this day he almost pitied the discipline they would face at nightfall when, awakening, they staggered into town to rejoin the ranks and met their angry, red-faced sergeants and captains—though more than a few of those, he suspected, were already half drunk as well.

Cartridge boxes, most of French issue, rested on right hips, and if his orders had been followed, each was packed with twenty-four freshly drawn rounds of .72 ball for their muskets. Veterans all, their weapons were as highly polished as their French comrades', locks well oiled, sharp fresh flints in place, with several spares wrapped in oiled cloth and tucked into the bottom of the cartridge box, and dangling from the right hip, all now had bayonets, polished to a mirror sheen and razor sharp. The years of drill with the army's beloved von Steuben, now awaiting them along with Lafayette down in Virginia, had trained them well with the bayonet. It was far more a weapon of the mind than it was ever actually used in combat; the sight of a disciplined line, advancing at the double, bayonets glinting in the sun, rarely drew blood, but, instead, would usually break an opponent's line when presented with such a terrifying sight.

As the entourage trotted past the waiting column, cheer after cheer erupted, and this time Washington did acknowledge it with nods, lifting his hat in salute as he passed regimental standards and the national flag. As they passed, behind them commands echoed, men falling back into columns eight men wide on the broad road into the city, flags, fifers, and drummers to the fore. He gazed with delight at Henry Knox's fine display of artillery, brass and bronze guns polished to a shimmering glean, limber wagons washed clean of dust and mud, even their sadly mismatched teams of horses cleaned and curried. In front of them were his small detachments of dragoons, most of them well mounted so they could match any confrontation with British and Hessian raiders. In that department, at least—though severely outnumbered—his men were definitely the match for anything the enemy or even their French allies could put in the field. "Light Horse" Harry Lee, a distant cousin to both him and Martha, was at the head of that column, and most of the men of his command were well trained horsemen from Virginia and the Carolinas, where the mark of a gentleman was that he knew good horseflesh and could keep his saddle whether it was on the hunt or battlefield. It was an elite outfit and they showed it with well maintained horses and equipment. Though well-trained with sabers, most had learned that a brace or two of pistols and a short-barreled musketoon loaded with buckshot, though less gentlemanly, were far more efficient at dropping their foes in the constant give-and-take of skirmishing along the picket lines and in irregular warfare.

The road ahead was now clear of troops, they were less than a mile from the center of Philadelphia. Eager civilians flooded the streets ahead. Mad Anthony Wayne, hero of so many battles, awaited him at the head of the column flourishing a salute. He had arranged the procession with the flair of a showman, a score of drummers and an equal number of the army's best fifers at the fore, led by an honor guard of picked infantry, one man from each regiment, well groomed, towering in height, some over six-foot tall, nearly matching the height of their commander. There were two flag bearers at the fore: the white and fleur de lis standard of France and King Louis XVI, held rigidly aloft by a giant of a man in a sparkling white uniform, flanked by two French soldiers on either side of exactly equal height and splendor; and beside them a soldier of Pennsylvania, bearing a clean but obviously battle-scarred flag of thirteen stars and thirteen stripes, flanked by four chosen soldiers from Jersey, Maryland, Virginia, and New York.

Wayne came up to his side with sword drawn and offered his salute, his normally fierce demeanor for once giving way to a grin of delight.

"All is prepared exactly as you ordered, sir," he cried with delight.

General George Washington rode on, with the Marquess Rochambeau by his side, slowing their pace, and from behind Anthony Wayne. Their staffs fell in a few paces after them, followed by the flag bearers, the drummers, and fifers. The crowd ahead parted as they approached, and for a moment there was actual silence in response, men taking off their hats, women quiet, and there was a terrible flash of memory.

From 1777, the humiliating defeat at Brandywine with his army, morale shattered, staggering through the streets of this same city. Not a civilian in sight, windows were shuttered, doors barred, and not a single flag was visible. Congress had already fled, finding out later that at least someone had remembered at the last minute to snatch their original signed copy of the Declaration from a clerk's desk, and had hid it in a wagon following the caravan of their retreat. The wounded and sick were piled into more wagons, to be left behind to the less than tender mercies of the victors, who first confined them in an unheated barracks for most of the autumn and winter, before taking them up to the prison hulks on the East River. Chances were that less than one in twenty of those he had been forced to leave behind were still alive.

It had been a bitter moment of humiliation and defeat. Now this.

Part of him did feel a touch of cynicism. How many of these same people had locked their doors four years earlier—or worse, had hung out Union Jacks and cheered when Howe and his men marched up this same street in their triumph? Yet, as he tried to still that thought, what else could so many of them have done? Their army had been shattered, most thought at that moment that the Revolution was dead, and he recalled the lament of one of his soldiers, caught as a deserter, whom he had spared from execution when the man, looking him in the eyes, had quietly said "Sir, I am a Patriot, but I am also a father. My wife is dead of the smallpox and I have four children starving at home with no one to take care of them. What would you do?"

He had spared the man . . . but he had died of frostbite three years later at Morristown after both of his feet were amputated.

I must end this war, he thought, as he gazed at the still silent civilians. If we are doomed to lose this campaign, and all odds are against us, we shall go down fighting, and by losing that way, perhaps inspire a future generation, maybe a hundred, two hundred years hence to attempt to stand yet again for their rights and the rights of their children. It must end now, he thought. This campaign must end it and I am venturing all on this single throw of the dice, not just for my army, which has stayed loyal, but for all these people as well.

Then the cheering started. An elderly man stepped out into the cleared street, where local militia now lined the road to hold back the gathering crowds. The old man took off his hat, bowed low to Washington, then turned back to the assembled observers and tossed his hat high in the air, crying: "Three cheers for General Washington, our gallant lads, and our noble allies!"

The cry was picked up, echoed down the street. Washington looked over at Rochambeau, who could not suppress a grin of delight, bracing back as well.

Leading their grand army of nearly ten thousand tough and hardened veterans, they returned in triumph down the main thoroughfare into the heart of Philadelphia, the capital of a nation still being born.

Cheer after cheer greeted them, crowds surging forward, at times breaking through the cordon of Philadelphia militia trying to hold them back. Washington, more than a bit embarrassed and with Rochambeau laughing with delight at his embarrassment, accepted a bouquet of flowers from a beautiful young lass who raced up beside him handing the flowers up. He quickly handed the flowers off to a grinning Alexander Hamilton riding just behind him.

The crowds were teeming—six, eight deep as they approached the main plaza at the center of town. His heart swelled, when for the first time in more than three years, he caught sight of the state assembly building "Independence Hall." Two flags fluttered atop it in the hot August breeze—the flag of France, and the thirteen stars and stripes of America. He had a flash thought, wondering who had started the legend that he had sat with a seamstress with the name of Betsy Ross to design the flag, and that she had personally stitched the first one together. It was a little exaggerated, actually, but when legends gave strength to his cause, he would not dismiss them.

On a raised platform stood those members of Congress in the city this day, the delegation headed by Laurens of South Carolina, president of the Confederation, and he knew this moment would bear great symbolism. He turned aside from the head of the parade and rode straight toward them, the crowd falling somewhat silent.

Across the years since the terrible winter of Valley Forge, and the plot to remove him by General Gates and some of the very men standing on the platform, there had been rumors that a day would come when, like Caesar, he would ride into this city at the head of an army, bring down the government at the point of the bayonet and seize control. More than a few—in fact, many—in the ranks marching behind him actually wanted such an event. For years, many members of Congress had mismanaged this war, and some had lined their own pockets and grown rich, while his men suffered, fought, and died by the thousands. Many died for want of but one decent meal or a warm shelter for a single night, a pair of shoes to spare them from the agony of midnight sentry duty in freezing rain, or on the long icy march to Trenton or Morristown, or a few extra cartridges at Monmouth, where, when out of ammunition, they had stood defiant against the charges of the enemy.

He approached the dais, and knew that more than one gazing down at him did so with a wary glance. There had even been rumors reported to him that several in Congress were saying that was exactly what he planned to do this day and the campaign to the South was just a cover for what would be a coup. Several averted their eyes, either out of fear or shame for how they had wronged him and his army in the past.

He slowly dismounted. There was a distant cry of a lone voice, "We're with you, General." He knew what that voice was actually saying.

After a momentary pause and then with full ceremonial flourish, he removed his hat, and bowed low in salute. Then, standing erect, Washington raised his sword and presented it in salute, a salute of recognition that he was but a soldier of a republic, acknowledging the leadership of those whom the people of his nation had chosen to be their elected representatives. For good or bad, for better or worse, it was these men to whom he had to answer in all things because, ultimately, he was but a soldier, and they represented what it was he fought for, and was willing to die for.

A gasp arose from the crowd and then, within seconds, a thunderous applause erupted.

Laurens gazed down at him, beaming. Laurens's son, a most trusted member of his own staff, along with the rest of Washington's staff, had dismounted, and following the example of their general offered salutes as well, and the cheering of the crowd redoubled.

President Laurens beckoned for Washington to step on to the platform and as he did so, Laurens made the gesture of coming halfway down the steps, extending his hand and then embracing Washington, whispering, "God bless you this day, sir," his words barely audible so loud was the cheering.

Rochambeau, in a gesture that was almost humble, was still astride his mount, but with head lowered, and it was evident there were tears in his eyes.

Laurens removed his hat and held it aloft.

"Vive la France!" he cried, and that cheer was picked up by the crowd, and he motioned for the French general to join them as well.

Rochambeau dismounted, stepping up on to the dais to stand on the other side of Laurens, and was greeted with thunderous applause. The general removed his hat, waving it and grinning with obvious delight.

The parade of ten thousand men, bound for what all knew was a final defiant gamble of victory or defeat, pressed forward, flag bearers, drummers, and fifers already passing, while the combined staffs of the American and French generals dismounted as well and stood before the assembly on the platform.

Next came Harry Lee and his dragoons and light cavalry, followed by Knox and his several dozen fieldpieces, the battery of six pounders, recruited out of this city, drawing loud cheers and then laughter as a woman, obviously expecting childbirth within days, waddled into the middle of the street to be swept into a loving embrace by a young gunner, the two crying with delight in this brief moment of reunion. The gunner looked to his officer who gave an indulgent nod, and the gunner, struggling to lift his wife and carry her, disappeared into the crowd to be greeted with cheers, laughter, and more than a few ribald comments.

Then came the infantry, led by the 1st Continental Regiment of

Foot, men of Pennsylvania, and the crowd went wild with ecstatic cheering. Women burst through the cordon. For a brief instant Washington feared he might actually lose most of that regiment, a few men slipping off for reunions with wives, mothers, and children, but in general, discipline held as most of the men stayed in their ranks, their colonel offering a formal salute as they filed past.

Then regiment after regiment filed by in formal review. Though their greeting from the citizens of Philadelphia was somewhat less passionate, there were still formal cries for "three cheers for the lads of Maryland!" and for the men of Jersey, Virginia, and New York. As each regiment passed it offered formal salute to the Congress and the two generals standing with them, until all four thousand of them had passed.

Then there was a lull, the street empty for a moment, the crowds and even members of Congress leaning out, looking up the thoroughfare to the north, wondering if it was over, but soon a thunderous ovation began to echo down toward them. Now the French army came into view at last. With a dramatic flourish, a dozen mounted trumpeters were in the lead, and had the crowd gasping at this glittering display of white uniforms of the Royal Guard of King Louis XVI, uniforms glittering with a score of golden buttons each the size of a Spanish doubloon.

Perfectly timed, they held their trumpets up, saluting the dignitaries, then blew a fanfare that echoed through the streets, and as they did so they formed ranks six across and continued to sound the fanfare as they led the parade. It was so typical of the French, Washington thought, and smiling he looked past Laurens to his comrade who was obviously filled with pride, smiling back. It was, as actors would say, a "scene stealer" but one that he was more than happy to grant this day, since without their noble allies, none of this would now be happening. There would be no mad gamble, no final desperate hope and lunge, which behind all this fanfare was the real reason they were parading down this street.

First came the battalion of the Royal Guards, and at the sight of them the crowd really did give way to wild cheering. They were splendid in their dress uniforms, all officers at the front, mounted, wigs powdered, some sporting the rather strange (to his eyes) makeup and "beauty marks" still popular with the royal court, but nevertheless fierce, tough soldiers, who, if ever mocked for such display, would readily reply with drawn sword in defense of their masculine honor and the honor of France.

Behind them, in perfect rigid lines, marching in perfect step, came the ranks of the guard, muskets at the shoulder, bayonets sparkling in the sunlight. These, he knew, were not parade ground soldiers, fit only to march around in front of a royal palace for the entertainment of the nobles and their mistresses. They were, man for man, the match of any equal number or even double the number of the elite Hessians. They had faced them before on many a battlefield of Europe and would die to a man to defend, if not necessarily the cause for which he fought, at least the honor of their regiment, their country, their general, and the king who had chosen to throw his nation and their national fortune into the American cause.

Behind them came a dozen more regiments, resplendent, of course in white, but each regiment marked with the various colorings of cuffs, collars, and trouser striping to distinguish their individual units.

"I fear many of our ladies of Philadelphia are falling in love," Laurens said to Rochambeau, for more than a few of the young women of Philadelphia, swept up by the splendid display, were forcing their way through the cordon of militia, dashing up to kiss a very happy soldier of France on the cheek and offer a flower, and perhaps a quickly whispered name and address.

Rochambeau offered the classic Gallic gesture of a shrug and a beaming smile.

"C'est l'amour," he said smiling and all around him laughed good naturedly, though Washington could sense that more than a few members of Congress were not so amused, and once this ceremony was over, would race home to check on the status and whereabouts of their daughters.

Then, the last regiment of France marched by. A vast encampment area had already been arranged just south of the city, something
Washington had insisted upon, with the strictest of orders, days before. There would certainly be a fete tonight, well deserved and most
definitely a morale builder for these men, both American and French,
who had endured so much without the attention of so many fair ladies across the years. But in a sense, it was a false triumph, unlike the
legendary parades of returning Roman heroes from far Carthage or
Germania, their wars won. They were marching to a battle, problematic at best, and in harsh reality a potentially forlorn hope, for even now
de Grasse might be sailing in a direction opposite of the one promised, driven by hurricane storms a thousand miles away. Or worse still,
the Royal navy, so confident and used to victory—a confidence well
earned—might have already met and defeated him, and on some far
away coast in the Carolinas, at this very moment thousands of bloated
bodies of French sailors might be washing ashore.

All hope and future would be gone for them—and gone for the
republic as well. The men standing about him now would then, in a
matter of weeks or months, crawl to Clinton in New York and beg for
peace, while he and the hard-bitten veterans who had just paraded
before him turned westward. That was his secret, never written down:
He would go into exile on the frontier of the Ohio rather than submit
to humiliation and surrender.

But at this moment? Let this city, this Congress, and this army cel-
ebrate. Though tomorrow, once new supplies and pay had been drawn
to further boost morale, the march southward would continue. So they
would encamp tonight just south of the city. There would be many a
man who by dawn could barely stand, and barely march, and he knew
some would no longer be in the ranks, having come this far, but at the
sight of home and family, after so many years of exile in North Jersey
and New York, their resolve weakened, would have slipped away for
home.

Most, and, he prayed silently, nearly all, would remain with their
standards and the march would continue, but for this night they

deserved, though cordoned off from too many temptations, a night to bask in glory, and at least some semblance of adoration.

Behind the parading troops now came the rather inglorious sight of a two-mile-long column of supply wagons, loaded down with spare rations, extra ammunition, medical supplies, and tents for field hospitals and the burdensome, but for the French, essential, "impedimenta" of their culture—choice food and drink for the officers and even some few treats for their enlisted men.

The crowd began to break up as suddenly disheartened teamsters and guards for the supply train shouted appeals for a least a kiss from the lasses or a bottle of rum, which triggered laughter and even a few friendly offers in reply, but nowhere near the showering of praise heaped upon the main troops of the line of the Continentals or especially those of France.

"General Washington, sir."

He turned and saw Robert Morris. He gladly took the man's proffered hand. He had doubted this man's true patriotism before this campaign, but not now, knowing that whatever profits Morris had made in the war, he had personally ventured in support of this campaign.

"General, sir, we must talk this evening, it is urgent that we do so. Would you accept the honor of dining with me?"

"I am at your beck and call, sir," Washington replied, feeling a bit of a chill because it was obvious by his demeanor that Morris was anxious.

"Sir, about the pay and supplies you and your men expect tomorrow," Morris whispered without preamble, "there's a problem . . ."

Ten

FOR ELIZABETH RISHER IT HAD BEEN A MOST SPLENDID AF-
ternoon. She had taken the red, white, and blue cotton and silk from
several dresses, now long out of style, to create a new dress for the
occasion, complete to a sash of blue with white stars. There was a
time in her life when such was not necessary; when a mere charming
smile to her indulgent father would have sent her packing for the latest
style to the seamstress down on Market Street, the same one who al-
legedly had made the first national colors, but that was before the war.

Half trusted by some, despised by many, and not fully trusted by
anyone, it had been a lonely life. She had sealed off most of their once-
vibrant home, except for her bedroom, the parlor, and the kitchen
where she made her own meals. It was existence on the edge, not a
life. Like so many, she never would have believed this war would have
dragged on for six long years.

Though the patriotic parade of this afternoon had created a new surge of morale—it was the first time since the summer of '78 that thousands of troops of the Revolution had paraded through the city— she was savvy enough to know that they were all bound on a desperate bid to end this conflict before winter. The city had been teeming with rumors ever since the spring that the Czarina of Russia had offered mediation, that both the French and English governments had expressed at least some interest in a settlement, and that more than a few in Congress were eager to see an end to the war, even if it meant only limited freedom, as long as there were pardons for all leaders involved. If this campaign should end in disastrous failure, the rumormongers were always ready to speculate. There were stories already that all was dependent on some sort of movement by a French fleet, and with more than three hundred miles yet to go on a march into Virginia, that would be the end of it. By the following spring it would be over with, a negotiated peace—a negotiated defeat.

This afternoon there had been a spirit of celebration, and tonight the city would be tumultuous, filled with soldiers who had managed to slip past pickets and provost guards. There was to be a grand illumination (and even fireworks) in front of the city hall.

Walking down the alleyway to her back door, Elizabeth fumbled through her clutch bag for the entry key. The early evening was boiling hot and once inside she looked forward to just locking the door behind her, opening the upper floor windows to try to create some draft, and perhaps even taking a sponge bath to cool off. She felt the cool barrel of the small pistol she kept in her clutch bag, always ready. That, of course, would never be beyond grasp at any time, even when asleep. She was a young and lovely woman who, too many were aware, was living alone, and on this night of what would certainly be a drunken debauch for many, once darkness fell, this city was not the safest place to be.

As she drew out her key, her other hand rested on the grip of the pistol.

"Elizabeth?"

Startled, she dropped the key, drew the pistol out of her clutch bag, and cocked it.

There was a sigh from within the carriage house.

"Am I such an enemy now?"

"My God. Allen?"

He stepped out of the shadows, hands held wide to either side, and she saw that smile of his, that sad, charming smile of his that was always so overwhelming to her soul.

They stood silent, staring at each other in disbelief, her hands shaking with the shock of surprise and now, also, at his mere presence.

"Perhaps turn the pistol to one side," he suggested. "The trigger is rather light on some of them."

She lowered the weapon and then looked nervously to the windows of her neighbors on either side. No one was home in either adjoining house; nearly the entire city was down on Market Street celebrating.

"In the name of heaven, what are you doing here?"

"Perhaps we could talk inside?"

She nodded, bent over to sweep up the key, opened the door, and motioned for him to dart in. Slamming the door shut behind them, she stood gazing at him. They were only inches apart and then, driven by mutual impulse, were in each other's arms for a long embrace. Elizabeth was shaking, struggling to hold back tears.

Their lips brushed lightly and with that she finally broke the embrace, suddenly fearful of her own reaction and what might happen next. Now the two were several feet apart, both a bit shy, nervous, hesitant.

"You didn't answer me," she finally gasped. "Exactly what on earth are you doing here? Last I heard you were still a damn Loyalist stationed in New York."

"Damn Loyalist? I recall you at many a fete when we were stationed here."

She did not reply.

"You still are a Loyalist?" she asked tentatively.

"Yes, I am in service to the Crown."

"As what?"

"I think my being here now makes that obvious."

"A spy."

"Rather a nasty and dishonorable word, spy. Prefer to think it is loyal service to a just cause."

Her gaze swept his garb. Of all things, he was dressed as a man of the cloth, dust covered, face sweat streaked, smelling of horse, obviously having ridden long and hard this day. He did look a bit absurd in the garb of a Congregationalist minister and she had to suppress a smile, but still there was a ripple of fear.

"If you are caught like that, you know they will hang you."

"The Rebels seem to take a certain pleasure in hanging," he replied sharply.

She knew to what he was referencing.

"I am so sorry about your friend John. He was a true gentleman and deserved a better fate."

"Washington didn't think so."

"Allen, he was caught behind the lines in civilian garb, as you are now."

"Thanks to that bitch friend of yours Peggy," and now there was a flash of anger.

She shared his disgust regarding Peggy Shippen and the role all suspected she had really played in turning her husband, Benedict, into a traitor. Perhaps even drawing a former lover into the scheme as well, but she did not react.

"Why in God's name are you here?"

He sighed, taking off his hat to wipe his brow.

"May I trouble you for something cool to drink first? I am parched."

Elizabeth hurried down to the cellar and debated for a moment as to whether to fetch one of the few remaining bottles of wine or rum, but she decided Allen needed to keep a clear head and came back up with a cool pitcher of buttermilk, pouring him a glass, which he took almost greedily and gulped down. She went into the parlor and cautiously looked out the windows. A few half-drunk revelers were out in the street. A fifer staggered by, playing a poor rendition of "Chester," but no one noticed as she opened the windows, closed the shutters, and then pulled the windows back down. Then she called him in to sit down on the sofa, where she settled in by his side, tempted to lean in close against him, but fighting the urge down.

"Now tell me why you were hiding in my carriage house?"

"In hopes of seeing you," he offered back forcing a weary smile.

"No, seriously. Not a single word from you since your letter a year ago . . ."

"I sent more than a dozen," he said.

"Well, only one got through," and she said it with a bit of pique.

"I'm sorry, Elizabeth, but, after all, there is a war going on and no longer a daily coach or postal rider between New York and Philadelphia."

"What happened today? Were you seen?" she snapped. "My God, if you are spotted you are dead."

"I was spotted."

"Go on," she said nervously.

He began his story, telling of observing the troops crossing the Hudson, reporting this to Clinton, then without orders venturing a foray as far as Chatham in Jersey and nearly being captured by Peter. Rather than wasting time crossing back to New York with what Clinton would dismiss as a dubious report at best, he had sent Jamie across with a written dispatch. He stole a minister's clothes in the hamlet of Mill Burn, forged a pass that he was to be allowed through the lines to attend to the funeral of his father in West Chester, and had actually crossed the Delaware river on the same boat as a company of New York troops. He had then ridden on this morning straight into Philadelphia. Before even arriving in the city, all was clear to him: Washington's still-rumored but obvious destination, and how many regiments of Continentals and French troops were in the line of march. He had even watched some of the parade, until a suspicious glance from a Philadelphia militiaman, who approached him and openly accused him of being a British officer who had occupied the city three years before and a friend of the damn traitor Peggy Shippen, had sent him fleeing. A hue and cry had gone up that there was a damn Loyalist spy right in the middle of the procession, most likely bent on murdering General Washington or some other such mayhem.

If that had been his intent, it certainly would have been easy enough. For a brief moment, in all the swirling confusion and back slapping and hand shaking after the parade had passed, he had been within easy pistol-shot range of their general. Even if the opportunity had been presented to him, he would have refused it without hesitation. The general had shown him pity after the death of his brother at Trenton, and treated him with courtesy the year before, even though the appeal he carried for Andre had been refused out of hand. If Washington was fated to die in this war, let it be with the honor the man deserved, even though he was a sworn enemy leading a cause Allen opposed.

He knew that any attempt to find refuge in a tavern or public house was far too risky, and, though he would not admit it to her, this was the one place he knew he could find safe hiding. He also wanted to see her after being so long apart.

She listened to his story without saying a word, interrupting to fetch him another drink of buttermilk and a thick slice of ham, which he devoured with a pale attempt to conceal just how hungry he was after two days of hard riding. He had stopped only to water and let his mount graze a bit before pushing on, for every inn along the main pike was packed with boisterous militia, and the risk was always that the closer he came to his birthplace in Trenton, someone might recognize him. Besides, no true Congregationalist minister would set foot into a tavern to seek sustenance.

"What will you do now?" she finally asked.

He looked at her, his exhaustion evident.

"I have all I need to know for certain. I counted the troops as they passed, the artillery, the dragoons, even the supply wagons." He reached down to his boot, slipped his hand in, and pulled out a soiled folded up sheet of paper and unfolding it, held it up.

She glanced at it in horror.

"For God's sake, Allen, give me that," and she snatched it from his hand.

He was startled by her gesture.

"You have it memorized."

"Not really."

"Then do so now. You get caught with that in your boot and you'll die like our friend Andre. Memorize it if you must."

He scanned it several times and finally nodded. She grabbed it back, crumpling it, and went into the kitchen where a low fire, in spite of the summer heat, smoldered in the oversize brick fireplace. She threw it in.

Elizabeth came back into the parlor, and gazed at him with hands on hips.

"When was the last time you slept?"

He shook his head wearily.

"I don't know, I think two days ago. I did have a brief nap in a field this morning north of West Chester just before dawn."

"You must be absolutely befuddled, Allen, to do something so stupid as to write down that note. Some spy you are! Now follow me."

He stood up and she took his hand, leading him to the stairs.

"Where is everybody? Your mother, your servant Ben?"

"I'm alone. Mother died last winter as did Ben."

He looked into her eyes. "I am so sorry," he said. "I didn't know."

She did not reply as she led him up the stairs, opened the door to her bedroom, and guided him in.

"At least wait until dark. By midnight most of the town will be drunk and you should be able to slip out unseen."

"I don't dare go back to fetch my horse. I left him at a stable several blocks from here, but chances are the word is out about me and they'll have someone waiting there."

She took that in and then actually chuckled.

"You know, you look absolutely absurd in that minister's cloth. It doesn't even fit you right."

He tried to smile.

"Here, let me help you," she said as she unbuttoned the heavy woolen coat, turning him about. His shirt was plastered to his body, drenched with sweat.

"Let me fetch a basin of water and a sponge. Get that shirt off, and I'll be right back."

She returned several minutes later, carrying a china washbasin filled with cool water from the outside well, and was a bit startled to see him standing there, knee breeches and stockings still on, but bare chested. Their gazes locked, then both lowered their eyes in embarrassment.

She soaked up a sponge full of water, wiped down his shoulders, and he actually sighed with relief, then started to turn back around to her, eyes wide. Fumbling she drained the sponge in the basin, soaked up more water and handed it to him, stepping back, hands trembling.

"Thank you, Elizabeth."

"Allen . . . ?" her voice trailed off.

There was silence for a moment as he sponged down his sweat soaked chest, then held the sponge over his head and squeezing it, letting it drain out, and sighing with relief as the cool water ran down his neck and face.

"A day hasn't passed when I have not thought of you," he finally said, breaking the silence.

"Nor I, you," she whispered.

There was a long pause again, as he stood by the side of her bed.

She finally stepped forward.

"Sit down, let me help you with your boots."

He did as ordered and she knelt down, sliding his boots off, recoiling slightly. It was far too obvious he had not been out of them in days, perhaps a week or more.

She felt a sudden wave of temptation . . . but no, she could not, not now. Not with so much dividing them at this moment. And yet . . .

She sighed and stood back up, as she did so gently taking his legs, helping him to stretch out atop the comforter of her bed.

"Sleep for now," she told him. "We'll talk later."

He looked at her with a smile and with longing. He held a hand up, a gesture to sit by his side, but against her own will and desire she backed away and tried to laugh.

"Behave like a gentleman now, Allen van Dorn. Get some sleep, we'll talk more about this later."

In spite of his obvious desire, he did not need to be told. She had barely settled into a chair in the corner of the room to keep watch over him, when his eyes were already closed. He had collapsed into exhausted slumber, so deep that he did not even hear the knock on her front door a few minutes later.

She did not think much of it as she slipped down the stairs, and went to the door, assuming it was her neighbor, old Mrs. Tennent, who, taking pity on her since the death of her mother, would often send a servant over to invite her for tea and dinner.

When she opened the door there was a moment of such complete shock, she knew it had to show.

It was Peter Wellsley, in the uniform of a lieutenant colonel of the headquarters staff of General Washington. She had not seen him in the parade and had no idea he was in town.

"Good evening, Elizabeth. I pray I am not intruding."

She knew her expression of shock was evident and a second later, she stepped forward, embracing him. "Peter Wellsley," she cried.

She stepped back slightly, actually trembling, but let her hand slip into his.

"Look at you, an officer, a colonel no less if I know my rankings," and she pointed with her free hand to his epaulette.

He smiled in return, eyes fixed on her.

"If it is not too bold, may I step in for a few minutes."

She could not hesitate, pleading some false rule of etiquette and decorum, for in her heart, she knew why he was here.

"Oh, but of course, of course," she said, and stepped back from the door, motioning for him to come in. Standing in the main corridor his gaze drifted past her to the parlor, to the jug of buttermilk on the table before the sofa, the empty mug.

"You must be hot and thirsty," she said quickly, "I was just refreshing myself when you knocked; may I offer you something cool to drink?"

"Thank you, that would be most kind."

She hurried into the kitchen and came out a moment later with an earthenware mug. Peter was already in the living room, holding the empty one, looking at it, and at the sofa, where she knew he could see the sprinkling of dust from Allen's jacket on that sofa and floor, and perhaps could tell even that two people had been sitting there only minutes before.

She took the pitcher, filled a fresh mug, and handed it to him.

"Won't you join me?" he asked, handing the other mug to her, the lip marks of someone having drunk from it clearly visible. She took it, half-filled it, and with a smile he raised his up in a token of salute.

"To seeing a dear old friend, and confusion to our enemies," he said and she repeated the toast.

He remained standing looking into her eyes.

"Your family, Peter?" she asked. "All is well?"

"I saw them briefly as we passed through Trenton, and yes, all is well."

Without comment he stepped past her and back out into the main hallway, looking into the dining room, which was now completely bare. Last time he was here she had sold off only the grand mahogany table, but gone now as well were the side boards and the cabinet that was once filled with precious silverware and real china from the Orient.

She followed him. He was obviously looking about, and she remained silent. Could she, as a lady, protest if he decided to go upstairs?

He stepped into the kitchen without showing the courtesy of asking permission and went to the fireplace, and to her horror she saw that the sheet of paper that Allen had been carrying had smoldered on the edge of the fire, but had not burned to ashes. He nudged the paper with the toe of his boot, looking down at it, the movement of it enough to finally trigger a smoky flame.

"Burning old love letters?" he asked looking back at her, his features unchanged, still smiling.

She deliberately let her features change.

"If I was, is that your business, Peter Wellsley?"

"No." He paused. "But then again, perhaps."

"How so, dare I ask?"

"I received a report."

"Of what?"

"Why don't you guess?"

She turned about, and motioned back to the parlor, not bothering to look back to see if he was following, sitting down on the exact spot that Allen had occupied only a short while before.

He sat down where she had been sitting.

"Something is going on, Peter Wellsley, now out with it."

He sighed.

"I received a report that Allen van Dorn is in this city, even now."

"So?" and she felt at that moment that she had put on the acting performance of a lifetime, even though he was staring straight into her eyes looking for the slightest flicker of emotion.

"He was spotted by someone little more than two hours ago," and Peter actually chuckled, "dressed, of all things, in the garb of a Congregationalist minister."

He fell silent, just staring at her. "I know his feelings toward you, and you admitted you returned those feelings last time I was here in the spring." His voice trailed off. "Elizabeth, I am here doing my duty as a soldier, please understand that. This is not personal."

There was a long moment of silence.

"Peter Wellsley, regardless of what some might say about this town,

I am a loyal Patriot. If you doubt that in the slightest, go find Dan Morgan and ask him about my servant Ben. Throughout the occupation, I was sending information through the lines via Ben regarding everything that transpired in this city, including the information that Clinton was preparing to abandon the city and retreat to New York. No one else knows now, except you, because I do know what your position is now. I believe some of those reports wound up in the hands of General Washington himself, and you can ask him to vouch for what I've just said."

"I do not doubt that, and in fact I already know it. I spoke with him about it only yesterday."

Again a pause.

"Elizabeth, was he, or is he, here?" he finally asked.

Feigning outrage she stood up and pointed to the door.

"I suggest Peter, that you leave here this instant. I will not be insulted this way."

He did stand, but then did not move.

"I have reliable reports that Allen is somewhere in this city and waiting outside are some militia that have been pursuing him today. I have been trailing him for nearly four days now, clear back to just outside of Morristown. God save him, he is not in uniform, and therefore not afforded the honors of war. You know what that means."

"So you would hang your closest friend of childhood if you catch him, is that it?" she asked, and she was furious with herself that her voice did catch with emotion.

He broke eye contact and looked away from her.

"I've placed a watch on every tavern in this city where he might seek lodgings. Every road out is guarded, and his horse, a rather fine gray stallion that easily outran me several days back, was found in a livery stable so that way out is barred now as well."

He fixed her with his gaze.

"I can think of only one place in this city, today, where he would know he would find a safe hiding place."

"And you are saying here?"

He did not reply.

She took a deep breath.

"Then go ahead and look," she challenged him. "Tear the house apart. You might even find him in my bedroom at this very moment, waiting for me to return to his side."

She could see those words struck him hard, his gaze lowered, but, as if to take her up on her offer, he walked out of the parlor, out into the main corridor, and looked up the flight of stairs. She stood silent in the parlor, heart now pounding. He finally looked back at her, smile gone.

"Have you ever seen a hanging, Elizabeth?"

She nodded. Who had not, in this city, across the years? Before the war, it was the usual criminals, and since then, the spies and traitors to one side or the other, depending on who occupied the city at the time. Drawn by childish curiosity, she had always stood at a distance when young, but not in recent years, not since this damn war had descended upon them.

"Allen and I stood only feet away when his friend Major Andre was hanged," he sighed. "You could hear his neck snap when he fell off the cart and the rope went taut. It is a fate I would wish on no man.

"But," again he paused. "It is what war does to us and I have seen far too many men die in far worse agony from gunshot, frostbite, small-pox, and fevers. Hanging could almost be seen as a mercy at times."

"Would you hang your old friend if you captured him?"

He fell silent, looking back at the flight of stairs, obviously debating whether to ascend them or not. He finally sighed and looked back at her.

"The secret is out by now," he said, his voice barely a whisper. "Once this army is clear of this city and the Delaware River, there is nothing on earth that Clinton can do to stop us on the march. It would take two days at least to report back what transpired here today, by then the army should be below Wilmington and at the head of the Chesapeake Bay.

"No matter how tight the cordon I've put out, others have, without doubt, reported back by now and will continue to do so. In ten days' time, Lord willing, we will be where we intend, and then it is up to fate. It will be for God, the winds, the strength of these men, and General Washington to decide."

He held her with his gaze.

"The report of one more bedraggled spy will change little now."

She said nothing.

He had turned to one side while looking up at the staircase, and as he turned back to face her, she saw he had a light pistol in his hand, cocked.

He uncocked the weapon and tucked it into his belt.

He bowed slightly.

"I wish you well, Elizabeth," he said, and started for the open door.

She followed him, coming up to his side.

"Peter," and her hand slipped back into his.

He gazed at her, eyes cold.

"Not a word, Elizabeth. Not a damn word. Whatever I felt for Allen, that is now dead. It is purely pragmatic now. What harm is a report long after we are gone? If anything, it will only sow panic and confusion, and knowing all I do about Clinton, yet more councils of war between generals and admirals, and yet more days will pass. In a week's time they'll read about it in all the Philadelphia newspapers— how this army marched through, right down to the exact number of regiments and pieces of artillery. It doesn't matter now."

Yet, she could see he was lying.

"God protect you, Peter Wellsley," she whispered, leaning up to kiss him on the cheek.

She felt a tremor of emotion from Peter and his eyes misting over. He swallowed hard, and then as if driven by impulse, he embraced her.

"Always remember what I said to you back in the spring. My feelings for you will never change."

Choked with emotion she slipped out of his embrace, thinking of the man she loved sleeping in the room above, but at the same time her feelings for Peter were there as well, reinforced by the realization that he was betraying his own code of honor with what he was now doing.

As she looked back into his eyes she saw his features had hardened.

"I never would have believed that even you would offer aid to a damn Tory," he whispered. "Maybe when this war is over I'll see it differently, but not now."

"I think you already do see it differently."

He looked back at her crossly.

"One more word and I will go back up those stairs."

She remained silent, her silence, she could see, all but a signal that he did, indeed, know the truth but would not act upon it.

He stepped out onto the stoop where, for the first time, she noticed that several Pennsylvania militiamen waited, muskets unslung and at the ready.

"You're mistaken," he announced. "He didn't flee here. Let's go."

He didn't look back even once as he stalked off, the three militiamen following, one of them looking back crossly at her. That one must have trailed Allen here, she realized.

"God protect you, Peter," she whispered.

She closed the door and locked it shut. Going to a shuttered window, she peeked out for several minutes to ensure that no one had stopped and gone into waiting at the corner or nearby alleyway. Meanwhile the street was increasingly filled with revelers.

The house was stifling hot as she went out into the kitchen, bolted the back door, and paused for a second to look at the fireplace. The note—the writing on it must have been visible—was now crumbled to ashes.

She then went up the stairs and slipped into her bedroom. Allen was actually fast asleep, oblivious to how close he had come to capture and death. At the sight of him her heart swelled with joy and relief. Yes, she had used him long ago to gain information, but even then that feeling had changed. Now, after three years of separation and these long months of living alone, no one from either side really trusting her, the decision was not difficult at all as she loosened the stays of her corset, slipped out of it, still modestly keeping her long skirt on. She slipped into her bed by his side and held him close. He did not stir from his exhausted sleep—perhaps that was for the best— nor did he notice or feel the tears of relief and happiness on his shoulder as she held him and drifted off to sleep by his side, knowing what would happen when both awakened.

Eleven

PHILADELPHIA
EVENTIDE
AUGUST 29, 1781

SIGHING, GENERAL WASHINGTON LEANED BACK IN HIS CHAIR, the wooden legs creaking. He looked away from Robert Morris and back to the half-empty glass of claret, the heavy crystal goblet sparkling in the candlelight.

Morris's dining room was richly appointed, and it was apparent that at least one French ship running supplies past the British blockade carried as well cases of the best of wine and champagne from France. Somehow the richly upholstered chairs, the silver setting for twelve, silver candelabra at the center of the mahogany dining table, the medieval tapestry of unicorns adorning a wall, and even the polished brass tools for the fireplace, had replaced those confiscated during the British occupation.

Though the table had been set for twelve, the only other man, sitting to the other side of Washington, and who Morris had insisted place himself at the head of the table, was President Laurens. Laurens had remained silent except for a few polite comments now and again, while the meal, a saddle of lamb with all the trimmings, had been served.

He had little appetite for it now, and was glad when it was removed. He refused the brandy offered so he could keep a clear head, and merely took a light sip now and again from his wine, refusing a topping off of his glass.

"I know this news comes as shock, General Washington."

He looked back at Morris. There was a time when he had held this man in the lowest regard, since he had obviously made great profit from this war, and was rumored for a while to have been part of the Gates conspiracy to have him removed from command. While having gained position as treasurer of the Confederation, a post that had been left vacant far too long because of Congress's obsessive fear of "centralizing too much power in one man," Morris had, indeed, come through the previous fortnight with the first real pay the men had seen in more than half a year, and supplies purchased and stockpiled along the route of march. He had come through.

But to come this far, and then hear this news!

"Sir, to call it a shock is an understatement," Washington finally replied, keeping his voice calm though ready inwardly to explode.

Morris looked over at Laurens for support.

"Sir, the treasury is bled dry. We marshaled every shilling to be found just to underwrite the cost of moving the army this far. It is bled dry."

"If I am to accept that," Washington replied, and now there was a touch of anger in his voice, "perhaps the only recourse left is to stop the army in place here and go no farther."

"What?" Laurens was obviously shocked by this statement.

"Exactly that, sir."

"How?"

"It is not a question of how," Washington replied, carefully choosing his words so as not to imply the slightest threat. "Most of the men, up until your efforts of several weeks back, had not seen any real pay, other than useless paper, in years. What they did receive was a month, maybe two months at most. That raised their spirits somewhat, but as they marched here, rumors swept the ranks, rumors I could not contain, that once in Philadelphia more pay would greet them."

Laurens sighed, shaking his head.

"Do not take this as even the slightest of insults, General," the president of Congress said, "but they do know what they are fighting for, don't they?"

Washington did take it as an insult, but kept it contained. Surely this man, whose only son was on his staff, understood the issue. A lucky few, such as the Laurenses, had homes, even plantations that could support them, even in time of war, but the rank and file? Most were either small farmers, shopkeepers, or laborers before the war started. The issue of pay was not directly about them, it was about families back home, some behind enemy lines, some with homes, farms, and stores looted and destroyed, families dispossessed and living on the charity of others, while husbands and sons stayed with the army.

He took a deep breath.

"Gentlemen. I beg to know that you are fully aware of where my own heart stands on this, where my role as general of the armies rests in relationship to this government."

He looked at the two who thankfully nodded in agreement.

"Yet I must press to you the case of the men who look to me for leadership. Yes, they know the cause they fight for, but they also read letters from home that unless there is some pay, something to at least buy food with, their families will starve come winter. I've been shown letters in which wives, mothers, daughters, loyal to our cause for years, are now lamenting that unless given succor, they will appeal to their men to lay down their arms and come home, otherwise by spring there will be no home to return to. What do I say to them tomorrow when after ordering them to shoulder arms and press on to Yorktown, they cry out for pay, a just pay for all they have endured, and will still endure?"

"Surely they will continue on regardless?" Laurens replied as if to reassure himself.

Washington sighed and set his glass down, and to his embarrassed dismay, he fumbled the glass and it spilled over on the table. Morris started to call for a servant, but Washington already had his napkin out, and, angry with himself that his pent-up emotions had manifested themselves with such clumsiness, mopped up the drink, though it had stained the embroidered tablecloth.

"Do you know what more than one of my men did with their pay last week?" he asked, gaze fixed on Laurens.

"Sir?"

"There was a soldier with a New York regiment. Discharged due to consumption and unable to make this march. The men of his company, some cut the coin they received in half, entrusted it to him, and asked that it be given to their family. More than one man just handed over the entire coin."

The other two were silent.

"Patriotism, gentleman, is noble for the soul and warms the heart of any good and honorable man, but it does not feed the empty stomach of a child at home. There have been times when I was tempted to block all mail coming into the encampments because the day after it was delivered, at morning roll call . . ." He sighed and looked off as if to some distant place. "There were morning roll calls where I had lost more men in a single night than in a battle. I saw the letters that drove them to this, pleas for them to come home after six years of service in a war with no end in sight, families impoverished, thrown out of their homes, and forced to the dishonor of living off the charity of neighbors and friends. Wives have died with no husband there to mourn them or tend to their children who were now living off of public charity. That is something no man of honor can bear, that children

were starving, and children they had never even seen had been born
and then died . . ."

His voice trailed off for a moment.

"There was a time," he whispered, "that when forced by the necessity of war I have with the greatest reluctance ordered a deserter
to be shot, but no longer. Not when a noble man stands before me in
tears, who has been with me since Long Island, who stood at Trenton, Princeton, Brandywine, Germantown, the winter of Valley Forge
and the triumph at Monmouth, and tells me to go ahead and shoot
him dead for desertion after all of that. Then to strip his body bare
of his tattered uniform and send that uniform home to his wife and
children so that they can perhaps sell the buttons for food."

He lowered his head and feared that for the first time in years
someone other than Martha would see him in actual tears. He was
exhausted beyond all measure, not just from this fatiguing march in
boiling August heat, but from all of the years of this war.

"That is a true story. I faced it not two months ago, gentlemen,"
and his voice was near to breaking.

"I could not shoot him. I was forced to order a dozen lashes," he
hesitated, "and I had word sent to the quartermaster applying the
lashes to do so lightly."

He looked at Laurens and then back to Morris.

"That man is still with the ranks. I saw him pass in review this
afternoon, his eyes meeting mine as if saying 'See, I am still here
though my uniform is in tatters, I am barefoot, and my children have
not seen me in years. I am a Patriot and still here.'

"Gentleman, I could barely face his gaze. Although, Mr. Morris, I
do thank you that the largesse of the last pay will at least keep his family in food for a week or two, if it ever reaches them. They live in territory that is within enemy lines, and no one will take pity on them. I
pray for his sake that some decent Christian will smuggle the money
through to his family.

"Gentlemen, we have staked, as was written in our Declaration, our lives and our sacred honor upon this cause, as we must and should have as its leaders. But to the thousands of men in my infantry of the line, and the men who follow Knox and Harry Lee? They, too, have staked their lives and tens of thousands so far have given those lives up upon the altar of freedom, but their families, gentlemen? I plead now not for a coin just to be dropped in their pocket. Frankly, I would not give a single shilling's worth for any man who fights solely for his own pay and prospect of booty. Let our enemies have such values, though I suspect more than a few in their ranks, if given the freedom of choice, would turn aside from this war if they could.

"But for our men? Something, anything, so that they can rest assured while braving this venture fraught with peril ahead of us, that they, at least, have a grateful nation that will see to the welfare of their families, whether they live or die in the weeks ahead." He felt he had spoken too much and lowered his head.

There was a long silence during which Washington picked up his now empty crystal goblet, but refused Morris's offer of a refill.

Laurens looked over at Morris.

"We've managed at least to gather some supplies in Maryland," Laurens replied, nervously clearing his throat, "but that is slim at best."

"And Virginia?"

"Mr. Jefferson said he will redouble his efforts. I know you heard he was almost captured recently by Tarleton's raiders, escaping only minutes ahead of them."

Washington could not help but smile at the thought of it. His respect for Thomas was boundless. It was his genius more than any other that had drafted the Declaration, but after six years of war, when a soldier heard of the momentary discomfort of a civilian administrator, the feeling was that, at least, it gave a taste of what those on the front line faced every day.

Something that did mystify him was the fact that raiders had not been dispatched to loot and burn his beloved Mt. Vernon. In moments of more generous contemplation of his opponents, he had to admit that there were still some "rules" to this war. Benedict Arnold was responsible for much of the mayhem this year in central Virginia, and he did wonder if some remaining shred of a now-lost friendship had resulted in a quiet order that protected his home and Martha. Regardless, standing orders still remained that if Arnold was ever captured he was to be summarily hanged, having already been found guilty in absentia, and condemned to the rope.

"The citizens of Fredericksburg have promised a full day of rations for ten thousand troops, as have the citizens of Richmond, in spite of, or should I say in revenge for, the pillaging they've endured, but beyond that, sir," and Laurens was again silent.

"It is not good enough," Washington sighed.

He was no longer playing a game of bluff, something he was known to be a master at, both on the battlefield and in negotiations, and in a spirited hand of whist; it was deadly real this time. He still had more than three hundred miles to go.

"At least we still control the waters of the upper Chesapeake," Laurens offered, "and boats are being gathered, sparing the men a long march and cutting the time of their journey to but a few days once they reach Head of Elk."

"I have been told though that there are not enough boats for all the men, and a fair portion will still have to march. That still does not address their pay."

"What about the French?" Laurens asked.

"I will not go to our allies, yet again, hat in hand and beg money from them as a pauper," he replied sharply. "The fact that they are venturing their main fleet, which costs more to operate in one day than my entire army does for a month, is a blessing. The fact that General Rochambeau has ventured his entire land forces here in North America on this venture as well is proof of their commitment and courage. You suggest I go to him tonight and ask for another month's pay for our men, or should I say a year or more of pay, which is what is justly owed them?"

He slapped the table with a clenched fist.

"No, sir, I cannot and will not. They have done far too much already. You know the reports from France as well as I do. Their government has risked bankruptcy in support of our efforts. If word goes back to France that we are now reduced to begging their government for a year's pay for all our troops in the field, it might very well tip the balance against us, gentlemen. President Laurens, your own son reported to you that the mood is turning against keeping their forces here, it is all but bankrupting them as well."

"They have gained much from it in their own right," Morris replied softly, "capturing more of the Spice Islands of the Caribbean. Their near success with the Spanish at Gibraltar . . . there are even reports they might drive the British out of India."

"Maybe so, but one reversal at sea and they risk that for us, and everything they have gained will be for naught. Let us face this fact, gentlemen. They gain not a single livre by maintaining more than ten thousand troops here and supplying us as well. The only gain is diverting their natural enemy to fight here as well and perhaps stripping him of thirteen of his former colonies. From their perspective, the efforts of Rochambeau and their fleets would be far better spent in taking Gibraltar or securing their hold on India."

He sighed.

"That is why I will not, unless directly ordered by you, ask for one livre more in order to pay our troops. We must do that ourselves. General Rochambeau has been the most gracious of allies any man or country could ever pray to have, but he is not under my direct orders, sir. He has been magnanimous in playacting but we all know, if the whim should seize him tomorrow to turn his troops about and march back to Rhode Island and from there take ship home, he could do so under his own authority, and there is nothing we can do to stop him. I will not add to our ledger of debt or perhaps even provoke a reaction by going hat in hand to him tomorrow morning."

He was tempted to add one more sentence but his judgment prevailed. It would be foolhardy to say he would resign if ordered to do so. There could always be a plot behind all of this, and without doubt, some in Congress would leap at the suggestion, still fearing his private goal was to become a Caesar before this war was done.

Morris half stood up, leaned across the table, and fetched the bottle of brandy, motioned to Washington, who again shook his head in refusal, and this time, forgetting all proper etiquette Morris poured his own brandy sniffer nearly to the brim and drained down several ounces in one gulp.

He sighed, leaned back, and stared at the ceiling, his features turning red from the impact of the very stiff drink.

"You won't have the money tomorrow, nor the full amount," he finally said.

He sighed deeply, his gaze now shifted to President Laurens.

"We will, however, promise a few months more within forty-eight hours."

For a moment Washington wondered if the man was drunk, and now deciding to joke with this somewhat cryptic statement.

"There is still money to be found in Philadelphia," and now Morris looked over at Laurens.

"Where?" Laurens asked.

"I'll just loot every bank clean and every merchant in the city I've not already tapped out."

"We already have."

"There's always more," Morris replied, "and, damn my soul, if I don't know every trick in the book, gentlemen, how the hell do you think I got rich to start with?"

"What guarantee of repayment will you offer if you actually do find this money?"

"Well, I could do as Caesar once did," he replied and now he was looking straight at Washington as if to gauge him. "I'll just have them condemned as traitors, executed, and all their property confiscated. I recall that is how Caesar helped fund his last campaign against Pompey."

Washington saw no humor in that, in fact he thought the words to be absolutely ill-advised, even in this private conversation, and his expression showed it.

Morris sighed and drained the rest of his drink and then looked back up at the ceiling, as if this were a necessary part of a ritual for the alcohol to take full effect, before he spoke again.

"I'll offer my personal voucher in repayment, and my stock in those ships of mine running the blockade as collateral," he said softly as if about to choke on his own words.

"My God, man," Laurens replied, "you did that with the last payment. You are already in over one hundred percent, everything you own is mortgaged."

"Only you and a few others know that, sir. The rest do not. So I'll be bankrupt twice over," Morris now laughed, "they can only throw me in debtors prison once, and by the way, I think once this war is done, a law should be passed outlawing debtors prisons. It is a stupid system. A man goes bankrupt then you lock him up so he can't earn his way out of it."

He now laughed out loud.

"I'd propose it myself that a man cannot be thrown into prison merely for bad debts, but if I did so, it might look self-serving. Heaven knows we are setting precedents and Congress should never appear to be self-serving with the laws it passes."

Neither Laurens nor Washington laughed at his attempt at humor.

Now he looked from one to the other, a bit bleary-eyed, but deadly serious.

"No one will trust a note from the government of this Confederation, as we call it now, but until the word gets out, my notes on my personal assets are still worth something. I know at least a score of men who have held back, when I went knocking on the doors of their counting houses last month. Give me until the end of tomorrow and they shall be persuaded. Good God, the way our men looked today as they marched through the city, compared to the French behind them, that should have at least stirred a few hearts. A rumor or two as well that if the men are not paid the army just might mutiny, loot the city clean, and declare Washington emperor will scare them to turn out their pockets as well."

"Sir," Washington's voice was cold, and obviously filled with personal insult, "never joke on that subject using my name, or even remotely use it as a threat to get this money in."

He did not add, though the three of them knew without saying, that the potential of that was all too real at this moment. All it would take would be a few disgruntled men, drunk, refusing to fall into ranks when ordered to continue their march south, and the tension was running just high enough that like a spark in a dry forest, it could explode into flames. To even offer a rumor that such a threat was real might actually trigger the event.

When planning this march, he had actually contemplated bypassing Philadelphia completely, marching around it to the west out of just such a concern, that his troops, many of whom were already drunk tonight, might turn ugly. Every officer had received the strictest orders to remain cold sober and on the watch throughout the night.

Morris bowed low while remaining seated.

"Apology most properly asked for and most humbly offered in reply, sir. I meant no disrespect and let me blame it on this fine brandy, if you will. I will be frank, sir, and perhaps the brandy has loosened my tongue a bit too much but there was a time I did fear you might harbor such thoughts. I was purged of that affliction long ago, as if Doctor Rush himself had given me a physic, and though I know relations between you and the good doctor are strained at the moment, due to his aligning with Gates, he himself has said that you value your code of honor more than any man in our republic. I know you are a man who would fall on his own sword first, rather than ever raise it in a dishonorable act, and please believe that though I am without doubt drunk at this moment, I beg apology of you."

"Accepted, sir," and Washington let his features relax.

"It might be helpful if some of your men, the dragoons of Light Horse Harry, were posted to guard the exits of the city. Our local militia, being known to my brothers in the financial and legal world, can easily be bribed with half a crown to let a man pass. We just seal the town for a day or two, so our wealthier friends cannot find some excuse to wander out to the countryside to visit their farms and estates or cross over into Jersey, and I'll do the persuading. If we do that . . ."

His voice trailed off again as if he was mentally calculating sums, and then he looked back at Washington.

"I can promise a month's pay in hard cash, with luck maybe two months, to be shipped down to Head of Elk in three days' time at most."

"Nothing more?"

"Unless we take the books of the ancient Torah as literal and tomorrow we look to the heavens and manna—or in our case gold doubloons and nice fat guineas—tumble from the sky, I fear at best a month's, perhaps two, pay."

"Will your men march out of the city with that promise?" Laurens asked hopefully.

"Some of them will march with no promise. I know those men almost to a man . . . many have been in the ranks for years. Our men are Patriots, but even of a Patriot, willing to give his life, we are asking too much. They need to be paid if we are to ask them to put their lives on the line for this desperate gamble."

"You do think it is a desperate gamble, don't you."

"All of this is based on one letter, sent by a French admiral, who, at the time he wrote it, was more than two thousand miles and still a month away. For all we still know, we could arrive before Yorktown and instead of seeing a French fleet there we see thirty ships of the line flying the British Royal ensign and all of this will be for naught.

"We must think of what Admiral de Grasse is thinking this very moment. Did his message get through? He must surely worry about that. We are two forces moving blindly, in total darkness relative to each other. The odds are long, very long, indeed."

Then he forced a smile, looking at Morris and extending his hand to take Morris's.

"You have narrowed the odds ever so slightly, good sir, and for the rest of my life I shall be indebted to you."

"Do you think we can actually win this one?"

There was no sense in playing any games with these two.

"A chance. I will say in private only to you two that there is a chance, but that the odds in reality are against us."

"If this does not work?"

Washington looked at the bottle of brandy, and held out the empty glass that had held his claret and motioned for a drink, letting Morris pour but a few ounces, which he drained in a single gulp, something he rarely did.

"Then we have lost the war, gentlemen."

Laurens and Morris exchanged glances.

"You know, sir, the efforts by Catherine of Russia."

Washington nodded, remaining silent.

"I have been approached by more than a few to send an envoy accepting her offer to at least consider negotiations."

Washington shifted uncomfortably.

"Gentlemen. I am a soldier of a republic. By ancient tradition, politics must not be my realm, it is you the elected members of government that control that."

"But you do know of it?" Laurens pressed.

"Yes, sir, of course I do."

"If you think this venture is such a desperate gamble, am I hearing you in some way suggesting that I consider opening negotiations?"

Washington stared straight at Laurens so that the man lowered his eyes.

"If we are defeated in front of Yorktown, I plan to retreat back into western Virginia, if need be beyond the Bull Run or Blue Ridge range, while ordering what few forces I have left in New York to retreat to West Point and if pressed, to withdraw up into the frontier as well. If need be I can keep a small force alive out there for years until the embers of liberty are rekindled, although that will mean another generation will have to suffer because of our failure. Those of us who signed the Declaration, you can go over the mountains with me into exile. I recall that the king swore a solemn oath that those who signed will find their end dangling from a rope in London. Though perhaps the way some will be willing to negotiate, it just might be exile to some South Sea island in the far Indies.

"I will of course resign my commission to this government if such transpires and will not disobey orders while I still hold that commission, but I will not submit, sir, nor will many still in the ranks. That is all I can say on the subject, sir, as bound by my own sense of duty and code of honor."

He said the words with sharp emphasis, still staring at Laurens.

"You have made yourself clear, sir," Laurens whispered.

Morris nervously cleared his throat and raised his goblet and refilled it again.

"I don't like hot climates," Morris announced. "Well then, a play on Mr. Franklin's words about death and taxes: A proper hanging is certainly one way to avoid your debtors, at least in this world. I don't see myself as doing well out on the frontier, where it is said prisoners are burned rather than hung."

Laurens finally looked back up to meet Washington's gaze.

"I will not negotiate as long as you offer me some hope of victory this year, sir," he finally said.

Washington stood up, the brandy not having affected his balance or sense of proper manners and decorum.

"Gentlemen, I have duties yet to attend to: staff meeting, planning the order of march, and the distribution of rations. I will write out an order to be read that promises payment at Head of Elk."

He paused looking down at Morris.

"I am putting my name on that promise, sir," he announced, his intent clear in his tone of voice.

Morris stood and clasped his hand.

"I saw those men today, sir," and now his voice was choked. "The way you describe that one poor man struck me hard. Not to sound like a rank sentimentalist, but my wealth came at the expense of his suffering. If I am one day to stand before God, I do not want that man's starving children there ahead of me. You have my promise, sir."

Twelve

To Allen's absolute amazement, young Jamie was actually waiting for him at the dock as he disembarked from the small rowboat that a Loyalist ferryman used to get him across the Hudson. He gave the man a shilling as promised in payment for his service.

"What, in the name of good heavens, are you doing here?" Allen asked, unable to contain himself, all but embracing the lad.

Jamie, smelling as he always did from not having bathed in years, was obviously embarrassed.

"Well, sir, you told me to wait for you here."

"That was what? Five days ago?"

"Six, actually, sir."

"You are insane and belong in bedlam," Allen said with a weary laugh.

"Sir, if they had caught and hanged you, then where would I be? Jamie a-thieving back in the streets again and doomed to the gallows as you predicted the night we met?"

"So you sat here for six days as if that would make a difference?" Jamie smiled.

"Nothing better to do. Besides, if I went wandering about without your protection someone might remember a past offense, or I might be tempted to try something stupid again, so I figured, Jamie boy, it was best just to hang about here and wait."

"Anything happen?" Allen asked wearily, hoisting his saddlebag that Jamie then insisted upon taking. He regretted abandoning that horse, but Elizabeth had given him another, the last poor bony crea-ture in the family stable along with one of her father's old suits, which loosely fitted his slender frame. There was even a cover letter that was in the saddlebag, conveying sympathy for a departed relative in Newark, and two pounds sterling as a gesture to help the family—or if need be as a bribe. She actually had something of a forger's hand and had created a reasonable pass in case he was stopped by militia. The ruse had worked several times.

Elizabeth. Throughout the long ride back he could not stop think-ing of her, of what had transpired in the hours after he awoke to find her sleeping by his side, and then her willingness to help him escape. She had told him about her encounter with Peter, and he could see that it visibly upset her, perhaps even tore at her sense of loyalty. Was it to the Loyalist cause or just him? he now wondered. That did give him pause as he questioned her several times about that encounter, in which Peter had held the balance.

That was the other question that had troubled him on the ride back to New York on a half-dead horse. Did Peter let me go out of some old sense of friendship, or did he deliberately want me to go now with the report of what was transpiring? Perhaps was it both? Or perhaps it was even out of love for Elizabeth that he sensed from the way she spoke of him with a certain sadness, and that must have torn him as well. That thought was secondary to Elizabeth, who he knew would haunt his waking moments and his dreams henceforth. The ferryman said he would see to the horse for a week, but sell it if Elizabeth's father failed to find a way to get it through the lines over to New York, and send the money to her. The man was a good Loyalist and just might see to it, but in the middle of this chaos of war, he would not hold his breath.

"Did you get my report to headquarters?" he asked Jamie as they turned the corner down Mulberry Street to his lodgings.

"Yes, sir, I did deliver your report as you ordered to Clinton's headquarters."

"To Colonel Smith?"

Jamie shook his head.

"They didn't let me past the front door and some sergeant took it. Sorry, sir, I tried but that is far as I ever got."

"Damn it to hell."

"I'm sorry, I tried, sir."

He took it in and gave the boy a reassuring pat. Exhausted, he all but staggered up to his room, calling for the innkeeper, who had just awakened to find him something to eat. Jamie had to help him change into his regular uniform, a blessed reassurance after the adventures of the last couple of weeks. It almost felt like a noose had been removed from his neck, now that all he needed to fear was a musket ball in the stomach, or a bayonet or sword. After what they had done to John, he had come to fear that death more than any other, though it appeared that John had felt no pain, but he would never forget how the man's face turned purple in death, tongue lolling out, eyes bulging. Not a soldier's death, damn them.

Bolting down a slice of warmed ham and two boiled goose eggs he suddenly realized he had lost his horse in Philadelphia days ago. Technically the army would provide him with a new mount, but that would take days to accomplish with all the usual paperwork and exasperating sighing of a bloated quartermaster about the cost of the king's property, as if it were his own personal possession. So leaving Jamie behind—the lad definitely would not help with any impression at headquarters—he went over to where a company of dragoons was housed and stabled, talked it over with their captain whom he had wisely provided with drinks on occasion, and finally had a mount for half a day. Wearily, he made the journey up the Broad Way, to Clinton's headquarters in the middle of the island. The morning seemed no different than any other now, some officers heading out with their "ladies" for some escapades in the forested hills of Harlem Heights, the usual drunk soldiers coming back late for morning parade. It was, he knew, a foreshadowing.

GENERAL CLINTON, WITH COLONEL SMITH SITTING IN HIS chair, as if the two had not moved an inch since last he saw them, looked down at his hastily written report and silently passed it over to Smith who examined it more carefully.

"So you have had quite the adventure, young sir. Upon my word, ten days behind the Rebel lines, no less. I shall see to it that when this is all over, you shall be mentioned in a dispatch."

Allen merely nodded his thanks, saying nothing.

There was a long uncomfortable silence until Colonel Smith, with an audible sigh, set down Allen's brief report. "Now let me understand this," Smith asked, while Clinton just sat back in his chair, holding Allen with his gaze. "You actually witnessed this parade, counted the troops, including all the French regiments that you have noted down, then just calmly turned about and came straight back here with this report?"

"Well, sir, I did have a bit of a problem with one of their officers for intelligence that delayed me until early the next morning."

"That was not in your report," Clinton said. "Why not?"

"I did not think it pertinent to the matter at hand, sir."

"So what did happen?" Smith asked.

"I was recognized by one of their militia shortly after the parade had passed and was briefly pursued. Apparently there was a bit of hue and cry so I hid until three in the morning after the moon was concealed by clouds, feeling it was safe then to slip past their pickets, return, and cross at Bordentown to avoid Trenton, where I would be recognized, and then straight back to here. It only delayed me a few hours."

"How and where did you hide?"

He had learned his craft well across the years, but he fumbled slightly with his story of hiding in a barn and taking the horse.

Smith gazed at him without comment.

"Sir, to be truthful, let us just say that the honor of a lady, loyal to our cause, is involved and thus I hesitate to speak further upon that subject."

"So you hid in the home of a beautiful young lady that you met while stationed in Philadelphia?" Smith asked and there was the flicker of a smile.

"Something like that, sir."

"A good Loyalist?"

"I found out later that a Continental officer had in fact come to the house to question her but she kept the secret that I was concealed on her property."

Clinton actually chuckled slightly.

"Her bedchamber perhaps?"

He tried not to let his flash of anger show. It was never wise for a colonel to show that kind of emotion to the commander of all forces in North America. It could mean a very quick posting, indeed, to some damn fever-ridden island.

"Relax, sir," Smith interjected, chuckling. "I pray the interlude was a pleasant one, a reward richly deserved, before you returned to your duty."

"My duty did come first," he replied icily.

"Of course, as it does with all of us," Clinton said, and again it was wise to say nothing. The number of Clinton's mistresses, one of them a married woman with her husband living in the city, was no secret to either side in this war.

"May I surmise that this Continental officer was an old acquaintance of yours, Colonel Wellsley."

"That is correct, sir."

Smith looked over at Clinton and placed the paper back before Clinton.

"My compliments, sir, on your report. We do not question it in the slightest," Smith continued.

Clinton glanced back down at the paper.

"Thank God we've already dispatched Admiral Graves. Combined with Hood, he should be able to contain those damn French."

"Graves has left, sir?" Allen asked.

"You didn't notice?"

"I crossed the river while it was still dark, changed, and came straight here. I must confess I did not stop to look down the bay."

"They weighed anchor four days ago, to link up with Hood at the mouth of the Chesapeake."

Allen nodded with approval at this news.

"The French fleet based in Rhode Island is gone as well," Smith now replied. "They departed four days ago as well."

So much had transpired in the ten days he had been wandering about New Jersey and into Pennsylvania.

He did the calculations and realized that all depended now on whether the British fleets were the first to unite and turn on one of the French fleets, or whether it would be the French who united first. All of that was dependent entirely on the vagaries of war at sea, on wind and tides, on clean copper bottoms or weed choked ones, and on the nerve of admirals being willing to venture their fleets in a line encounter. There was a time when he had held the British fleet in awe. He had grown up on the stories of their great triumphs. During three years here in New York, however, he had seen that Graves was all but afraid of his own shadow, unwilling to act unless given clear written instructions. Perhaps the greatest mistake of their fleet across this century was the dishonoring and execution of Admiral Byng. In the opening days of the Seven Years War (what he and his boyhood friends knew as the French and Indian War) Byng had failed to follow up on a partial victory and turn it into a decisive defeat of the

French, and suffered death by firing squad for a sin that was not his fault.

That had thrown ice water on the initiative of most every admiral since. They now insisted upon clearly written directions, right down to detailed orders of under what conditions they would be permitted to actually engage an enemy. All of the famed aggressiveness of the Royal navy seemed to have drained away. To earlier and, he prayed, to later generations of British admirals, the presence of Barre's fleet, so close by to New York, would have been a call for aggression, offensive, venturing all. While Graves had just safely followed his orders to protect New York harbor and their line of communications back to Halifax and England. Gone were the days when an admiral with a stomach to risk all would load his ship full of marines from every other vessel in his fleet, wait for a moonless night, load them into rowboats, and storm straight into the enemy anchorage to either "sink, burn, or make a prize of war," of the entire lot.

Wars were not won by defensive actions.

As he looked at Clinton now, he wanted to cry out. If ever there was an opportunity to catch Washington out in the open and not locked up in his fortress of West Point, it had been these last ten days, his army strung out along fifty miles of road. A sortie in force would have cut that army in two like a sharp knife slicing through a thread stretched taut. They might not have been able to defeat them as they once so easily could, but they surely could have battered him, stalled him, perhaps even turned him back. Instead, officers were off with mistresses to Harlem Heights, drunk soldiers wandered back late for parade, shrugging off the dozen lashes lightly applied. The entire city seemed locked in timelessness, as if the war no longer seemed to have any real beginning or end, that it would just be like this forever.

He had clearly seen that Washington could not wait forever. He was bent on a mission, in his heart, without doubt, the same watchword driving him forward as it had at Trenton: Victory or Death.

"When do you estimate they will reach Yorktown?" Smith asked, breaking the silence.

"Sir, they should be at Head of Elk on the Chesapeake within a day, two at most. From what I could hear, sir, but this was more gossip than seeing actual reports, and thus is not in my report. There are not enough boats to move the men from there."

"How many, though?" and now it was Clinton who asked.

"Maybe enough for a third of the infantry. Of course, artillery and heavy supplies will receive priority for the boats they have. The rest will continue on foot. If the weather holds, and I have heard the main road down through Virginia is well maintained, or at least it was before the war, the bulk of the army will most likely arrive by around September 20, if they hold to a pace of fifteen to twenty miles a day."

"It should all be over by then anyhow," Clinton said, looking over at Smith. "Graves links with Hood, together they smash those braggadocio French and what they call a navy. Communications are resumed with Cornwallis, who can easily hold there through the winter if need be, and then we decide whether to move and reinforce, or just pull Cornwallis back to here for the winter. Then we just leave Washington stranded in his precious home colony with an army that will melt away in disgust after having dragged themselves five hundred miles for nothing."

It was the most he had ever heard Clinton say about his plans so openly, and even with a touch of animation.

Smith looked back at him and shifted, slightly turning a shoulder to Allen as if he was not supposed to hear.

"Sir," and his voice was low, so that Allen actually did step back several feet in a gesture of politeness, but nevertheless he could still hear every word as he stared off, eyes raised from the two of them, fixed on a painting behind Clinton of a pastoral scene with two lovers with the usual naked cherubs flying about above. He remembered Elizabeth had such a painting in her dining room, and he always thought it highly amusing. How could anyone concentrate upon attempting to make love with naked babies flying over one's head?

That thought triggered yet again the memory of being with Elizabeth. Even as he dwelled on that thought, the two officers, but feet away from him, continued to speak, their voices lowered as if he was not to listen.

"May I point out, sir," Smith whispered, "that your statement has several assumptions of which we have no knowledge yet: that Hood and Graves do unite, that they do meet and defeat the French, if they can engage them before the French first gain the approach into Chesapeake where they will have a vastly superior position against any naval force trying to force its way in from the open seas. We now have certain knowledge, thanks to the bravery of this officer, that at least ten thousand American and French troops are speeding down upon Yorktown as we sit here. When combined with the forces already there under Lafayette, Cornwallis will be vastly outnumbered.

"Proper fortifications are a multiplier of four to one against any frontal attack," Clinton replied haughtily, as if annoyed by Smith's comments.

"That number is cancelled if Cornwallis is cut off, and Washington, following procedures that his army has learned well in the last six years, and backed by the best of French engineers, builds proper siege works and traverses to slowly tighten the noose on Cornwallis."

"Tightening the noose," the mere mention of that shattered his reverie regarding Elizabeth, causing Allen to inwardly flinch, thinking of the sound of his friend's neck snapping.

"I urge you, sir, we must move," Smith said insistently. "You stated before Graves departed that you would not commit our army to Virginia as long as there was doubt as to Washington's intent. It is not likely that this maneuver across New Jersey is an elaborate ruse to strip out our forces here to send to Cornwallis aid and relief and then Washington and his French allies turn back to take this city. Yet with that thought still in mind, we allowed Graves to sail without a single additional regiment of infantry of the line to aid our gallant friend in Virginia or better yet, some heavy artillery of which we have a surplus here, to counter any siege attempts against him."

Allen could sense Clinton bristling. A good adjutant was supposed to have the freedom to offer alternatives, suggestions even to debate a decision already made, but it was always a delicate line and many an adjutant, with a few ill-spoken though correct words, found himself at the end of his career on some damn remote island or back home languishing on half pay.

All knew there was no love lost between Clinton and his second in command, the far more dramatic and aggressive Cornwallis. Allen thought that Smith had made a bad move with how he had worded his argument.

"Sir," Smith continued, and now extended his hand in a gesture of appeal. "This gallant officer standing before us has delivered to us the proof you yourself asked for at our council of war before Graves sailed. Washington and Rochambeau are bound for Yorktown. North of us, at best they have left behind four or five thousand men as skeleton guard to throw us off, and the usual rabble of militia on the Jersey coast. What they have left behind are not their prime troops. Sir, a thousand, fifteen hundred of our men left behind at most, joined by citizens of this city who are loyal, could easily repulse any action they might make. As you yourself just said, good defensive works are a multiplier of four to one. This city could stand against an assault by six thousand or more of their best. I beg you, sir, we have the transports still in the harbor and enough light frigates and sloops to guard them. We could embark tomorrow with the bulk of our troops and all the Hessians if you gave the order now, join with Cornwallis, and end this war once and for all in our favor in front of Yorktown."

Smith sat back, and Allen dared to give him a glance and made eye contact with the colonel. He could sense the man's frustration, that he had just ventured all, and Allen agreed with him fully.

Clinton, finished with his breakfast, leaned back in his chair, taking his mug of tea, from the scent of it liberally dosed with some brandy, and sipped the brew. Then ever so slowly shook his head.

"You say that my reaction is filled with 'ifs' but so is yours, Colonel Smith. I thank you for the candor and your personal sense of duty and courage to offer such advice that you know runs counter to my thinking."

He actually offered a smile of reassurance and reached out to pat Smith on the hand.

"It is one of the reasons I retain you; I need men like you to propose alternatives for me to consider. I shall take it under most serious consideration."

He looked back down at Allen's brief report and then back to Smith.

"I'll dispatch a courier ship today to our good friend Cornwallis," he said, and Allen could hear the touch of disdain in his voice, "to inform him that we have confirmed information that the combined arms of the French and the Americans, to the total of at least ten thousand, are now marching upon him. We shall advise him to prepare proper works to withstand a siege, which, of course, a man of his experience must already be doing.

"Still, as to moving this garrison south to Virginia based upon this?" and he pointed to Allen's report as he shook his head.

"Yes, I do believe that Washington, in his foolishness, is now embarked upon this venture, but it is just that, a foolish and desperate folly. Backed up by our navy Cornwallis could withstand four times their number, and let the rabble and their lily white–clad allies bleed themselves out. I will not risk all that we hold here in the north of this damn land to defeat an army on the edge of collapse anyhow, somewhere down in the fever swamps of Virginia. Good God, we could lose ten times as many men to the ague or yellow fever, which is still present there until the first heavy frost, as we could to any poorly aimed shot of one of their rabble."

He slapped the table lightly with an open palm.

"No, my garrison here in this city is the one rock of stability our king holds on this continent and I shall not dare to risk that on assumptions. Besides, we have plenty of time to still decide."

"Based on what, sir, may I beg to ask?" Smith's voice clearly indicated exhausted defeat.

Clinton smiled.

"Let us first consider that our noble friends in the navy have not properly disposed of the French fleet. Can you imagine the slaughter if I embark my men and our Hessians on to the transports you refer to, and somewhere down the Jersey coast we run afoul of Barre and his ships of the line? It would be a slaughter. For that reason alone, I will not risk this garrison. It could be that Cornwallis is in no crisis at all, our fleet already having defeated the French navy, but if I follow your advice and then lose this army at sea and thus lose the war?"

He shook his head like an angry bear.

"No, sir," he snapped, "I will not have history remember me as the army's equivalent of Byng. No, sir."

Smith did not reply.

"Write out a dispatch to Cornwallis this morning. Inform him of our latest intelligence and tell him to expect the arrival of Washington and Rochambeau with ten thousand men under arms in a fortnight. My orders are to properly coordinate holding his position at Yorktown, with the navy of course responsible for securing his lines of communications and supply. If the situation warrants that he personally feels he cannot hold, he must then clearly inform me of his distress or fear of failure, and then, and only then, with proper discretion, will I transfer men of this command to reinforce him. When he personally and specifically declares in writing that he has boxed himself into a situation that requires me to intervene on his behalf, then I will do so."

He looked up at Allen.

"You, Colonel, please rewrite your report clearly, with proper hand, on decent paper as you were trained to do. That report will be included in the dispatch sent to Cornwallis."

Neither Smith or Allen spoke for a moment, though the glances exchanged between them spoke volumes. The general was covering himself, and putting onto Cornwallis the onus of asking for support to rescue him. If those reinforcements were then ambushed at sea and lost, and with it New York, it would be Cornwallis who must face the king and a possible court-martial, and not Clinton. If then reinforced, finally, and victory achieved, it would be Clinton who had come as the savior to pull Cornwallis's chestnuts out of the fire, as the Americans say, and the glory to Clinton as well.

Allen stiffened.

"A request, sir."

"And that is?"

"Let me go with the dispatch ship and report directly to General Cornwallis all that I observed. I think a firsthand report to him from someone who actually observed and followed the enemy forces would be of far more value than a mere written report."

Clinton took that in, and just continued to gaze at him.

"Why do you volunteer like this?"

He, of course, did not say what he felt in his heart. That he was sick to death of all of this, of three years here in New York, of the way his friend John had died in a miserable effort of stealth to snatch West Point, that a bold force led by a bold leader could have achieved in a damn good proper stand-up fight. He was sick of all of it, and if there was to be action that decided this war he wished to be there where his services would be of greater value.

None of this he said.

"Sir. I think my duties in New Jersey are no longer necessary. It is held by a few militia and nothing more. The main army will be in Virginia and perhaps my experience can be of service to General Cornwallis given the knowledge I have of them."

Clinton actually forced a smile.

"Not jumping ship are we?"

"No, sir, of course not; the thought never has crossed my mind." His years of work had taught him to at least be a halfway decent liar some of the time.

"Go then."

He formally saluted, catching the eye of Colonel Smith, and thought he caught the flicker of a smile.

"I'll arrange a courier ship to depart with the tide this afternoon," Smith said. "Remain here for now and once I've finished the dispatches you can carry them. God go with you, Colonel van Dorn."

Withdrawing, Allen was glad to be out of that room, already sti-fling with the rising morning heat. To get out of here would be a damn blessing, he thought as he walked down the steps of the man-sion, out onto the lawn. Looking about he thought to hell with deco-rum and a proper display at all times of a proper officer in service to the king. He picked out the shade of a willow tree not unlike the one in the painting of the two lovers. He knew it'd take several hours for all the dispatches and orders to be written out and properly stamped and sealed.

To hell with propriety, he thought as he leaned back against the tree. The view across the East River could almost be considered romantic, except for the fact that down the river, within view, were where the accursed prison hulks sat. Fortunately the wind was not coming from their direction and carrying with it the fetid stench of that hell.

He took off his hat, wiped his sweating brow with the sleeve of his heavy wool uniform, leaned back, closed his eyes, and thought of Elizabeth—what it would be like to have her by his side now, as she was but a few days ago—and he drifted into an exhausted sleep.

ON THE ROAD BETWEEN HEAD OF ELK, MARYLAND, AND CHESTER, PENNSYLVANIA
SEPTEMBER 5, 1781

He still felt guilt over what he had done. Perhaps it was the perverted hunger in the eyes of the Philadelphia militiaman, never obvious in a real battle, but the sick kind of man who took delight in watching another man die, the type that enjoyed a "good hanging."

Did he spare him out of a friendship he could not fully break? Was it pity for the fear in Elizabeth's eyes, a cousin he had loved at a distance since still a lad and the war had yet to come? Was it disgust with the all but drooling militia man eager to see a killing, or as he tried to assuage his guilt now, a sense of what General Washington had implied the night before at a council of war that he had attended? The army had cleared New Jersey without incident, and it no longer mattered what Clinton knew, if anything, in New York. He kept trying to tell himself that had been the reason. It would have taken Allen a day and a half, more likely two or even three days, to get back to New York, if he could successfully dodge the patrols. By then they would be on the march again, approaching the northern shore of the Chesapeake. Let Clinton then wander into New Jersey after them; they had a two-week lead. The deeper Clinton ventured into Jersey the more he would be dogged by militia cutting up his supply lines. Let them. If Clinton turned north to try to take West Point, that was a risk he was willing to take. If he now tried to reach Cornwallis and the French fleet failed to appear, or worse yet, were destroyed, then all was moot anyhow. So let them know.

Perhaps, he reasoned yet again, that is why he did not go up that flight of stairs. The general was all but saying they were clear of the deadly threat of marching directly past Clinton in New York. They had not stirred and now nothing could stop this army from linking up with Greene and Lafayette in Virginia.

"Rider coming."

Peter stirred from his depressed musing and looked up. The day, like nearly every day of this march, was one of oppressive heat and dust. The column of the American troops was stringing out, standard march discipline having broken down from the heat and exhaustion. Men shuffled along at their own pace, step after step, a thousand paces to the mile, five hundred miles, one million paces. Those broken down from the heat and illness lined the road, especially around bottomland muddy creeks, where they could find cool air and a soak to cool off, before donning gear and falling back into the ranks.

Thanks to the miracle of Robert Morris, the talk of refusing to advance farther had been stilled. Though when the men had formed up to be paid, and only received on average a month and a half's worth in hard cash, it had been enough to still the voices of some who had been whispering about marching back on Philadelphia and looting the "rich bastards" clean and then go home. Of the men remaining in the ranks, everyone was there because he was there to make the march, and unless dropped by exhaustion, would press on. Washington had given orders for provost guards to go lightly, to issue passes freely if need be, and more than one provost had surrendered his saddle, often with two exhausted men mounted, while the provost held the bridle and led his mount. He had seen many a good officer, doing the same, surrendering the symbol and privilege of rank to an exhausted young private. That was now another thing about this army of Revolution. The haughty officers, the ones so full of themselves with their rank and privileges, men like Gates and Charles Lee, had long ago been driven from this army. Those that remained were men who knew how to lead and inspire. Sergeants, which was too often the rank of bullies in other armies and had been in this one at the start, were now mostly older men, often of fatherly demeanor, who shouldered a staggering private's musket and pack to encourage him to try for just for a few more miles and stay in the ranks.

The rider could be seen, coming up the middle of the road at a full gallop, standing in his stirrups, riding like a madman, waving his hat high. Peter, the only other mounted man visible, drew to one side of the road, and at the sight of him the rider began to rein in, but did not come to a full stop.

"General Washington?" he cried.

"I think about three miles or so behind me," Peter replied, turning his mount around and falling in beside the wide-eyed courier.

"Take me to him!" he shouted and spurred his lathered mount back up to a gallop.

Something was up, and Peter felt he at least had the excuse to ride by his side, having been asked to guide, and, of course, curiosity filled him. He did feel a tremor of fear. Perhaps the man carried word of disaster, that Cornwallis had broken out, defeated Lafayette, and was even turning back toward the Carolinas. Thus tauntingly offering a long, stern chase, with the advantage on his side that he could loot supplies as he retired, and leave broken bridges, poisoned wells, and burned houses and barns in his wake. That, or maybe the French fleet had abandoned their effort, or worse had been destroyed by storm or battle.

"What is it?' Peter cried, coming up by the man's side, his mount still relatively fresh.

"Orders for the general only!" the rider shouted, leaning forward, spurring the sides of his poor mount so that the horse was bleeding.

Turning a bend in the road, Peter saw Washington was not directly on the road, having moved into an orchard for a noonday break. The rider would have gone past him without noticing, so wild was he to press forward. Peter shouted, pointed, and the rider turned his mount, still at the gallop, as if to try to jump the fence, but wisely chose instead to angle along the side of the split-rail fence to an opening and then dashed through, Peter just behind him.

Still fifty yards off, he again stood tall in his stirrups, the troops who had been shuffling along the road to either side stopping, looking, some turning back to find out what was afoot.

"It's the French!" the rider shouted. "The French navy!"

The long night of planning out the day's march, of sending foragers ahead to try to bring in supplies to set by the side of the road for the passing regiments, to bring in fresh beef that he had promised to Rochambeau and his men, had left Washington exhausted. He had felt fine starting out in the morning, but though he was a Virginian, the heat of midday had begun to tell and he had accepted Alexander Hamilton's insistence that "the general" at least rest for a half hour or so before pressing on. The orchard looked inviting, it reminded him of home, and the rich scent of ripening apples was soothing as he stretched out under one of the trees for a short nap. The horses were let loose to crop on the grass and the first of the fallen fruit.

"Rider coming in," Hamilton had announced at the man's approach, followed by young Wellsley, tasked this day with staying close to the head of the march and through his New Jersey past, to help with negotiating with neighboring farms to part with precious supplies for the army staggering by.

He stood up, his staff coming to their feet around him.

"It's the French!" He heard the cry and his heart froze at that instant.

Disaster, he thought. De Grasse was not coming or had been destroyed. Word had come in yesterday that the English fleet in New York had sallied forth. With a good following breeze they might already be drawing close to the mouth of the Chesapeake, but it was far too early for any news of that coming up from the south of Virginia. If Hood had decided to face de Grasse alone, though, with the vagaries of action at sea, who could tell the outcome? He felt his stomach knot up. If the French had been defeated or decided to retreat, here he had an army halfway between two points. To turn them about now, to march back through Philadelphia would be an act of utter humiliation, and after the near collapse over lack of pay but a few days past, the city was, indeed, stripped clean of every last shilling to be found. The men knew that, and the thought of now marching them clear back to New York through land stripped clean by their passage was impossible. Press forward? Backed and supplied by the enemy fleet, the siege would drag out forever, the land there stripped of supplies as well, winter would come, and the army would disintegrate, the gamble lost.

He waited and the rider, looking like a man who had just escaped from a madhouse, suddenly appeared to realize the nature of his mission and position. He slowed, reined in breathing hard, Wellsley coming up by his side, a glance to the young colonel showing he knew nothing of what this was about.

The rider, realizing he was now before Washington, came to rigid attention and saluted, swaying a bit in the saddle as if half drunk.

"Reporting, sir, from General Lafayette," he cried and started to fumble with the dispatch case by his side, unable now to open the latch.

"Well, out with it, man," Washington snapped, "just tell me, surely you know."

"It's the French, sir."

"I already heard you."

"Sir, General Lafayette begs to report that the fleet of Admiral de Grasse, twenty-six ships of the line, is at this moment anchored within the mouth of the Chesapeake Bay having blocked all access in or out by the Royal navy and at this moment has successfully sealed the forces of Cornwallis encamped at Yorktown from all resupply or retreat by sea."

Washington stood silent as if struck by a bolt of lightning and was now welded to the earth.

"May I see the dispatch, now," he finally asked, his voice a hoarse whisper.

The rider, hands trembling, fumbled with the latch until Peter just leaned over, grabbed the pouch, tore it open, snapping off the latch, reached in and pulled out the folded sheet of paper, and leaping from his mount, handed it to his general.

Washington broke the seal, opened the note, scanned it, and his eyes clouded with tears.

"It's true," he gasped. "Praise to God in Heaven, it's true!"

As he spoke his words changed from a gasp to a shout.

"It's true, the French fleet led by de Grasse is with us!"

Seconds later wild hysterical cheering erupted from the staff, Hamilton running down to the edge of the fence row, climbing atop it, lifting his hat, troops along the line of march having stopped to see what all the commotion was about.

"Boys, the French are here! Their fleet is blockading Cornwallis and his bastards! They're trapped like rats in a barrel and waiting for us to finish it! Three cheers for France and to hell with Cornwallis!"

The word instantly leaped down the road, sweeping through company after company.

Unable to contain himself, Washington shouted for Billy Lee to mount up and bring his horse and saddle up.

"Where is General Rochambeau?" he cried. No one was really sure other than that he and some of his command were last seen on a barge just north of Chester, moving down the Delaware River to dis-embark on the far side of the town to start the short trek across Delaware state to the headwaters of the Chesapeake.

Washington set off at a gallop.

Across six years, no one had ever seen their stoic, phlegmatic general like this. The sight of it actually frightened some. Perhaps after the stress of all these years, some overwhelming news of disaster had at last broken him. He galloped full out, barely slowing to weave around a laboring team of horses dragging a heavy twelve-pounder, hat gone, but as he passed his cry, his thunderous voice echoed the word.

"The French are with us, lads. Their fleet has arrived! The French fleet is with us!"

Knox, leading his column, watched thunderstruck as Washington charged past him, not even slowing to offer a customary salute, and in fact not even recognizing his portly commander of artillery. The cry reached Knox, who turned his poor overburdened mount gasping as he spurred it to fall in with the wild, hysterical with joy officers charging back up the road.

"The French are with us, lads!"

More than a few of the heat-exhausted infantry, misunderstanding at first, grumbled and cursed that yes the damn French are with us. With money in their pockets and in their gaudy white uniforms they had certainly been with them in Philadelphia, their Gallic charm winning over more than one lass during their stop there. Finally the word trailing behind their general, who seemed driven to some insanity, arrived, cheers echoing behind Washington, and seconds later any cursing of the French changed to shouts of joy.

He reached the outskirts of the south side of Chester, the docks lining the river with barges offloading a regiment of French infantry.

"Rochambeau!" It was Washington shouting over and over. White-clad troops stared at him at first with disbelief at his strange behavior, then pointed up the river where a heavy barge approached bearing the general and his staff, turning in from the flow of the river and approaching the dock.

"Something is wrong," and General Jean Baptiste Rochambeau stirred from his musings, his inward cursing of the blasted heat of this country, the swarms of mosquitoes that were an endless torment even out in the middle of this river that smelled almost as bad as the Seine in the middle of Paris. One of his staff was pointing to the dock and the sight that greeted him was, for a moment, actually amusing.

A tall man, an American officer, hatless, wig gone, was actually dancing a mad, insane jig, reminding him of the way a trained bear would dance at a circus. He capered about, waving his arms, jumping up and down. Other American officers were now galloping up, leaping from their mounts, and joining in this strange mummery. The only thing missing was some jugglers and a fiddler or two to provide music for their show. For an instant he wondered if some drunken soldiers had decided to entertain his arrival, and then with a shock he recognized the man.

It was his Excellency General George Washington leading the bizarre display.

"My God," someone whispered, in shocked disbelief, "the poor man, the strain of it all. It has driven him mad. Now what do we do?"

"Quickly," Rochambeau cried, "get us ashore!" and the crew of the barge waited till the very last second to drop sail, coming in so swiftly that Rochambeau was knocked off his feet as the barge slammed into the dock, anxious staff tumbling about, while trying to prevent their general from falling head over heels into the muddy slime of the river bank in a most undignified manner.

Soldiers of one of his regiments on the dock, recognizing the potential embarrassment of their beloved leader, leaped into the water, chest deep, to brace the barge. Eager hands reached out to all but lift him on to the shaky wharf. Clear through the press, to the giant of a man who was the leader of the Revolution, shouldering his way, still waving his arms, shouting with such animation all Rochambeau could grasp was, "You did it, France did it!"

"Did what? Rochambeau shouted.

"My God, you haven't heard."

"What good, sir? What?"

"You did it. God bless France and may our friendship last a thousand years. De Grasse is in Chesapeake Bay! Even now Cornwallis is blockaded and under siege. De Grasse has come!"

Washington, still wild with absolute total abandoned joy after so many anguished years of suffering, turned to look at the men of Rochambeau's command, who stood gazing at him wide-eyed, not understanding a word tumbling out of him.

He took a deep breath, as if struggling for composure and a return to his normally grave and formal manner, then simply shouted with his thunderous voice, "Vive de Grasse, Vive la France, Vive Louis!"

With the first words all understood the reason for his mad excitement and the cry was picked up with a thunderous cheer so loud that civilians in the village were now pouring out into the streets and toward the commotion.

Then Washington turned back to Rochambeau. For a brief moment, he regained his normal sense of decorum and gravitas, and offered the most formal of gestures, bowing to his comrade.

"Joy to you, sir, to all of us. I bring word that the noble Admiral de Grasse has arrived true to his promise."

It was the first, and perhaps the only time they had ever witnessed such a display, tears streaming down the face of George Washington. The George Washington who had led the numbed retreat from New York five years ago but refused to admit defeat. He who had led the freezing night march on Trenton more than half convinced he was leading his ragged band to a death like Leonidas's at Thermopylae but, at least, willing to die fighting, who had endured so much for six years, now, at last, all restraint broke away in this moment of joy.

Before Rochambeau could take all this in, it was Washington who stepped forward, arms extended wide, and swept the French general into a bear hug embrace.

"May this day be remembered between our two nations for a

thousand years to come and may the gratitude of my nation be eternal to our friends in France. If we are blessed by God to win this war, it is you who stood by our side, and it must never be forgotten."

Rochambeau was awed to realize that the general was actually in tears and the sight of such emotion stirred his heart to tears as well, as the two embraced with joy and laughter. Around them, by the hundreds, soldiers of France, soldiers and civilians of America, cheered and embraced with joy. A cry soon was picked up and repeated over and over.

"On to Yorktown!"

Part Three

THE BATTLE OF YORKTOWN

SEPTEMBER–OCTOBER 1781

Thirteen

THE ROOM ABSOLUTELY REFUSED TO STOP SWAYING BACK and forth. A cold sweat was beading Allen's brow, and he feared he might just suffer the ultimate humiliation of vomiting in front of the British commander.

General Cornwallis looked up at him, and there was a bit of an indulgent smile.

"Ah, Colonel van Dorn, are you feeling unwell?"

Several of Cornwallis's staff chuckled and he wondered if he did, indeed, look that sick.

"Sorry, sir, it is just that I have not yet regained my land legs."

"We understand, sir," Cornwallis replied, "I have suffered from the mal de mer many times. If the need overcomes you, please excuse yourself—no need to ask permission."

Allen swallowed hard and whispered a thanks.

He had known Cornwallis from a distance when the general was still stationed in the northern theater of the war. More than a few believed that when Howe was recalled, it should have been Cornwallis that took over, but he had unwisely insisted upon a leave to return to England to winter there with his wife and thus had not been on the spot to take command. To the disappointment of many including Allen, Clinton was then slotted in instead.

All knew that he and Clinton had little love or respect for each other, perhaps one reason Clinton so readily agreed to a division of the dwindling forces in North America. When Cornwallis proposed to take the war into the Carolinas, since it was so obviously stalemated in the North and Clinton was not seeking active battle, his superior readily accepted. Many saw that even though Clinton gave up nearly half his troops to Cornwallis, he was glad to be rid of him and see him sail away to Charleston.

Though his independent command in the Southern theater had ultimately proven a failure and had led now to this dire position, at least Cornwallis had always displayed far more aggressiveness than Clinton, which Allen admired. During the campaign of 1776, he had performed a feat every bit as daring as Wolfe at Quebec, by crossing the Hudson at night and personally leading an assault force of light infantry up the towering cliffs of the Palisades, literally under the gaze of the American garrison of more than five thousand holding Fort Lee. If discovered at any point as they went up the near-vertical cliffs in the middle of the night, a detachment of drummer boys or drunk militiamen could have slaughtered all of them merely by dropping rocks over the side. Yet gaining the heights undetected, he had then patiently waited while cables were dropped back down to the bottom of the cliffs so that sufficient artillery could be hauled up, reassembled, and prepared, to present to the Americans at dawn a force ready to assault them from behind.

It had triggered a mad panic, an absolute rout, the entire American army breaking and fleeing westward, abandoning nearly all their equipment and supplies. Cornwallis had pursued them relentlessly

and if given his own head, he would have pushed across the Delaware and finished what was left of Washington's broken ranks. The
thought of that, even as it flashed through Allen's mind, triggered a
mix of emotions because, after all, his youngest brother had been
with that fleeing force, had stayed loyal to their cause, and had died
doing so. Howe had reined Cornwallis back in, ordering the army to
go into winter quarters, and then split up into a score of small detachments across central Jersey. One of those garrisons was the Hessian
force that occupied Trenton, and to which Allen was first attached as a
Loyalist volunteer, to act as guide, scout, and translator.

Cornwallis could have ended the war that winter, or at least radi-
cally altered its course, and Allen could imagine the frustration of
that must have nagged his dreams of lost recognition and glory ever
since. His feat, if performed against French or Spanish forces, would
have won him a peerage at the very least, but against "rabble"? Never
would his name be linked with the likes of Wolfe or Marlborough.

Allen, of course, knew the contents of the dispatch entrusted to
him. Colonel Smith had obviously been less than pleased with writing it out, explained it to him that if necessity at sea demanded that it
be thrown overboard, he must try to somehow escape to bear the
message through enemy lines.

Then he had endured days of pure hell as the light and supposedly swift courier sloop encountered contrary seas, a day-long chase
in the opposite direction from a French frigate, which had nearly run
them down except for the cover of darkness, then a day of what the
sailors laughed off as being becalmed, but for him had been worse
than any torture as the ship lurched and rolled without any wind to
press them forward.

They had finally encountered a badly damaged brig, limping north,
and bearing with it the ill news that the French fleet had, indeed, arrived off of the mouth of the Chesapeake. Also that Hood and de
Grasse had met in what at its absolute best could be called an incon-
clusive action off the cape. With de Grasse luring Hood into slowly

following him to the southeast, the action allowed Barre to slip in with his ships along with additional supplies, the entire train of heavy siege guns, and several thousand more French troops.

It was all a complete muddle, climaxed with Hood declaring that he and Graves thought it best to retire back to New York, to refit and resupply after the action before venturing another throw. Of course, it was a decision that meant he would not lose any ships, had followed what could be argued as the proper course of a prudent admiral, and would not, perhaps, face a firing squad as he might have if he had decided to boldly press in and attack, regardless of loss, in order to break through to Cornwallis.

No officer of the fleet would dare to voice a word of complaint or protest in front of a mere officer of infantry, especially one who was not even an Englishman but an actual colonist as well. He could sense the mood aboard the ship as they finally approached the entry to the Chesapeake, especially when in such close quarters aboard a sloop he could hear every mutter and curse of the common sailors as they went about their duties. The commander of the ship was, however, of stouter heart than his superiors aboard the retreating ships of the line. Familiar with the waters of the bay, he had ventured to run the French blockade at night, dodging past their patrols, slipping through the cordon of towering ships of the line, and gained the harbor of Yorktown before dawn, a masterful show of seamanship, aided by a strong nor'easterly blow. It made the waters of the bay as sickening to Allen as the open sea for one final bout of what Cornwallis called the mal de mer, made nearly as agonizing now because he was on solid land, but his stomach told him the land was pitching back and forth.

He was trapped in that terrible agony of starvation after days of being unable to keep anything down for more than a few minutes, yet the mere thought, even the scent, of food cooking caused his stomach to churn in rebellion.

Cornwallis had already read the dispatch in silence and handed it back to his adjutant, the dismay of the man obvious as was that of the other officers the general had called in to hear the news from New York.

He motioned for Allen to sit down at the table next to him.

"I see in the dispatches a note that you are to report to me as well your own observations. That apparently you boldly ventured behind enemy lines for more than a week scouting their ranks and strength. I also seem to recall that you served with the lamented Major Andre."

"I did, sir."

Cornwallis shook his head sadly.

"A brave man, perhaps too brave with that venture. You do know that Benedict Arnold campaigned here this spring, but is now back in New York."

Allen said nothing.

"I must say his actions made the situation here more than unpleasant. The pillaging and looting that he said were now the only way to bring the Rebels to their knees, only served to arouse their wrath and turn out yet more militia."

Allen made no comment about the reports coming back from the Carolinas that the same atrocities had been committed by Cornwallis's troops as well, a war that was now truly devolving into ever-increasing barbarity.

"I find a mild chicken broth can help settle you down a bit," Cornwallis said kindly, "please, sir, attempt it."

Allen weakly smiled and nodded his thanks.

"At least, I think we do have a chicken about or in the pot someplace around here," he added.

A moment later a bowl was placed before him. Allen took a few sips while Cornwallis and his staff talked among themselves in the far corner of the room. Allen could overhear more than one foul oath, though the general did order the men to fall silent.

Allen ventured a few more sips and found it did help, slightly. Cornwallis finally dismissed the rest of his staff, obviously angry over the dispatch that Allen had just presented.

"I understand you have a somewhat more private report to present to me."

"Just some general observations, sir."

"Let me ask, why did you feel it necessary to come with the courier ship? You could have written your report down and stayed out of this," he hesitated as if carefully choosing his words, "this situation."

"I felt what I saw myself, conveyed to you personally would be of better service."

Cornwallis nodded.

"If anything of dear Major Andre rubbed off on you, it was that you sought action, and I dare say the inaction up in New York must have been tedious."

"I think it important to share with you what I saw and learned while trailing their army," Allen replied, not taking the bait.

"Go ahead please. Is your stomach settling?"

Allen wished he had not reminded him. It had not, but he pressed into his report. Describing what was the obvious subterfuge, well thought out, of moving troops and boats toward Staten Island, which was obviously a sham, even to the touch of a bakery in Chatham, implying a major shift to that area and really not necessary to support an army rapidly moving through the area a dozen miles farther west.

"Those Rebel troops moved by boat down the bay have already disembarked, the boats returning back to pick up more along the line of march," Cornwallis offered. "My reports indicate that nearly all of them, and from what you said it is at least ten thousand or more, are even now, this very day, filing into place but several miles from here, thus sealing me off."

He looked again at the dispatches Allen had delivered and then out the window. All was silent, it was hard to believe that over twenty-five thousand men of opposing forces were digging in, even as they sat here, preparing for an all-out confrontation, while but a few miles to the south a French fleet with over twenty-five thousand more men had gained what an army would call the high ground within the bay, and even now were off-loading hundreds of tons of rations, entrenching and siege equipment, and the deadly heavy artillery that would have been impossible to drag over the back roads of Jersey, let along the three hundred or more miles beyond to this place. "I think the American phrase is that our good friend General Clinton has left us like a pickle in a barrel."

He didn't correct him that it was fish in a barrel but the analogy was appropriate.

"Let us enter a confidence you and I," Cornwallis said, and standing, he went to a sideboard, opened it up, started to pull out a bottle of French brandy but then looking back at the green-faced colonel, he reconsidered and drew out a half empty bottle of burgundy and without comment poured two glasses, pushing one over in front of Allen.

"I have found that a dry burgundy is a tonic that can settle even the most upset of stomachs, try it please."

Allen took a sip and then another, and it did seem to work for the moment.

"I see your color returning already," Cornwallis announced with a smile, "now as I was saying, sir, shall we have an exchange of confidences."

"Thank you for your consideration, sir."

"Then please a reply. I must insist before allowing you to take a much deserved rest. First off, is General Clinton aware of the dire straits we are now in? If he had given me freedom of action earlier this summer, do you honestly think I would have sat in this rat hole? I was assured the full support of His Majesty's Royal navy, that if need be I could embark and be done with this damned Virginia, and leave it to the continued ravages of Benedict Arnold and company. Instead Arnold has pulled back to New York, I am left here and promised full support, but bounded by orders to remain here with these blandishments of reassurance. If I had even suspected that this would be the situation, I would have turned back into the Carolinas. At least there, I still had a secure base at Charleston and would have raised hell along the way, Greene or no General Greene in my path."

That was a lot for Allen to digest, and he sipped at the wine, even feeling a touch of pleasure as the drink radiated through him and did, indeed, settle his stomach a bit.

"Sir, to your first query I have no answer. The courier ship departed New York harbor even while the confrontation between Hood and de Grasse raged. I would like to think that if General Clinton were aware of that outcome his actions at this moment would be far more forceful."

"Go on."

"Sir, I am not sure there is much more I can answer."

"Is it fair to assume that General Clinton did not bestir himself because he believed the French fleet, in strength, and now reinforced by Admiral Barre's additional ships and supplies, would never arrive here? I did receive a report that sometime in mid-August, Washington knew of this arrangement that prompted his remarkable march to the outskirts of this town. If he knew, then surely Clinton knew it."

"Sir, we both know the vagaries of war at sea. In defense of General Clinton," and now he chose his words as diplomatically as possible, "I believe he assumed that either the French message to Washington was a ruse and that New York might be the real target for a coordinated assault by land and sea, supported by de Grasse, or that surely our own navy would meet and destroy de Grasse long before he arrived in these waters."

"Our navy meeting head on and destroying a fleet of twenty-six ships of the line?" Cornwallis snorted with disdain while draining his glass of burgundy in a single gulp and refilling it. "That is asking for risk, sir, and good God, sir, to actually put a ship of the line at risk?"

It took no reader of minds to sense the frustration and rage of Cornwallis at this moment. He had walked into a trap, but had believed he would be supported by the navy that had fled. If he had but known this fate only two weeks ago, there still would have been plenty of time to brush Lafayette and Greene aside and storm back into the Carolinas. If he had positioned himself at Petersburg instead of here, as the infamous Arnold had urged him to do, but a day's march would have taken him into open countryside with numerous routes to choose from in order to evade his pursuers and gain ground to maneuver, with Washington and Rochambeau left looking like fools in his wake. Instead he was now trapped in a bottleneck with an enemy fleet the stopper in the bottle.

"Will Clinton come to my aid?" Cornwallis asked, refilling his glass.

"Sir, I do not know if I am in position to answer that."

Cornwallis chuckled softly. Turning to one side he took a sheet of blank paper, picked up a quill, inked it, scratched a quick note, then pushed it over to Allen.

"Colonel Allen, I am hereby accepting your service to volunteer to serve on my staff as an adviser, promoting you to rank of full colonel in the regular forces and not just as a Loyalist volunteer, and tasking you in all things pertaining to the gathering of intelligence of enemy forces here in Virginia. I'll include a dispatch later, if it ever gets through, informing General Clinton that I have pressed you into my service, against your will if need be, given the situation of the moment. Once this campaign is completed, you will receive honorable mention in dispatch to our king."

He smiled conspiratorially and drained another glass of burgundy, motioned the bottle to Allen who politely refused.

"Now, sir, an answer without prevarication since you are now officially part of my staff and no longer serving directly under our dear friend General Clinton. Will Clinton venture all, knowing that he has no real enemy to face in New York now that Washington is here. Will he now rally all his forces, British and Hessian, and come to my relief?"

Allen surprised, stunned actually, looked at the sheet of paper and back at Cornwallis.

He drained the rest of his glass and taking the bottle poured a second drink, then took a deep breath. As the old saying went, in for a penny, in for a pound.

"No, sir," he replied forcefully and struggling to hide his bitterness at this mad folly. "Win or lose, this fight is yours and yours alone. Clinton will not come."

"Thank you for your frankness, Colonel, I look forward to our association, and know I can trust you."

He actually smiled now.

"You still do look decidedly under the weather, young sir. You are dismissed. Ask my adjutant to find you appropriate lodgings here at my headquarters. I suspect you will be in need of relief of your poor stomach in a moment or two, and then take the day to rest. You are dismissed."

Less than a minute later Allen was leaning over a fence railing, disgorging the wine that Cornwallis had so adroitly used to loosen his tongue.

Exhausted, he collapsed into the bed he had been assigned and slept the rest of the day away, interrupted only once by another bout of the malaise when he began to dream that he was again aboard the tossing ship at sea.

FLAGSHIP OF THE ROYAL FRENCH
NAVY *VILLE DE PARIS*
SEPTEMBER 18, 1781

The piping of the bosun's whistle truly hurt Washington's ears. High pitched sounds usually did that to him. Maybe it was a throwback in his memory to the minutes just before the disaster with Braddock in the last war. Throughout the morning of that ghastly disastrous day, the British regiments had insisted upon marching in formal order, even though they were following a forest track through the dangerous woods of western Pennsylvania. As an "adviser" to Braddock he had, several times, tried to tactfully suggest that maybe they should stop the damn musical accompaniment of fifes and drums. Instead, throw out a heavier screen of light infantry to probe ahead and break the target-rich column, which even a blind man could hit just by the sound of their marching into a looser formation.

He had never asked, but he wondered if some of the older staff with Rochambeau, now his trusted ally and friend, had been there that day on the Monongahela.

Fifes and drums had been part and parcel of this war, but at times the high squealing did trouble him and he was glad at this instant not to be an officer serving in any navy as the bosun's pipes shrieked and echoed, picked up in salute by the other ships of the line anchored fore and aft of the flagship of de Grasse's fleet.

As he gained the deck, he remembered the coaching of one of his staff, turning first to salute the ribbon-bedecked officer of the watch, saying in French "Permission to come aboard, sir," which was warmly greeted, then turning to remove his tricorner hat and bowing low to salute the flag of France fluttering astern, then finally turning to face Admiral de Grasse for the first time and saluting him as well.

His first impression of this man, upon whom the very outcome of all their efforts had depended, was a most positive one. Nearly as tall as himself, he cut a splendid figure in full formal uniform, though inwardly he did think that it certainly was gaudy compared to English custom, with several sashes of embroidered silk from left shoulder to right hip, an eight-sided star nearly as broad as the palm of his hand adorning his left breast, full wig, properly powdered and curled, and that most strange, curious practice of French nobility of white makeup and beauty mark on the cheek. Any effeminate aspect of that makeup was instantly belied as de Grasse came forward with a quick step, hand extended in traditional greeting that an instant later pulled Washington into a firm and warm embrace, complete to a kiss on both cheeks, though he knew the admiral's rouge had without doubt stained his own cheeks.

At that exact instant, the deck of the flagship leaped as a full salute was fired from both port and starboard batteries to be picked up and repeated by every ship of the fleet. The waters of the Chesapeake were rippling from the blasts of hundreds of guns. He could not help but run a quick calculation in his mind of how much powder per gun had just been expended, with the conclusion a few seconds later that such a display could have kept his entire army supplied for several hours of pitched battle. He remembered a time, as they went into Trenton, when his ragged few thousand, on average, had but five rounds of musket ball per man.

Crying, "Oh, mon Général!" and releasing Washington from his embrace, which left light stains of makeup on both cheeks, de Grasse rushed to salute and then hug Rochambeau in turn, while lower staff officers of the navy and of the American and French armies received similar greetings from de Grasse's staff.

The staff, with repeated bows and compliments, led the way through an ornate double door, which Washington could not help but note was scored by a cannonball shot and several musket or grape shot rounds, into the admiral's comfortable quarters. All was gilded or polished wood, though it was obvious that a score of carpenters must have been hard at work these last few days, repairing the damage from the action of the week before. One cannonball, he judged it to be a twenty-four pounder, was actually lodged firmly in the starboard wall, and it was pointed out to all jokingly as a shot that had missed one of the admiral's stewards' head by mere inches, the poor man wetting himself. There stood the steward, grinning weakly, the object of amusement. Yet Washington made it a point to go over and pat the man on the shoulder, and struggling with his command of French, complimented the man with what he hoped came out that though his britches might have been wet, he, without a doubt, had a stout heart.

His words elicited warm laughter, but in turn de Grasse, not to be outdone, went to his sailor and clasped his hand, saying he was a brave man who stood to his post throughout the fight. There was now a shocked and embarrassed look upon the face of the formally attired steward. Washington knew that if sailors were even remotely like soldiers, by day's end every man on this ship would know that the "bon général américain" had personally complimented the man, had erased his shame, and from there word of it would leap to every ship of the fleet.

The formal dinner that followed was a tedious ritual Washington knew had to be followed before a single word could be exchanged regarding the reason for his formal visit and the news that had turned his elation of but days before to one of deep concern.

Course followed course. If sailors "forward of the mast" had to sustain themselves for months on end with hard bread and salt pork, rare was the admiral that suffered the same. Though on this day the entire ship was filled with celebration. Cases of wine had been slung up from below, two bottles to each mess table and a bottle of brandy, fresh beef, and soft bread for all those forward. Junior officers of the American and French armies were welcomed aboard for the celebration, while their seniors feasted on fresh lamprey and caviar of James River sturgeon, roasted Chesapeake goose, fresh greens, and Indian corn. This was a luxury for men who were often at sea for months at a time, followed by a traditional American apple cobbler drenched with rich cream.

The last of the plates were cleared, Washington grateful that the stern windows had been opened to allow a touch of a breeze to cool the room, stewards setting out bottles of choice wines, brandy, and even some Scotch captured from a ship taken from the British fleet. As always, and especially when there was a potential for rough negotiations ahead, Washington drank sparingly. His friend Rochambeau gazed over at him with a sly look each time the bottle was passed. His fellow French general had finally admitted that more than once he had attempted to put Washington off his guard with brandy before a tough point was to be settled between allies, but never had he fallen for the ruse.

Another round of formal toasts were offered to the king, to President Laurens, to His Majesty's navy, and the gallant American army. Then Washington finished the rounds by standing, bowing to Admiral Barre, who had remained silent throughout the small talk of dinner, and raising his glass, announced, "To our gallant friend and ally, Admiral Barre, who so bravely brought to this distant place the siege guns necessary for the destruction of our foes, while your noble fleet blocks their escape from the trap we have laid. If our foe does attempt to escape, the fox will surely fall into the snare you have so gallantly set in place, and all glory shall be yours."

He chose his words carefully, this time offering it in English while his dear friend of so many years, young General Lafayette, provided the translation. There was a murmur of approval, all raising their glasses, Barre offering just the touch of a smile and bowing from his seat, but saying nothing.

Washington sat back down and knew the toast would now allow him at last to raise the issue that had left him in shock since word of it had first been given to him the day before, upon his arrival by land to where he would place his headquarters near Yorktown.

"I think, my dear friend," de Grasse said, now gazing thoughtfully at Washington, "there is a matter we must discuss."

"Thank you, sir, for raising it," Washington began, Lafayette having risen from his seat, standing between the two of them to translate. Rochambeau, sitting on the other side of the table, would glance at Washington, but otherwise kept his gaze fixed on the admiral. Barre feigned indifference. Washington knew the tension between the two admirals as to exactly who had precedence and command over the other. De Grasse was the most recent to come from France, bearing direct orders from the king, but technically Barre still had seniority. With de Grasse having no orders to follow his command, Barre was forced to defer. It was obvious that did not set well with him. On such points victory had often been thrown into the jaws of defeat.

Washington nervously cleared his throat. Less than two weeks ago he had, indeed, been insane with joy. Awakening the following morning he had overheard some of his staff still chuckling about his emotional outburst. Of course, they had fallen silent when he had emerged from his tent, but it had reminded him of just how wild and undignified his outburst had been. Throughout the day as he trotted along the road, heading south, more than one wag in the ranks, waiting until he was safely past, would cough loudly and there would be a muffled "Heard you dance a handsome jig, sir!" or some such thing.

He knew it was a call of affection, actually. Unlike the darkest days at Morristown and the tense days after leaving Philadelphia with men openly calling for their pay, even before he had passed. He would be forced to ride on stoically, looking straight ahead, not replying.

This was a different army than any of this age. Men of the British, French, and especially Hessian and Prussian ranks would have been flogged unmercifully for such effrontery, but this army? In part this is what these men were fighting for. Army discipline or not, it was the freedom of speech, the freedom to be heard, and he knew as well that to punish or suppress one man for thus speaking out would only serve to arouse five hundred more to do the same. This was the army of a free republic, of free men, all of them volunteers, not one of them pressed into service, or dragged out of a prison and offered the choice of enlistment or the end of a hangman's noose. This was an army of freedom, not the army of a king, and this army required at times forbearance and silence on his part rather than the tantrum display of an autocrat. He knew, in turn, that the men respected him the more for such moments of forbearance, and often he would hear the echo of another soldier calling for silence, that their general would see it through fairly for them.

"Sir," he began, again clearing his throat before continuing, "I read with great interest, but I must confess concern as well, your note of yesterday that so graciously welcomed me to this theater of operations that I must say, first has only been made possible by the bravery of you and all those who serve beneath you."

De Grasse nodded warmly and raised his glass as if to offer a toast but Washington now pressed forward, not wishing this to turn into another quarter hour of compliments, self-congratulations, and what he feared even more, the possibility of a long-winded speech lubricated by drunkenness.

"There is, however, sir, a point of concern."

De Grasse nodded and sipped at his brandy as Lafayette translated.

"My orders regarding the time allotted to me here," de Grasse interjected, in a rather un-Gallic gesture cutting straight to the point.

"Yes, sir," Washington replied softly, almost deferentially, for after all, he had no position of strength to argue from. If insulted or if a variant mood suddenly struck this admiral, there was nothing to prevent him with the coming of the next tide to weigh anchor and sail away, thus dashing all his hopes, and in reality, ending this war in defeat after all these years of sacrifice and struggle.

All now rested on what would transpire in the next few minutes. He spared a sidelong glance at Barre, who was just staring off with indifference to the conversation as if it were no concern of his, but he sensed the man would be perfectly happy if de Grasse just suddenly announced orders contrary to Washington's wishes and dreams.

It did not help that with the stern windows open, even out here in the middle of the bay, mosquitoes had found likely meals and annoyingly buzzed about.

"Sir," Washington continued, "your welcoming letter, so joyful to receive, however, did give me momentary pause when you concluded with the statement that your orders, upon departing France in the spring, were to campaign in the Caribbean until the onset of the hurricane season. Only then were you at liberty to sail northward in search of enemy shipping for not more than six weeks at the ending of which you were to come about and carefully return back to the Caribbean for the winter."

"Those were my orders when I left Brest. Yes, those were my orders from the admiralty and from my king. I was to venture this fleet northward for six weeks only, and then return to protect our possessions in the south."

"Orders that of course are sound advice," Rochambeau now interrupted, speaking in French so that Lafayette had to quickly shift to English so that Washington understood what was being said. "But surely, sir, if our good king knew of your glorious victory here a week ago in these very waters, that your presence here now blocks the British navy, which has scurried, with its tail between its legs back to New York like whipped dogs, and that by being here you block any thoughts they might have of harrying our rich possessions to the south. Surely His Majesty would be the first to congratulate you."

De Grasse nodded his thanks for the compliment.

"Your presence here as well, now traps over seven thousand elite troops of England, that if freed from your blockade, could do much harm to our interests, let alone that of our noble allies. I am confident our king would now see things differently."

De Grasse smiled.

"If only this war did not divert the genius of your Benjamin Franklin, I dare say he would have, by now, applied his mind to harnessing lightning itself, to find some means of employing it so our voices could leap with the lightning bolts back and forth across the ocean, so that my king could hear this conversation and offer his sage opinion and give proper orders."

All chuckled goodnaturedly over the witticism and absurdity of the wish.

De Grasse extended his hands wide and shrugged his shoulders in a typical Gallic gesture of despair.

"But such is not so, and my orders were clear, sir."

For a moment Washington feared that de Grasse would stand, indicating that the conversation was at an end. He had departed the Caribbean early in August, it was now the middle of September; if he followed his orders to the letter, he would leave these waters by the end of the month.

The army with its full strength had finally arrived only yesterday after nearly a month of hard marching in broiling heat and with short rations. They needed several days of rest, at least, before being set to the hard task of beginning to dig the siege lines forward. It would take weeks, nearly a month, for those lines to be completed, according to the estimates of the ever-accurate von Steuben and his master of artillery Knox, agreed upon by Rochambeau's own engineers.

If moved to absolute desperation they could attempt a "forlorn hope" of a direct frontal attack against Cornwallis's well-prepared works. It would be a forlorn hope, indeed, von Steuben said that chances were it would turn into the bloodiest attack of the war within minutes. To expect casualties as high as 50 percent or more, with but one chance in ten at most of carrying the enemy position and winning the day.

If de Grasse was now announcing he would stand by the rigid orders he had sailed with in the spring, he would have to launch that forlorn hope, with himself in the lead. He would rather die at the head of his troops, than face the defeat that would come if the attack failed. Or far worse, if he did not do a damn thing at all, and then stand impotent and watch as the French fleet sailed away, leaving the back door open for Cornwallis to either escape, or perhaps see, within a few weeks, transports bearing Clinton's army, fresh and well supplied to shatter his ill-fed and exhausted troops.

"Sir," Washington struggled to keep a sense of dignity to his voice even though he was bargaining here with no cards in his hand to play out other than a personal appeal, "you have achieved in these waters the greatest naval victory of the war."

That was more than a bit of an exaggeration. Only one enemy ship of the line had actually been sunk, in reality scuttled by its own crew when the rest of the fleet retired, and one other ship captured, the vast bulk of the British fleet easily retiring northward. It was, after refitting in the naval yard at New York, still a potent threat. De Grasse's fleet had no shipyards here for major repairs, the careening of ships to scrap bottoms, to replace spliced masts and shattered yardarms. Another encounter and though fewer in number the British would have the advantage and surely that was weighing upon de Grasse's thinking.

"There is the absolute potential here for an even greater and far more glorious victory," Washington hurriedly pressed ahead, Lafayette barely able to keep up with the translation.

"You, sir, have bottled up nearly half of all the main line infantry of the British empire in North America here, in this bay."

He pointed out the window and he thanked God that the wind had shifted this ship around in its anchorage, so that as he pointed dramatically, off in the distance the peninsula of Yorktown and Williamsburg was in view.

"More than seven thousand of their elite infantry who have terrorized the Carolinas for two years and that my dear Generals Lafayette and Greene have forced from the Carolinas," and as he spoke, he nodded to his beloved young French comrade, who had played such a crucial role in creating this moment.

"Think of it, sir," and now he allowed enthusiasm to come to his voice. "A dozen of their finest regiments and all their standards, sixty pieces of artillery, carried with the greatest labor from England to here. Consider when you return to your dear king and our friend Louis, you, sir, personally could present those colors of humbled regiments to your king. What then? Sir, it would be the greatest triumph of this war," he hesitated, "and fitting revenge for the last war."

He was not sure if he had overstepped with mention of that last war. For after all, he had fought against France and gained his reputation doing so in that last conflict.

"I hear, sir," de Grasse replied smoothly, "that you were quite the hero in that last conflict. That it was you personally who led Braddock's men out of the trap laid by some of the very men you march alongside of now. That you gained quite a reputation then, and would boast that you would not rest until the last Frenchman was either dead or driven into the Great Lakes or the sea."

Washington held his gaze but felt his color rising. There was no denying his role or his boast. Then he gave Lafayette a sidelong glance almost in appeal for the young man to come up with some comforting and diplomatic reply.

But de Grasse chuckled and patted Washington's hand resting on the table, breaking the momentary tension.

"You were a noble foe in that last war, sir. We know your reputation: fierce in battle but magnanimous in victory, and the first to offer aid to a fallen foe even if he had been the enemy but moments before. That you spared my fellow countrymen who were prisoners and insisted they be properly exchanged. I heard a legend that years afterward a noble savage chieftain you met, who had faced you in battle, said that he ordered his men not to waste any more lead shooting at you, because their god, who obviously respected you, had put his hands about you and no bullet would ever strike you. That you and this chief then did that strange custom of theirs of smoking a pipe together in friendship."

Embarrassed, he simply nodded in reply.

"Is it really true that in the battle against Braddock, your uniform had thirteen bullet holes in it, but you were not touched?"

Washington, now truly embarrassed, only shook his head.

"Four bullet holes in his uniform and two horses shot dead beneath him that day," Lafayette proudly announced without waiting for him to speak, looking back at his friend with open admiration.

"Those days are long past," Washington said awkwardly, "now we are friends united in a common cause."

"Seven then," de Grasse said with a smile.

There was a moment of silence, drinks poured for several and, of course, Washington put his hand over his glass politely indicating refusal.

"I will come to the point," Washington now said, his voice gaining strength.

"I already know your point but do proceed," de Grasse replied.

"I implore you, sir, to extend your time here until we have, as we Americans are fond of saying, 'the enemy in the bag.'"

There were polite chuckles.

De Grasse did not respond. Attention now fixed on his goblet of brandy, swirling it about and taking a sip.

"Four additional weeks, sir, will see the job done," he hesitated. "I will swear that to you as my solemn oath, sir. Extend for four weeks, until the end of October. If we cannot achieve our final victory by then, I promise you upon my oath, sir, I will not ask for a single day more."

De Grasse looked up at him over the rim of the brandy sniffer.

"You realize, sir, you are asking me to go against the instructions given to me by my king and the board of the admiralty. I was granted six weeks discretion and no more."

"They are in Paris, nearly four thousand miles away," Rochambeau interjected. "My friend, we are here. We are entrusted with our ranks not just to blindly follow, but to judge as well when God grants us fair opportunity. I believe this moment is such a chance. Such a chance might not ever come again in our lifetimes."

"If we live through this," Barre interjected, his mood now clear. "The English fleet fully refitted could be back in a fortnight from New York while our ships still need a proper naval yard for repair."

De Grasse looked over at him and nodded as if accepting his advice and for an instant Washington's heart sank, but as he looked at Rochambeau he saw the flicker of a grin, the way a partner in a hand of whist or hearts might signal that an opponent had just made the wrong play.

De Grasse's gaze shifted from Barre back to Washington.

"I agree with you, General Washington. Four additional weeks, sir, but not a day longer."

Washington struggled to contain himself. After his display in front of Rochambeau, he could not afford another such outburst, ever again.

Rochambeau and Lafayette made up for it, both rising to their feet with loud exclamations of joy, each grabbing a hand of de Grasse, shaking it, then hugging him as he stood to return their enthusiasm with proper grace.

All Washington could do was just stand, head bowed, though not about to dance another jig, he feared his emotions might swing the other way to tears of relief. It had all hung in the balance yet again.

He could see the dour look of disapproval by Barre. It was obvious the man wanted out of this campaign, if for no other reason than the fact that de Grasse was for it, but it was time for a noble gesture. He reached across the table and extended his hand to Barre, who looked up at him in surprise.

"Sir, without your gallant transporting of additional supplies and especially the siege guns all of this would be moot. Sir, your efforts will forever be remembered for enabling us to batter Cornwallis into submission or his grave. I shall never forget that."

Lafayette hurriedly translated while still embracing de Grasse and to Washington's inner delight he saw his words had worked the proper effect, at least here, and Barre rose and took Washington's hand, nodding his thanks.

The group of commanders finally returned to the main deck, their enthusiasm evident, and at the sight of them, the crew, after word had come that the meeting had drawn to a successful conclusion, were now drawn up in formal ranks. Though nearly all were swaying or barely standing from the generous outflow of spirits, their cheers resounded, picked up by the crews of ships up and down the line, and again another thunderous broadside upon broadside in salute. Which made Washington wince as yet again he thought about how much powder they had just expended. But now? He stood listening to it with delight and hoped that Cornwallis could hear it as well.

Fourteen

GENERAL WASHINGTON CLICKED HIS POCKET WATCH OPEN, for the tenth time within the hour, a sure sign to all gathered with him that the anticipation was all but overwhelming. Hamilton was holding a hooded lantern, shielded from the sight of the enemy line by his cloak.

"Two minutes," Washington whispered, struggling not to let his emotion, his raw excitement, show.

It had been over three years, three long years since Monmouth Court House that he had actually started an action and the anticipation of it all was nearly visceral, made even more tense by the near-maddening stress of the previous six weeks. He usually felt a strange inner calm descend once action was joined; it was what he was noted for in all three armies on the field and behind fortifications this night. Even the British who had seen him in action later commented how he moved about in a near-placid state, as if oblivious to danger or the other extreme of being overcome with battle lust.

At this moment, he felt a deep inner frustration as well. In the shadows he could see Dan Morgan, actually leaning forward, like a greyhound ready to sprint into action, and how he longed to go with him, as he once had in his youth. He had even muttered such a suggestion but an hour ago, and the response was near-instant rebellion from Hamilton, his guards, Lafayette, and even "Ole Dan," who grumbled, "Just you do that, sir. Just fine. Dressed up as you are. You stop a bullet and till my dying day everyone will curse Dan Morgan. So no thank you, sir, you go forward and I'll stay here and command the army while you try and get killed."

That comment, from any other man, would have drawn a rebuke of stony silence, but from Dan, who all knew had been the general's comrade in battle since youth, with Dan acting as the elder, in spite of rank, triggered soft laughter.

He knew he was boxed in and would lose all dignity if he tried to argue the point. Besides, Dan was right. This was a night action, which tended to disintegrate into confusion, and his place was here, behind the lines. All knowing his location if in need of orders, or if a decision had to be made to send more troops in, the thousands of men behind him concealed and waiting out the night in the marshes.

He silently was counting off the seconds. Rochambeau's timepiece was even finer than his, varying only a minute or two a day, and the two had compared watches and set them together at the evening staff meeting.

He counted off the last seconds out loud, unable to conceal his excitement any longer, turned, and looked at Knox, who insisted upon performing the duty himself.

"Send it up," he announced.

Knox, grinning, stepped away from the knot of officers, and taking a lit cigar from his mouth, walked up to three metal tubes stuck vertically into the ground, and bent over at the waist.

"That sight alone should terrify the enemy if they was awatching right now," Morgan chuckled and Washington could barely suppress a laugh. Poor Henry Knox, at over three hundred pounds, was used to being the object of joking. How he kept his weight even at Valley Forge was a source of wonder, conversation, and humor, which the poor man had always tried to endure with good will.

"Just get a little downwind from me next time you say that," Knox retorted, and now there was laughter.

He touched the lit cigar to a fuse protruding from the base of the metal tube, then quickly stepped to the second and third tubes and did the same.

"Stand back," he announced, moving hurriedly even for one of his bulk.

A rocket snapped heavenward from the first tube, followed a few seconds later by the second and third. The damp light breeze wafting in from off the bay drifted the smoke around Washington, a smell he actually loved, that of burnt gunpowder. The rockets soared heavenward then burst one after the other, three reds.

All turned to look north and seconds later three more rockets, from the French line, burst in reply.

"Go!" Washington shouted as if the hunt was finally on, which in a way it was.

Dan, grinning like a schoolboy let out on a vacation, looked to his general, saluted, then dashed off into the shadows.

"I know you wish to go with him, my general," and Washington turned to see Lafayette by his side.

"Yes, indeed," he replied with a smile, "but that old buzzard is right and I must stay, damn it. My place has to be here."

"There will be action enough in the days ahead," Lafayette offered.

Washington sighed.

"It is one thing to go into a fight, it is, as you have learned, young sir, entirely another to give the orders but then stand back behind the line."

"It is your plan, your battle, and will eventually be your victory, sir."

Washington tried to chuckle and put his hand on Lafayette's shoulder in a fatherly gesture of thanks.

"My plan for years," he whispered, "or should I say my dream. Thank God for our allies over there," and he nodded toward the French position, "your countrymen.

"This is it, gentlemen," he announced, looking around at those gathered by his side. "After so many years we have come to this moment, this beginning of the end I pray. You have all done your duty superbly well these last six weeks. My compliments to all of you, for without you and our allies . . ."

His voice trailed off. There was nothing else to be said. They dreamed of this moment with as much fervor as he had across the years. It had begun and now all he could do would be to wait and see what came next.

He was never one for waiting, but six years had taught him much. Patience, as his plans were at last set in motion, was one of the hardest virtues he had been forced to learn.

A veteran of six years of this war, and seven in the last, he knew how often even the best of plans went astray. Dear God, after so much agony and suffering by so many, please let this one work.

"Skirmishers forward," the command was whispered along the line of battle even before the rockets had snuffed out, and Peter Wellsley felt a thrill run down his spine. Gone was the "game" that he had been tasked with for far too long. He was still officially on the headquarters staff of the general, but was now something of a man without a mission since New Jersey was hundreds of miles to their rear. He had offered what services he could to his Virginia counterpart, who had of course politely accepted, but Peter had not heard a word from him since. He most likely would have reacted the same way. Each man had his own way of doing things, his own organization, and did not need a counterpart of equal rank who might prove to be a second-guesser and nothing but trouble.

Hanging about headquarters, he was delighted when old Dan Morgan actually recognized and remembered him as one of the "brave lads" who had guided the army at Trenton and took over command of a regiment of militia at Monmouth. Seeing him unemployed he invited him to join "in the fun," and, of course, Peter gladly accepted.

It had taken more than ten days since their arrival at Williamsburg to get ready for this moment. Hundreds of tons of siege equipment and supplies had to be off-loaded from French ships and put in position. Unlike the Americans' arrival at Valley Forge with only fifty good axes at hand for the entire army, the French truly did think of everything. All the equipment necessary for a prolonged siege had been delivered: sharp doubled-bladed axes, this time by the hundreds, shovels, picks, small two-wheeled carts that could be pulled by a couple of men, wheelbarrows, all the tools for a siege that, more than anything else, was about digging. Half a million rations were on hand, enough to feed the armies for the next month and a half, either salted and preserved or still on the hoof, purchased from farms fifty miles around with French money. Enough ball ammunition so that every infantryman had twenty-four fresh rounds in his cartridge box and a hundred more laid up in dry bunkers and barrels filled with a hundred thousand musket and pistol flints. Most crucial of all, however, was artillery. Nearly a hundred pieces, from the light field four- and six-pounders hauled the long distance by Knox, who would be damned if he ever left a gun behind, up to heavy long-barreled twenty-four pounders and the massive sixteen-inch-bore mortars, which would not be brought forward until the siege lines had been dug to within killing range, for not even the French had a limitless supply of shot, shell, and powder for these, the most destructive guns deployed in land in this war.

Now the army Washington had brought down from New York had reunited with their comrades whom Greene and Lafayette had deployed here more than a year ago. The Continental line numbered nearly eight thousand strong, backed up by more than three thousand militia who had come swarming in.

Even for Peter, who had grown inured to so many of the horrors of this war, the sights that greeted the army as they arrived in this theater of war had shocked him and triggered rage throughout the ranks. Cornwallis, apparently anticipating this outcome, had ordered the scorching of the earth as they pulled back in upon Yorktown. It was no longer just the looting of barns for supplies. Hundreds of farms had been wiped clean from the earth, everything destroyed. He could not believe that Cornwallis himself had grown so hard and bitter in this fight, but some under his command surely had. Dozens of civilians had been executed, left dead by the smoldering ruins of their homes, and in one horrific case a pregnant woman was found dead, her baby disemboweled with a note scratched on the wall that this "bastard will never grow up to be a Rebel."

Outraged, Washington had sent Hamilton himself through the lines under a flag of truce to file a vehement protest and Cornwallis replied that if the culprits were found, they would be publicly hanged within sight of the American army. Everyone was still waiting for that hanging and the mood among more than a few was so bitter that orders had to be passed repeatedly that the rules of war would be obeyed, enemy prisoners and wounded treated humanely.

If there had been some insane purpose to that obscenity it had surely turned against the British as word of the atrocity spread across the countryside. The ranks of volunteer militia had swelled as a result, the same as they had when a similar incident had happened just before the Battle of Saratoga.

The skirmishers, light infantrymen mixed in with detachments of Morgan's rightly feared long riflemen, set out from the edge of the marsh to which Washington had moved all his infantry, Americans on the right flank, according to Rochambeau the position of honor on any battlefield and that he insisted Washington and his men were to have. Close to eight thousand French, their numbers increased by the regiments transported by Barre, were deploying out to the left. It was a battlefront several miles wide that had waited out the damp chilled night. The building of fires was forbidden, with the silence broken only where some Virginia boys had kicked up a nest of wild pigs and decided to give chase for their breakfast. The commotion had not caused the outer line of British pickets, half a mile away, to bestir themselves.

Peter stayed close to Dan Morgan, figuring at least he could fall back on his old role of courier if need be. Beside Dan was a curious character who had taken a liking to Peter, calling him lad, even though Peter was officially a lieutenant colonel, and the old man addressing him was a private. It did not bother him in the slightest. Old Mose was very much a legend. Peter had even read about him before the war. Taken by the Shawnee in the Ohio country, he had faced death by torture, a favorite ritual that if properly done could take several days of hell. If one broke or begged for mercy, the man was handed over with contempt to the women of the tribe, who were truly to be feared.

They had burned most of the flesh off of Mose's feet and his response was unrelenting taunting back with suggestions, including scalping him while still alive, even offering to perform the act upon himself if they would give him a knife.

His tormentors had quickly shifted from hatred to outright admiration, spared the man, and adopted him into their tribe, where he lived with them for more than a year while his feet gradually healed. Then one night, in the dead of winter, he just simply walked off, leading his somewhat startled and less than amused adopted family on a weeklong chase clear back to Fort Pitt. After the hostilities of that war had passed, Mose was eventually an honored guest with his old family, and would frequently drop in for extended visits. He was treated with awe as the man who, though his feet were little better than charred stubs, had outrun them for nearly two hundred miles. Bent now with age, shuffling like a wounded bear, he was a constant companion of Dan's. No one would ever dare to say it to Dan's face but in recent years his vision had begun to fail him, but it was said that Old Mose could still spot a flea riding on the back of a horsefly a hundred yards off and shoot the flea off without even nicking the fly.

Peter felt honored to be in their company this day. A crescent moon marked the eastern horizon off to his right, the sky shifting from darkness to indigo, then to the first streaks of deep red and gold. They drifted around the ruins of a farmstead that once must have been prosperous, but all of it gone except for charred timbers and broken-down fences. There was the sickening stench of a dead ox, bloated and having burst open after a week in the Virginia heat, causing even some of Dan's hardened men to gag and curse under their breath at the senseless waste of it all.

The British picket line was now less than a quarter mile off, at least their campfires were that distant. It was fair to assume that they should at least have some men out forward and that was who Dan and the light infantry were now hunting.

At last it was Mose who stopped, putting up his hand, the signal silently passing down the line, the skirmishers halting. Peter could see him point; he himself saw nothing, just shadows. All stood silent as Mose shouldered his rifle and took careful aim, his finger at last brushing against the trigger.

The flash of the powder in the pan of the rifle was startling, blinding Peter for a second. He had, as if still a green militiaman, been looking straight at Mose, rather than averting his head, or at least closing and covering one eye. The sharp crack of the rifle thundered, echoing across the open plain, greeted a few seconds later by a startled cry of pain.

It had begun!

Within seconds rifles and muskets began to crackle up and down the long open formation, and, finally, after some obvious confusion on the far side of the open pasture, a scattering of return fire, no balls hitting, but one did hum by between Peter and Old Mose, who was reloading his rifle.

"Shouting like a stuck pig he is, must have just winged him," the old man announced.

"Come on Dan, let's go see what we bagged!"

Dan motioned for the line to press forward. In the few intervening minutes the light had risen enough to reveal British light infantry, standing up in the high pasture grass, some firing off a quick shot, others turning and just running.

A wild taunting cry rose up from the riflemen, bone chilling, like the sound of wolves on the scent of blood, as they dodged forward, some pausing to fire a round, others just pressing in on the chase. The entire encampment line of the British pickets was now astir and obviously confused by this sudden onslaught. They were definitely not heavy infantry, who would have formed into volley line for this kind of fight, but instead were deploying out as skirmishers in open order. Most were already giving ground, abandoning their position as they fired and retreated.

Mose angled off to the right, Peter following him. Someone was sitting up in the grass, cursing, clutching his right arm at the elbow. The soldier, not much more than a boy, looked up at them wide-eyed and began to fumble for his musket. Peter leveled his pistol and cocked it.

"Give it up," he said coolly, and obviously terrified the boy let his weapon drop.

"Don't shoot me," he began to beg.

"We don't shoot wounded prisoners."

"Sergeant Patrick said you'll geld all light infantry, that's what your Mad Anthony promised," and he began to sob. "I wasn't even there."

Peter realized he was referring to the Paoli Massacre from back in '77, that after the battle and forever after any British light infantry that fell into the hands of the survivors of that night under Anthony Wayne's command could expect rough treatment. The passions of that had cooled somewhat during the three long years without much action after Monmouth, but in the Southern campaign of light infantry against partisans led by men like Francis Marion there were many dark rumors.

Mose knelt down by the boy's side, pulling his hand back from the lad's elbow.

"I must be getting old," Mose sighed, "I was off by a good foot or more to the right," and he shook his head.

"What does he mean?" the boy cried, looking up at Peter, who had a cocked pistol aimed at the boy.

"He means what he said. He's the best shot in the army, and he was aiming for your heart. You're almost a disappointment to him."

"No scalp," Mose muttered, turning his head to one side to spit out a stream of tobacco juice, but then fished the wad out of his mouth, slapped it onto the wound, and taking the boy's free hand, guided him to hold the wad in place.

"We'll cut your arm off, laddie, but you'll live, but damn me, that's the worse shot I've made in quite awhile, especially at this range."

"It was still dark," Dan Morgan interjected to soothe Old Mose's wounded pride, coming up to look at the wounded soldier, while ahead of them the skirmishers were continuing to press forward.

"You're Dan Morgan, aren't you?" the boy asked, looking up at him wide-eyed. "I had nothing to do with that farm over yonder or that woman, I swear it."

"I didn't accuse you," Morgan said coldly, "but don't lie to me now, boy. What regiment are ya."

"The 44th."

He nodded.

"Licked them before, will lick them again. Now, on your feet."

The boy weakly tried to stand. Peter uncocked his pistol, holstered it, and helped him up.

"Colonel, perhaps he's worth you having a chat with as you take him back to the surgeons."

"I'm not going to lose my arm, am I?" and the boy was stifling back sobs.

"Sure are," Mose announced, "better than you with a busted heart and your scalp on my belt, now get along with you."

Dan was smiling as Mose, muttering under his breath, turned and pressed forward to catch up with the advancing skirmishers.

"Someone to keep your skills up with, Colonel, while you take him back. If you want some fun later, come back on the line and I'll loan you my rifle for a shot or two."

"Thank you, sir."

"Later then," and Dan set off at a slow trot.

"Come on now," Peter said, helping to brace his prisoner up as he pointed him back to the rear.

"What did he mean about practicing your skills? You aren't going to torture me or something are you?"

Peter could not help but chuckle, but then again, could understand the lad's terror after talking with him for but a few minutes. From the streets of London, caught as a petty thief that he swore he was innocent of. Rather than dancing at the end of rope, he had taken the king's shilling, swearing it had all been a set up by a corporal who said he had tried to pick his pocket, and after a quick trip to the magistrate, had his new recruit for the day.

Peter pulled out a flask, offering it over, the boy first asking if it was gin, but taking it anyhow, grimacing from the taste of sour mash. With the rising dawn the sight that confronted them as they crested over a low rise back of the destroyed farmstead caused Peter to stop in awe.

The advancing lines of American and French heavy infantry were a sight to behold. He had not seen anything like it since Monmouth, and the three years of training since showed. They were not expecting a fight this day, only moving forward to stake claim to land for what would be the first siege parallel, laid out just beyond the range of British artillery. It was also a bravado display to let the British clearly see what they now faced. Muskets were unslung, bayonets fixed, glinting red in the dawning light, the men moving easily but keeping disciplined formations. Now that dawn was breaking he could catch glimpses of the white uniformed French, a mile or more away to the left. Fifers were playing "Chester" or "Yankee Doodle," drummers keeping the beat, officers forward and mounted.

He saw General Washington at the center, a white-clad rider beside him, without doubt Rochambeau, and he could only imagine what they were thinking at this moment after so many tension-filled weeks of wondering if all their elaborate plans would be in vain. This display of power, of their combined armies marching together in battle formation, was something unseen in any war on this continent, and it filled both friend and foe with awe.

Leading his captive through the lines, several men taunting the poor boy as they passed to the rear, Peter guided him into the low marshy ground, where thousands more were now busily at work, nearly all of them the militia guided by the engineers of the American and French army. In the previous days thousands of trees for miles around had been dropped, thinner logs split in half, the heavier ones laboriously sawed into planks If only a sawmill had been nearby, the work would have been easier, but the British had made sure to burn that in their retreat. Though even now, men were laboring to repair it, and fetched inland for replacement blades. Causeways big and strong enough for supply wagons and even artillery up to the heaviest of the siege guns were now being constructed out of the split logs and planks. With thousands of men at work, the plans carefully laid out days before, officers briefed on what was expected, even surveyors carefully marking out the routes, the roadways were already under construction though the day was barely an hour old.

Peter guided his prisoner along, offering as much as he wanted to drink without letting him get truly drunk and his skills, as Dan had put it, worked, gaining the boy's confidence that he would protect him. Yes, he would send a letter to his mother letting her know he was safe. Soon Peter knew the dispersion of the regiments to either flank, their strength, the fact that a fair number of men were down with the bloody flux and summer ague, barely able to stand for inspection let alone engage in an open-field fight, and that the boy had only joined the army as a reinforcement early in the spring.

"I heard in the court in London and God strike me if I am being untrue, good sir, that a fellow was caught up just like me," the boy slurred, "same ruse, got taken before the magistrate, offered the rope or the king's shilling, and he said to give him the damn rope! He had been in the last war, wounded twice, and he'd rather dance with the rope than come back to this godforsaken wilderness to get scalped by Indians than burned alive the way his brother was."

With that the boy looked at him, wide-eyed.

"Are there Indians with this army?"

"A few."

"You're not going to give me to them are you?"

"Just tell me the truth when I ask a question, lad, and I'll protect you from them."

Peter laughed and patted him reassuringly, the boy looked at him face pale. He began to cough and then, suddenly, there was a flood of bright red blood frothing out from between his pale blue lips.

"Lay down, boy," Peter ordered.

He gently moved the boy's arm up, the lad crying out with pain, and he saw the hole drilled into his side and drilled into his chest.

"Am I dying?" the boy asked, eyes wide with terror.

"No, lad, no. I'll get you to surgeon, and we'll get that bullet out in no time."

"I'm dying, ain't I."

"No, lad, not while I got you."

He tried to lift him back up, but the boy cried out in agony, and more blood came gushing out. Now the youth began to weep.

Peter stood up, looking around, for though a scrawny lad out of the slums of England, there was no way he could carry him all the way back alone.

SOME MILITIA CAME BY, LEADING A CART THAT HAD BEEN loaded with spilt logs for the laying out of the corduroy causeway across the marsh and had dumped off the last of the load.

"Can you men give me a hand getting this boy back?"

"Son of a bitch," one of them grumbled, "leave the bastard out here to die, or if you just turn your back, sir, I'll finish him."

Peter stood up about to argue, but knew it was one he couldn't win, even if he did try the stupid routine of pointing to the epaulette on his shoulder. The man was more than twice his age, brawny, covered in sweat from his labor, and could undoubtedly knock him cold with a single blow to the cheers of his comrades.

"Bastards burned my farm out before you sharp looking boys with those Frenchies came struttering down here. Why should I help him or you?"

"Then why are you here?" Peter asked.

"Pay them back."

"Then help me get him back to the surgeon before he bleeds to death. He's spilling his guts to me like a frightened girl. I'm on Washington's staff, I'm supposed to find things out from prisoners, and he's my first one."

"Come on, Josiah, he's right," one of the other militiamen said, and the older man simply picked the boy up and unceremoniously dumped him in the back of the wagon as they turned it about, the jolt of it stirring the lad half awake, a groan of pain escaping him.

"I'm not a frightened girl," the boy whispered, looking up at Peter.

"No, you aren't. You're a good soldier. You'll get good treatment, and then later we'll talk over a drink. I promise you."

The boy looked up at him, gasping as the wagon bounced and swayed over the corduroy road through the marsh. The night air was thick with mosquitoes swarming about them.

The boy began to blather, something about his mother, a woman named Johanna, said he couldn't write, a snatch of a prayer about laying down to sleep, and then he just began to sob softly.

"Tell him to . . ." the brawny soldier snapped, but a look up from Peter still him.

"For God's sake, show some pity," Peter whispered.

"He's right," the other driver replied and the brawny man fell silent as the boy struggled to sit up, gasping that he couldn't breathe.

"Write me mother," the boy whispered looking into Peter's eyes and then fainted away.

"I promise I will," Peter replied.

They had reached the edge of the marsh. In a tent by the side of the road illuminated by torches was a hospital area.

"Just help me get him up there."

The brawny man seemed to have relented, and he reached into the cart and lifted the boy out, paused, then looked at Peter.

"He's a dead un," the man said, and then just laid the body down by the side of the road.

Across the years of war, Peter had seen hundreds die, but this one seemed to him to be so pathetic, so futile. The boy's death would not change the outcome one iota. Inwardly he cursed all the bastards who had dragged him to this place to die.

Peter looked down at the body, so pathetically small now.

"You get the laddie's name?" the other driver asked.

"No."

"Then no letter to his mother then," the brawny man replied, but there was now a touch of pity in his voice.

"Damn war," he continued, and reaching into his pocket he pulled out a flask and handed it to Peter.

"Think you need a drink, son."

Peter nodded his thanks.

"First time you seen a man die like that?"

Peter took a long pull on the flask. "If you only knew," was all he could say. Peter offered the flask back but the man refused.

"Keep it. Call it an apology for what I said earlier."

"Thank you."

The militiaman turned and walked off, Peter put the flask in his haversack, slowly walking through and around the thousands of laboring men, the causeway gaining yards with every passing minute. Coming at last out of the far side of the marsh, he saw that the main battleline had come to a stop, a good quarter mile closer in to York-town, while a quarter mile beyond them a lively duel between skirmishers now ensued.

Off in the distance he saw Washington riding along the line, pausing to chat with officers and men as they waited for the order to continue the advance. He wondered yet again what the general was thinking and feeling at this moment. Most likely joyful as he should be, as any general would be after so many years of struggle and the agony of the long march here, and in the equation of all of that the death of a British soldier was just one more step closer to victory.

An occasional musket ball hummed past the general, but he paid it no heed, he rarely did, and would be stunned when after a battle someone would point out the number of bullet holes in his coat, a shattered canteen, a bent saber scabbard, a ball clipping his hat. During the blessed times that Martha had stayed with him in winter quarters, if bored, she would rummage through his uniforms for something to darn and then cry out with horror when she discovered another near miss. She would then lecture him sternly, even bringing his staff in on several occasions, yelling at them to keep better watch of their "beloved general."

Of course, old Billy Lee would always side with her and she would lovingly patch his poked clothing. Billy Lee, ever-present, was up to his usual routine of trying to ever so casually move himself between his general and the incoming fire and if confronted too crossly would fall back on the defense. "Sir, Missus Washington, she ordered me to do this, and you and I both know we don't go against her word." No one would dare laugh if within his sight, but he knew the response would always draw chuckles behind his back and nods of approval and encouragement from his staff.

Today with Rochambeau by his side, Billy Lee was up to his usual routine, and Washington could not help but note that on Rochambeau's staff, several were doing the same, though with more than a bit of French bravado, striking heroic poses as in a painting. Though there had been a moment of levity when one ball had nicked the mount of one of his staff, poor animal had its nose badly creased. The animal had bolted off in a panic, finally throwing the now-frightened young officer. Rochambeau, ever the gentleman and concerned officer, had leaped from his mount and gone to the side of the shaken and now thoroughly embarrassed young man. The old line infantry behind them struggling to contain their laughter, while Rochambeau made a great display of praising him, patting him on the back, offering him a drink, and then diplomatically sending him to the rear with some trivial dispatch.

"Our boys," Rochambeau had said when mounting up beside Washington and speaking in English, "we must look out for them, and when this is done, send them back safe to their mothers."

Washington could only nod in agreement. He had written far too many letters to mothers and wives in this war.

"He is humiliated today, but I guess, fifty years hence, he will proudly tell his grandchildren how his mount stopped a bullet meant for me and a proper portrait will be commissioned to memorialize the moment," and the two chuckled at the thought of it.

The skirmishing ahead was brisk, the range having spread out somewhat as Hessian Jaegers, their riflemen, came into the line, causing the musket men with their short-range weapons to pull back and let the professionals duel it out. All the time, Dan Morgan would keep the pressure up, his men getting up to sprint a few dozen yards closer in, and all the time the enemy line kept retiring back when the pressure truly told.

Washington thought, and Rochambeau agreed, that their counterpart, Lord Cornwallis, was on the far side, a mile or so away, telescope raised, observing the fight, this opening skirmish, just as they were.

The day was growing hot, and he had sent word back to his heavy infantry to settle into the high grass, and to send runners back to keep fetching more water from what his own surgeon had said was a safe source of spring water on the far side of the marshes. If the British were suffering from the flux, as young Colonel Wellsley had reported to him earlier in the morning, it could be dangerous. In a matter of a few days it could take half of his army, so carefully gathered from New York and as far as France, out of the fight and kill thousands.

He had hesitated to expose the army to the bad humors and vapors of the marsh the night before, and prayed the exposure was short enough that flux and ague would not strike them down. He was now glad to be free of those deadly elements, and under a hot sun that would evaporate such influences from their bodies.

He had actually hoped that this display of his main battleline, the combined forces of heavy infantry of the Continental line and the elite regiments of France, might actually provoke Cornwallis into an all or nothing duel, out in the open. It was all but a direct taunt, and if this were an earlier age, he would have sent a gallant young knight forward with his gauntlet and a note of challenge to a fair fight under a noonday sun, in the sight of God to settle the matter today. The victor would host the defeated, if both were still alive, for dinner.

Yet this was a modern age, of modern war. Cornwallis was outnumbered. Now surely his young aides were carefully scanning his lines, noting regimental flags and counting numbers. That was deliberate on his part, to show that opening hand. Because any veteran on their side could count as well, and whereas a month ago they would have fought with some advantage of numbers on their side against Lafayette and von Steuben, now they could see they were surely outnumbered, and any hope of a stand-up, breakout fight would be a desperate gamble. He knew soldiers, and he knew that as the British infantry sat around their evening campfires, the officers off in their tents eating the best of rations as they always did, while they chewed on rancid salt pork and hard bread, they would whisper among themselves as to the odds of living out this fight.

The fight had pushed forward. The French and his own engineering officers had already gone forward, taking sightings, scanning the ground, and he finally passed the word back for his men to form up and resume the slow but steady advance. Another couple of hundred yards forward, another halt, no complaining from the lines. Though the day was decidedly warm, and they had been ready for an all-out fight since dawn, it was now well past noon and they could sense the

British would not oblige by coming out of their trenches and redoubts, so the tension in them unwound like a clock spring winding down. With the next halt, and with orders to hold ranks but sit down, many of them just simply laid out in the grass, ate their cold rations of soft bread, a true luxury, coming from French bakers no less, and slabs of cold beef, pork, or mutton, prepared the night before by French cooks and handed out just before dawn. It was a rare meal for the American infantry, and filled them with praise for their allies.

More than a few had, of course, managed to fill their canteens with strong brew, but only half a dozen or so men had to be arrested and taken to the rear for drunkenness. Most had downed just enough, along with the good food, and the apparent prospect that they would not be in a fight this day, to just quietly go to sleep. He sent word back, as well, to just let the men relax. It was a day good for their morale as long as they behaved and those who were drunk remained quiet.

As they settled into this position there were flashes and puffs of smoke from several of the British redoubts, the range obviously too far, the balls striking hundreds of yards short, bouncing lazily, striking a second and third time and then just tumbling through the grass and rolling to a stop. Several hundred yards short. One lad, filled with bravado, broke from the ranks of the main line and dashed forward. As an officer cursed him soundly, the lad raced up right into the edge of the skirmish line, looking around for a moment in the tall grass, and then holding the eighteen-pound solid shot aloft like a trophy, he paraded back with it. Washington looked over at him sternly, but the boy just grinned, obviously a bit feebleminded. As he rejoined his regiment, he was greeted with a rousing cheer, even as his officer delivered a solid kick to his backside, which resulted in yet more cheers.

Rochambeau laughed good-naturedly and Washington finally relented and smiled as well.

Why did they fire, he wondered? Did they deliberately put a lighter charge in the guns to try to lure him into what could be killing range,

No, he decided against that. Though far more used to the capabilities of four-, six-, and twelve-pounders, the largest guns his army used in the field, he could sense even their long eighteens and twenty-four pounders were just about at maximum range. If not, as the besieged with limited supplies on hand, they would not waste powder and ball on harassing fire with little chance of doing serious damage. They would be waiting until their enemy was, indeed, close.

Rochambeau was apparently debating that same issue with one of his engineering officers, who was pointing out the redoubts that had fired upon them and then handing up a hand-drawn map pegged to a wooden board, which the French general examined, nodded, and handed to Washington.

"General," Rochambeau announced, as Washington looked at the map, "my chief of engineers humbly suggests an advance of two hundred more paces, with a partial refusal of our left."

He nodded agreement. The skirmish line ahead had driven their Jaegers back, a few casualties limped to the rear, and near a low bramble of bushes a dead Hessian was sprawled, shot between the eyes. He gazed at the man for a moment, wondering, as he often did, what terrible fate had led this man into a war that was none of his business and why he would continue to fight in it. This was now the ending of it. Would his family ever know of his fate?

"Shall we continue, mon Général?"

He did not reply, just nudged his mount to a slow trot, Billy Lee, of course, out forward chatting amiably with several of Rochambeau's young officers. He wondered if either understood a word of the other.

The lines were rousted up, those who had fallen asleep rubbing their eyes. A few, who had actually passed out from the sun and too much corn liquor or rum, were being hoisted up by loyal comrades so they would not face arrest, and the vast array of over fifteen thousand men moved forward another two hundred paces as suggested.

A few more cannon shots, one of the balls actually rolling the last few hundred yards into the ranks, a veteran yanking back an obvious green recruit, who cried he wanted to catch it and tried to step in front and crouched down. Such stupidity had killed or taken off the leg or arm of more than one man, not realizing that though rolling slowly, even a six-pound shot could still crush a limb or, if it bounced up, cave a man's head in like a rotten pumpkin.

They were now atop a low rise of ground, not much, barely a dozen feet higher than the surrounding pasturelands and cornfields that had been razed by the retreating British. Yet a dozen feet often made all the difference in a battle when it came to clear fields of fire, and a slight downward slope gave tremendous advantage to defense, if they were trained properly to aim low, at the knees, and von Steuben had ceaselessly drilled that into his men ever since Valley Forge.

"Good ground this, sir,"

Turning he saw Knox and with him, the man who had done so much to transform his army into a professional fighting force, von Steuben, by his side. Both of them were smiling, talking to each other, von Steuben saying something in German while pointing at the British works and obviously delighted.

"What say you, gentlemen?" Washington asked with a smile.

"Ya, dis be good ground, sir," von Steuben announced, to which Knox agreed, laughing with the thought that they were within extreme range of the heavier guns but let them fire away and waste their powder and ball.

He looked over at Rochambeau, who addressed something to von Steuben in French, the two of them laughing in agreement, von Steuben coming over to the side of the French general, saluting him formally and then extending his hand that Rochambeau warmly took.

"You know they faced off against each other in some battle in the Seven Years War," Knox whispered. "Our baron says he thrashed Rochambeau's regiment, but I doubt if he is saying that now."

Apparently there had been some reference to it as the two talked hurriedly, with Rochambeau pointing out a nearby regiment of his army. Von Steuben saluted again, bowed, and then galloped off toward that regiment, and Washington wondered if his old comrade had been a bit too heavily into the schnapps and there was a moment of worry. Alliances had fallen apart in the past over the most trivial of incidents or supposed insults. Rochambeau, however, just watched the old German with a smiling gaze as von Steuben rode up before the regiment. He was too far away to be heard, but it was obvious he was delivering some kind of short speech, then dismounted, bowed low, went up to their regimental standard, saluted it, took a corner of the flag in his hand, and reverently kissed it.

There was no orchestrated three cheers that greeted his gesture. It was a spontaneous roar, hats going in the air, men holding their muskets up over their heads, officers racing up to embrace von Steuben warmly, the colonel of the regiment actually offering to help him remount. Von Steuben, grinning broadly, trotted back toward Washington, looking a bit ridiculous, his face covered with powder and rouge from the kisses of so many French officers, tears streaming down his face. As word spread down the line of French regiments, the cheering picked up, his name echoing and reechoing across the open field.

Men of the Continental line, all of them holding the eccentric German in highest regard, began to cheer him as well as he rode past them, hat off, held high in the air in salute.

"War certainly does make strange bedfellows at times," Knox whispered, chuckling with delight.

"Dis is good ground!" von Steuben announced, "and with our gallant and noble allies we start here to thrash them bastards good and proper. Ja?"

Washington looked over at Rochambeau who was obviously honored and delighted by the noble gesture of a former foe.

"He is right. Here is where we begin."

Washington turned to look back at his staff.

"Order the men forward to this ridge," he paused, "if we can call it that. Order all men to stack arms except for a guard detail from each regiment. Bring up the entrenching tools. This is where we begin the siege of Yorktown."

LORD CORNWALLIS LOWERED HIS TELESCOPE. HE HAD BEEN observing Washington, Rochambeau, and now some display by their officers that had triggered cheering so loud that the sound of it reached even to his own lines.

He turned to survey the outer works, so laboriously built by his men, and the hundreds of African slaves that had been rounded up from nearby plantations and promised their freedom in exchange for work. Once the works had been completed, however, he simply bade them to leave, not wishing to expend rations on them now that the backbreaking work had been completed.

When laid out he had expected, at most, to be facing an equal number of foes. This overt display of their numbers, which without doubt was a ruse with far more still concealed, had, indeed, unnerved him. It was true that proper defenses were a force multiplier that gave a fourfold advantage, but one had to have men to hold those defenses. Leave one spot weak, if your opponent perceives it, he focuses all his strength there, and then your line is pierced, your entire force in jeopardy when forced to flee to the fall-back position. In such a rout, for that is what it could turn into, the defender's army could be entirely overrun.

"This will not do," Cornwallis said aloud, turning to look back at his staff.

They were silent. They had been watching this slow, but steady, advance toward them for hours. Initially they had welcomed it. Perhaps their foes, filled with bravado, would dare to launch an all-out frontal assault by day's end, which would certainly prove to be the bloodiest day of the war. The numbers would again be even and the morale of Washington and the damn French shattered. Some even voiced out loud that after one such attack ending in failure, surely the two sides of this alliance forged in hell would turn upon each other with recriminations, each blaming the other, and by day's end the French would be off the line in a fit of pique, march back to their fleet, and sail away.

It was evident now no such foolhardy attempt was being contemplated. The troops by the thousands on the far side of the field were preparing to dig in, while behind them, wagons were already coming up with lumber and tools, and behind them the causeways across the marshy low ground between Yorktown and Williamsburg were pushing forward at a rapid pace. This was not an attack; it was preparation of a siege line. It would be completed by tomorrow. They would then start to dig their traverses closer and closer.

If he had but the forces he should have been given, he could have, at least, launched a spoiling raid, a show of bravado on his own part. But the risk was too great, and throughout the day, he had been forced to just watch, with an ever-growing sense of frustration and outright humiliation.

Cornwallis gazed at the staff, but he seemed distant, remote.

"Pass the order. All regiments to withdraw from the outer works, except for the bastion on our right, and to pull back to the inner line."

There were looks of consternation, but none dared to protest.

"Damn all to hell," his inner rage at last exploding in front of his men. "Clinton promised me reinforcements. Instead I have received but one lone courier bearing a message for me to hang on. We were to see how things develop over the next few weeks, for my good comrade of a general still feared that this is all a diversion, and that the main blow will still fall upon him in New York."

Angrily he turned back and pointed to the fifteen thousand or more men confronting them.

"Does anyone here call *that* a diversion!"

No one dared to speak.

"I am confronting the full strength of the Continental army, backed up by the full strength of France in North America, and am blockaded as well. We do not have the men to hold the outer perimeter against such force. We will pull back to the inner lines now. There, at least, we will have the density of men, still well enough to hold a musket and stand in the trenches, to hang on until my dear friend Clinton decides this is where the war will be decided."

"But, sir," an adjutant ventured. "At least let us wait till nightfall, do it under cover of night. It will shatter morale to do so now in broad daylight, under the eyes of those damn Rebels."

"Now, gentlemen, now. We try this at night, it will be mass confusion, and if the enemy senses it and decides to attack us at that moment under cover of darkness, it will trigger a panic that will stampede our entire army straight into the bay. Let the damn Rebels see us fall back, but once inside our inner works they will think twice. Now, do as I've ordered, damn it!"

IT WAS DAN MORGAN HIMSELF WHO CAME UP BEARING THE news and though Washington had known this man clear back to their youth on the frontier and the disaster with Braddock, which both had clearly foreseen, at first he wondered if, indeed, the man's eyes were failing him as some whispered, that or he had broken his promise to the general and had gotten into the corn liquor again.

"May I suggest the general come forward himself if he doubts me," Dan replied, a bit of a hurt tone in his voice that any of his reports would ever be doubted.

"No offense, Dan, but let me ride forward."

"May I suggest walking it, sir, some of those bastard Hessians are rather good with a rifle, sir."

Washington smiled. After such a comment, the last thing he would do would be to dismount. He nudged his mount forward and to his dismay Rochambeau, in full ceremonial white uniform for this day, fell in by his side insisting he had to see as well. That triggered a mad flurry of activity as staff mounted, Knox and von Steuben insisting on joining in. Lafayette, who had been over on the ridge, galloping up as well, gleefully shouting out the same report as Dan's.

"Now they've got one hell of a target," Dan snarled, looking up at

Washington as he trotted alongside him. "Can't you order these men back?"

"You try to order them back, Dan."

"Well, don't blame me if all of you are eating dinner in hell tonight."

"I pray our fate would be a different dining room table with a better view, and far better company." He smiled. "And smell better than you as well."

Dan chuckled, spat a stream of tobacco juice, and kept up his pace, famed on the frontier where he supposedly could run more than thirty miles in a day through the wilderness. A feat Washington recalled with awe, because he had once tried to keep up with him, and finally staggered into where Dan was camped, hunkered over a good, nearly smokeless fire proper for survival on the frontier. Dan had bagged a turkey that was roasting and awaited Washington and the rest of their men. Dan had just enough book learning to boast that if he had been with "them Greeks," he'd have delivered the message of Marathon "proper like, and not dropped dead at the end of the run."

They came up to the skirmish line, men arrayed along it looking up with surprise, Old Mose coming up to the general's side.

"Sure is good day's hunting, young sir, personally bagged two of 'em," he announced and rather than saluting, he held up a chaw of tobacco that Washington made a show of accepting, mimicking he had taken a bite. The habit actually disgusted him, but with Old Mose, a man who had, indeed, taught him so much about survival in the wilderness, formalities had to be observed. He actually smiled and looked over at Rochambeau, gesturing with the twist of tobacco. The French general's eyes filled with horror at the mere thought of it, and Mose laughed, muttering something under his breath.

Everyone else in this army, at least he prayed so, had come to accept and now openly admire their old foes from the last war, but Mose? He suspected if given the chance he would gladly indulge in a little target practice, maybe not to kill, but at least to knock an epaulette off a French general's uniform.

Washington handed the plug of tobacco back to Mose. There was no need to unfold his field telescope to survey the outer line of the British defenses. Some of Dan's riflemen and the light infantry were already through the chevaux de frise, entanglements, the moat, and up on the outer wall, rifles and muskets resting atop the wall as they poured out a harassing fire.

"They are retiring all along the line," Lafayette cried with a near-childlike enthusiasm. "They are running for their inner works!"

He could plainly see it. The redcoated columns pulling back, no flags flying though, their colors cased for such a humiliating maneuver, in full view of foes, who they once held in contempt and would chase while sounding foxhunting calls on their bugles.

"We capture any artillery?"

Dan shook his head.

"They got them all out. Hooked up right quick, and were on their way."

Washington took it all in, as several puffs of smoke erupted from the inner line, and Billy Lee looked back nervously at the general and the knot of staff and officers around him. They did present one hell of a big target. A cannonball struck the ground a hundred yards off, directly ahead and for a fraction of a second, Washington did feel a flutter of concern for his staff, which had not noticed the impact, except for Knox, who gave him a quick glance, but the ball bounced high, humming over their heads, striking down again a hundred yards behind them.

"Their bowling is off today," Knox announced and there was a scattering of nervous laughter in reply.

Washington, grinning, turned and looked at Rochambeau.

"May I suggest we order our men to stop digging and to move forward in force. It appears our friends in red have already built our first siege line for us."

Rochambeau took it all in. His features showed absolute astonishment. In the European tradition, an enemy did not concede his outer works in a siege until his opponent had at least dug and fortified an outer line and started pushing the first traverses forward. Since the days of Vauban, a hundred years earlier, a ritual had developed for such things, observed and honored by both sides in the minuet-like dance of wars between kings. Such a hasty retreat was, to the eyes of European professionals, unheard of.

"Your words are not a suggestion to me, mon Général. They are an order I shall fulfill with joy. May I congratulate you on your first victory of this campaign."

"Our campaign, my friend, but may I add," he said, showing his very American pragmatism, after so many years of disappointment and defeats, "we must remember this is only the opening move."

Turning about, they galloped back, to be greeted by the cheers of fifteen thousand men, who with barely a casualty or the turning of a single spade full of dirt, now held the outer siege lines of the enemy.

Fifteen

YORKTOWN
THE NIGHT OF OCTOBER 6–7, 1781

THE COOL AND STEADY RAINFALL WAS PERFECT FOR THIS
night's work, Washington thought, masking any moonlight, the rainfall
deadening any sound. During the previous week, after the shocking
display of the British abandonment of their works, which his army now
occupied, without barely having to fire a shot, he eagerly accepted
the advice offered by the French professionals, truly the world's masters when it came to siege works. Rochambeau had even predicted
that their mass display of advancing as they did might, indeed, trigger
the British to retreat, which had happened. The French, the recognized masters of the world when it came to laying out siege lines, had
surveyed the entire front, offering suggestions as to the next step
that he noted down with ready acceptance.

There had been jubilation throughout the ranks at the sight of the
ignominious withdrawal of their enemy, and morale had soared to
heights he had not experienced since the heady days of July 1776, right

after the public readings of the Declaration, and before the debacle of the fight for control of New York City had begun.

The men set to now with an extra will and with the rations provided by the French, they were actually happy with their lot, in spite of the plague of gnats, biting flies, and mosquitoes. The long march, most of it under good weather, the plentiful rations, even the labor at hand caused men who seemed on the point of physical collapse or desertion but weeks ago to now throw all they had into this effort.

His army felt absolutely vibrant, and this was no false bravado of men who had not yet seen the reality of battle. They smelled victory, a true victory in the air, and the enthusiastic talk was that once they had driven the bloody British into the bay or into prison camps, they could all at last go home.

He did nothing to still such talk right now. He needed that sense of destiny in them, if the siege dragged out till the end of the month, and he was forced to order an all-out assault along the entire front before de Grasse turned his fleet south, or—his other fear—that a British fleet would appear and this time truly look for an all-out fight to relieve their trapped men.

After so many years of ceaseless worry about where the next day's rations would come from, how was he to hold this army together for another month, he felt at last he had an army under his command that would see this thing through to a final glorious victory.

The causeways crossing the marshes, hastily built the first day, had been reinforced. They were covered over and tamped down with earth, sand, and gravel, able to support the hundreds of wagonloads of supplies an army of fifteen thousand in the forward lines needed to maintain a proper siege, and to provide roadways as well for the heavy artillery yet to be moved forward.

The newly captured outer works, which, of course, had faced toward an enemy approach, had had to be refortified now that they faced inward. The British had, indeed, expended a fair amount of their precious artillery rounds harassing his men at work, who had lookouts posted for whenever a gun aimed in their direction was fired, the result being only less than a score of casualties for hundreds of rounds fired. To instill morale, he had followed the French lead, and offered a bounty of a shilling in silver for any man who retrieved a fired British solid shot in good enough shape to be reloaded and fired back. He actually did regret that offer, because after each shot had lodged in the earthworks or bounded to a stop, a dozen or more men would drop picks and shovels and scramble about, laughing, yelling, and at times brawling with each other as if from rival regiments, to retrieve the bounty sent over by their enemies that was worth a good jug of corn liquor in trade. Young Wellsley, laughing, had reported that the price of liquor had gone up significantly now that the British were providing payment for it.

Two men eventually had to be flogged, lightly though, when they were caught trying to steal a caisson load of shot from Knox's artillery camp to dole out as "captured" British rounds. With a stern warning that the next fool who attempted that, Knox would personally deliver three dozen lashes.

Literally thousands of trees for miles around Williamsburg had been cut down, to provide lumber for the building of roads, to reinforce revetments and trenches, and even, under the supervision of carpenters from the French navy, the dropping of many a stately old oak. These were used for hasty repairs to broken "knees," siding and planking for French ships of the line damaged in their engagement, now called the "Battle of the Capes," while stately pines that were dead and well-seasoned were sought out for replacement spars.

Every morning he awoke with the fear that during the night the Royal navy had returned and this time, under sturdier command, was spoiling for a fight to the death, behind them transports laden with the garrison of New York as a relief force. Each morning the first report was one of reassurance, delivered personally by de Grasse, that all had passed well during the night and offering words of encouragement that the French navy would see this campaign through to glorious victory.

There was no light except for a single, hooded lantern. One of his men, covered in mud, grinning, handed him a pick. He had not originally thought to participate in what struck him at first suggestion as a somewhat foolish ritual but von Steuben strongly urged him to go forward and do so.

"Da men, mein General, all will speak of it and work twice the hard. Even King Frederick, ja, would do such things."

He took the pick and liked the heft and feel of it. There was a time in his youth where he could hold a long handle ax out at arm's length in a bet with friends, standing absolutely rigid for long minutes while others competing against him would, with sweat beading down their faces and arms trembling, let their axes fall, while he just stood smiling, but, of course, keeping well hidden the pain of doing so.

He raised the pick, swung it back and forth a few times to gauge its heft and weight. It was a good tool, typical of the French in so many things, who even when it came to siegecraft made their tools with precision and skill.

He raised it on high, and with a solid reassuring thump, swung it down, cutting deep into the forward wall of the trench, pulling back a full spade load of dirt that fell to his feet. There were muffled words of approval that "His Excellency" still had the strength of a laddie half his age.

He stepped back, unable to hide a grin of delight that he had not looked foolish and missed his blow.

He handed the tool back to one of his men of the line.

"Here you go soldier, what's your name?"

"Jerry Clark, sir, 1st Continental Regiment of Foot, been with you, sir, since Long Island. Wounded at Brandywine and at Monmouth, and still with it."

"What do you think of this, Clark?"

The man grinned with delight.

"Sir, after we push them lobsterbacks into the bay, I'd be honored if you'd have a drink with me, sir."

"Mr. Clark, you are a true Patriot and may America always remember the service men like you have given to her. Yes, I will join you in that drink."

Clark looked back at his comrades who had gathered round.

"Now to work, men!"

They set to with a will, and within a few minutes the outlines of the long traverse were already dug out. It would sink down into the earth at a gradual angle. The French engineers had crept out at night, watchfully accompanied by Morgan's riflemen and Mose, ever hopeful that he could "bag another one," to drill out core samples of the subsurface. They had assured him and Rochambeau they could go a full eight feet below the surface before hitting the water table, the bane of more than one siege effort, learned by hard experience by both the French and English when campaigning in the fields of Flanders. It would be twelve feet wide, and covered over with timbers, which by the thousands had been stockpiled behind the lines, and when completed, would stretch an amazing two thousand yards, to nearly within killing range of the inner British works. Once there, a parallel line trench would be cut across the face of the British lines with deeply placed revetments for the heavy mortars and howitzers, which would then pound the town of Yorktown, if need be, into rubble.

It would provide, as well, firing positions to hammer the small fleet of light British ships, bottled up in Yorktown harbor. This fleet was essential for them to maintain a line of supply and communication to their secondary line, north of the York River at Gloucester Point. That was held by the infamous Tarleton, according to reports by Washington's intelligence chief for this campaign, and a brave but damn near-foolhardy reconnaissance raid led by Peter Wellsley, that had fetched that news back. Tarleton had attempted a raid out of that line to try and pull in some supplies and spread general mayhem, but had been repulsed. It was fair to assume, though, that he would attempt so again, or at least order others to do it. Veterans of the campaigns in the Carolinas, on their own, had raised a fund of ten pounds sterling, in real silver, for any man who brought in Tarleton's head, with emphasis that it only had to be the head.

Though he officially disapproved of such sentiments, Lafayette had made it clear he had put five pounds of his own money into the fund, and, in a rare defiant mood, had made clear he would not withdraw the prize money, no matter what his general might say. Many grumbled that if only Arnold were still here, the fund would have leaped to a hundred pounds sterling.

He watched the men laboring away with a will. For those digging at the front, their French comrades had promised a healthy ration of good brandy when relieved, which was a tradition with their army. Behind them, men by the hundreds were in place, ready as relief forces, others already manhandling up timbers to lay across the top of the trench and cover over with the earth that had been dug out. That was a dangerous job, and would become increasingly dangerous the following night, when the British would, unless totally blind, see the traverse heading toward them. Flares would be sent up, and, if they still had sufficient grit, skirmishers would be slipped out to shoot at the men aboveground when illuminated. It was a slow type of warfare that he chafed against when compared to an open fight in the field, but it could be just as deadly. One mismanaged move, one mistake, and swarms of British light infantry and Hessian Jaegers gaining the traverse would be slaughtering men by the score and in a few hours tearing apart a week's worth of work, and if given sufficient time, actually seizing and holding the traverse, forcing their enemies to try somewhere else.

Always the clock was ticking away. All were of good heart, morale was the highest he had witnessed since the early days of the war, before the disasters at Long Island and Manhattan. He marked off every day on the calendar as one less day that de Grasse had promised him. A promise that could be shattered if a bold English fleet suddenly appeared off the Capes and aggressively sought battle. There was a time, a time when he still defined himself as an Englishman, that he had read with pride of how a sharp and gallant move by but a few ships of the Royal navy had disrupted the plans of empire by Spain and France.

It would truly shatter the morale of his army if after the years of suffering, the exhausting march of August and September to come to this place, that at the last minute, the French fleet was defeated. Worse yet was, as later dispatches would declare, "and thus the fleet was forced to withdraw out of military necessity," the standard line of any commander covering the fact that rather than venture all, he had fled.

Washington knew that ultimately the French had nothing to truly gain by holding this bay four weeks longer, other than the potential glory of then claiming they had helped to bag an entire English army in the worst defeat inflicted upon them since the Hundred Years War. If an English fleet, even a small raiding force, should seize but a few islands of the sugar islands of the Caribbean in exchange for this, de Grasse would be recalled in disgrace. He owed that man much. As he watched his men dig, with shovels, picks, and tools provided by their ally, he found himself praying that no matter what might happen in the future, America owed much to this gallant ally, and if ever asked to repay them in some future war, perhaps on their own soil, we would not hesitate to answer that call, and they, in turn, would remember the eternal pledge made here as allies.

Seeing that the work was proceeding at a brisk pace, his ceremonial task completed, he turned aside and started the long walk back to return to his headquarters. The trench was lined with men, coming to their feet as he passed, offering salutes, raising hats, but no shouting out all had been repeatedly ordered to remain silent, but more than one whispered "General number one," as he passed, reaching out to touch his arm as if he were a talisman.

It could not help but move him, and again he prayed that this campaign would end without a frontal charge upon hearing that the French fleet was withdrawing, and that within hours the English would be relieved, if not destroyed that day. The prayer even went to his enemies as well, because if unleashed in a forlorn assault, by even the European rules of war, the begging for quarter at the last instant was often near impossible to achieve after such slaughter. He did not wish his nation to be founded upon such a legacy.

Clearing the main redoubt line, he ventured down the now covered causeway, at last reaching the marsh, where to his amazement, he found an extremely upset Lafayette awaiting him.

"It is infamy, sir, absolute infamy, and you must send a protest to Cornwallis!"

"What is it, my friend?"

"Infamy, that is what it is. I never dreamed they would sink to such depravity."

He felt a momentary flutter of concern. Had Tarleton raided out again and committed some atrocity? He was still angered, deeply angered that though Cornwallis had promised to investigate, no reply since had come back regarding the murder of the pregnant woman, and his respect for the man had plummeted as a result.

"They slaughtered all of them. Well, nearly all of them!"

"Slaughtered who?" he cried, fearing to hear the grim news that might trigger his own army into a rage of bloodlust that could not be contained.

"Their horses!"

"What?"

"Their horses, sir. Cornwallis had every horse in the army, except for those belonging to officers and their dragoons, driven down to the bay, and there they slaughtered them all."

"Horses?"

"Yes, sir, Cornwallis ordered all of them killed."

Washington stood silent, not sure how to reply. As a horseman of some renown in Virginia, in his younger days admiring friends said he was the finest horseman in the colony; be it on fox or boar hunt, or on the race track, his heart was close to horses . . . but this was war with all its tragedies and he was not sure what to say.

"Hundreds of them. Sir, may I beg that you send a letter of protest to Cornwallis, or at least give me leave to do so."

"May I ask why, and what would you wish different?"

"Sir, we could have arranged a cartel, an exchange of their horses for something, anything."

"And what would you have proposed? There is no sense to it now, my dear comrade, the deed is done. But pray what would you have proposed in return?"

Lafayette extended his arms in a typical Gallic gesture of frustration.

"A question, my friend."

"Yes, sir."

"I am confused by this, why not eat them instead? It would have given the army fresh meat for a week or more."

Lafayette looked at him in astonishment.

"Why they are Englishmen! Everyone knows Englishmen do not eat horse."

"We did, at Valley Forge and Morristown."

Lafayette dwelled on that for a moment and sighed.

"I see your point, sir, but we could have given them to my fellow countrymen."

"For what purpose, sir?"

"Why to eat, of course. We do not have your, how shall I say this, prejudice against horseflesh properly stewed or slow roasted over an open flame."

He could not reply.

"The English, they are all stupid, they killed perfectly good rations," and sighing and muttering to himself, Lafayette walked away.

Washington stood silent, and then going up to where Billy Lee had patiently waited for him, holding the bridles of their mounts, he paused for a moment and rubbed the snout of his horse.

"Hope you didn't hear that," he whispered into his mount's ear while fetching a handful of corn out of his pocket as an offering. "I'll starve before I'll eat you."

HEADQUARTERS OF CORNWALLIS
AFTERNOON OF OCTOBER 7, 1781

He sat alone, stunned with disbelief. In one night, under cover of the storm now sweeping these accursed grounds, the enemy had started a traverse of nearly a half mile. It was still shallow, just deep enough and wide enough to provide cover for a few diggers at the front, but behind them he could see hundreds of spades rising and falling, widening the trench, and back near its starting point, it had already been covered over with timbers. They were already beginning to branch out with parallel lines definitely within the range of their deadly riflemen. One in particular seemed to appear like a ghost at one place, strike down one of his officers, who was incautiously peeking up over the lip of a trench, shout an obscene taunt, cackle, and spit, then an hour later kill or nearly hit another of his men.

It was impossible, simply impossible. The best of his engineers had assured him that such a traverse would take four days, perhaps a week to construct, and once spotted, proper countermeasures could be taken. Either a direct counterassault by light infantry at night, or a counter-traverse, to meet them in the middle of the siege grounds, and there, man to man, the light infantry backed up by grenadiers would surely hurl them back.

It was now, however, an accomplished fact. They had burrowed ahead like moles, digging deep enough to provide cover for their damn riflemen and skirmishers to get within killing range. Several of their regimental flags had been hoisted up out of the trenches at dawn and waved defiantly, greeted with huzzas and jeers toward his own men, who stunned, were all but silent, hunkered down behind their earthen walls. As he walked down their battle line, though roused by officers to come to attention and salute, few showed the enthusiasm and eager cheers that had once greeted him when, triumphant, he had ridden up Market Street of Charleston, fifes and drummers playing.

Damn Clinton, damn him, he sighed.

Yet there was no use in damning him. He was hundreds of miles away, and that despite the reassuring message slipped through the blockade that even now he was mounting a rescue force that, God willing, would arrive by the end of the month.

A sheet of paper, vague promises, and that was it.

He sat in silence. The gunfire of his batteries, ordered now to conserve ammunition to but ten rounds a day per gun and fire only if all but certain of a kill, thumped. The French and American guns did not reply, and he knew what that meant as well. They had a surfeit of ammunition, but would not fire one round until all was in place. Washington had, indeed, matured into a commander worthy of any European battlefield, unlike the man who he had thought was an amateur, a bumpkin so easily routed at Long Island. He had matured into a trained professional. He would patiently wait the few more days until the parallel was well established with gun emplacements well dug in and masked with a single night's digging. His estimates were they had near to a hundred pieces on hand, without doubt the heavy siege train that Hood and Graves had let slip past them within the hulls of Admiral Barre's ships. He would wait until every precious gun was in place, well secured against anything but the luckiest of hits, and then unleash them all at once in a withering barrage that would last for days and tear open his inner line and shatter what little will his men still had.

The noose was tightening with every passing moment, and if he did survive this, a day would come when he had to face his king to explain what happened here, while Clinton standing to one side would but shrug and have his excuses ready. History, as it usually did with such affairs, would all but forget Clinton's name, but forever remember him as the general defeated and humiliated.

Tarleton had tried a breakout a few days ago and been soundly repulsed. In one, at most two, days from now their parallels would place into position a battery of guns that would drive out of Yorktown bay the small fleet of light ships still at his disposal. Breakout here on this front would be impossible.

To try for a breakout, yet again, in a night action. If a hole could be cut in their lines on the north shore, at Gloucester, spike his guns, abandon this line, and in what would be a last hope, cut his way out and into the open countryside of Virginia.

It would be at least some sort of force intact, that by living off the land could survive until the Royal navy, bearing Clinton and his men in their hulls, did show up for the rescue, which, of course, Clinton would claim as his own action. To hell with him. At least it was a slim hope in the face of what was now utter humiliation and ruin at the hands of the upstart Washington. He still had one card up his own sleeve in response, and it was time to play it.

Cornwallis rose up, stepped out of his private chamber, the grenadier guards posted to either side of the door coming to rigid attention, and out in the corridor his staff came to their feet.

"Send for Tarleton and," he paused for a moment trying to remember a name, "that Loyalist Yankee, what's his name . . . van Dorn. He apparently knows these kinds of operations, let's give him something to do other than draw rations, I'm certain he'll be delighted to lead it."

Sixteen

HEADQUARTERS OF GENERAL WASHINGTON
NIGHT OF OCTOBER 8, 1781

HE LOOKED AROUND AT HIS ASSEMBLED OFFICERS. ALL WERE grinning, their delight obviously enhanced as well by the case of brandy sent over with the warmest of compliments by Admiral de Grasse, a note attached, yet again, assuring Washington that the navy of France stood in amazement at all that had been accomplished since their last meeting and would stand by his side even if the entire British fleet now did suddenly appear.

He nodded to General Knox who now stood.

"All is prepared, sir, as per your orders. Ninety guns are in place along the line, including those of our French allies. Proper reserve bunkers have been dug for speedy resupply of every piece along the siege line, with batteries of light field artillery ready to move out and deploy at a moment's notice if the enemy should attempt a sortie. We have a hundred rounds per siege gun moved forward, and, as you have ordered, steady fire shall be maintained starting just before sunset tomorrow and continue throughout the night. Sighting sticks have been set out so the fire will be accurate enough to strike their works in spite of darkness, and flare rounds for the mortars are in place as well if illumination is needed. We'll expend just under five thousand rounds of heavy fire throughout the first night."

"God's grace, how many rounds did we have at Trenton?" Greene asked.

Knox looked at his old comrade and grinned.

"Just under a hundred rounds total for all guns, sir."

"Pray continue," Washington asked before another round of self-congratulations and toasts erupted, even though he was awed by the numbers. The armies had close to a hundred rounds per heavy gun in reserve, nearly fifty thousand rounds, and de Grasse had promised, as well, that extra ammunition would be provided by his fleet if need be. Six years ago such profligate expenditures were beyond his wildest dreams, recalling a day, the day this Revolution had started, when the British had ventured eighteen miles out of Boston to Concord, to try to snatch a few four-pounders, a couple of barrels of powder, fifty round shot, and twenty grapeshot hidden there.

If only they had known what it would ultimately cost them, if only we had all known, he realized, recalling the thousands of unmarked graves after Trenton and the long bitter winters at Valley Forge and Morristown. Boys and youths thought that if it was their fate to die as a soldier they would die gloriously upon some battlefield, a relatively painless death, as he was told Andre had said, "but a momentary pang." For each who died thus, and few of them painlessly, most of them screaming their last breaths out under a surgeon's knife, ten would die of smallpox, flux, ague, consumption, or locked within the damnable stinking prison hulks on the East River of New York.

"Sir, as with the turning of the first blade of soil, all of my command begs of you the honor that you will fire the first shot of this final bombardment."

He nodded, half listening, as Knox told him the time and place, and that an honor guard would be sent for him and Rochambeau to guide them to the proper bastion where all would be prepared for them.

Would Cornwallis so abjectly and tamely submit upon his knees to this fate, he wondered. If it was he, at this very moment he would be planning some final riposte, even if but a desperate lunge.

He interrupted the self-congratulatory celebration as Knox heavily settled back in his chair.

"Gentlemen, I want every regiment along the line to stand to this night. Half to be on guard, bayonets fixed, muskets loaded, while the other half rests. Guard to then be changed every two hours, all men ordered to clean out their musket pans, and wipe their flints clean of moisture from the night dew. Every regiment to double their skirmisher guards forward with clear orders that if they spot a sortie to withdraw silently back into their lines. Every gun along the line to be charged with a double load of grapeshot, artillery men to have hot lintstocks ready and burning. Every hour on the hour the breech charges of all guns to be wiped clean and replaced with fresh powder."

The room fell silent with his words of caution.

"Let us not grow complacent, my comrades. There is no need to pass this along to the French on our left. They are professionals as we are, and without doubt at this very moment General Rochambeau is passing the same orders. Cornwallis must know what tomorrow will unleash upon him, and if all was reversed, I would order an all-out assault shortly after midnight and attempt a breakout, or least such a disruption of our position and the spiking of the siege guns to set our efforts back a month or more. We know if he succeeds in that, and the Royal navy arrives, all can still be lost. So do not let us grow too fat and complacent, my friends."

Knox blushed slightly, always sensitive about his three hundred pounds of girth. Washington looked at him reassuringly and smiled.

"A master of artillery needs those few extra pounds in order to single-handedly manhandle his guns about, as you do."

Henry threw back his head and laughed good-naturedly at his own expense and again there were relaxed chuckles.

"It will keep our men on their toes and besides, let Cornwallis come and he will receive one hell of a welcoming in the middle of the night."

The room relaxed after the stern tone of Washington's words.

The bottles of brandy were passed around, their general as usual refraining, along with a young officer at the far end of the table.

"General, sir?"

It was Peter Wellsley. Few in the room actually knew his true role; some recalled him as a youth who had bravely guided them flawlessly against the Hessians at Trenton and again at the second battle of Trenton, and Princeton the day after. Others had vague recollection of him at Monmouth or standing alongside a British officer to witness the execution of Major Andre.

The way Washington nodded for him to go ahead and speak, displaying utmost respect, was clear enough indication for the celebratory gathering to fall silent.

"I have some concern about the Gloucester front, sir."

"Go ahead."

"It is the back door as we all know, on the far side of the river and where their leader of dragoons, Tarleton, is in command. It might be a back door, sir. I know they tried a few days ago and our men guarding that approach gallantly repulsed them, but I must caution that if I were Cornwallis I just might try there again for a breakout."

"Go on, sir, I am listening."

Peter nervously cleared his throat.

"We have advanced our lines along this main front and it is obvious to all on both fronts where the main blow shall now fall. Therefore, sir, I suggest that Cornwallis, or at least this beast Tarleton, as he is called, might have orders to attempt to open a breakthrough. Or even without orders and upon his own."

"Exactly what that bastard might try," Morgan snapped. "Excuse my language, sir, but the lad is right. It'd be like him to try to bolt and run, and maybe cut a hole wide enough for the rest of them scoundrels to follow. He knows every man who fought in the South has sworn an oath to put a bullet in him."

"If they can open a line of escape," Peter continued, "before we can shift our main forces across the river, if they abandon all heavy equipment and just take what each man can carry, thousands could escape, bring low our efforts here, and ravage the countryside in a bloody and senseless slaughter."

Washington realized the young man could be right.

"What leads you to this conclusion?"

"Five long years of war in my home state of New Jersey," Peter replied calmly, and no one offered a sarcasm or rebuff after their celebration of but moments before. He had presented them with a scenario that just might be true, and could lead to the deaths of thousands, perhaps even a denial of ultimate victory and a vicious degeneration of their war that could then drag on for additional years.

"Your suggestion."

"Shifting of at least the militia in reserve to that front. They might not be able to stand against a well-coordinated assault by heavy infantry, but I doubt it would be coordinated. Once free of a trap they most likely would break apart. In that department, sir, as I witnessed repeatedly, militia can, indeed, be most efficient, and remorseless, and most certainly deadly.

"They would then buy the time for our main line troops of the Continental line to shift across the river, contain the breakthrough, and drive it back into the river."

No one spoke for a moment.

"I wholeheartedly concur, sir," Morgan finally said, breaking the troubled silence.

Washington extended his hand as if almost in salute to Peter.

"I concur as well, Colonel Wellsley, and humbly thank you for this caution. It is wisely suggested. I hereby authorize you to pass the order, which I shall draw up immediately, to our militia units to transfer to the north bank of the river to reinforce our position behind the lines, forming a cordon to block or at least slow any attempted breakout. You are brevetted to command of those forces until the ending of this siege."

Peter stood up, bowing low, saying nothing in reply.

"Alexander," Washington said, pushing aside the plates and bottle of brandy set before him, "help me to draw those orders up immediately."

ALLEN CROSSED OVER THE ENTRENCHMENTS THE HOUR BE-fore dawn, picked Hessian skirmishers and light infantry, all of them volunteers, moving in open line through the predawn day. The Hessian riflemen insisted upon wearing their uniforms. They knew the odds, this was not their war after all, and if captured or dropped wounded, they wanted the rights of any infantryman of the line, to fair capture and fair and honorable treatment. Tarleton, to his disgust, had, at the last moment, just simply said he would lead the main breakout rather than accompany Allen. They knew the gambit was far more desperate. After two bitter years in the Carolinas, and for some nasty atrocities all the way back to Paoli, their chances of surviving capture were problematic at best, if even one Rebel on the other side remembered and now sought vengeance. As the siege line had drawn closer, within taunting range, threats had been shouted across that honorable surrender would be offered to any man of the main infantry line, but if any of the bastards involved in the murder of the pregnant mother and child were found, orders or not, their suffering, after being handed over to some of the Indians with their army, would drag out for days. They were so terrified, most of them lads swept up from the gutters of English, Scottish, and Irish cities and pressed into service, free of any guilt, except for the few, that the risk Allen offered them seemed the only alternative left.

The plan discussed with Cornwallis was straightforward enough. To don the uniforms of Virginia militia or civilian clothes, breakthrough a weak spot he had observed in their lines, and head for open country beyond. According to the plan to which Tarleton had simply nodded agreement, and that van Dorn realized now, that that officer, expecting his rank to preserve his own hide, would only make the vaguest of motions to follow up on, Allen would break through, secure good ground behind the enemy lines, and signal back that he had secured a breakthrough point. Tarleton was then to attack with all his forces while Allen struck back into the rear of the enemy to sow confusion and alarm. Once a breach had been secured, the rest of the army would cross the river and proceed up and away from Yorktown.

It was a mad hope for somehow that was all but "fey" as the Irish in the ranks called it when first he briefed them, but at least it was something. He reassured them that he had done such operations in New Jersey a dozen times before, and just walked away scot-free.

Even as Jamie begged to come, he had ordered the lad to stay behind, and was now horrified to find him loyally following as they crept through the predawn darkness. It was too late to hiss and order him to fall back and follow orders.

A Hessian in front of him did the hard deed he himself always shied away from. Surprising the forward sentry, who was actually asleep, the Hessian slipped into his position, knife drawn, and cut the old man's throat, hand over his victim's mouth. Then, almost gently, laid the body down, and to Allen's surprise actually muttered a prayer and made the sign of the cross before pushing forward and up over the main entrenchment line.

As he had learned at Paoli, he ordered the seventy-five men with him to advance with loaded muskets but pans empty, and to do their task with bayonet and knife only. They gained the revetment and stormed over it, but some of the Continentals holding this line, not caught completely off guard, opened fire. There was a vicious minute of close infighting before they had cleared the trench for a span of a hundred yards.

They could only hold it for minutes, the alarm already being sounded. He had a hooded lantern with him, unmasked it, held it up while standing atop the battlement, and waved it back and forth.

There was no response; no follow-up wave of dragoons to open their hold.

There was a moment of hesitation on his part. Had that bastard Tarleton just ignored Cornwallis's orders, decided all was lost anyhow, and was now turning coward and not following through as agreed?

"We fall back, ya?"

It was one of the Hessians, a man he recognized from years before and had befriended after the fight at Princeton.

Surely Cornwallis must be watching this operation and would eventually order Tarleton to push straight in regardless. They had a breach; had cracked their surprisingly weakly held lines wide open on this other shore of the harbor. If they pulled back now, this effort was, indeed, lost.

"Press forward," he snarled. "The woods over there," and he pointed to a farmer's woodlot two hundred yards to the American rear. "We hole up there if need be. We can play hell with them. You riflemen, harass their rear until Cornwallis finally does something, damn it."

Those still with him followed as Allen sprinted for the woods. In all the confusion they had triggered, and an adroit lie on his part to a nervous sentry, who stopped him for a moment, that the enemy had broken through and he was ordered to fall back and hold the woods. Most of his band gained the temporary safety of the stand of chestnuts and oak. Three quarters of the woodlot had been harvested for the building of the entrenchments, but there were still several dozen acres standing, cut through the middle with a deep ravine where hopefully they could hide until the follow-up attack came to their rescue.

The dawn was rising; it was chaos along the line as swarms of Continentals came in from either flank to close off the breach. It was as if a vast iron door was closing behind him.

Tarleton had betrayed him, he would not follow through.

He ordered his men to withdraw deeper into the woods and down into the ravine. Those wearing Continental uniforms were to form a cordon at the edge of the forest and divert any inquiries. If they could hide thus throughout the day, once darkness fell they would strike back to the river, strip down, and try to swim back to safety.

The ruse held for nearly half a day. He actually managed to doze off after a sleepless night of planning and worry. The dream was a lovely one. The war was over, he was returning home, to his parents' house. Strangely—though it did not seem strange in the dream—his youngest brother, dead after the battle literally fought on his doorstep, was there to greet him with open arms, his parents weeping with joy. The greatest of joys awaited him within the doorway. Elizabeth, beaming with absolute ecstasy, leaping into his arms, smothering him with kisses, as she had during their one night together. He was so overjoyed tears flowed, and tears were flowing as he opened his eyes, and it was young Jamie kneeling over him and shaking Allen awake.

"Sir! Sir! Something's going wrong."

He sat up, Jamie pointing back toward the enemy line.

He followed Jamie back to the edge of the woodlot. All was clear to see. A heavy line of infantry was drawing up, bayonets fixed, someone before them, pointing toward the woods, and an officer drawing saber and pointing in their direction.

"Sorry, sir, guess I didn't sound right."

It was one of the men he had posted as a cordon around where the rest of them were hiding with orders to these guards to be taciturn but blunt, that "secret supplies" were concealed in the woods and not to be disturbed until nightfall when they would finally be moved forward into the main line. Far too many of these men, straight from their homelands, could barely sound like a proper Yankee, but if pressed they were to say they were from Massachusetts and thus perhaps throw off any inquiries from Virginia militia.

"I was flustered and blurted out Liverpool when he asked me what town I was from," the frightened youth said. "He didn't say nothing, sir, but then took off at a run saying there weren't no town named such in that whole damn Yankee state."

The Continentals, several companies strong, were deploying out to cover the entire width of the woodlot, bayonets fixed.

Allen looked at his now thoroughly frightened command.

"There's nothing left for it, lads," he hissed. "God bless you, and run for it."

He grabbed Jamie by the shoulder, turned, and started to run. Light infantry men wearing Continental uniforms began to tear them off, hoping that if caught in just breeches and shirt they might be shown mercy. Hessians, having wisely insisted upon full uniforms, just began to stand up, but then taking their much beloved rifles and smashing the stocks against trees, shattering their weapons before tossing them aside and stepping out of the woods with cries of "Kamerad! Nicht schiessen!"

For those who had followed his suggestion of civilian garb, there was nothing now but panicked flight.

"Stay with me, Jamie, we've always talked our way out of this before!"

Bolting out of the north side of the woods he set off at a full run, and for the next three hours actually did manage to dodge his way a couple of miles toward the rear. He mimicked an angry farmer, his old routine of having brought up a couple of jugs of good liquor to sell and been cheated by those damn regulars, pulling a bottle of rum out of his haversack and offering it as proof and a bribe. Shorn of that trick, he was an angry father with his son, looking for his trollop wife who had taken off with an officer. He even had Jamie strike him a blow that had broken his nose to make the ruse look more convincing, now whining about being beaten up for his efforts to fetch his wayward wife back. Some militia who had stopped him let Allen pass with mockery and disdain. A final effort was to first try and talk his way past two sentries, and there seemed to be a swarm of them about the countryside, that he had been in the fighting, chasing down some lobsterbacks who had tried to cut their way through, had his nose broken and his son was now helping him home to his wife and five children, who he wished he had never left.

Jamie had worked his way around the one sentry, and knocked him cold with a single blow from behind, and to his horror, Allen had been forced to knife the other one. He prayed not fatally, but the man had sat up howling with pain as they ran off. The hue and cry was now following them, like a pack of blood-hungry hounds, that they had two lobsterback spies on the run.

They had run another half mile northward, and he was sickened to see one of the men who had followed them the night before had somehow managed to make his way ahead of them. He was dangling from the end of a rope at a farm-lane crossroads. His death had not been sharp and clean. They had hoisted him up to strangle slowly, and the men who had done it were standing about, admiring their work, their victim's face contorted with agony from his final death struggle, as he slowly kicked out his life, and with every jerk the rope had tightened a bit more to strangle him.

One of the killers spotted them, shouted, and the pursuit was on again.

Jamie was beginning to flag, gasping for breath, begging for a halt, but he would not leave him behind for the obviously bloodthirsty militia, half dragging him along as they dodged around a farmstead that had somehow been spared from burning. The bay was visible, just several hundred yards away.

"One more sprint, Jamie, then into the water, swim out into the middle of the bay, and we're safe."

"But I can't swim, sir."

"I'll hold you up, lad," he cried in desperation.

Then he saw them: mounted regulars, cutting down along the edge of the bay ahead of him. He stared in disbelief. He could always recognize Peter who still rode as clumsily as ever.

Looking back to the farmstead and its barn, still intact, he pushed Jamie into it. There was a hay loft. Perhaps, dear God, show mercy at least to the lad, perhaps they will think we ran past it, not so stupid as to seek refuge within.

"Oh, God in heaven," Peter sighed, watching with disbelief as Allen, pushing someone ahead of him, staggered into the barn. Surely he would not be so foolish as to be caught this way.

The alarm had been up since dawn that a group of several

hundred of the enemy had broken through the main line, as he had predicted, and then disappeared. The militia units under his nominal command had all but gone to pieces with excitement and the chase, running about, damn near shooting him at one point when they declared his Jersey accent sounded English to them. He had finally dismounted, displayed all his dispatches and orders, and was actually dragged before their colonel. His captors were clearly disappointed they would miss out on the hanging, when the colonel finally conceded that Peter was who he claimed to be.

It had delayed him nearly two hours and for a few minutes he actually thought they would string him up, one hell of a way to end his career in the army. Terrifying as well, when he did pass some of their handiwork, a man dangling at a crossroads, the object of jeering from half a dozen militia who had just finished him off. He could only pray the man had been an enemy, trying to slip past in civilian garb, thus, at least, nominally deserving of his fate. He had scattered the executioners with vehement curses and cut the body down, haunted as he did so that the way Major Andre died, at least, had some dignity to it, even mourning from those forced by the necessities of war to perform such a grisly task, rather than this leering mob.

He had finally acquired a guard of mounted dragoons to ride with him. An offering from Morgan, who had been searching for him most of the day, with the express orders to stay with him and guard him, fearing the fate he had almost faced with men on his own side if he rode about on his own with his strange Jersey accent, and for which, after his near brush with a hanging and seeing the dangling corpse, he was, indeed, grateful.

"My God, it is Allen," Peter sighed, as he rode up to the barn and dismounted, followed by his guard detail, short muskets or pistols drawn.

From the opposite direction a swarm of militia was closing in.

"Stay out here," Peter ordered, looking back at his escorts.

"Sir. He is a damn lobsterback out of uniform," one of them snapped in angry reply, "and General Washington's orders were clear to us. If we fail to bring you back safely, he'll personally flog the lot of us."

"Then face the damn flogging, but you are ordered to stay here. Tell him those were my orders."

His cold gaze stilled further protest. "Fine, sir, it's your neck, and only our backs."

"Keep those damn militia back."

Drawing his pistol and cocking it, he stepped into the cool darkness of a barn that was rich with the scents that conjured so many memories of childhood, of cows and sheep, and fresh mown hay, and apples newly harvested. Memories of many a childhood lark on an autumn afternoon with his friends, the three van Dorn brothers, and how the eldest always protected and stood up for him if the younger tried to tease or pick on him while they snuck into a farmer's barn to filch some fresh milk or a slice of smoked ham before wandering on in their childhood games of war, and Indians, and knights, and dreams of future glory.

He paused for a moment, letting his eyes adjust to the dim light. The lower floor of the barn was empty. Cattle, pigs, and sheep having been driven off long ago to feed the hungry maw of war, whether English or Continental, French or Hessian, no longer mattered.

He prayed silently that his wily friend had simply dodged in here as a ruse, had somehow slipped past the militia. They were already on the other side of the building shouting protests as his escort ordered them to stand back and away, crying it was they who had cornered the damn Tories, and it was time for another hanging.

With pistol raised he cautiously slipped through the lower floor of the barn, looking into each empty stall, and then his gaze shifted upward to the hay loft.

Merciful God, surely not there, not there, not so amateur a move now. Surely he had figured out some other way to escape this trap.

He was tempted to turn away yet again, to just step outside, say no one hid within, but he could hear the arguing on the other side of the thin walls. Someone was declaring that he was a captain of militia and if the regulars didn't have the guts to search the barn properly, they sure as hell would, and string the bastards up after what they had done to that poor woman down in Williamsburg.

Heart pounding, Peter cautiously climbed the ladder to the upper floor and stepped out onto it. A mound of hay was all that was up there, actually pathetic looking, a final effort of some poor farmer to at least bring in a little something for beasts that no longer existed after both armies had foraged through his land. As always, the price of war for those caught in its grasp, no matter which side they were on.

He leveled the pistol at the mound of hay in the corner of the barn. "Allen, I know you are in there. It is Peter."

Silence for a brief moment and then the fresh mown hay seemed to have a life of its own as it stirred, parted, and Allen stood up, a pale-faced trembling youth behind him.

His pistol was cocked and raised, pointing straight at him.

"Allen," he sighed, and for a moment his eyes clouded with tears.

"Yes, Peter."

"It's over, Allen."

He just stood silent staring at him, while outside the crowd of militia was growing in size and volume of protest, demanding that the prisoners belong to them, and would receive the treatment they deserved.

"You hear that?" Peter asked, and there was a beseeching note in his voice.

Now he could see tears in Allen's eyes.

"Do you remember Elizabeth?" Allen asked, voice trembling.

"Of course I do. And yes, I knew you were upstairs that day."

A momentary pause.

"You know what to tell her," Allen whispered softly. "You know what you have to do, my friend. We both saw John Andre die. For God's sake do it for me, for Elizabeth."

He smiled sadly.

"Peter, I've seen things and done things most would not believe in this war, but at the end I thought of her. Tell Elizabeth, I thought of her in my last moments. Now do it."

Allen turned his pistol aside and squeezed the trigger. The explosive roar in the confines of the barn startled Peter, and in the next second he aimed true, as he would for any friend.

Allen tumbled backward, chest shattered, and was dead even before he collapsed into the freshly mown hay.

Jamie tried to catch his friend as he fell. He looked up at Peter with wide-eyed fury, and charged toward him. Peter reversed his grip on his pistol, the barrel now warm, and caught the lad on the side of the head, knocking him cold, grabbing hold of him, and gently lowering him down to the floor.

With the explosion of the two pistol shots the militia swarming outside the barn, now pushed past the regulars, and charged in.

There they found Peter, cradling their quarry in his arms, holding him close, softly crying.

"Damn all, he killed 'em," one them said with disappointment. "But at least one is still alive."

Peter looked up at them and, recocking his pistol, he leveled it even though it was empty.

"Damn you all to hell, when will this ever end? Haven't you had enough of it? Haven't you had enough?"

They fell silent, backing up.

"He's my prisoner. He's just a frightened boy. Now leave us be."

He barely heard the soft but sharply clear orders of his escorts to clear the hell out. There were whispered comments from the floor below that they knew of this man, and he had just shot and killed his childhood friend to spare him from the hanging mob.

The shadows lengthened as he held Allen close. Off in the distance there was a muffled rumble of a single cannon shot, something registering within that it was General Washington, whom he had once led to Trenton. The general had just fired the first shot of what was the final siege. Seconds later came the thunder of nearly a hundred more guns, followed by volley after volley greeted with distant cheers.

At last he came down, bearing Allen's body, before him a dazed and frightened boy, quietly sobbing.

One of his guards took the body.

"We'll see he's buried proper, sir," one of them said softly.

He looked up at the man, old enough to be his father. Peter Wellsley could not reply.

"Back to headquarters then, sir?" the old man asked.

He nodded slowly.

"Then, when free at last of all of this, to home," he whispered. "My war is over. I've done my duty for my country."

Cheer after cheer erupted up and down the entire length of the siege line. If far enough back from musket and rifle fire, men had climbed out of their trenches to watch the show.

To Billy Lee's dismay, he was one of them, and at the sight of their commanding general, standing atop a revetment to watch the bombardment, more cheers erupted.

"By God we are giving them hell, General!" Hamilton cried excitedly, all but jumping up and down like an excited schoolboy.

Washington struggled to contain himself because he, too, was tempted to let emotion show. To leap with excitement as Hamilton did. Across six years of war he never dreamed he would see such a sight, a scene of such firepower, pouring down upon their enemy, rather than being on the receiving end of it.

Along the entire front, every artillery piece, from four-pounder field guns to the giant sixteen-inch mortars, was firing as rapidly as possible. Both he and Rochambeau were in full agreement that the first day's bombardment should be unrelenting, guns pausing only long enough to let barrels cool rather than risk bursting. There was to be no holding back ever again.

The fire was concentrated on several of the key British redoubts, he had at first ordered. No shots were to be aimed into the town, but when Knox had come to his side, and he truly was in an ecstasy of delight, and pointed out that several of the buildings were, indeed, being used as headquarters, Washington had given approval to fire upon them as legitimate military targets. Besides, any civilians who had remained in that town, even though they might be Loyalists, were, without doubt, down in basements or hastily dug bombproof shelters.

Dozens of shots slammed into the buildings, the first volley aimed that way, striking away nearly an entire side, and seconds later, dozens of tiny figures in red uniforms came scurrying out and ran off to seek safer shelter, eliciting gales of laughter from the gunners and observing infantry.

Heavy mortar shells, with fuses sparkling in the twilight sky, arched up high, then came screaming down into the British redoubts, great fountains of earth leaping upward seconds later. Plumes of dirt showered up from the earthen walls of the redoubts, support timbers splintering, spinning off through the air, sections of wall already beginning to collapse under the relentless pounding.

He still thought it incredible, hard to believe that his army had fifty thousand artillery rounds on hand, when the Battle of Trenton had been fought with little more than a hundred.

Knox promised him that the rate of fire would continue unabated through the night, preventing any of the British engineers and sappers from attempting repairs.

"By God, General Washington," he turned to see Dan Morgan, rifle cradled in his arm, coming up the side of their revetment to join him. "I seen many a fireworks display and a few damn good bombardments that we was always on the receiving end of. I almost pity those poor bastards over there. But by God, sir, we'll remember this the rest of our lives!"

He heartily clapped Dan on the shoulder in an open display of affection.

"By God, sir, you are right! We'll remember this day the rest of our lives!"

He now knew without any doubt he would remember this day the rest of his life because only one result would come of this now. Cornwallis had no choice left but to surrender. If he attempted to sally now, his men would be slaughtered by such massed firepower undreamed of throughout the war. He could sense that the morale of, as Dan said, those poor bastards over there, would soon be so shattered that they would refuse any order to commit such suicide by some foolhardy attempt to break out.

He took the moment in. He would never forget it. He prayed none here would ever forget it, and remember as well all that it took to arrive at this moment of triumph.

Seventeen

YORKTOWN
OCTOBER 19, 1781

THE ASSEMBLED FIFERS AND DRUMMERS OF ALL HIS REGI-
ments led the way, repeatedly playing what, long years ago at the
start of this war, had been a song of derision of the British against
their colonial bumpkins, "Yankee Doodle." In the previous hours,
French engineers had cut an opening through the battered inner defensive works of the English to allow passage wide enough for troops
arrayed eight abreast to pass. The hastily laid out road from the American lines into the British was now lined to either side, French to the
left, Americans to the right, shoulder to shoulder, half a dozen ranks
deep. Though he expected no last-minute subterfuge, which would
have been viewed as a dishonorable act of the lowest kind, some regiments were kept in reserve behind their own lines, muskets loaded but
unprimed, just in case, along with four batteries of Knox's deadly light
field guns. Just in case. Some could still recall with horror the base
betrayal after the surrender of Fort William Henry in the last war,
when a British regiment, having honorably surrendered that bastion

in upstate New York to General Montcalm, had been brutally slaughtered by the native irregulars accompanying the French. It had been reported that some of the British soldiers, especially after some of the atrocities committed in the Carolinas and in their pullback to this position, expected the same treatment once they had laid down their arms.

Tensions were still high enough that Washington had personally sent an assurance to Cornwallis, on his word of honor, countersigned by Rochambeau, that all honors as agreed upon would be observed. Several points were different from the agreement that Gates had, rather foolishly, signed after Saratoga. Unlike then, all enlisted personal would be held until England should formally sign articles of peace, though officers would be allowed to be paroled upon their word of honor not to engage in further action in North America or the Caribbean, and return back to England. That had caused some bristling, but he held firm on that, actually it was Rochambeau who absolutely insisted upon it. If this entire army was paroled and allowed to go home, what was to then prevent them from relieving or reinforcing other forces at Gibraltar, still under contention, or free up troops there, who without such a pledge might return here next spring. Besides, separating the officers and letting them go free would just increase the divide between the two classes, and without doubt, more than a few of their enlisted men, when comparing what they would return to in London or Dublin, would in the end ask for asylum in this new land.

Loyalists, however, were to be removed from the main ranks and detained separately, and he had received reports, from a now strangely distant Peter Wellsley, that this had triggered a panic with scores of them actually attempting to swim the bay to escape, one group of them commandeering a small brig to try to run the French blockade. He had Wellsley's report of the running down of several dozen such men, who had tried to slip out in civilian garb, as he had so wisely predicted, and that a dozen of them had been caught and summarily hanged for being out of uniform, or worse yet, attempting to pass while wearing

Continental uniforms. It was not until several days later, that Morgan
had come to Washington with a report as to why the young officer, so
energetic and diligent, had withdrawn into total silence, unless directly spoken to by him, apparently in some sort of malaise or state of
shock.

He had given Wellsley a position with his staff to witness this
moment, the young man riding behind him, but he saw no exuberant
open joy as there was with everyone else. As the cavalcade of victo-
rious officers passed between the assembled ranks of French and
Continentals, discipline all but broken, cheer upon cheer resound-
ing, though he had passed strict orders that there were to be no overt
displays once the British came marching out. Again, a breach of proper
formality and protocol, fueled by a little too much liquor that had
without doubt flowed in his camp, and was rumored to be rampant in
the English camp. He had been informed that a frightened, leader-
less mob of English troops had broken into a supply warehouse filled
with liquor, reserved for officers, and a couple of them had been executed to restore order. It was just such things that could turn the
ceremony ahead into violence that would forever bring shame to his
cause. An area had been cleared just forward of the enemy bastion,
smoothed out, even covered with sand so their mounts would have
firm footing. Rochambeau parted from his side, going to the left, to
take position at the front of his columns of assembled troops. Arrayed
behind him were the proud regimental standards carried into battles
here, and as far away as India, while Washington moved to the right.
Washington took his final position, his staff dismounting, horses led to
the rear, flag bearers of all regiments that had fought in this campaign,
moving in behind him, proudly holding shot-torn standards aloft.

Knox was speaking half aloud, and most proudly pointing out the
horrific damage "his guns" had inflicted on the enemy works. Over
thirty-five thousand rounds had been fired since the opening of the
bombardment on October 9. The first shot, of course, fired by His Excellency the general, and legend was already afoot that the round he

fired had actually crashed into a gathering of English officers, shattering the table they sat about and had sent them scattering.

Washington was still amazed at what the more cynical and insensitive had always called the "butcher bill" now that the battle was done. Less than a hundred dead for the combined French and American forces and three hundred wounded. When this campaign had started, he had, with the cold pragmatism of the price of war, anticipated ten times as many lost before Cornwallis was subdued, if he could be subdued.

On the British side, there had been half a thousand killed or wounded, most fallen victim to the unrelenting artillery barrage, the rest sick with ague or the flux. Artillery was not just a killing weapon; it was a morale destroyer as well for those suffering under its blows, even if unharmed. The redoubts to either side of where the generals now waited had, indeed, been pounded into rubble, artillery rounds striking with such unrelenting fury that no work parties at night dared to venture out to attempt repairs. The few that did were driven back into their works or scattering when a single deadly rifle shot out of the dark killed a sergeant directing the work.

Old Mose was part of Washington's invited party, standing behind him alongside of Dan Morgan, the shuffling bearlike figure at least cleaned up somewhat by Dan, with a fresh hunting shirt on. He was under the strictest of orders not to say a single word to the surrendering British about the fourteen he claimed to have hit, and definitely not any kind of baleful glance at their French allies on the other side of the road.

Then, at last, they heard them and it sent a shiver down Washington's spine, as it always did.

They played several pieces as they approached, "Scotland the Brave" in honor of the regiment from the far north of the British Isles and then, strangely, an old popular drinking tune, "The World Turned Upside Down."

The irony of it was all so obvious and he wondered if it had been chosen deliberately, or had been just a random choice of their drum major. For on this day, the world had, indeed, been turned upside down. "A rabble in arms" of free citizens, with but a handful of them ever trained to war, had risen up in defense of their rights as free men, had finally triggered a global war as a result, lost countless battles, but always kept coming back for more. Now at this very moment, before them, humbled and humiliated, would pass the finest infantry in the world in abject surrender.

Perhaps that was the true reason for all this, he mused. When free men stand against those dragooned into the service of tyranny, in the end, free men will keep coming back, again and again, to either die or win with sacred honor what it was they believed worth dying for. Whereas the slave of a tyrant? What would he fight for when pressed to the wall?

If all had been reversed, he would have fought until bled out to hold the outer line, then withdrawn to the inner line, and if need be, his men reduced to eating the boiled marrow of their horses and belt leather rather than submit to this. When freedom was pitted against tyranny, he prayed, that henceforth and forever, those fighting for freedom, for the rights of man, would, if need be, hold to the last man, and if fated to fall, before doing so, they would train their sons to remember them and to continue that fight. He thought of the bitter atrocity of the pregnant woman. Cornwallis had yet to reply to that, but he would press to investigate, and at that moment he offered a prayer to her fallen soul that her spirit was here, with that of her un-born child, to know that their suffering had insured that others would never suffer the same fate, for good and honest men, aroused to pro-tect innocence, had come to the side of their cause for this fight. She, poor suffering woman, had contributed to this victory, and he prayed history would not forget her, and that those who did such a cruel deed would stand before God and her to beg forgiveness.

The drum major, the fifers, pipers, and drummers passed, and now came their officers. To his shock and, yes as well, his disdain, Cornwallis did not lead the march, it was their second in command,

General O'Hara, a decent opponent, most definitely not Tarleton or Grey. Yet it was not Cornwallis, and what respect he still had for the man was shattered at that moment, never to return.

O'Hara caught his glance, but then, and this was yet another shock, averted his gaze. He had heard O'Hara, whom he had never faced in battle, was an honorable man, who had been severely wounded at Guilford Court House and had lost his son in that action. O'Hara angled across the road and reined in directly in front of Rochambeau.

"Sir, I regret to say that General Cornwallis is indisposed due to the ague," O'Hara cried so that all could hear. "I therefore bear his sword that I now present to you as token of our surrender to your forces."

There were gasps of protest from those around Washington. Lafayette, Knox, von Steuben, and the son of President Laurens, Colonel John Laurens, returned from France, who had served as the direct agent negotiating the surrender. Dan Morgan and his lifelong companion Old Mose, and a host of others, including the young silent Peter Wellsley, threatened to ride forward at this effrontery, but a gesture from their general held them.

He smiled, knowing what his trusted friend and ally would do.

Rochambeau, with a wave of his hand so beautifully French, made a gesture of disdain, and then stood in his stirrups and pointed directly at Washington.

"There, sir, there, is my commander and the architect of our victory!" he cried, first in English and then in French, so that all understood his words, and a gasp of delight went up from the men of the Continental line who were close enough to see and witness this grand gesture. Many of their French comrades on the other side of the road silently raised their hats in salute, and with flourishes, then bowed to the American line on the other side of the road.

Washington, so rarely prone to open emotion, struggled for control. It was the single most gallant gesture he had ever witnessed, and one he swore he would never forget.

Taken aback, abashed, O'Hara, red-faced, turned away from Ro-chambeau's haughty rebuff, turned his gray mount about, and now faced Washington, his emotions composed and within him now, a building anger. Either Cornwallis should be here or should have hon-orably died in battle, as he knew he had chosen to do more than once in desperate actions, to either win or die. But to hide behind this poor man, burdened with his sword?

"Sir," and for a moment O'Hara's voice choked with obvious shame, "I present to you the sword of . . ."

Washington raised his hand swiftly, a sharp command for silence.

"Sir," he announced slowly, carefully enunciating each word. "Since the general, of equal rank to my own, has decided to suddenly be," he hesitated then realized never to let his anger hold sway, "indisposed, then I refer you to my gallant comrade, General Benjamin Lincoln, who shall accept the sword of surrender."

Lincoln looked over at him with astonishment. He had been in command of the garrison that had attempted to hold back the sur-prise arrival of Cornwallis, backed by a British fleet in Charleston Harbor, the opening move of the bitter campaign for the Carolinas. Forced to concede the city, Cornwallis had ordered the most hu-miliating of terms to allow Lincoln to surrender and withdraw, com-pletely outside the rules of their version of traditional warfare that an honorable foe, who had put up an honorable fight, was to be acknowl-edged as such. Lincoln had fought in the backwaters for more than two years, haunted by that humiliation, his staff fearing at times he would take his own life as some sort of Roman-like atonement for that day.

Now the man just stared at Washington, who by surprise had selected him for this honor and this atonement before friend and foe.

O'Hara formally held the sword in its scabbard, hilt pointed to Lincoln, who reached out, took the weapon, and with a brief flourish held it up so that all could see, but something in his gaze and that of Washington stilled any spontaneous cheering. He then leaned

318   NEWT GINGRICH AND WILLIAM R. FORSTCHEN

forward, and there were gasps of surprise when after all this man had endured, Lincoln handed the sword back to O'Hara.

"You have fulfilled your duty, sir," Lincoln said. "The surrender of all the king's forces and those who serve him is now accepted and the terms of surrender honored by us. Keep the sword."

He hesitated.

"Keep the sword for yourself," he finished, his voice now edged with bitterness, "you presented it to me as your duty demanded. I have returned it to you personally, in token of friendship to you an honorable soldier, and it is now yours to keep."

The double meaning of his words was obvious and there were mutters of approval from the staff behind Washington. O'Hara took the scabbarded blade back and cradled it under his left arm. He raised his hat in token of salute, first to Lincoln, then to Rochambeau who returned the salute, and then, at last, to Washington, bowing low as he did so.

Washington, remembering all that this war had done to his land, his people, his comrades, neighbors, and now fellow citizens, touched the brim of his hat in reply.

O'Hara turned his mount and with gaze fixed straight ahead, trotted forward, the pipers, drummers, and fifers falling in behind him, and again they played the tune all would comment on later as so ironic, "The World Turned Upside Down."

Emerging from the fortifications came rank after rank of once-proud British infantry, who for nearly a century, ever since the campaigns of Marlborough in the War of the Spanish Succession, held themselves to be the elite of the world.

Their colors were cased and would be confiscated, a term Washington insisted upon in spite of the counterthreat of a few British officers that they would fight to the death rather to accede to such a dishonor, but his demand had held firm.

After the humiliation of Lincoln and his men, who, as they finally abandoned their works in what they had thought was honorable surrender and withdrawal, had, instead, their colors snatched from them and passed through a gauntlet of jeering men. The same men were now surrendering, but would not face such a gauntlet. He remembered as well, the Dante-like hell reported, regarding the prison hulks that still rotted in the East River. The enlisted men this day would go into captivity until this war was ended, but would do so out on the Pennsylvania frontier, with the agreement that British agents would be allowed to attend to them and to supplement their rations transported through the lines, a request he had made more than once to Howe and Clinton for his men held in captivity, and always had been rebuked.

There was a political side to his decision regarding the flags as well. He would later present them as trophies of war to de Grasse, Barre, and Rochambeau to return to France and display before their king. Such things carried great weight and honor in the courts of Europe, and the gesture would be long remembered

Rank after rank of them marched by, some staring straight ahead, some obviously drunk and shamed, helped along by their comrades. The Hessian contingents marched out, their riflemen without weapons, for nearly all had smashed them rather than surrender their precious arms, and they did look about nervously, fearing retribution, for rumor had spread with them that they would be held to account, blamed for atrocities not of their fault. Washington had already detailed some of his men from Pennsylvania of German descent to fall in with them, once clear of the surrender ground, to reassure them, and to offer them pardon if they would remove their Hessian uniforms, offer parole, and settle in as laborers on the farms of their German cousins around Lancaster, Reading, and York. Many would take that offer, and then try to find means to bring their families here. Their petty princelings had sold them into this war, and with this final defeat, in their bitterness, many were now asking, why return to Europe, when such an offer was being made of forgiveness and to stay here in this new land?

Of light infantry not a man was to be seen. Hours before the surrender, Laurens had reported back that all men of those ranks, and grenadiers as well, along with Loyalists, who had not decided to just try and take their chances with escaping and instead hid within the ranks, were being issued fresh uniforms of infantry of the line and merged into the ranks. Washington had decided not to press the issue, yet again, fearing that even now, a formal ceremony of peaceful surrender could still go awry in a panic. They might have been to the bottom of the barrel with ammunition and rations, but some paper pusher in England, months before, had made sure an entire shipload of five thousand new uniforms had braved the Atlantic and the threat of French capture, to run the new uniforms in just before de Grasse had closed the gate.

It took several hours for the column of over seven thousand men, the largest prisoner haul of this war, to pass down by the marsh where they stacked muskets, cartridge boxes, and flags, and were stripped of all regimental insignias from belts and caps. This followed at the end by the pitiful sight of half a hundred wagons drawn by horses provided by the Americans, since they had slaughtered their own, containing within the suffering wounded and dying of this broken army.

The road into Yorktown was empty, except for the refuse of an army marching to surrender; some broken muskets of men too proud to surrender the weapon, the symbol of their pride as a soldier for years; thousands upon thousands of pieces of paper of cast-off letters, some of it, perhaps incriminating, if taken in a search of a man's pockets; even the glint of the king's shilling, pay they would rather toss aside than have looted from them later by some Rebel.

The road into Yorktown, the goal of so many months, what he once thought little more than a dream, now lay open to Washington and his men. All around him were silent, some openly weeping with joy at the sight of it.

"I want sufficient rations for whatever civilians still are within the town to be brought up immediately," he announced.

He crossed the road, extending his hand to Rochambeau.

"Come, my friend, let us take our city back."

"Your city, mon Général," Rochambeau replied, "your city, your dream, your country."

"But not without you," and he pointed the way. "Sir, I demand the honor that you shall ride in first after all that you have done for America this day."

Eighteen

PHILADELPHIA
NOVEMBER 11, 1781

IT HAD BEEN A DAY OF TUMULTUOUS CELEBRATION UNLIKE
any witnessed since perhaps the day when the Declaration had first
been read aloud to cheering crowds on the Glorious Fourth, now five
years past. Read, even as the British invasion fleet, with thirty thousand sent to suppress that Declaration, had sailed into the outer approaches to New York harbor.

The entire city had prepared for days for this moment. Patriotic
displays of fresh-cut garlands of pine arched over Market Street Banners stretched across the road up from Wilmington proclaimed, "All
Glory to Our Gallant Heroes of Yorktown," "Philadelphia Welcomes
Our General Washington and His Men," and even a few in French,
honoring the men of Rochambeau.

Word had, amazingly, arrived in Philadelphia only three days after the surrender, carried by post riders an exhausting three hundred
miles, and the city had erupted with joy after weeks of anxious worry.
There had been a startling rumor that Clinton had bestirred and as

a countermove was marching upon the capital of the rebellion with the threat to raze it to the ground in retribution, and yet again, the more skittish of Congress had prepared to flee the city. The rumor, of course, had proven false. Clinton had, in fact, bestirred himself at last, loading more than five thousand of his garrison of New York into transports and, accompanied by the refitted ships of Graves, at last sallied to the relief of Cornwallis. While still off the coast of Virginia, a Loyalist, who had escaped the trap and somehow dodged all the patrols and reached the coast, actually managed to steal a small fishing boat and sailed out to the grand fleet, slowly riding down the coast facing contrary breezes, bearing the news that the entire army had surrendered the week before. Then, Admiral Graves, spotting the combined fleets of de Grasse and Barre, had declined battle since, after all, they did have nine more ships of the line than he did.

With that, the entire flotilla had turned back to New York, and as all of America was now taunting, did so with their tails between their legs.

Clinton's report, it was said, was already winging to England aboard a packet ship, bearing news of the disaster and soundly denouncing Cornwallis for not holding out as any English officer should have until relief, as he had promised, arrived, rather than so basely and abjectly go into captivity.

For a city that had endured three quarters of a year of haughty occupation by these same men, it was yet further cause of merriment and delight to welcome the triumphant hosts of Washington and Rochambeau, their victory at Yorktown complete, and finally now marching back north at an easy pace to resume their watchful surrounding of the last bastion of England in North America, the city of New York.

De Grasse had, within recent days weighed anchor. His promise was fulfilled and he was returning to the Caribbean to resume harrying British possessions there and to guard France's precious and wealthy gains in those waters. His fastest frigate had already been dispatched to France, which might have arrived even now, bearing word of the glorious victory, the greatest humbling of British arms in this century. Without doubt, the English Parliament that, at best, had always been lukewarm about this war, with some even voicing support of it as a righteous rebellion defending the rights of true Englishmen everywhere, would now rise up en masse and demand a negotiated end. That end would be full independence at last.

The procession had started precisely at noon. Given that it was a fair, crisp autumn day, unlike the boiling heat of little more than two months past when this same army, exhausted yet proud, had marched through these same streets to an uncertain future, they now came forward proudly: Their morale was even higher, because with this great and stunning victory, even Robert Morris was shocked to discover that his combing of the city for every last shilling and doubloon and Dutch thaler to pay these men had not turned up all. His credit was now honored, though he was—something he would never admit publicly—in debt for well over 300 percent of his assets. Suddenly Morris had pressed into his hands enough for two more months of pay in actual coin, at 8 percent interest, due quarterly of course.

So not only would this army bathe in the glory of a true triumph, they would be granted liberty as well for the next two days, and the shrewdest investors knew that barely a piece of eight would leave their fair city and thus enhance their own economic interests as well.

It was truly a triumphant host, as if from the ancient days of the Romans, that marched up Market Street under the noonday sun. First had come patriotic displays borne on wagons, thirteen of them, each symbolically representing their thirteen states of the Union. Each, of course, had fine young ladies aboard, decked out in finest silks, the wagon representing Massachusetts carrying a boat with banners proclaiming all honor to the men of Lexington and the boatmen, who had carried their army across the river to Trenton and rescued it from Long Island. Of course, the display for Pennsylvania drew the loudest applause, requiring a full team of sixteen horses to pull it along. At the fore of the long open wagon a tableau representing the signing of the Declaration; behind them on a raised platform Betsy Ross herself, the stuff of a legend, joyously waving a thirteen-star flag; behind her a fairly good imitator of their beloved elder citizen Benjamin Franklin, currently in France; and all four corners of the wagon posted with sentries decked out in full frontier attire of fringed hunting jackets posing with Pennsylvania long rifles.

Next came some of the captured booty of the campaign, British artillery, wagons stacked to overflowing with Brown Bess muskets, and a proud member of the 1st Continental leading a fine stallion, a sign dangling from either side of the saddle proclaiming that it was, indeed, the horse of Cornwallis. There had been suggestions that, at least, let a dummy representing him be mounted, but Washington had outright refused that indignity.

At last they came, marching twelve abreast, drummers and fifers marching before them, the only overt display Washington would allow of his enemies humiliation. The once-proud flags of their regiments, now unfurled, carried by an equal number of Continental and French troops. Flags that upon many a battlefield had once struck terror into the hearts even of veterans as they saw them, above the battle smoke, relentlessly bearing down upon them. Now the object of derisive cheers and a few of the more drunken and boisterous pelting them with "horse apples," and shouting imprecations. For those who carried them, the reaction was actually disturbing. They had faced these colors on many a battlefield across six years, and such disrespect now troubled some of them, and they shouted for the crowds to leave off.

Behind the drummers and fifers, flags, booty, and patriotic carts now came the true objects of adoration this day, the army of Yorktown and the generals who led them.

At the fore were Washington and Rochambeau, riding side by side, and the ovation was thunderous, deafening. As George Washington took it all in, yet again there was a flash of memory. The days after Brandywine, his broken army staggering down this same road in defeat, barely a citizen visible, Congress having fled. But today? Young girls and fair ladies by the scores raced forward to throw garlands of autumn flowers and wreaths before them so that the road was carpeted with their offerings.

"My God, my friend," Rochambeau declared, looking over at his comrade. "This is even better than returning in triumph to Versailles!"

"Your men deserve it this day," Washington replied, voice thick with emotion. "We will never forget that without you and our gallant friend de Grasse, on this day," he paused, "on this day, of November 11th, all would be different. May we never forget."

Yet again, that typical Gallic display took hold and as they paused in the center of town, the Independence Hall up the street and towering above them, Rochambeau leaned from his saddle to take Washington's hand and clasp it firmly.

Cheer upon cheer redoubled as they dismounted, to again climb the dais and this time, rather than an obviously nervous Congress to greet them, they were swarmed with congratulations and well wishes, joined in turn by their staffs and comrades, Lafayette, von Steuben, young Laurens, who eagerly leaped into the embrace of his father, the president of this Congress, the two weeping with joy, and all the others who had accompanied them across six bitter years of war.

Now the troops of so many proud regiments began to pass in review, and even while others cheered Washington stood silent with hat raised, heart filled with emotion.

The celebration was, indeed, glorious, but there was still much to be done. This triumphal victory had not truly ended the war, as many now claimed or wished to believe. He sensed that never again would there be a campaign or battle, but nevertheless there would be a long final dragging out, the enemy hoping to wear them down through negotiations now that it was obvious they could not defeat them on the battlefield. The enemy hoping that if they dragged out negotiations long enough, the will of America could still be broken to accept some sort of settlement, and not the one he had now fought for, a free America, all of it, from the Atlantic to the Mississippi. The time of soldiers standing in volley line might have passed at last at Yorktown, but months, perhaps bitter years, of negotiation still lay ahead until, at last, Clinton took the last of his regiments and fled back across the sea.

Much was still to be done, to keep this army intact once the joy of this moment had passed, and the dull tedium of winter quarters, spring watch, standing guard on hot summer nights, and chill autumn rains passed, and passed perhaps yet again. Until the last of the British had left and his land was free and he free as well to place his uniform back into a cedar chest, as any true citizen of a free republic would do. Then return at last to the loving embrace of Martha, and to home, where, at this moment he prayed, he could live out his remaining years in peace, having done his service to his country.

PETER STARED AT THE DOOR, FROM WHICH FLECKS OF PAINT were peeling, steeled his nerves, and knocked.

There was silence from within. Shutters were drawn in, curtains within pulled down, and his heart sank.

He knocked, and then knocked again more insistently. No reply, no answer from within. Heart sinking he began to turn away and then he heard a bolt being unlatched.

His disappointment of but a second before now replaced with nervousness . . . anguish.

Elizabeth opened the door.

She gazed at him in obvious disbelief and the sight of her shocked him. Her once-glowing features had paled, cheeks sunken in, eyes dark rimmed, hollow, and he recognized that look from years of winter encampments, the poor pathetic girl was malnourished, starving.

"Peter, is that you?" she whispered in obvious disbelief.

"Yes, Elizabeth, may I come in?"

She opened the door wide and silently beckoned for him to enter.

What greeted him within was a shock. The once-ornate parlor was devoid of any furniture except for a couple of straight-backed chairs. Everything, furniture, ornate wall hangings, even the brass andirons and tools for the fireplace gone.

"What in heaven happened here?" Peter gasped.

"Taken," she whispered. "I was accused of harboring a known Tory after you left. One of their militia men testified against me at the hearing. My father's sentiments were already known, of course, and he dare not return from New York to try to defend our property or me. I was declared a traitor, our property forfeited and confiscated to support our cause. It was taken the day after word arrived of our victory at Yorktown. The house has already been sold at auction; at least the buyers took pity on me, and said I could have till the end of the month to vacate and head to New York."

"This is infamy," Peter snapped, his mission forgotten for the moment so bitter was this outrage.

"This is war," she whispered. She began to choke up. "I think I have enough tea," she whispered, trying to appear brave and nonplussed, "would you care for a cup?"

He followed her into the kitchen, stripped out as well, though there was a fire of a few sticks to ward off the chill, a chair drawn close to the smoldering flames where she had obviously been sitting to stay warm. A single kettle was suspended over the flame, and reaching into a near-empty cabinet, she drew out a small jar, opened it, and sprinkled the precious leaves into the kettle, then turned back to face him trying to force a smile.

"Give it a few minutes to simmer."

"Elizabeth."

"Yes, Peter?"

He had rehearsed this moment in his mind a thousand times during the long weeks of their return march. Thinking upon it while riding, trailing behind Washington and his joyous staff, lying awake at night in the open fields whether star-studded or cloud-covered and raining. He had tried to rehearse it a thousand times.

"Regarding Allen."

She actually smiled.

"Yes, Peter. He was here. I hid him that day you were here and I bless you for it," she paused, "he was in my bedroom even as you and I spoke in the parlor and you so nobly, God bless you forever, turned and walked out the door. And Peter, I knew that you knew and have blessed you every day for your gallantry and compassion."

"Elizabeth."

Her eyes widened and he tried to force the words out but his voice broke into a shuddering sob.

"He's dead."

It was all he could say. No gentle building up, no flowery statements, no explanation, just those two words escaping from him.

Her features paled so that he feared she would faint. He reached forward to brace her up, but she slapped his hands away.

"How, how? My God, how?"

"The war."

"How?"

He struggled for control, lowering his head, tears streaming, dropping to the floor.

"I killed him."

"What?" and even as she cried out that one word she strode forward and began to strike him again and again.

"How? Why? My God, why?"

He blurted out the description of what happened as if confessing the darkest of sins to a mother torn apart with grief and her blows finally ceased.

"I had to," he cried, finally daring to look back into her eyes. "I did it because I loved him. We played at being soldiers once, and, oh God, how different our dreams of what war is were then. We played it so many times as boys and thought it to be all glory and painless death.

"If I had not," and again sobs wracked him, "those bastards outside would have hanged him and after what I saw with John Andre, I would not, I could not give my friend over to that . . ."

He began to cry again and now rather than blows, her arms were around him, holding him close.

"Bless you, Peter," she sighed, holding him close pressing his head against her shoulder. "Bless you, Peter."

"I had to tell you. I could not feel absolved until I told you."

There was a long moment of silence, and then she drew in her breath.

"Peter, I am with child."

Still holding her close he put his hand under her chin and raised it. Her eyes were shining with tears, but there was just the flicker of a smile, the smile nearly all women have when they know new life is within them.

"That night, after you left us, Peter. I am with child, Allen's child."

He drew her into his embrace.

"I am more than two months along. I know no one else knows," and she actually shuddered out a soft laugh, but then began to cry again. "Only you know, but you know what they will do. I am already accused of being a Loyalist, and now I will be branded the mother of a bastard child of a Loyalist."

Then she did, indeed, begin to cry, long wracking sobs, for her lost Allen, her baby who would be branded the bastard of a traitor.

At that moment, somewhere in the depths of his heart he sensed that he knew this all along. That on the night he had turned away from her doorstep, to spare the life of his friend from the rope, to spare his distant cousin from the humiliation of harboring a Tory, he somehow knew why this had happened after all. That Allen sensed the result of that one night together and thus his final appeal, just before Peter drew careful aim and then snuffed out his life to spare him.

He leaned down and kissed her all so gently on the forehead.

"No, Elizabeth."

She looked up at him confused.

"No, Elizabeth. You carry my child."

"What?"

"My war is over. I asked my general for leave after six years of service and he granted it to me. I think someone, God bless him, told him the truth of what happened between Allen and me. Washington bade me to sit with him and I told him everything."

He struggled to control his emotions as he remembered how his general had reacted only the night before when he had been ordered to report. Washington had drawn his chair closer and put a fatherly hand on his shoulder, then asked him to speak plainly about all that had transpired.

"You did the right thing," Washington said softly as Peter, voice breaking, finished his narrative. "I could not have spared your friend, you know that. It would have been horrible, ghastly. You spared him that out of love for an old friend. And yes, I recall as well your friend as a man of honor, with a brother, who alongside you was crucial to our victory so long ago at Trenton."

Not a word was shared for several minutes as Peter broke down in front of his general, and then Washington had placed a hand on his shoulder.

"You've been in the army how long now?" he asked.

"Since I was seventeen, sir, I joined back in '76."

"And this young woman you spoke of, who hid your friend?"

"Elizabeth Risher," he replied woodenly.

Washington sat back, and nodded.

"Go to her."

"Sir?"

"You have done splendid work, Peter, and you must know that I have dozens of others who did and still do such work for me as well."

"Sir?"

"She has always been a Patriot, Peter. She was crucial in giving us information while Philadelphia was occupied, and if she stands accused now of being a Tory, that is false and you must help her."

Washington smiled.

"This war is over for you, young sir. You have done enough, as has she. You will hold your commission until the army is demobilized, but I think it is time you went home to rest, and to peace."

"What are you saying, Peter?"

He smiled and drew her close in an embrace.

"It is our child, Elizabeth. I have always loved you. Remember my one feeble attempt to dance with you so many years ago before this war, and you said I was a clumsy oaf?"

She actually smiled and nodded.

"I have loved you from that day. And I loved Allen, the brother I never had."

"Peter, do you know what you are saying?"

He smiled.

"Of course I do dear, Elizabeth. We leave for my home in Trenton and will marry tomorrow. He will be our child, Elizabeth. The war is over for us and young Allen will be born an American."

Epilogue

FRAUNCES TAVERN
NEW YORK CITY
DECEMBER 4, 1783

THE ROOM WHERE HE HAD ASKED TO BE ALONE FOR A FEW moments to gather his thoughts and prepare for the brief ceremony ahead was quiet, at least relatively quiet, when compared to the tumult just outside his third-story window. General of the Armies of the United States George Washington had to stand several feet back from the window, because if observed by the jubilant crowd on the street below, there would be renewed calls for a speech, something he felt absolutely incapable of doing on this most emotional of days.

The war had ended at last.

It was just over two years to the day since he personally gave his report to Congress in Philadelphia of the triumph at Yorktown. There had been wild prophecies by some, claiming that the war was over then and there.

The months after Yorktown had been heralded as the beginning of the end, but as a student of history and war, he knew better than most how many times a final victory had been snatched away at the negotiating table.

The news of Yorktown, of course, echoed resoundingly across Europe, and members of the British Parliament, some of whom had defiantly and openly expressed support of the American cause from the start, now called for an end to it all. Serious negotiations in Paris had at last begun, but it had taken nearly two years of that to see it through to this conclusion today.

For two more winters, his army, nearly as ragged and poor as before Yorktown, waited it out. The infusions of cash by Robert Morris, which had kept the flame of liberty alive on the march down to Yorktown, had totally exhausted any reserves left throughout the thirteen states. His men endured two more cold winters of scant rations, many of them shoeless, uniforms in tatters, after a grueling five-month campaign and nearly a thousand miles of marching. What he had feared might be a fatal blow that would reverse everything gained over the previous year were the orders from Paris the following spring, recalling his staunch ally Rochambeau and the entire French navy to Europe or deploying them to cover their possessions in the Caribbean. Rochambeau had openly wept with shame when he presented his orders to withdraw, and their parting had been a sad and bitter one, the parting of two comrades. Never would he forget the French general's proud and haughty gesture when offered Cornwallis's sword. He had refused it, pointing to him and announcing, "There is the commander of this army, present your surrender to him." It was not just an acknowledgment of Washington himself; it was an acknowledgment of a new nation.

The announcement triggered fears that France might fold at the negotiating table and thus encouraged, England would just decide to let the war drag on forever by keeping a garrison in New York until hell did, indeed, freeze over. Bitter conflict still flared in the Carolinas and Georgia. One of the victims at this late stage, killed in some senseless skirmish, was his trusted aide, the son of the president of

the Confederation, Colonel Laurens. Just as dead if he had fallen leading a "glorious charge" at Monmouth or Princeton, but instead gunned
down in an ambush on a back-country lane, that would have no bearing on the outcome of this conflict, but dead, nevertheless. Some
congressional representatives from New England had whispered that
conceding the three most southern states to England in exchange for
independence for the other ten might not be such a bad deal after all.
He thanked heaven for men such as Benjamin Franklin, who had at
this moment of renewed crisis pushed the negotiations forward in
Paris. Franklin conveyed the impression to King George that even
if standing alone again, America would be a wound that could never
heal, would consume if need be a hundred million more pounds and
fifty thousand more troops, with the other powers of Europe sitting
back and smiling as English power was sapped away by this interminable struggle that could go on for generations. If they wanted another Ireland or Scotland, this one a hundred times worse, then let the
struggle go on.

The threat worked. Even while negotiations in Europe dragged
out, through "indirect" communications with General Carleton, who
had replaced Clinton in New York City, an "understanding" was
reached, that if one did not seek aggressive action the other would
refrain as well, and let the diplomats sort it out.

Within his own ranks a true crisis had come during the winter of
'82–'83. A group of officers, actually loyal to him, had hatched a plot
to simply give power to their commander, march on Philadelphia,
throw Congress out on its heels, and just let Washington handle
whatever was to come, starting with pay for those still in the ranks
and supplies to keep them alive. It became known as the "Newburgh
Conspiracy."

He felt he could always recall that moment now with true pride
in his response. If ever there was a temptation, the offer of a Faustian
bargain such as Cromwell and so many others had grabbed hold of, it
was that moment. Of course, the temptation was there to play along

in innocence as others paved the way for him to be Cromwell or Caesar, but it was impossible. Men such as Cincinnatus and the hero of his favorite play, Cicero, had been his models since childhood, not Caesar.

He had rebuffed the "Cabal of Newburgh" with a simple gesture. When a brief speech denouncing the plot failed to draw the response he sought. Washington resorted to a bit of "stagecraft" by drawing from his breast pocket his spectacles. Few, except his closest aides, had ever seen him wearing them, a symbol appropriate for an intellectual such as Franklin, or an aging minister, statesman, or scholar, but certainly not for a general still robust and apparently in his prime.

The room had fallen silent at the sight of this gesture and with true humbleness he had said, "As you can see, I have gone old and near to blind in service to my country. I did not fight George the Third to become George the First."

The potential rebellion had collapsed before he had even left the room.

As much as the memory of so many battles fought filled him at this moment with a sense of pride, it was turning aside that ultimate offer of power that he felt he could be proudest of.

Come spring, when it was clear that negotiations in Paris were coming to a successful conclusion, Congress ordered him to start the demobilization of his army. He knew it was to cut expenses, but there were some lingering doubts as well that he just might change his mind about the offer of an army, giving him the power of dictatorship. That any would believe such of him after so many years of service was an insult, but, as always, he obeyed.

As each regiment mustered for the last time, under their faded, shot-torn standards that they had carried before them in victory and preserved in times of bitter defeat, Washington had stood before them. His voice often choked with emotion, extolled them to return to their homes as free men, as honest men, that their pay was the glory they had won on so many battlefields, and the honor that they would be held in by all generations of Americans to come. They had heard him and gone home with barely a word of protest. He had clasped the hands of many thousands in those months, and could never forget the look in the eyes of so many. Poor, ragged, worn after eight years of war, they were free men, men of honor and pride, who looked him straight in the eye as he thanked each for their service to America.

Now it was time for him to go home as well.

Word had arrived on November 24 that the treaty of peace had been signed in Paris. A secure America, from the Atlantic to the Mississippi, had been won.

The proper protocols and messages had been exchanged between him and General Carleton with the arrival of the notice of this Treaty of Paris. The final act would be the last British soldier embarking by the morning of December 4 for England.

The evening before he crossed the Harlem River via the "Kings Bridge" to the tip of Manhattan isle with his army, now less than a thousand men under arms. Shallow sunken graves still pockmarked the land, from the battles fought back in 1776, a final resting place of many a Patriot.

Dawn had come bright and clear, with early winter weather, but with the promise of a springlike warmth by midday as they marched down from the wooded heights, past farmsteads, some overgrown and abandoned by Patriots who had fled the British occupation and were now following along to reclaim their land and rebuild. As they came off those heights, in the distance, in the upper bay between Staten Island and Manhattan, all could see a small convoy of ships taking on the last of the British army, which had arrived here more than seven years ago with boasts that in three months' time they would crush the rebellion and be back home by Christmas. If the wind was swift and fair, they just might make it back at last for this Christmas. Mingled in with them were thousands of tragic refugees, who, at this moment, he no longer bore ill will toward. Refusing to accept or trust in the treaty that promised insurance of their property rights (for those who even still held property), the Loyalists were now going into exile, most to Canada, some all the way back to England.

As the army started to disband throughout this year, there were many farewell ceremonies. His old friends and comrades Lafayette and Greene had come north after the British evacuations of Charleston and Savannah, and there had been a quiet evening of talking of future hopes and recollections of their past, in crisis and in the rare moments of triumph. Lafayette, imbued with a bit too much wine, had mused on how history might remember them, and what statues might someday be erected.

He had rejected the idea out of hand. They had fought to create a free republic, not an empire with statues of Caesars and conquerors. The argument had flowed back and forth, with some saying a republic needed models of heroes of the past, which history might someday record them as. Washington had finally conceded that at the least he could accept a statue to Benjamin Franklin, who all universally acknowledged was the intellectual leader and chief negotiator of their liberty. The topic had shifted to the various battlefields, Lafayette and Greene urging at least a statue of a soldier, dressed in rags but defiant, in the now abandoned winter grounds of Valley Forge, to mark the graves of the thousands who had died there during that terrible winter. Then had come the question of Saratoga.

There was a long moment of silence. The subject on their minds was Horatio Gates, the purported commander of the armies there, who was a pariah to all present. He had all but attempted an open coup against Washington during the Valley Forge winter. His supporters in Congress had finally forced through his command of the armies in the South, where at Camden, he had nearly thrown away the Revolution in a disastrous defeat, out of which Greene was dispatched to retrieve the situation.

"If our grandchildren someday decided upon statues at Saratoga," Greene had mused, "what of Benedict Arnold? For even we must acknowledge that his gallantry that day turned defeat into glorious victory."

Lafayette sighed, looking into his glass of claret, the wine the color of blood.

"I wish the bullet had been aimed but a bit higher," he finally whispered, breaking the embarrassed silence.

"Which bullet?" Greene had asked.

"The one that struck his leg."

Lafayette looked back up at his friends who were gazing at him curiously, not sure of his meaning.

He chuckled softly.

"I could think of no finer fate, after a few more years of life of course, and with children and grandchildren to remember me," and those around him chuckled softly, "then to die for a cause such as we have fought for."

There were nods of approval.

Then he sadly gazed back down at his glass of wine.

"If I were Arnold, for the rest of my life, I would wish that the bullet that had struck me in the leg at Saratoga had winged but a bit higher and struck me in the heart. For in that death my name forever after would be spoken of with reverence and honor. He did not fall upon the stage of this life when fate would have been most kind, and shall now live out a life alone, despised here as a traitor, mistrusted in the land to which he has fled to by those who faced us as soldiers who understood honor."

There were nods of approval from some.

"If they someday erect statues to us," Lafayette finally concluded, I pray there is one for Arnold as well, for we all know that at that moment at Saratoga our cause hung in the balance, and it was he who tipped the scales to the conclusion we have now today."

"I would place no wreath at such a place, sir," Greene snapped, "and if there is one for Gates, I will be certain to purge myself before going to honor it."

Lafayette had nodded with understanding, for it was Greene who had to rebuild the demoralized wreckage of the army that Gates had left to him.

"Then at least this," he finally said with a forced smile. "A statue of just his leg?"

"Pray why, sir?" Greene retorted.

"Because it will be the part of him that will forever bear two wounds, won at Quebec and Saratoga, that shall forever remind us he was once a man of honor."

As he recalled that conversation now, he smiled at the thought of it. The typical romantic gesture of a Frenchman.

"SIR, I DO THINK THEY ARE WAITING FOR YOU."

It was the ever-present Billy Lee, interrupting his thoughts, holding his blue and buff uniform jacket, freshly brushed, the epaulettes sparkling in the light streaming through the window.

He looked at the clock. It had chimed noon and he was so deeply lost in thought he had not even heard it.

He nodded thanks to Billy, who helped him don the jacket, motioned for the uncomfortable wig that the ceremony of this moment required, reaching up to adjust it slightly. Billy stepped back, dark eyes surveying his general from head to toe and nodding approval.

Billy opened the door, smiling.

"I'll see that the horses are ready, sir," he said softly.

He actually dreaded what he now faced, fearful that emotion would take hold, and uncharacteristically, he reached out to grasp Billy's hand.

"Thank you, I'll be along shortly," he whispered.

Billy went ahead of him down the flight of stairs. Two of his personal guards, the last of his detail still in his service, flanked the door leading into the meeting room. Both snapped to attention and presented arms. He looked to each of them and felt a lump rising in his throat, for both had tears in their eyes.

He paused, extending his hand first to one and then the other.

"Sergeants Felton and Hurt, you have been with me from the beginning and I shall always remember your faithful service."

The two fumbled, not sure how to react while at attention with present arms, as they had done a thousand times before, at last nervously taking his hand smiling as he grasped them warmly. Felton, unable to speak, opened the door into the meeting room where they were waiting for him.

These farewells had been going on for weeks, months, ever since the congressional order of the spring that started the demobilization of the army. Now there were only seven of his officers left to say a final good-bye. Their fellowship of nearly eight long years was at an end. They were all standing, waiting in anticipation. He had thought to prepare a few words since he, along with all those closest to him, knew he was nearly a failure when it came to giving an impromptu speech or eloquent statement. Perhaps that had served him as one of his greatest strengths in the end. Unable to speak loudly, glibly, or richly such as men like Franklin, Jefferson, or even Greene, his response was usually silence that he had come to learn lent him an air of gravitas, so that when he did speak but a few words, all listened.

"Gentlemen," he began, "with a heart full of love and gratitude I now take leave of you. I most devoutly wish that your latter days may be as prosperous and happy as your former ones have been glorious and honorable."

He fell silent for a moment, unable to continue as he gazed into the eyes of the last few of his beloved comrades from whom he would part this day. A decanter of wine had already been passed around, all were on their feet and, raising their glasses, they toasted him and their new nation, the United States of America.

He joined in the second half of the toast, scanned their faces, many streaming with tears, and smiled at General Knox, who was standing directly in front of him.

"Gentlemen, I would feel obliged if each of you will come and take my hand in farewell."

Knox did so first, a shudder running through the rotund man as he embraced his general, then each in turn followed, most unable to speak, a few whispering "God bless you, sir," "Thank you, sir," and then stepped back.

He was unable to reply, except for the grasp of the hand, a warm pat on the shoulder as they embraced, fearing he truly would disintegrate into uncontrollable tears. So strange war. We so fervently beg for its ending, and yet when that ending comes, and we gaze upon trusted comrades for the last time, we somehow wish we could linger but a few more days, share one more campfire, even share one more moment of the thrill of triumph.

But this is what we fought for. This moment and now it was at hand.

Never again would they sit about a campfire on a chilled snowy night, sharing a single bottle of brandy between them that Lafayette always seemed to have tucked away in his luggage, to make desperate plans for the following morning, not sure if the next day would be their last or if they would have the joy that next evening of seeing each other still safe and sound. Never again would there be summer nights, under the stars, walking through camp, lingering in the shadows, listening to the talk and gossip of their men to gauge their morale. Nights of hope, of fear, of dashed hopes, and then belief that still all will be set aright. Never again would they share such moments together, a bond of brotherhood that only those who had endured such and shared such could ever truly understand. Now, mere words at this ending could never express all that was felt as they looked into each other's eyes, bidding farewell.

He wondered if he would ever see any of them again in this world. In his own heart his future course was clear: It was to Mount Vernon, to Martha, to home and whatever years the good Lord still might grant to him.

He was never one for dragging out such moments, and even as they bid their farewells, the waiting crowds in the street below could see them through the windows, and cheers were rising up nearly drowning out the few words exchanged.

He could not speak, offer any final words, and with a simple nod of his head, he turned for the door, taking a deep breath, wiping the tears from his eyes, and descended the staircase to the ground floor. The doors were wide open and as he stepped out into the noonday sunlight a tumultuous cheer rose up from the thousands who were gathered and had waited for this glimpse of him.

He had made sure word had been spread that there would be no ceremonies, no formal speeches on his part or that of any other. The governor of New York and various officials of the city were gathered on the steps of the tavern, obviously eager for just such an event and a chance for a speech on their part as well. He did not afford them the opportunity to indulge, rapidly going down the steps, politely shaking their hands. Several tried to cling to that quick grasp, but long practice with such things allowed him to graciously slip their attempted bond, and move to where Billy Lee waited, holding the bridle of his mount.

He lifted himself into the saddle, grateful that the few hundred troops who had accompanied him into the city, thinking ahead, had formed a cordon, an honor guard that opened a narrow path down Pearl Street, and to the flank of the heavily fortified battery at the tip of the island.

How many memories were tied to this place as he rode along the flank of the high-walled stone and earthen fortress. Of course, the British had removed all the guns, so that the gun ports were empty, and the world being as it was, someone in Congress would now have to figure out where to get guns to replace them, but at the moment, that was no longer his concern.

A broad-beamed ferryboat awaited him, festooned with pine wreaths and a hand-lettered sign "All Praise to Our Glorious General Washington."

He and Billy Lee dismounted, and the boat hands were eager to take the bridles of their horses. As soon as they were aboard, the stern railing was raised up, rudder locked back into place, and a large lug sail raised to catch the gentle, nearly warm southwesterly breeze coming across from the Jersey shore.

NEWT GINGRICH AND WILLIAM R. FORSTCHEN

The crowds poured down to the wharfs and landings, and lined the wall of the battery fortress, offering cheer after cheer that gradually faded, and he was grateful for that. It was the type of demonstration he knew he had to endure at times in his office, and at times actually did welcome, when it was raised by disciplined regiments of his men, who were ready for a fight, but on this day, it filled him with discomfort.

He knew that a boat had most likely departed from the same dock perhaps only an hour ago, bearing a swift dispatch rider, who was even now racing along the postal route to Philadelphia and from there on clear to Annapolis, where Congress had decided to convene this year, bearing the news that General Washington had, indeed, fulfilled what he had promised.

He had disbanded his army and was now going home.

He was no Caesar, no Cromwell. His only desire, his final duty was now simply to go home.

He shaded his eyes against the sun, and saw the British ships, one after another, running close hauled as they cleared the "Narrows" between Staten Island and Brooklyn. It conjured to memory the sight of seven years past, where many of those same ships had so boldly and arrogantly sailed into this same harbor bent on swift repression and defeat of those whom they derisively called "a rabble in arms."

A light sloop, running before the wind, actually bore down upon them, and the ferrymen watched it with a leery eye, one of them muttering in near panic that they were coming to take them.

He ignored their comments, standing calmly, and could see several officers on the fantail. As the sloop came about one of the officers lowered his telescope and then raised his cocked hat in salute.

Of course, he returned the gesture.

This war was over and he thanked God it was closing now with some civility after so much bitterness.

Those on the New York shore had witnessed the moment and greeted the gesture with cheers. He gave one final look back, raising a hand in salute, then turned with face to the wind. The War of Independence was over. He was laying the burden of duty aside to return to Mount Vernon, to Martha, and what he believed would be years ahead of peace in quiet, honored retirement, his duty to his nation completed at last.

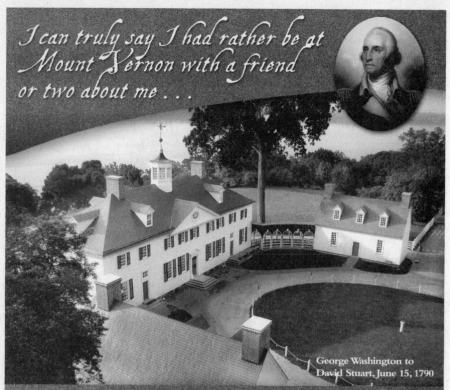

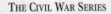
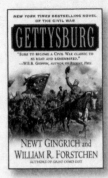

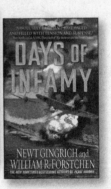